## ABOUT THE AUTHOR

When *USA Today* bestselling author Alissa Callen isn't writing, she plays traffic controller to four children, three dogs, two horses and one renegade cow who believes the grass is greener on the other side of the fence. After a childhood spent chasing sheep on the family farm, Alissa has always been drawn to remote areas and small towns, even when residing overseas. She is partial to autumn colour, snowy peaks and historic homesteads and will drive hours to see an open garden. Once a teacher and a counsellor, she remains interested in the life journeys that people take. She draws inspiration from the countryside around her, whether it be the brown snake at her back door or the resilience of bush communities in times of drought or flood. Her books are characteristically heartwarming, authentic and character driven. Alissa lives on a small slice of rural Australia in central western NSW.

### Also by Alissa Callen

*The Long Paddock*
*The Red Dirt Road*

# THE
# ROUND
# YARD

## ALISSA CALLEN

**mira**

First Published 2019
Second Australian Paperback Edition 2019
ISBN 9781489281043

Published by
Mira
An imprint of Harlequin Enterprises (Australia) Pty Limited (ABN 47 001 180 918),
a subsidiary of HarperCollins Publishers Australia Pty Limited (ABN 36 009 913 517)
Level 13, 201 Elizabeth St
SYDNEY NSW 2000
AUSTRALIA

A catalogue record for this book is available from the National Library of Australia
www.librariesaustralia.nla.gov.au

Printed and bound in Australia by McPherson's Printing Group

*To Luke*

# CHAPTER

# 1

Neve Fitzpatrick walked out the front door and into a scene of mass garden destruction. Dismay anchored her boots onto the dusty veranda floorboards. No wonder the two willie wagtails perched on the nearby wooden fence had been scolding.

The three-year-old girl she carried on her hip stopped wriggling. The five-year-old sister standing close beside her stilled. They all stared at what had been ordered rows of vegetables filling the raised beds in the right corner of the garden. Now, carrots and strawberry plants littered the red dirt path and the rows of staked tomatoes slumped as though they suffered from heatstroke. The scent of crushed rosemary tinged the breeze.

'Uh-oh.' Maya slipped her small, sticky hand into Neve's. Her chatterbox voice lacked its usual volume.

'Uh-oh,' Kait repeated in her high-pitched tone, shaking her head so her red curls glinted.

'Uh-oh, all right.'

'We need Mr McGregor who chased Peter Rabbit,' Maya said with a frown.

'Or a better fence.' Neve sighed. 'We have a bigger problem than rabbits. Make that two big problems.'

Loud crunching sounded. The grey-and-white donkey feasting on a carrot turned to look at them with large amber eyes. The taffy pony beside her snatched at a head of lettuce before peering at them through his long blond forelock.

Neve shook her head. To think she'd been worried about locusts, when the threat had been far closer to home. She'd watered and nurtured the rows of vegetables through the summer heat and now, just when the cooler autumn weather had arrived, she'd have to start over again.

'Don't give me that innocent look, Sebastian,' she said to the pony as a lettuce leaf hung from his mouth. 'I know it was you who busted you and Delilah out.'

The pony took a second bite of lettuce.

'Bassie's going to get a tummy ache.' Worry pinched Maya's heart-shaped face and her hold on Neve's hand tightened.

A brain tumour had robbed the sweet sisters of their mother last spring. On the days they spent with Neve, while their father worked in Woodlea as a livestock agent, she made sure she provided stability and fun. She pressed her lips closed against the emptiness that didn't seem to fill despite the calendar pages she turned. She knew firsthand how losing a mother could strip the warmth from the sunshine and dull even the brightest of blue skies.

Neve released Maya's hand to place an arm around her delicate shoulders. 'He'll be fine and if he's not we'll call Ella.'

The concern straining Maya's expression eased. Both girls knew and liked the local vet, as she'd looked after their kelpie when he'd fallen off the farm ute. Ella was also the reason why Neve had a shaggy donkey and a sassy pony in the paddock of her rented farmhouse. Both animals had been neglected and in need of a loving home.

As a child Neve had been horse mad and she hadn't outgrown the dream to one day have a horse of her own. She just wished Ella had sent out a how-to manual along with the bales of hay. Growing up in the city hadn't exactly equipped her with the skills to outsmart her two escapees.

Kait wriggled on her hip and Neve bent to set her on the veranda beside Maya. With their burnished curls, big brown eyes and pale, round cheeks, the sisters were a mirror image of each other. When she took them to town they'd often been mistaken by tourists for her daughters, except her auburn hair was a lighter, more strawberry blonde and her eyes were green.

Footsteps sounded in the hallway behind them before the screen door opened.

'Sorry, the hospital calle—' Fliss stopped, her mouth rounding. 'Not again.'

Neve moved to take hold of the tray of iced cupcakes that tilted in the local doctor's hands.

'Yes. Again.' She set the tray on the nearby outdoor table. They'd have afternoon tea before she attempted mission impossible to return the donkey and pony to their paddock. 'This time they didn't just eat the hedge. I was sure the extra row of electrical tape would work.'

'I was too.' Fliss ran a hand through her glossy, dark hair. 'It's time your free-spirited duo met their match. If Denham and Tanner can sort out that chestnut bully of Old Clarry's, they can handle a big-eared donkey and pretty-boy pony.'

'Thanks, but Denham's busy with his wedding and I've not met Tanner.' She poured water into a plastic cup. 'I'll work it out.'

It didn't feel right relying on others. Usually, she was the one offering to problem-solve and to help. Life had taught her to be self-sufficient. After her father had died when he'd fallen from a ladder, it had only ever been her mother and her, and for a too-brief while, her grandmother.

Fliss helped Kait into a chair before passing her a cupcake on a blue plate. 'Tanner's home from droving and Denham would welcome any distraction from working out table-seating arrangements.'

'I couldn't ask Denham. It isn't just the wedding keeping Cressy and him busy, they're also getting ready to go away for their honeymoon.'

'Which leaves Tanner. He'd be able to keep Bassie and Dell in their paddock and work with them to make them easier to handle.' Fliss smiled at Maya and Kait. 'Bassie's also supposed to be broken in. You'd like to ride him, wouldn't you?'

Both bright heads bobbed.

Neve didn't realise she was chewing her bottom lip until Fliss glanced at her. She turned away to sit beside Maya. 'I'm sure Tanner knows what he's doing. But it's fine. Really.'

To her relief, Fliss also sat and the conversation lapsed. Wings *whoosh*ed as a flock of cockatoos landed in the old gum tree that threw shade across the trampoline. Dell and Bassie weren't the only ones who'd been eyeing off the ripening strawberries.

Silence settled over the veranda as everyone enjoyed the cupcakes iced in white and sprinkled in edible pink glitter. The girls liked baking and Neve made sure they cooked recipes that reminded them of their mother. A mouthful of cake lodged in her throat. One day she'd cook her own mother's favourite vanilla cake recipe.

Avoiding Fliss's gaze, she stifled a cough and reached for her water. Her new neighbour was far too perceptive and had already done enough to help her keep busy. Three months ago, she'd organised for Neve to look after the girls five days a week until Graham found a more permanent arrangement in the spring and before Maya started school.

Kait giggled as Dell plucked a fresh carrot from the garden bed and Bassie tried to steal it from her.

Fliss laughed softly. 'I know those two are incorrigible, but they really are cute.'

Neve joined in with the laughter. 'I'll remind myself of how adorable they are when it takes me at least an hour to get them into their paddock.'

'I can help.' Fliss selected another cupcake. 'I'm not on night duty, so I'm not in a rush to get home.'

Fliss and pickup rider Hewitt lived at nearby Bundara, and the house Neve rented was on their second farm. It was no coincidence she'd chosen the small town of Woodlea to move to. Bundara had been her mother's family home and she lay buried alongside her parents in the historic local cemetery.

Thanks to kind and generous Fliss, Neve had since been a frequent visitor to the bluestone homestead she'd visited as a child. Sometimes the memory of her mother's laughter would echo as she walked through the high-ceilinged rooms. The summer scent of white gardenias took her back to eating Anzac biscuits on the cool veranda with her grandmother.

Neve took hold of the empty water jug. 'Which means you can spend a quiet night in with Hewitt.'

'Wouldn't that be wonderful. He's been working late on the new adventure playground so I've barely seen him.' Fliss's hazel eyes searched her face. 'Are you sure?'

She nodded, ignoring the way Bassie threw her a sly sideways look. There'd be a battle of wills as soon as her boots hit the lawn.

Fliss dug in her jeans pocket for her phone. Neve stood and headed inside before Fliss could again mention Tanner and offer to text him. If she was honest there was more to her refusal to enlist his help than her ingrained independence. If Denham wasn't so busy she'd possibly ask him, but Tanner was a definite no.

Tanner was Woodlea's man of mystery. His name was usually mentioned in wistful tones or with a dreamy expression if it was a young cowgirl speaking. When he wasn't away droving, it sounded as though the horse trainer only hung out with a few select mates and rarely attended social events. From the variation in the stories murmured about him, it was obvious the majority of the district hadn't personally met him.

She'd only seen him once, but it was enough. Edna Galloway was justified in having the broad-shouldered cowboy at the top of her future-husband list for her daughter. Even from across Main Street, his easy grin as he'd greeted Denham had caused Neve to forget what she'd been heading to the grocery shop for.

It wasn't only Dell and Bassie she was ill-equipped to handle. Good-looking, single men also ticked such a box. It wasn't so much the combination of his dark-blond hair and tanned, sculptured features that triggered her need for self-preservation, but how he carried himself. Confident and in control, he wore his self-assurance as well as he did his faded denim jeans.

Water jug full, she turned to retrace her steps. Sure she'd had boyfriends, but between university and her mother's multiple sclerosis, and then starting up her Sydney occupational therapy practice, relationships had been put into the too-hard box. Being an introvert hadn't helped either when she'd sold her business to become her mother's full-time carer. She hadn't wanted to waste a moment of their final two years together by going out on yet another awkward date.

Her shoulders squared. She had enough to deal with without feeling tongue-tied around an eligible bachelor who'd think her useless for not coping with her new charges.

Before she reached the front door, Fliss entered holding Maya and Kait's hands. Pink shimmered on the girls' cheeks and chins. Fliss held up the sisters' hands; they too were covered in glitter. 'Turns out Bassie and Dell like being fed cupcakes as much as they like carrots.'

'Why doesn't that surprise me?' Neve said with a laugh as Fliss disappeared into the main bathroom with the two grinning little redheads.

Neve went to clear off the outside table and to check she didn't have a donkey and a pony making themselves at home on her front veranda. When she returned, a clean Maya and Kait played in the toy corner, while Fliss stood at the sink.

The tall brunette turned with a grin. 'I know … I'm not supposed to do the washing up.'

Neve opened a drawer to take out a folded tea towel. 'I didn't say a word.'

Fliss's laughter filled the small kitchen and the lonely crevices of Neve's heart. The farmhouse hadn't felt like a home until she'd started babysitting the girls, and Fliss, her sister Cressy, and Ella had befriended her. Now the house was busy, noisy and a riot of colour. Just how she liked things. Light caught in the pink specks scattered across the kitchen bench. And today it sparkled.

She smiled and took hold of a plate to dry. Fliss glanced at her. 'All this glitter reminds me of the hoof polish the ponies wore in the trail-ride parade. I'm sure the girls would love some for Bassie and Dell.'

'I'm sure they would too.'

'I'll ask Kellie where she got her pink polish from when we see her at the small-hall festival. You're still right to go?'

'I won't have the girls and Ella's determined I come along.'

'Trust me, if Ella's set on you going, you'll have no hope of backing out. She's dragged Cressy and me halfway around the countryside to make sure we had some fun.' Fliss placed a bowl in the dish rack. 'I can't wait to see the Reedy Creek Hall decorations. It always looks so different to when it's used as an emergency control centre. Touch wood, there're no more floods and that Drew Macgregor's header is the only thing to go up in flames.'

Neve nodded. She was still to meet many of the locals, but she'd heard about the flooding spring rains as well as the Christmas harvest fire.

Gravel crunched and a diesel car engine chugged. She glanced at the clock. Graham was here early to pick up the girls. Usually, she'd give them dinner and a bath before he took them home.

She didn't need to call out to Maya and Kait. Toy horses in their hands, they raced out the door and down the veranda steps to hug the man walking along the garden path. Bassie and Dell stood in the shade of the garden shed and barely flicked an ear as Graham passed by. If only they'd stay so placid. Who knew such short, stubby legs could move so fast.

Graham picked up Kait, and then, holding Maya's hand, joined Neve and Fliss on the veranda. He assessed the destroyed vegetable garden beds. 'Someone's been busy?'

Neve grimaced. 'Yes, but don't worry, the girls and I will still make the carrot cake we promised you. You're here early.'

'I thought I'd take the afternoon … off.'

As he looked down at his daughters, Neve swapped a concerned look with Fliss. The anguish of losing his wife was imprinted on Graham's weary face. Fresh silver glistened in the cropped brown hair at his temples.

He dipped his head at Fliss. 'That Hewitt of yours has been hammering up a storm in the adventure playground.'

'He says another two weeks, and a final working bee, and it'll be done.'

Maya's smile beamed as she tugged at her father's hand. 'Neve's taking us. We're going to be the first ones to play on it.'

'That sounds like fun.' Graham's voice deepened and he paused to clear his throat before glancing at Neve. 'Thank you for all that you do for the girls. I don't know how we'd cope without you.'

She didn't immediately answer. She was the one who didn't know what she'd do without Maya and Kait. Their tight cuddles and cute chatter never failed to keep her loneliness at bay. The brutal ten months after her mother's funeral and before they'd come into her life had proved she wasn't used to being on her own or not having anyone to care for.

Even with packing up and selling her Sydney family home, she'd felt purposeless. She'd never made a decision that only involved herself. She'd never had spare time that required filling. Since she'd been at high school, she'd done the washing, cooking or shopping whenever her mother's joints had ached or she'd been unable to stand due to her poor balance.

Fliss slipped an arm around her shoulders. 'It was Woodlea's lucky day when Neve called to rent this place.' She paused to glance at the nearby pony and donkey. 'Especially for those two.'

Fliss's amusement dispersed the heavy emotion. Neve went inside to collect the girls' backpacks. Through the screen door she heard their excited voices filling their father in on what they'd done today. The knowledge that she'd kept them busy and made their day happy eased the ache in her throat.

After she and Fliss had waved Maya and Kait goodbye, Fliss turned to hug her. 'Thanks for afternoon tea. See you and Ella on Saturday night and … good luck with the destructive duo.'

'Thanks.' She crossed her fingers and held them behind her back. 'I'll have them out of the garden in no time.'

Even an hour had been an optimistic estimate of how long it would take to get Dell and Bassie back into their paddock. The usual bribery of hay failed to work, so Neve used their need to evade her to eventually direct them through the gate.

If either animal had been wearing a headcollar she would at least have been able to catch them. But the day after they arrived both headcollars had been removed. She hadn't been close enough since then to put them on again. She still didn't know who the clever culprit was who'd taken them off.

Once Dell and Bassie were where they belonged, Neve made sure the electric fence was intact and the red light of the charger blinked. As purple shadows dappled the lawn and the first blush of sunset brushed the sky, she went inside.

A coffee in one hand and her phone in the other, she settled onto the end of the living-room sofa. From such a position she had an uninhibited view of the electric fence through the large front window. She'd kept watch before, and if she had any hope of outwitting the terrible twosome, she needed to stay one step ahead. The only way to do this would be to discover how they escaped.

She was swapping texts with Ella about what to wear to the upcoming festival when Dell and Bassie approached the two strands of electrical tape that formed the gateway. The plastic-handled metal hooks that slipped into the loops on the corner post didn't carry any charge. Bassie and Dell appeared to sniff at the hooks. Dell then pulled the bottom hook free even before Neve realised one strand of white tape sagged onto the ground. If she wasn't so dumfounded, she'd have been impressed.

She sprang off the lounge and used her phone to film Dell ducking under the remaining wire and Bassie pawing the ground before he followed. The donkey and pony touched noses then ambled towards the pots of sunflowers growing alongside the garden shed.

Neve headed outside. Logic told her that Houdini Dell had more than one escape method as this was the first time the tape at the gateway had been removed. She had more hope of plugging holes in a bucket than of keeping Dell and Bassie where they were supposed to be.

Another hour and a half later, and with only the pale wash of moonlight to see by, Dell and Bassie were in their paddock. Neve double-checked the knots on the baling twine she'd used to secure the gate hooks.

'Sleep tight,' she said, rolling her shoulders to ease her weary muscles. Dell lifted a heavy eyelid to give her a placid look. Bassie ignored her. 'I know I will.'

But as Neve lay in bed, a loud bray from outside her bedroom window startled her. She groaned, rubbed at her forehead and reached for her phone on the bedside table. It didn't matter how awkward or out of her depth she'd feel around Tanner, it would soon become a safety issue if the girls were in the garden with Dell and Bassie. She also couldn't impose on an already flat-out Denham. Stomach swirling, she texted Fliss for Tanner's number before her self-preservation had a meltdown.

Tanner Callahan parked in the shade of an established cedar tree. He made no move to turn off the ignition of his blue ute. The V8 engine rumbled, masking the thundering of his heart. He stared at the woman and two young children waiting for him beyond the garden gate on the neat green lawn. Sunlight glanced off their auburn hair.

He could ride an unbroken brumby and offer carrots to a grumpy mountain of a rodeo bull, but he was in no hurry to leave his ute. Only two things unnerved him: anyone under four feet in height and small-town matchmaking. Not that the woman before him would threaten his bachelor status; she was already spoken for. He'd passed a man in a white four-wheel drive not far from the front cattle grid. When Fliss had given him directions she'd said no one else lived along this road.

He turned the ute key and the sudden silence magnified the pounding in his ears. In this woman's case, what dried his mouth was what she represented. The way she held one child and had her arm around the other conveyed her deep love and warmth. All the homely scene needed was a white picket fence and he'd be looking at the embodiment of a perfect family. He reached for his battered felt hat on the passenger seat and jammed it on, making sure the brim was low enough to hide his expression.

He may have found Meredith, his birth mother, and he may have worked through the childhood self-doubts associated with having been adopted, but his fears refused to fade. Abandonment continued to coil inside, striking out at any tentative sense of stability. Common sense argued that a woman to love, a home and children would fill the chasm within him. Yet, his self-control insisted that giving in to such yearnings would only make him a fool. He couldn't again risk having his trust, let alone his heart, broken.

He left the ute cabin and the warmth of the morning sun spilled across his shoulders. The well-oiled gate didn't make a sound as he walked through and past a bed of fragrant yellow roses. To his right were the remains of a vegetable garden, while to his left a pony and a jenny stood beneath a gnarled pepper tree. This was his first sight of whom he'd come to see and he'd soon know what he'd be dealing with. But his attention refused to leave the woman before him.

A gust of wind tangled in her long hair and she brushed the red-gold strands from her cheek. She shifted the smaller girl she held on her jeans-clad hip higher, before again draping her arm around her older daughter. From Fliss's earlier phone call, he knew the woman's name was Neve and she was new to town. From Neve's own phone call, he knew her voice was quiet and sweet. He looked away from the fullness of her lips and the way the breeze moulded her green shirt against her gentle curves. Her partner was a lucky man.

She greeted him with a smile that was gone even before it had begun. 'Thanks for coming so quickly.'

He stopped a body length away. 'No problem. Fliss said it was urgent.'

He didn't know if it was the effect of hearing Neve's voice in person or the unblinking brown stare of her daughters, but he couldn't walk closer. All his instincts said to keep his distance.

Neve nodded. The day's heat flushed her cheeks and tension creased a faint line between her brows. He could understand her concern at having a pony and donkey running amuck.

'Girls, this is Tanner. He's come to help us with Dell and Bassie.' She paused as she nodded towards the child she carried. 'This is Kait and this is ...' Her arm tightened around the taller girl, who wore a white dress and pink cowgirl boots. 'Maya.'

He didn't immediately reply. There had been a flash of apprehension in Neve's green eyes that didn't fit with her calm words or what he'd come here to do. Her hold on her daughters could just as easily be read as defensive as well as maternal. The older child stood too still and straight, as though she'd take flight if he made a sudden move.

'Hi.' He smiled to offer reassurance and to ease his own tension.

Neve blinked and the brown eyes of her daughters widened. No one spoke. Great. This was why he avoided babies and children. He had no idea what to say or do. It had only ever been his older, adoptive parents and him. He'd always lived in an adult world.

After what seemed like an endless second, Maya said, 'Hi.'

'Hi,' her younger sister repeated.

Unsure of how to respond, he gave each girl a quick nod.

'So … what do you want to do first?' Neve asked as she gazed towards the two offenders dozing in the shade.

To his relief, her daughters also looked at their pets.

'The first thing will be to make Dell and Bassie's paddock escape-proof.'

He made a quick assessment of the twin rows of white tape that formed the near side of the pony paddock that also doubled as an orchard. Just like Neve had explained, the other three sides were wire and in good condition. He returned to his ute for some portable horse panels.

While he dismantled the electric fence and assembled the panels, Neve and her daughters watched from a garden bench. Beneath the pepper tree, the pony and donkey continued to sleep. He wasn't fooled. The flicker of their ears betrayed that they knew exactly what he was doing.

He pinned the final panel into the ground and attached two small loops of blue baling twine at hip height. The sun's heat had strengthened, and from the row of trees beside him he could smell the scent of oranges. A few winter frosts and the fruit on the laden branches would be sweet enough to eat. He turned away. Everywhere he looked, this small farm reminded him of how much it had been shaped into a home by loving hands.

Neve and the two girls approached. When they drew near to the fence each girl reached out to touch the cold steel.

Neve's lips curved, but her smile didn't reach her serious eyes. 'Unless Bassie and Dell dig their way out, that has to hold them.'

'It will.' He bent to collect two dusty headcollars and lead ropes from the tub Neve had set near the old gateway. He'd spoken to Ella on the drive out and she'd confirmed that the pony had been broken in and that the donkey possessed far more manners than she displayed. 'Let's see how they like their new fence.'

Maya left her mother's side to walk up to him. He forced himself to stay relaxed and for his shoulders to not brace. Up close he could see the freckles across her small nose and feel the intensity of her fierce frown. 'Bassie's is the red one, he doesn't like orange.'

Unsure if her tone was bossy, upset or worried, he glanced at Neve.

She moved to rest her hand on Maya's shoulder. 'It's okay, sweetheart, Tanner knows who owns which headcollar.'

'I do.' He hesitated. Maya's frown hadn't eased. He held up the noseband of the orange headcollar. 'Dell's is bigger here to fit the shape of her donkey jaw.'

Neve's smile had him turn on his boot heels and head towards the pepper tree. The warmth and thanks in her gaze unsettled him almost as much as interacting with Maya had. Whenever Neve's eyes met his, he was torn between looking away and staring. Her irises were such a vivid sea green. He'd never seen such flawless skin or hair that burned with fire under the sun and glowed gold in the shade. Neve's partner wasn't just a lucky man. He was a *very* lucky man.

With every stride that Tanner took away from Neve and her daughters, the tension leached from his shoulders. He'd survived. Just. Things could have been worse. There could have been little-girl tears or Neve could be single and yet another woman he had to avoid when in town.

He slowed his pace as the donkey and pony spun around to face him. He was under no illusion they wouldn't bolt the moment he got close. The savvy pair were seasoned rascals. Intelligent and inquisitive, they'd be quick to learn bad habits. There was nothing he liked better than working with animals, the more cantankerous and badly behaved the better. Once he'd gained their respect and trust, their loyalty and love were unconditional. When he'd met his palomino mustang, Arrow, the horse had been hellbent on driving him out of the round yard.

Making sure he held the headcollars and lead ropes by his side, he altered his path to head off any dash the pony or donkey might make to the right. The toss of Bassie's golden mane identified him as the ringleader. Not looking directly at either of them, Tanner kept his posture relaxed as he approached Dell's left shoulder. He'd catch the donkey and then focus on Bassie, who'd backed up to ensure that Dell acted as a physical barrier between Tanner and him.

He drew near to the donkey, and when she swung her head away signalling she'd move, he took a step backwards. Dell stayed still and looked at him. He stepped forward again and when she turned her head, he stepped back. Using the pressure-on and pressure-off technique, he gauged her comfort zone. Soon she let him extend a hand to touch her neck and then allowed him to rub her withers. He made no move to slip on her headcollar. Instead, he leaned in close to give her neck a good scratch.

She stared at him, her oversized ears flickering. Taking his time, he draped the lead over her neck and put on her headcollar. From the corner of his eye he saw Maya clap her hands. He again scratched Dell's neck as positive reinforcement for her cooperative behaviour. Unimpressed, Bassie stamped his hard little hoof.

Dell followed Tanner over to the new fence, where he tied her to the blue baling twine. If either donkey or pony pulled back, the baling twine would snap before they hurt themselves or broke their lead rope or headcollar. He collected a curry comb from the tub and, talking quietly, brushed the dirt from Dell's shaggy grey-and-white coat. Bassie sighed and left the shade of the pepper tree. Making sure he again kept Dell between Tanner and him, he stopped to watch Tanner pick up Dell's feet.

After he'd made sure the donkey was quiet and the girls would be safe around her, Tanner turned his attention to Bassie. Thanks to using the same pressure-on and pressure-off strategy, the pony soon wore his red headcollar and was tied beside Dell. Once Tanner had assessed his temperament and was certain he too was safe for the girls to handle, he nodded at Neve and her daughters.

The two tiny redheads jumped off the bench. Neve smiled as she took their hands and slowed them to a walk. Tanner focused on brushing Bassie's taffy coat. He must have been alone for too long last droving trip. The beauty of a woman's smile shouldn't cause his chest to tighten.

Bassie peered at him through his long blond forelock.

'I know, mate,' Tanner said under his breath. 'I need to get out more.'

After the girls took a turn at brushing Dell and Bassie, Tanner let the pony and donkey out in the orchard. Until there were no more catching issues, their headcollars would stay on. He'd already checked that there were no taps or other hazards for the headcollars to snag on.

Neve laughed softly as both animals sniffed the fence and then strolled away to graze. 'They know the game's up. Usually, they wait for me to leave so they can bust out again.'

Tanner returned the lead ropes and brushes to the tub. It didn't matter if Neve's laughter was as easy on his ears as the tone of her voice, it was no excuse to make small talk. He needed to let Neve and her girls get out of the sun. Today was also the first day of many. Dell and Bassie might no longer be escapees, but there was work to do before the pony could be ridden. He looked beyond the garden fence to the rolling paddocks dotted with black cattle. Not that there was anywhere for the girls to ride. There were no easily accessible cattle yards or pony-sized paddocks.

He risked a glance at Neve. 'I'll text through a list of things that will help keep Dell and Bassie out of mischief. I suspect it's Dell who knows how to remove her and Bassie's headcollars. Donkeys can get bored and especially love toys.' Maya and Kait's smiles widened. 'I'll also set up a round yard that will give us a safe space to work and for the girls to ride. I have a spare set of panels and can drop them over tomorrow. I can either assemble them or … your partner could.'

Neve's eyes briefly left his. 'Sorry … I thought Fliss explained. Bassie and Dell are mine, but Kait and Maya aren't. That would have been Graham, their father, you passed on the road.' She held up her left hand that he'd noticed bore no wedding band, but not everyone who had children together formalised their relationship. Colour washed her cheeks. 'There's no partner … actually no anything. I'm here on my own.'

# CHAPTER

## 2

Saturday morning rush hour in small-town Woodlea was in full swing.

Neve waited beside the white picket fence of the sportsground for the stream of dusty cars to slow. Behind her children laughed as they climbed the play equipment in the adjacent park, while their parents browsed the stalls at the farmers' markets. The aroma of fresh coffee and bacon wafted on the breeze, but the combination failed to make her mouth water. She'd overindulged on a huge breakfast egg-and-bacon roll.

She transferred the heavy bag she carried to her other hand. She'd also gone a little overboard at the honey stall. The markets were on once a month and she tried to support the local small businesses as much as she could. Fresh crumpets drizzled in raw organic honey were on the menu when her hunger returned.

A horn honked and she waved as Denham and Cressy drove past in a white Land Cruiser ute. She checked the clock on her phone.

She had fifteen minutes before she was due to meet Cressy at the Windmill Café.

Taking advantage of a break in the traffic, she headed across the road with a group of locals. Three girls in hot-pink-and-black netball dresses walked alongside her, while two boys dressed in cricket whites surged ahead. It wasn't only the markets that brought everyone to town. Team sports also ensured that parking along Main Street was in demand. Which was why she parked up the hill near the craft shop. She'd head there now to leave the honey in her car.

A flash of royal blue caused her to frown and to take a second look at a man ahead who wore a wide-brimmed hat. Both times she'd seen Tanner he'd worn a blue cotton work shirt that sported the embroidered emblem of a horse and his name above his left pocket. Even though she knew he was at Rosewood putting up the round yard, her nerves tightened.

Despite his visit yesterday being a success with Bassie and Dell, she remained on edge. It was as though everything she'd said was on constant replay in her head. The more she revisited her conversation with Tanner the more she cringed. As if she'd needed to state the obvious and explain to the girls why he was there or expand on her single status. When the pedestrians ahead parted and she saw the man in the blue shirt and hat wasn't as tall as Tanner, she lowered her tight shoulders.

Now she'd met him, her need to avoid the cowboy had intensified along with her awareness that he was way out of her league. When he'd grinned at her and the girls, there'd been a moment when all she could do was stare. His eyes had been such a pure light blue and a disarming dimple had appeared in his cheek. But even when he'd smiled his jaw had remained as rigid as the granite that scarred the ridge.

She opened her car door and pushed aside the stirrings of curiosity. When Maya had approached him, Tanner had tensed. But no good would come of wondering why he'd reacted as he had. Just like she shouldn't read anything into his response to the news that she wasn't the girls' mother or even married. The muscle that had worked in his lean cheek could just as easily have been caused by Kait walking over and breaching his personal space.

With the bag of honey in her car, Neve navigated her way through the shoppers towards the centre of town. Outside the charity shop she stopped to pat a poodle-kelpie cross tied to the lamp post. The affectionate dog owned by old Will was the full sister of Cressy's energetic Juno.

She entered the Windmill Café and just like the street outside, Woodlea's only coffee shop was busy. The farm clothes, sports uniforms and the brochures being read identified the crowd as a mix of locals and out-of-towners.

Sally gave her a welcoming grin from behind the coffee machine. 'Latte?'

Neve returned her smile. It was such a simple thing having someone remember your order, but it reassured her that she wasn't as invisible as she sometimes felt. She'd drop everything again in a heartbeat to care for her mother. It brought her great comfort to know her mother had been surrounded by memories and the walls of her own home until the very end. But there had been a personal price to pay. The years by her mother's side had proved isolating. 'Yes, please.'

Cressy waved at her from the back of the noisy, crowded room. Smaller than her older sister, Fliss, Cressy shared her sibling's thick dark hair and hazel eyes. When Neve had met the no-frills cowgirl over dinner at Fliss and Hewitt's, she'd liked her straight away. They exchanged a hug.

'I keep forgetting how busy it is on a Saturday,' Cressy said as she returned to her seat. 'I usually don't come in on the weekend.'

'Yes, every man and his dog seem to be here this morning.'

Cressy's grin turned mischievous. 'That is everyone except a certain horse trainer.'

Neve failed to quell the rush of heat in her cheeks. There would come a time when she'd made up for her lack of social opportunities and wouldn't always blush. Her fair Irish skin revealed far too many of her emotions.

'No, Tanner isn't. By now, Dell and Bassie would have their very own round yard.'

'I take it everything went well yesterday?'

'I still can't believe Tanner simply walked up and caught them. I could run a marathon after all the exercise I've had chasing them.'

Cressy's soft laughter merged with the hum of conversation. 'I know I'm biased because he's Denham's cousin, but Tanner does have a way with horses.'

'And donkeys. Honestly, when he scratched Dell's neck I swear her eyes glazed over.'

Cressy laughed and pressed a hand to her ribs. 'Don't make me laugh. I did something to my side in the hay shed.' She paused to take a deep breath. 'Wait until you see what Edna does when she's around Tanner. Which reminds me, Edna's in town and she'll be looking for you.'

Neve glanced out of the large shop window at the busy Main Street, half expecting the social queen bee to be peering inside. Edna was a formidable town personality, but so far, apart from a five-minute inquisition when Neve had arrived, the local gossip had left her alone.

'Why? I made sure I gave her just enough of my life story to keep off her radar.'

Cressy began to laugh and stopped herself at a chuckle. 'Very wise.'

'Edna went to school with my mother and even our grandmothers were friends. I'm sure it's hardwired into my DNA to watch what I say around her.' Neve smiled at Sally as she delivered her latte. 'I've no doubt Edna's mother and grandmother also took a keen interest in other people's lives.'

Cressy also gave Sally a grin before the university student returned to the counter. 'Bethany thankfully seems to have broken with tradition. All she's interested in is finding a man her mother disapproves of.' Cressy spooned sugar into her cappuccino. 'Odds on Edna wants to see you now that Tanner's going out to your place because she'll be checking there isn't anything happening between you.'

'That's ridiculous. When she grilled me, I made it clear I didn't move here to find a man.'

'I know. Just be prepared if she tracks you down.'

Neve nodded and stared into her latte. There was zero chance of Edna's fears coming true. Even if she was ready for a relationship, which she wouldn't be while her life remained rudderless, Tanner could have any woman he wanted. She didn't exactly have a history of men queuing to date her.

'Neve ...' Cressy's serious voice broke into her thoughts. 'I usually don't meddle, but there's a reason why Tanner's so good with horses. He lets them get close ... it's very rare he lets ... people do the same. When he does it's only ever a short-term thing and this can, and does, lead to ... hurt.'

Not sure what to say, Neve nodded before steering the topic onto something safer than Tanner's love-life. 'So how are the wedding plans coming along?'

'Fliss has missed her true vocation. She might be a brilliant doctor, but she was born to be a wedding planner. All those to-do lists would do my head in. She's even found the most beautiful pair of handmade white cowgirl boots.'

Neve took a sip of her latte to hide her grin. Horrified that Cressy would wear her battered work boots with her bridal gown, Fliss had made it a priority to find the perfect pair of wedding boots. Preoccupied with the glimpse of a blue shirt out the café window, Neve slowly lowered her glass to the table.

Cressy turned to look at the people on the street. Aware that her face would have revealed her distraction, Neve nodded towards the delicate white crocheted squares decorating the smooth trunk of a plane tree. On each visit to town, there were new woollen creations draped over the streetscape. The mysterious guerrilla knitters had firmly put Woodlea on the tourist map. 'The recent yarn bombing seems to have a wedding theme?'

'Or it could be white for winter,' Cressy said with a twinkle in her eyes.

'True.'

Cressy finished her cappuccino. 'I'd better go and make sure Denham's survived his meeting with the glamping people. He said he was fine to talk to them on his own, but at the first mention of what cotton count the sheets were, he'll be grinding his teeth.'

Neve too finished her hot drink. 'The pop-up glamping village will be such a fun way to accommodate wedding guests at Glenmore.'

'I hope so.' Cressy stood and tucked her pink shirt into her jeans. 'Even Ella said she'd sleep in one and she likes her creature comforts. She's going to ask if you want to share.'

Neve came to her feet. She'd only known Cressy for three months, so hadn't wanted to presume she'd be invited to her wedding. She didn't try to hide the delight in her words. 'I'd love to.'

'I'm so glad. Make sure you keep the last weekend of May free.'

'I sure will.'

Once out of the coffee shop, they swapped a last hug and went in opposite directions.

Still smiling at knowing she'd be sharing Cressy's special day, Neve scrolled through her phone to find Tanner's list of things she'd need for Dell and Bassie. He hadn't been joking when he'd said donkeys liked toys. Luckily, she already had a hoop and a small ball at home. She also owned a large fitness ball that Dell would make better use of than she ever had. The other items she'd find at the saddlery.

The leaves on the plane trees rustled as she passed as if they were whispering to her. Soon they'd turn the yellow-amber hue of her honey. The white bell tower of the old church shone against the cloudless sky. It was inside the historic stone walls that her mother had been christened and her grandmother married.

This was why she'd left her city world. Out here where the breeze carried the scent of eucalyptus after rain and nature painted in bold, intense strokes, she was returned to a time she associated with family. Each step she took along Main Street followed a path her mother and grandparents would have taken. Each building she entered they too would have frequented, even if the train station now housed the library and once occupied buildings stood empty.

Being in Woodlea anchored her and connected her to something bigger than she was. The town reminded her of the people she'd loved. She could only hope it would also help her find her place in an unfamiliar world in which she was now the only one left.

She pushed open the saddlery door. The timeless smell of leather enveloped her. The shop owner smiled from where she was helping a mother and daughter buy a pair of boots.

Neve headed for the back of the shop where a coloured array of leads hung on the wall. She was right for a saddle and bridle as Fliss had borrowed what Bassie would need from her young friend Zoe, who'd outgrown her pony. From the lunging leads, Neve chose a deep purple and from the saddle cloths she selected a red colour to match Bassie's headcollar.

But as she stood in front of the rugs, she had no idea which sizes would fit or whether she needed the combo design, let alone rip-stop fabric. The shop owner was still busy fitting boots on the tiny cowgirl so Neve sent a text to Ella.

While she waited for a reply, she browsed through the shelf filled with horse books. But when there was no message from the vet she bit the inside of her cheek. She really needed to keep moving. She didn't usually have the girls on a Saturday, but Graham mentioned he might need to go to Dubbo after lunch. Before she could even think it was a bad idea, she texted Tanner.

She eased out a tense breath. Communicating by message was far less nerve-racking than talking face to face. There was far less risk in typing a few short words than stringing together a sentence. He also mightn't text back as his phone could be in his ute while he finished the round yard.

His reply was almost immediate: *Are you in the saddlery?*

*Yes. In front of the rugs. What size is Bassie?* she responded.

*I'll come over. I'm across the road.*

What had he been thinking? Tanner tunnelled a hand through his hair as he jogged across Main Street towards the saddlery. It hadn't been his brightest idea to call into Woodlea, even if the latest issue of his horse magazine was in the newsagent. Both Edna and Neve were in town.

But he couldn't not help Neve. He never went back on his word and he'd said he'd sort out her pony and donkey. He could text through Bassie's rug size, but it would be quicker to see for himself what options the saddlery had. He stepped onto the footpath and headed towards the shop.

He'd had time to deal with yesterday's curve ball that Neve was single. Everything would be fine as long as he kept his distance. Last week he'd helped Sally load her groceries into her car. By that afternoon the town grapevine had hyperventilated with the news that despite the decade age gap, they'd secretly been an item and had moved in together. All it would take would be a careless, too-long look into Neve's green eyes and people would sense how aware he was of her.

Not only had he noticed far too much about her, he didn't need someone like Neve to unearth the loneliness he'd buried deep inside. Warm and kind-hearted, she'd love her own children as much as she cared for Kait and Maya. He'd carved out a hard-won contentment at being on his own that he couldn't afford to lose.

He entered the saddlery and the first thing he saw was the back of Neve's auburn head. Today she wore a white dress with black dots and like yesterday her loose hair fell down her back. The red-gold strands caught the overhead light and reminded him of the wash of a sunset across a winter sky.

As if sensing his presence, she half turned. 'Hi. Thanks for coming. I hope I haven't dragged you away from anything?'

It was just subtle, a hint of warmth in her cheeks and a breathlessness to her voice, that suggested she wasn't as relaxed as she appeared.

'No worries. I was across the street.' He broke eye contact to scan the shelves filled with an assortment of folded rugs. 'There're quite a few to choose from.'

'You can say that again.'

'This is the size we need for Mr Bassie.' Tanner pulled out a royal-blue rug. 'This rip-stop canvas will also cope with your barbed wire fences.'

Neve took hold of the rug. He didn't miss the way she made sure their hands didn't connect. 'Great. What about Miss Dell?'

'Clare will need to order her a special one along with a fly mask.' He moved away to collect a box of worming paste. Yesterday he'd thought it had been the roses in Neve's garden adding a floral perfume to the air. Now he wasn't so sure. The longer he stood near her the more the fragrance of summer flowers filled his lungs.

When the rug and saddle cloth slipped from Neve's grasp he moved forward to catch them. But she stepped back as she adjusted her hold on the bulky items. 'Thanks. I've got them.'

The careful tone of her voice reaffirmed his impression that she valued her independence. She'd tried to manage Dell and Bassie by herself. She also hadn't wanted him to carry the tub of lead ropes and brushes over to her house. If she'd known how, he was certain she'd have put up the round yard. He moved away, respecting her message.

Over at the counter, Clare handed the little blonde cowgirl a bag containing her boots. While Neve browsed the grooming kits and brushes, Tanner spoke to Clare about ordering Dell's donkey coat and fly mask.

As Neve paid for her items, Tanner's phone pinged with a new text message. Denham had seen his ute and wanted to know if he'd come for a drink at the Royal Arms. He'd just spent the past hour discussing the softness of sheets and the décor of portable bathrooms.

Tanner texted he'd be there in five minutes. He glanced sideways at Neve as she brushed her hair off her shoulder and laughed at something Clare said. He also could do with a drink. Being around Neve, even for a short amount of time, made him feel restless and on edge.

But as he held the door open and Neve walked through, the sound of heels clicking on hard concrete warned him that having a cold beer would have to wait. A woman bore down on them. Her perfectly coiffured grey hair had to be the result of a visit to Taylor at the hair salon. Pearls gleamed around the woman's neck. Her lips curved in a satisfied smile as her gaze zeroed in on Neve.

'Have you met Edna yet?' he asked, resisting the urge to take Neve's arm and cross the road.

She only had time to give him a quick nod before Edna's strong perfume engulfed them.

'Tanner ...' The notorious gossip extended her arms and embraced him. From long practice, he avoided breathing until she'd released him.

'Edna.' He glanced at Neve. 'You know Neve?'

'Of course.' Edna air-kissed Neve's cheeks. 'Our families were old friends. Which is why I have a duty to fulfil.'

'Duty?' Scepticism added a wry edge to his tone.

In an emergency Edna was indispensable. Her efficiency, local knowledge and zest for being in charge had seen Woodlea weather a mini-tornado as well as spring floods. But when it came to unselfish acts of goodwill, the jury was out as to her true motivations. Some locals swore she had a heart of gold, but others, like Tanner, suspected Edna usually had an agenda.

'Yes.'

Tanner braced himself. The gleam in her sharp gaze usually preceded an indirect order to come to Sunday lunch.

Edna turned to Neve. 'I worry about you out at Rosewood all by yourself.'

'That's very kind of you, but I'm not on my own. I have the girls.'

'I know. It's been such a relief to Graham to have them so well looked after. But you also need adult company.'

Tanner didn't miss the way Edna shifted so she now stood between Neve and him.

The older woman touched Neve's arm. 'Which is why I've organised for you and that nice young pharmacist, Michael, to have dinner tonight. My treat.'

'Thank you, Edna. That's so thoughtful.' The sweetness of Neve's words had Edna raise a hand to her chest in false modesty. Then Neve's chin angled. 'Unfortunately I'm busy.'

Edna blinked. Tanner masked a smile. Neve's tone was as resolute as the steel of the round yards he'd work Bassie and Dell in tomorrow.

'Busy?' Edna's frown would have stopped a saddle bronco mid-buck.

Neve's expression remained serene. 'Yes. *Very* busy.'

'Well then, let's make it next Friday.'

'Sorry. I'm busy then too and the weekend after.' This time Neve patted Edna's arm. 'I really appreciate you looking out for me, but Tanner will be around for the next few weeks should I feel lonely.'

Admiration filled him. Neve might be all big eyes, creamy skin and soft words, but she was whip-smart with a strength of will to match.

Edna's gaze sharpened as she turned to him. 'You haven't spent *weeks* working with Bethany.'

He held Edna's stare. 'Bethany's only ever had the one horse to work with.'

Edna pursed her lips as she glanced between Neve and him. 'I see.' Her expression cleared. 'When you're done at Rosewood, keep your schedule clear. Bethany's always talking about getting another project horse. I think now would be a good time.'

He kept his expression neutral while he worked out how soon he could organise a new droving job. The season out west continued to be dry and help was needed to move hungry stock along the travelling stock routes. 'I'm sure it will be.' He glanced down the street to where the white wrought iron of the two-storey Royal Arms gleamed. 'Nice to chat, Edna, but Denham's waiting. I'd best get moving.'

'I'd better go too,' Neve said, swapping the oversized bag she carried to her other hand.

While Edna air-kissed Neve's cheek, Tanner moved a safe distance away.

Knowing Edna was watching him, he briefly looked at Neve. 'I'll be out at nine if that suits?'

'I'll be home.'

Tanner nodded at Edna. 'I might see you next time I'm in town?'

Edna's smile grew smug. 'I'm sure you will thanks to your blue ute. I always know when you're here. It's the only one of that colour.'

Without another look at either woman, Tanner strode away. He scraped a hand over his stubble. Next trip to town, he'd park in a side street or he'd borrow Phil's farm ute. Small-town matchmaking never failed to make him feel like a wanted man.

His tension must have shown on his face, as when he walked into the Royal Arms Denham didn't say a word, just slid a beer across the table towards him.

'That obvious?' Tanner said with a grimace as he took a seat and curled his fingers around the cold glass.

Denham touched his beer to Tanner's. 'Yep.'

Tanner sighed and relaxed into his chair. The familiar smell of alcohol was universal in all the bush pubs he'd visited in his search for who he was. Thanks to the church bell tower, the only clue he'd had about his birth mother, he'd found the answers he was looking for. Now, the only pub he visited was the Royal Arms.

Denham grinned, his blue eyes brimming with laughter. 'Cressy might have also texted that Edna had you and Neve cornered outside the saddlery.'

Tanner took a swallow of beer. 'It's all right for you. Your ute is white and you're a soon-to-be-married man.'

'I keep telling you, go out on some dates, have some fun. You might actually enjoy yourself. Once you're off the market, Edna will leave you alone.'

'That's easier said than done. My social skills are as rusty as the iron on the hay shed. Besides, I'm away so much it wouldn't be fair on anyone.'

Denham looked out the window as Edna's white four-wheel drive left town. When he glanced back at Tanner, the amusement had left his eyes. 'I know we've talked about this before. I also know the western district is doing it tough and needs drovers, but there's more than enough work for you here … if you wanted to stay.'

Tanner stared into his beer. Not only was Denham his cousin and best mate, but he was also his business partner. Denham ran the rodeo-bull-breeding programme side of their company, while Tanner dealt with the horse-training component when he was home.

Denham spoke again. 'Meredith's worried about you … and so am I.'

'I'm fine. I just need to … get away … sometimes.'

Denham didn't immediately answer, just studied him, empathy in his eyes. 'I'm here anytime you want to talk.'

'Thanks.'

He didn't say anything more. He had no words for what surged and seethed inside, even for Denham. The only thing that provided a respite from his restlessness and uncertainty was droving.

Out on the long paddock, there was just him, his horse, dog and a mob of cattle. There was no more unpredictability, complexity or heartache. Out in the space and bush solitude, a family didn't force a young mother to give up her son. Out in the red dust, an adoptive father didn't reject his son. And out where the stars blazed in the midnight sky, a woman didn't make promises she had no intention of ever keeping.

# CHAPTER
# 3

'I heard you had a very social morning yesterday,' Ella's cheerful voice sounded down the phone line.

Neve smiled into her mobile. 'Let's just say I've discovered a trip to Woodlea's never dull.' She told the vet of the date Edna had organised with the pharmacist.

Ella chuckled. 'I wonder if Michael knows of Edna's grand plans to get the two of you together?'

'I went to see him. He had no idea. Stranger things have happened, but Edna's intel was out of date. He has a girlfriend.'

'You're kidding. It's not every day Edna's wrong. At least there's one person she won't set you up with and that's Tanner.'

Neve banished an unexpected tug of yearning. Surely Edna hadn't been right? She didn't need any more adult company, especially of the cowboy kind.

'True. I thought Cressy was joking when she said wait until I saw how Edna acted around Tanner. I'm sure she fluttered her eyelashes.'

'I've no doubt she did. We might have to run a rescue mission at the small-hall festival … that's if Tanner goes.'

Neve gave in to her curiosity. 'You don't think he'll be there? Denham and Hewitt have already said they're going.'

'I know he won't be. You've more chance of seeing the white kangaroo out on Stoney Hill Road than you have of seeing Tanner at a social event. You're just lucky he's home at the moment to help with Dell and Bassie.'

'I am.' Neve looked out the kitchen window at the drive into Rosewood. It was almost nine and Tanner's ute would soon kick up dust on the gravel road. 'He'll be here in a minute. I'd better go.'

'Me too. Sorry I missed your text about Bassie's rug. It was a busy day. The sooner the brown snakes realise summer is over and it's time to hibernate, the better. I had two dogs come into the surgery with snake bites.'

Neve shuddered. 'I hope they were okay.'

'Yes, both had their anti-venom in time. Say hi to Tanner and see you on Saturday.'

Neve barely heard Ella's words. A fine red cloud drifted into the sky. 'Will do.'

She ended the call and stared through the window at the approaching blue ute. Uncertainty fluttered in her midriff. She wished for the tenth time since breakfast that she was looking after the girls today. There was safety in numbers. She could only hope that Tanner hadn't misinterpreted her remarks to Edna. Her comment that she had him around if she needed company wasn't designed to flag her interest or threaten his bachelor status. Edna already had him in her sights.

She headed to the front door. The comment had been simply an instinctive response to the hunted look that had darkened his eyes before Edna had thrown her arms around him. Neve was hardwired to help people, and in that moment Tanner had needed an ally.

She'd also wanted to signal to Edna that she didn't appreciate being manipulated or part of any matchmaking games. She tugged on her boots and grabbed a pink cap with Woodlea Veterinary Hospital on the front from the hat stand.

Tanner had parked beneath the cedar tree and now strode towards the orchard paddock. Today he wore his usual jeans, felt hat and blue work shirt. His loose, lithe strides and the relaxed line of his broad shoulders didn't fool her. Cressy's heads-up yesterday confirmed that his confidence and self-possession hid a vulnerability that if she wasn't careful would draw her to him.

Black-and-white flashed as a dog raced over from the ute to Tanner's side. She stifled a groan as the drover grinned and bent to pat the young border collie. She didn't need proof that Tanner possessed a gentle and tender side. He already was too good-looking for any single girl's peace of mind. Let alone one whose last date was so long ago she had trouble remembering the guy's name and where they went.

'Morning,' she said as she drew near. She'd see if he needed anything before hightailing it inside.

'Morning.'

His nod was polite and impersonal before he walked through the pony paddock gate to where Dell waited for him. As he scratched the donkey's neck, Neve didn't need to be a donkey expert to know the grey-and-white jenny was smitten. Bassie stood a body length away, his tail swishing.

Tanner led Dell over to the fence and tied her to the baling twine. 'I hope it's okay that I brought Patch. I knew the girls weren't here and wanted to see how Dell and Bassie are around him.'

Neve glanced at the long-haired border collie who had a black patch over his right eye. The dog was busy sniffing around the base of the iron bird bath Hewitt had welded from a rusty plough disc as a 'welcome to Woodlea' gift.

'Good idea. He looks just like Hewitt's dog, Max.'

'He's Max and Molly's son.'

Neve fought a hot wave of embarrassment and kept her answer to a nod. Yet again she'd stated the obvious. She passed Tanner the curry comb from the tub she'd earlier brought outside. When he moved in close to take the comb she caught the scent of sun-dried cotton and leather. His eyes briefly met hers.

Needing something to do, she picked up a soft body brush. What was wrong with her? She had no trouble being herself and feeling comfortable around Denham and Hewitt. 'I can brush Dell if you want to tackle catching Bassie?'

'Thanks.'

Using the same techniques she'd witnessed yesterday, Tanner approached and then took a step away whenever Bassie looked like he'd bolt. It wasn't long before Tanner had clipped on Bassie's lead rope and the pony was tied to the fence. As much as Bassie maintained his I'm-not-impressed stare, he closed his eyes as Tanner brushed a sweet spot on his shoulder.

As they groomed the pony and donkey, neither Neve nor Tanner spoke. The only sound was the screech of a cockatoo before its talons clicked as it walked across the tin roof of the garden shed. Neve snuck a glance at Tanner's face. His closed expression gave nothing away. She had no idea if he was as tense as she was. If she could she'd make witty small talk. But the methodical way Tanner moved and smoothed his hands over Bassie gave her hope that he wasn't uncomfortable, just focused on whatever he was learning about the pony.

Tanner broke the silence. 'Bassie's quiet, with no malice. He just needs a little attitude adjustment.'

As if knowing Tanner was talking about him, Bassie turned to peer at Neve through the long blond forelock that fell over his left eye. If she didn't know better she'd have thought him angelic.

She arched a brow. 'A little attitude adjustment?'

Tanner's lips twitched. 'Yes. I'll work him in the round yard and see what training he's had, but I'm confident he'll make a good leadline pony for the girls.'

Tanner led Bassie out of the orchard paddock. Not quite sure what to do but knowing she didn't want to miss seeing if the pony would try any tricks, Neve followed. Patch ran by her side and then alongside Bassie. Both Dell and Bassie appeared oblivious to the young dog's presence.

Tanner had assembled the round-yard panels in a perfect circle near an old gum. The spreading olive-green canopy provided shade as well as protection from the wind. Near the gate, three milk crates were secured together with zip ties, two on the bottom and one on the top. Neve guessed the step configuration would be to later help the girls climb into Bassie's saddle.

When Tanner and Bassie entered the round yard, Neve carried the mounting block deeper into the shade before sitting on the top step. Patch rested his head on her knee and she tickled behind his ears.

Tanner stopped in the middle of the round yard to gather the long lunging rein in his left hand. He moved in close to Bassie's left shoulder and lifted his right arm. The pony didn't move.

Tanner's deep chuckle sounded. 'You're not going to yield, are you, Mr Bassie? Stubborn has to be your middle name.'

Tanner moved closer and lifted his arm again, and this time Bassie moved his feet and swung around to face him. The drover rubbed the pony's forehead. 'See, that wasn't so hard. Now out you go. I know you know what to do.'

Tanner allowed the lunging rein to lengthen as Bassie moved to the edge of the yard. The pony then walked in a circle around Tanner. After he had completed several laps, Tanner spoke softly and Bassie broke into a trot. After a few more smooth laps, Tanner slowed Bassie to a stop, changed the lunging rein into his right hand and had Bassie walk, then trot, in the opposite direction.

All the while Neve watched and patted Patch. Even if she wanted to return inside, she couldn't. For the first time since she'd met him, Tanner appeared comfortable and relaxed. Whatever troubled him, he'd left at the round-yard gate. The wide brim of his hat hid his eyes, but his mouth had softened. The smile he flashed was the same easy grin she'd seen in town the first time she noticed him. Working with Bassie in the round yard made him happy. But as soon as Tanner led the pony out of the yard, the line of his jaw was again as taut as the wire fence that ran alongside them.

'It looked like the attitude adjusting went well,' she said, forcing herself to start a conversation. Tanner's retreat behind the wall he encased himself in almost made her feel … lost.

'Bassie's as wise as he's smart and stubborn. He knew the more he behaved the less work he'd do. Rule 101 of training is to always end on a positive note.'

'Which means when I lunge him, we'll be in the round yard until Christmas.'

For a moment Neve thought a real smile would break through Tanner's reserve, and then he looked away. 'He'll get hungry before then. I'll teach you how to lunge and he'll be a perfect gentleman.'

He tied Bassie to the baling twine, and as he ran his hand over the pony's caramel neck, Bassie leaned into his touch.

Neve swallowed. She didn't need further evidence that Tanner had a good and kind heart. She also didn't need to catch another glimpse of him content and at ease while he worked with Dell.

She spoke quickly. 'I'll head inside now. Thanks again for everything.'

'See you tomorrow.' Even though Tanner glanced at her, she couldn't read his expression beneath the low brim of his hat. 'I should be out after lunch if that suits?'

Neve nodded as she bent to give Patch a last belly rub. 'See you both then.'

Without a backward look, she walked through the garden to the veranda steps. But as she made pink sparkly playdough for the girls in the microwave, she snuck glances through the kitchen window to where Dell trotted around the circular yard.

It was only when Dell and Bassie were in their paddock and the dust had settled behind Tanner's ute that she abandoned any pretence of concentrating on what she was doing. She left the last of the dishes in the sink and sat at the kitchen table to open her laptop.

Her inquisitiveness about Tanner would only lead to trouble. But perhaps if she found out more about him he'd stop being of such interest? She typed in the name embroidered above his pocket. A website bearing the same horse logo filled the screen along with a picture of him riding a metallic-gold palomino.

In the photograph, Tanner had longer hair and his wide smile was full of carefree charm. When she looked carefully, she saw that it didn't quite reach his eyes. She clicked on the testimonials of his horse-training expertise and was surprised to see a number of American clients.

Further internet searching revealed he didn't have any social media presence, but he did have a public profile following a win in an American mustang-training reality show. She enlarged photos of him dressed as a cowboy in leather chaps and a vest as he jumped the palomino through a ring of fire. Not surprisingly, he also was voted the fan favourite. A title reinforced by the many photos of him taken with cowgirls whose eyes sparkled more than the rhinestones on their belts.

Neve clicked on a link so she didn't have to look at the proof that she wasn't the only one taken by his clear blue eyes and the indent of his dimple. The link led to an article from the local Woodlea paper. A single image showed a tall, elegant Meredith walking in Claremont's garden, her arm linked with Tanner's.

Neve leaned forward to better see Tanner's expression. In this picture his eyes smiled. The article explained how Meredith had been forced by her family to give up her newborn son after the jackaroo she loved had been killed in a fall from a horse. It had taken years of searching for Tanner to then find his way back to her.

Neve shut the laptop lid and took a shaky breath. No wonder Tanner's confidence masked an unexpected vulnerability. No wonder it was only animals he let get close. Tanner had had as much control over his life as the mustang he'd worked with. Both had needed to navigate a world they hadn't been born into.

She texted Fliss to say she was coming over for a cuppa and to help in the garden. She couldn't stay here on her own. Without her mother, the girls, or work to keep her busy, she had no distractions. She frowned through the window at the road Tanner had left on. She wouldn't be able to stop thinking about what he'd been through searching for his birth mother. It was already bad enough that he occupied her thoughts far more than he should.

$\infty$

Arrow's golden ears flickered as they rode the track between Claremont's custom-built rodeo yards and the stables. Tanner patted the gelding's velvety neck. Grey blurred to their left as a wallaby bounded through the bleached grass towards the grove of wattles that lined the nearby gully. The mustang might be a long way from his Montana birthplace, but no longer did the unfamiliar sight of a kangaroo, wombat or even an echidna bother him.

Arrow, with his strong will and fearless heart, was a steady constant in his life. Together they dealt with whatever came their way, whether it was a steer breaking away from the mob or floodwaters they had to swim through to rescue a trapped mare. They understood each other and their bond was unbreakable.

'Easy, boy,' Tanner said as Arrow's ears pinned back. 'It's just Reggie. It's not personal, remember?'

Dust tinged the afternoon breeze as a massive Brahman-cross bull lumbered over to the fence. Slab-shouldered, with thick, curved horns, Reggie's size was only matched by his don't-mess-with-me glare. As intimidating and grumpy as the bull was, when around Cressy or Fliss he was nothing but gentle. He also had an obsessive weakness for carrots. Tanner felt in his shirt pocket for the carrot he'd cut earlier. He slowed Arrow to a stop before leaving the saddle.

Fliss and Cressy believed Reggie was an excellent judge of character and that a man had to feed him carrots before he could be considered a prospective life partner. Such a 'test' was a current source of ribbing from Denham and Hewitt. It was all right for them, they'd passed and ended up with the women they loved.

Tanner strode towards where Reggie eyeballed him before pawing the ground. He'd have to put up with their jokes that he wasn't yet man enough for anyone until Reggie accepted carrots from him. As for him falling for someone special, even if they were beautiful and warm-hearted like Neve, it was out of the question. He only ever did casual in relationships and with women who felt the same way he did. He needed the freedom of knowing he could leave at any time.

'Okay, Reg. You know the drill. I have carrots. You like carrots.'

The grey rodeo bull allowed Tanner to reach the fence and then with a snort spun around and presented him with his rump.

Tanner sighed. 'Right. Today's not the day.' He leaned over the fence. Reggie mightn't accept him, but the bull hadn't ever tried to hurt him. He tossed several pieces of carrot so they landed on a clump of grass close to Reggie's front foot. Just like on every other failed carrot-feeding day, Tanner wouldn't make it back to Arrow before Reggie had crunched on the treats. 'I'll be back.'

Arrow whickered as he approached. 'Yeah, buddy, I saved some for you.' He fed the gelding the last piece of carrot and rubbed his forehead. 'Now the troughs have been checked, we'd better help Meredith before we head to Neve's.'

Once Arrow had been unsaddled and had ambled down to his favourite grazing spot beside the creek, Tanner left the stables. As it was autumn he didn't need to keep watch for the male magpie intent on protecting his mate's nest. His hat still bore the dents from where he'd been swooped last spring.

He walked past the jacaranda tree to the line of strappy agapanthus that marked the start of the garden. Huge shade trees sheltered the veranda-clad homestead that had been home to generations of Rigbys. Tanner stared at the eight chimneys silhouetted against the sky that once would have emitted curls of smoke. He'd spent so long not knowing who he was, he still couldn't believe that the blood of pioneering ancestors ran through his veins.

He caught sight of his birth mother as she knelt weeding a garden bed over near the fir tree. Not a day passed when he wasn't filled with gratitude for finding Meredith or for the way she'd received him. Warm, generous and uplifting, she'd opened her life to him. Even after eighteen months a wave of emotion still caught him by surprise and made his throat ache. She was everything he'd hoped to find, and more.

Guilt twisted inside. She could never know that, even after being reunited, a part of him remained displaced. In the short space of two years he'd lost his adoptive mother to cancer, the support and approval of his adoptive father and the woman he'd been hoping to spend his future with. He couldn't trust that life was done messing with him.

The radiance of Meredith's smile triggered a fresh assault of guilt. 'Hi, darling.'

'Hi.'

In honour of the memory of the gentle and unselfish woman who'd adopted and raised him, he couldn't call Meredith 'mum'. To his relief she understood.

Meredith came to her feet and brushed the hair off her forehead with the back of her pink-gloved hand. Even dressed in her gardening clothes she appeared graceful and stylish. It was no surprise Cressy said she'd once been crowned Miss Woodlea Showgirl. 'Any luck with Reggie?'

'No.'

'Not even with my homegrown carrots?'

'I still got his does-my-butt-look-good-in-this pose.'

Meredith's laughter chased away his tension. 'Maybe next time?'

'Maybe.' Tanner walked over to the laden wheelbarrow. 'The usual place?'

'Yes, thanks. Patch's still out with Phil. They'll be back from checking the cattle soon. He may be young, but Phil says he's got the makings of a great working dog.'

Tanner nodded, but didn't take hold of the wheelbarrow handles. Concern shadowed Meredith's blue eyes. He'd sensed she'd been wanting to say something over the past few days. Even though he shared the main homestead with Meredith and her husband, Phil, he lived in the granny flat in a side wing. Unless they had a meal together, there wasn't always an opportunity for a serious talk.

'Tanner ... we're really enjoying having you home.'

He fought the urge to fold his arms. 'It's good to be back.'

He didn't need to add *for a little while*. Meredith's gaze already searched his face.

'Do you think you'll be here until the wedding?'

Tanner had a flashback to the delight in Edna's smile when she mentioned Bethany taking on a project horse. 'No, but I won't leave for long. Denham's twitchy enough as it is.'

'Yes, he's been over more than usual for morning smoko.'

'As much as he groans about wedding plans, he can't wait until he says "I do".'

Meredith's smile grew tender. 'Phil was the same.'

During Tanner's first autumn at Claremont, Meredith and farm manager Phil had exchanged their vows in a small intimate garden wedding. A picture taken on the day of Meredith and him together was one of two photos Tanner carried in his wallet. The other picture was of his adoptive parents.

Shoulders tight, he took hold of the wheelbarrow handles. Photos could capture special memories, but they also provided a reminder of the realities of life. In the picture of his adoptive parents, his mother had looked healthy and his father had been laughing at something he'd said.

Meredith bent to collect a fallen weed and added it to the pile in the barrow. 'So how are Neve's pony and donkey going?'

Tanner stiffened. The lipstick target on his bachelor back was making him overly suspicious. Meredith didn't mean anything by her casual question, even if she threw him a quick look. It wasn't like her to play matchmaker. She often asked how his horse training was going.

'Good. They're no longer escapees.'

'That will be a relief to Neve.' Meredith moved away to pull a broadleaf dandelion out of the lawn. 'She's been just what those two girls have needed since they lost their mother. I suspect they're what she's needed too. I'll give you some jam drops to take over.'

Tanner nodded. Empathy flooded him for Maya and Kait's loss. Meredith's remark about Neve also validated his feeling that all wasn't rosy in her world. Unease fuelled his restlessness and he pushed the wheelbarrow over to the compost heap. Neve's life wasn't any of his business. Independent and self-sufficient, she wouldn't appreciate his concern.

But that afternoon when he handed Neve the container of jam drops, all thoughts about keeping to himself evaporated. Today she wore her usual jeans, bright cotton shirt and Woodlea vet cap, but she'd pulled her hair into a ponytail. It didn't matter if her smile was composed, dark smudges underlined her eyes. The pale curve of her nape and the delicate jut of her cheekbones further heightened an impression of fragility.

She took hold of the container with a brief smile. 'The girls will be excited. We love Meredith's baking.'

Now was the time to keep their conversation professional and talk about what he'd be doing with Dell and Bassie today. Instead, he placed a hand on his abs. 'Don't we all. I'm sure Arrow groans every time I get on him.'

Amusement kindled in Neve's green eyes. 'Arrow's a great name.'

'He's a straight-and-true kind of horse.'

'He sounds wonderful. What colour is he?'

'Palomino.'

Neve nodded before her smile ebbed. She turned to look at Bassie and Dell. 'So what's the plan for today?'

'Seeing as the girls aren't here, and if you'd like, you could lunge the terrible twosome.'

As he'd hoped his light tone returned the smile to her eyes.

'I'm warning you now, my horse experience is limited, but I'm game.'

'Great. Let's catch them.'

In the years since he'd graduated from his claustrophobic city law degree and gone in search of his dreams, he'd helped many horse owners lunge their animals. But never had a round yard felt so small and never had he been so aware of a woman. Neve stood at least an arm's length away, but all he could smell was the fresh scent of flowers. Her long ponytail hung down her back, drawing his attention to the curve of her waist beneath her loose purple shirt.

'Like this?' she asked over her shoulder.

He forced himself to focus on anything but her. 'Yes. Now lift your arm to signal to Bassie that he needs to walk away from you and out to the yard edge.'

When Bassie didn't move, Tanner said quietly, 'He's such a rascal. When he doesn't listen, make sure you have his attention and then add a little more pressure.'

Before he could suggest some techniques, Neve said, 'Bassie. Out you go.'

Neve's tilted chin and firm tone communicated she meant business. Bassie swished his golden tail before walking out and then around her.

Neve flicked Tanner a happy and relieved look. Her checking in with him communicated they were a team. He clenched his teeth.

Other clients had felt the same way, so why then did his heart hammer in his chest when Neve looked at him with trust and not a trace of wariness?

Bassie ambled a full circle and then walked to where Neve stood in the centre of the yard.

Tanner spoke quietly. 'He's still testing you. You're the one who decides when to stop. Give him a pat to reassure him and send him out again.'

Neve followed his instructions and this time Bassie didn't stop after he'd walked a full circle. Once the pony had circled her again and Tanner could see Neve adjust her position to always be behind Bassie's shoulder, he told Neve to ask Bassie to 'trot on'. The pony's mane and tail shimmered as his tiny hooves went up and down.

After Bassie had completed two laps, Neve sent Tanner a sideways glance. 'He's going well so this would be a good time to bring him in and to go around the other way.'

He nodded. 'It would be.'

Neve was a quick learner and she'd soon be able to handle Bassie and Dell without his help. The realisation brought with it relief as well as a sense of disquiet. Neve, with her sea-green eyes, her unselfishness and her secrets, had got under his skin. He should be counting down the days until he resumed his solitary life. Instead, the loneliness that he had no time for pushed itself onto his to-be-dealt-with list.

Knowing she wasn't focused on him, he passed a hand around the base of his neck. It wasn't just children or small-town matchmaking that dried his mouth. Neve Fitzpatrick was now number three on his list of things that terrified him.

# CHAPTER

# 4

'When's Tanner here?' Maya looked up from the picture she'd been drawing for the past half-hour. The brightness of her brown eyes matched the excitement infusing her voice. Tanner's visit was already the highlight of her day.

Neve liked to think that brushing Dell and Bassie and playing with Patch was what the five-year-old enjoyed. The truth was reflected in her picture. Maya had drawn a large cowboy in a hat alongside a smaller pony, donkey and black-and-white dog.

'Soon, sweetheart.'

Maya returned to colouring in.

Kait grinned from across the kitchen table where she played with a white toy horse. She'd given up on drawing after five minutes, but her anticipation at seeing Tanner hadn't waned. Expression hopeful, she kept staring out the window.

Neve withheld a sigh as she placed a pile of photographs of her grandparents' wedding day into a labelled envelope. She didn't

need any reminder of how Tanner had won over the girls as well as
Dell and Bassie. The taffy pony now waited at the gate with Dell
whenever Tanner's ute appeared.

'Tanner's nice,' Maya said as she chose a different pencil. 'Dell
and Bassie like him. He also knows Bassie has the red-and-black
lead.'

Neve gave in to her restlessness and left her seat. The girls'
desperation to see Tanner sent her nerves into a freefall. It was hard
enough as it was to not feel self-conscious around him without her
also looking forward to his visits. 'How about we catch Dell and
Bassie before Tanner arrives?'

Maya and Kait were out of the kitchen door before Neve had
finished speaking. She double-checked they had on boots and a
hat before they raced outside. She also made sure she filled a small
container with a chopped apple.

She followed the girls into the mid-morning sunshine. While the
days were balmy and the skies blue, the cool, crisp nights flagged
winter was on its way. Against the shed was a pile of wood Hewitt
had cut for whenever Neve needed to light the fire in the living
room. It wouldn't be long until the scent of wood smoke filled the
night air.

To her left the vegetable beds looked bare, but soon tiny green
shoots would push themselves through the watered soil of the two
far beds. She'd also get some seedling punnets on her next town
visit to finish off the last two beds. She just hoped all the local talk
about locust swarms migrating eastward wouldn't prove true. This
time she wanted to at least eat one vegetable from the garden.

Happy giggles sounded as Maya and Kait patted Dell and Bassie
as they pushed their noses through the gaps in the fence panels.
Despite their gentleness with the girls and Tanner having made
taming the terrible twosome look easy, Neve wasn't fooled. Bassie

regularly sent her a sly and sassy look. He'd revert back to being a rascal before she could even blink.

The girls turned to face her and held out their hands. She placed a piece of apple on each small flattened palm. When Tanner had instructed them on the safe way to feed Dell and Bassie, strain had etched his face, but his words had been quiet and gentle. He still avoided the girls as much as possible, but their high opinion of him said they saw through his reserve to the kindness within.

Once Maya and Kait had fed the pony and donkey their apple, Neve took the leads and headcollars and went through the paddock gate. The girls waited outside, brushes in their hands. Dell stood still while Neve slipped on her headcollar and then followed her over to the fence. Bassie looked like he was going to walk away, but then stayed where he was while Neve buckled on his headcollar. When it came to moving, he then didn't budge. His four tiny feet were planted in the red dirt as though they'd been anchored there for centuries.

Neve used the calm and patient voice that worked on her young occupational therapy clients who were reluctant to participate in their first therapy appointment. It usually only took a couple of swings in the colourful hammocks that had been suspended from the ceiling and she'd never have to use such a voice again.

'Bassie ... walk on.' She touched his shoulder like Tanner had shown her and took a firm hold of the lead where it clipped onto his headcollar beneath his caramel jaw. Bassie sighed and moved.

She tied him to the fence using the baling twine and made a conscious effort to relax. Tanner wasn't here; there was no reason to be so on edge. Bassie and Dell, and even the girls, would pick up on her tension if she wasn't careful.

She hadn't taken two steps away when Bassie suddenly lifted his head, leaned back on his haunches and pulled. The baling twine snapped. Lead rope trailing, and his hooves kicking up powdery dust, he galloped to the far end of the orchard.

Neve took hold of Dell's headcollar in case she followed, but the donkey didn't even look in the direction Bassie had bolted. The jenny would have seen Bassie behaving badly many times before.

The girls stared at Neve, their brown eyes large and round. She gave what she hoped passed as a relaxed grin. 'It's okay. Bassie didn't hurt himself. I'll go and bring him back.'

While Neve headed to the far corner of the paddock, she searched the winding gravel road into Rosewood. It was important she dealt with Bassie without Tanner's help. Her pace quickened as she saw a flash of blue and a wisp of dust.

Between using the tactics Tanner had taught her, and having the lead rope to grab hold of, she was surprised at how quickly she had Bassie retied to a new piece of baling twine. Before she moved away, she held his unblinking pony stare. Eventually, she'd be privy to all his naughty pony tricks.

Tanner drove through the front gate and parked in his usual place beneath the cedar tree. As soon as Patch was unclipped from the chain on the back of the ute, he leapt to the ground and bounded over to the girls. As wary as Tanner was of the two little redheads, Patch was besotted with them. The feeling was mutual. Neve's heart warmed as the border collie wriggled so much the laughing girls could hardly pat him.

A grin tugged at Tanner's mouth as he watched Patch with the girls. The curve of his masculine lips caused Neve's stomach to swirl. He had the most gorgeous smile.

Tanner nodded at Maya and then Kait. Even though he didn't say anything, Neve knew that when he greeted each child they'd felt like they were the sole focus of Tanner's world. She too felt that way whenever he looked at her. His gaze had an intensity and an honesty that, as much as she didn't want to admit it, connected to something deep within her.

His light-blue eyes briefly met hers as he held up the donkey rug he carried. 'I was in town. Dell might need this.'

'Thanks. Clare called to say it'd arrived.'

'Bassie up to his old tricks?'

'Let's just say this is his second time being tied to the fence.' She broke eye contact to stare at the pony. Holding Tanner's gaze for too long never failed to leave her feeling breathless. 'How did you know?'

'The snapped baling twine.' Tanner paused to scrape a hand over his chin. If she didn't know better she could have sworn it wasn't only the girls that made him uneasy; she did as well. But a man like Tanner would never be unsettled by someone like her. 'Bassie won't try that trick again now he knows he can't get away with it.'

Tanner headed for the tack shed before she could work out from his expression if it had been respect deepening his words.

Smiles wide, Kait and Maya followed him. Last visit Tanner had attached some wire saddle racks to the shed wall and one of them now held Bassie's small pony saddle. Neve noted the way Tanner shortened his stride so the girls didn't have to run to keep up with him.

Realising she was staring at the shed door long after Tanner and the girls had disappeared inside, she looked away. She had to stop being so preoccupied with Tanner. She'd never had any trouble relegating members of the opposite sex to the bottom of her priority list.

She picked up a brush and smoothed Dell's shaggy coat. Perhaps that had been her problem. She'd never made time to socialise even if her opportunities to go out had been limited. It had been a no-brainer. Go out on a date or stay at home with the mother she loved and who needed her. Even those precious years together now weren't enough.

Sadness pushed against her control. She still didn't know how she would fill the void losing her mother had left behind. The girls had given her a temporary sense of purpose, but when Graham found a more permanent arrangement next spring she'd need another distraction.

She also had to consider her finances once she stopped looking after the girls. Her nest egg wasn't supposed to be touched. She brushed the same spot on Dell's neck twice. She wasn't going to think about what would happen if she remained adrift and didn't start to reconfigure her life.

She hadn't registered Tanner and the girls returning until Tanner's quiet voice spoke her name. 'Neve?'

She took her time to turn. 'Sorry …'

His gaze swept over her face before he replied. 'It's okay, I was asking if Bassie has had his saddle fitted?'

Neve shook her head. Tanner had Bassie's black saddle over his arm while Kait held the red saddle cloth and Maya a dark-brown bridle.

While Tanner checked the fit of Bassie's saddle, Neve helped the girls pamper Dell. Perched on the milk-crate mounting block, they then watched while Tanner lunged Bassie. Just like every other time Tanner entered the round yard, his tension and reserve ebbed and his grin grew easy and relaxed. All too soon he led Bassie back to the orchard paddock to be unsaddled.

Maya looked at Neve and she gave her a nod. The two girls sprinted across the lawn towards the house. Patch followed before wandering off to sniff around the vegetable garden beds. Neve glanced at Tanner. Since the day he'd taught her to lunge, they hadn't again been alone. But if Tanner was aware they were by themselves, it didn't register in his body language or his voice as he shut the paddock gate.

'I'll bring Arrow next week and pony Bassie off him, just to make sure he's okay to be led. Then the girls can have their first ride.'

'They'll love that.' Neve looked over at the veranda, but there was no sign yet of Maya and Kait. 'Would … you like to come inside … for a cool drink? The girls have something for you.'

Tanner folded his arms even before she'd finished. She ignored the way the blue cotton tightened around his biceps and his rolled-up sleeve cuffs inched higher on his tanned forearms. 'I'd better head back.'

Neve linked her fingers together to stop herself from taking hold of his arm as he half turned. The tight line of his jaw reassured her it wasn't indifference that made him want to make a quick getaway, just uncertainty.

'The girls won't be long.' She lowered her voice as the front door slammed. 'Tanner, you don't have to do anything when they give their pictures to you … just smile and say thank you. That will make them happy.'

She didn't miss the relief that relaxed his mouth as he turned back to her. 'Thanks … I'm not very good with kids.'

She didn't have time to reply before Maya and Kait raced over, stopped in front of Tanner and thrust out two pieces of paper. Kait's paper was now filled with blue squiggles, which explained why they'd stayed inside.

Tanner accepted the drawings, studied each picture and then said a quiet, 'Thank you. These are … great.'

Neve took Maya's hand just as the five-year-old went to launch herself at the drover to give him a hug.

'You're very welcome,' Neve said and both little redheads nodded.

The tanned skin of Tanner's throat moved as he swallowed. 'I … like my hat in this one. And I like all the blue in this one.'

Maya giggled. 'That's because blue's your favourite colour.'

Tanner glanced at Neve, his eyes unsure and brow creased.

She gestured towards his shirt. 'Your shirts and your ute are blue.'

He didn't immediately reply. 'I guess the baling twine's blue too.' He nodded at the girls, a grin crinkling the corners of his eyes. 'Blue obviously is my favourite colour.'

As if conscious he'd stepped too far out of his comfort zone, his smile died. He looked around for Patch, who, body low to the ground, slowly approached a magpie. At Tanner's whistle the dog sped to his side. 'We'd better get back. Denham has a truckload of cattle arriving.'

'Okay. Thanks for your help today.'

'No worries. See you next week.'

Too late Neve saw Kait step forward and hold her arms up to Tanner to be picked up. He froze, the light in his eyes dimming to a troubled blue.

Neve let go of Maya's hand and scooped Kait up to sit her on her hip. Kait rested her head in the crook of Neve's neck and waved at Tanner.

He lifted a hand and waved in return before also waving at Maya. Then without looking at Neve, he turned on his boot heels and strode away. Just like they usually did, Neve and the girls watched until his ute disappeared through the front gate and Patch's barking could no longer be heard.

Neve only half listened to Maya and Kait's chatter about what they could make Tanner that was blue as they walked along the paved garden path. With every meeting, Neve glimpsed a little more about who Tanner was and unearthed a little more about him.

Instead of helping assuage her curiosity and disengage her interest, each new discovery only drew her to him more.

Today he'd admitted he wasn't good with kids. Yet he'd gone above and beyond what he'd needed to do to thank the girls for their presents. He'd put aside his own fears to make sure he didn't hurt their feelings. She stifled a sigh. And now it would prove even more impossible to stop thinking about him.

∽

'So this is where you've been hiding?' Hewitt's voice sounded before his boots rang on the concrete of the workshop that occupied a section of Claremont's machinery shed.

Tanner straightened to wipe his oily hands on a rag. 'My ag bike needed an oil filter change before I head out droving again.'

'I hope you're not heading off to the long paddock anytime soon. Denham's going to need some nights out at the Royal Arms.'

Since Hewitt had moved into Bundara with Fliss, he'd become a good mate. Tanner, Denham and Hewitt had all bonded over their mutual love of horses, cold beer and country life.

'I'm sure he will.' Tanner left the question about when he'd head off droving unanswered. 'He won't be the only one.'

Hewitt bent to pat Patch, who'd left his favourite corner of the shed to greet the pickup rider. 'You can say that again. Once Cressy and Denham tie the knot the focus will be on Fliss's and my wedding. I'll need just as many visits to the pub as Denham.'

Tanner ignored the ache of a long-ago pain. He too had once had a wedding on his mind.

'Count me in.'

Hewitt passed him the socket wrench. 'Have you got time for a ride? Garnet's going stir crazy.'

'I'm taking Arrow over to Neve's Monday afternoon so can call in on the way back?'

'Great. We can head up to the ridge before it gets dark.' Hewitt paused and the expression in his grey eyes turned serious. 'I wish I could do more to help Neve. It's tough having to adjust to a new life.'

Tanner's hands stilled as he fitted the replacement oil filter.

'New life?'

'Yes, she lost her mother last winter. It turns out her mother grew up at Bundara, so we have Neve over as often as we can. She hides her loss well, but it's only when she's there that she looks at peace.'

Tanner focused on finishing fitting the new oil filter. His adoptive mother might have passed away while he was at university, but the anguish associated with losing her remained. It had required a great deal of time to accept the new direction his own life had taken after her death.

When he replied he made sure his voice sounded casual. Hewitt was a man of few words, but he read people as easily as he did the rodeo bulls and buckjumpers. 'I can understand why Neve's moved close to a place that she connects with family.'

Hewitt nodded and Tanner didn't miss the way the pickup rider's stare stayed on him. The phone in Hewitt's shirt pocket vibrated and he checked his messages.

'Fliss wants to know if you need a ticket for the small-hall festival tomorrow?'

'No, I'm all good.'

A smile twitched on Hewitt's lips. 'No, as in you've got one, or no as in you're not setting foot in the same room as Edna?'

'No, as in I haven't given it any real thought.'

Hewitt raised a dark brow. 'You know if you don't go, Denham and I might take a wrong turn and end up in his man-cave.'

Tanner's laughter caused Patch's tail to thump on the floor. 'Do I have to remind you the last time you got *lost* Fliss and Cressy turned up at the shed, took your ute keys and personally chauffeured you to the book-club Christmas party?'

Hewitt groaned. 'I've never eaten so many mince pies in my life. At least if I was eating I wouldn't have to talk. Denham and I were the only males there.'

'So next Christmas, whenever book club is on, I'll pencil you in for a week away camping and fishing?'

'For sure.'

The sudden ebb of the amusement in Hewitt's eyes let Tanner know that even a few days away from Fliss would be too many.

Tanner returned the socket wrench to its position on the shelf. He'd told a half-truth. While he hadn't given the small-hall festival any real consideration, he had thought about it enough to decide not to go. His constant vigilance to avoid having his name connected with anyone single had worn thin. There also seemed to be a baby boom in Woodlea. Everywhere he looked there were either babies or women who were expecting. He avoided Hewitt's gaze as he faced him.

Most of all Neve would be there. It was hard enough being around her while working with Dell and Bassie, let alone engaging with her in a social setting. All eyes would be on them and he couldn't trust in his ability to hide his awareness of her. This morning when she'd recaptured Bassie, his respect for her determination to not let the pony win had deepened his voice.

'You're not going, are you?' Hewitt's solemn words sounded.

'Sorry, mate. You and Denham are on your own.'

'If you change your mind, you know where we'll be.' Hewitt moved forward to clasp Tanner's shoulder. 'See you on Monday.'

'Will do.'

Long after Hewitt had left, the knowledge of why Neve had come to the bush weighed upon Tanner. No wonder her smile didn't always last for long. No wonder she was kind and patient with the girls. She knew exactly what they were going through. Instead of losing her way in an unfamiliar world, Neve had opened her arms to children who needed her. And the knowledge humbled him. Neve possessed a depth and generosity that went beyond words.

The loneliness that was never satisfied with staying in the background coursed through him. On edge, he swept out the workshop and then, with Patch by his side, headed for the stables. He needed to feel the wind on his face. He needed the rhythmic sound of Arrow's galloping hooves to fill his head so he couldn't think of anything else.

He hadn't reached the shed when his mobile rang in his jeans pocket. His grip on his phone tightened as Neve's name flashed onto the screen. She usually only texted.

'Hi.'

'Hi, sorry to bother you, but Bassie's stuck in the fence. I can't get him out.'

He turned towards where his ute was parked beneath the jacaranda tree. 'You're not bothering me. I'm on my way.'

'Thanks.'

Patch jumped into the ute trayback and Tanner clipped the short chain onto his collar. As he drove the back road to Rosewood, he reminded himself that Neve's request wasn't personal. For her to ask for his help, Bassie must be well and truly stuck. Despite such a rationalisation, a hum of happiness refused to subside. He hadn't missed the warmth and relief in her voice when he'd said he was on his way.

Just as he'd suspected, Bassie had got himself into trouble. At the far end of the orchard an old iron gate had been used to reinforce the fence where the wire had once been cut. Somehow, greedy Bassie had wriggled between the fence and gate to reach the longer grass. He didn't appear to be in distress, which Tanner suspected was because his very round stomach was full. Neve stood inside the paddock next to him while the girls sat outside on two pink camping chairs. Dell grazed down by the lemon tree.

Tanner parked, let off Patch and collected wire cutters from the ute toolbox. He smiled at the girls as they patted Patch. Their serious little faces broke into grins.

Maya pointed at the taffy pony. 'Bassie's stuck like Winnie-the-Pooh in the honey tree.'

He nodded, despite only having a vague idea that Winnie-the-Pooh was some sort of bear. 'He sure is, but he'll be out soon.'

Kait gave him a thumbs-up sign he'd once seen Neve use.

Neve's strained expression didn't change as he approached. A faint blush bloomed in her cheeks. 'Thanks again for coming to help.'

'No worries.' He looked away to hide how much her appreciation touched him. 'Bassie's done a good job.'

'He can't move forward as there's nowhere to go and when he moves backwards his stomach gets stuck. I also don't have anything with which to cut the wire.'

Tanner reached over the fence to rub Bassie's forehead as he lifted his head. After assessing the pony for any injuries and finding none, Tanner bent to cut the wire that attached the gate to the fence. With each snip the tension holding the gate to the fence decreased.

Neve took hold of the rusted metal and carefully pulled it towards her, creating space for Bassie to back out. He did so as though he had all the time in the world. Then, once free, as if he hadn't created any drama, he peered at Tanner and Neve from beneath his long forelock.

Neve shook her head as the pony then wandered over to the fence in front of the girls in the hope of a treat. 'So much cuteness and yet so much mischief.'

Tanner laughed softly. 'You must admit, life without Bassie would be dull.'

For a moment he thought Neve wouldn't respond and then she too laughed. Her green eyes sparkled. 'You're right … it would be.'

Tanner busied himself with cutting the last of the tie wire securing the gate to the fence. He didn't want to examine the need to keep making Neve laugh until all the shadows were banished from her face. He lifted the gate over the fence so he could reattach it on the outside. He wasn't going to give crafty Bassie a second opportunity to wedge himself into a similar position.

Using a wooden post for leverage, he vaulted over the top fence wire. As he bent to reposition the gate, footsteps sounded behind him. The girls had left their chairs. As difficult as it was being around them, if he was honest, he no longer felt quite as panicked. But when a small hand tapped his shoulder he couldn't stop himself from tensing.

'What are you doing?' Maya asked as she stood close by him. He caught the scent of strawberries.

'Doing?' Kait echoed, standing beside her sister.

He slowly straightened. Even with their hats, the day's heat had turned their pale cheeks pink. The plaits that fell over their shoulders were the colour of campfire flames.

He looked for Neve, but she had her back to him, her attention on where Patch was barking over in the rose garden.

Mouth dry, he said, 'Bassie-proofing the fence.' At their blank expressions, he tried again. 'Fixing the fence.'

Both nodded.

Maya said, 'I want to help.'

'Me too,' Kait said.

Tanner hesitated. 'Sure ...'

He thought hard. There wasn't anything for the girls to do that didn't involve sharp wire. Last month when he'd bent over a water trough, his phone had taken a dip.

'Maya ... maybe you could hold this for me?'

He pulled his phone out of his shirt pocket and passed it to the five-year-old. Then he took off his hat and handed it to Kait. He wasn't prepared for the brilliance of their smiles or the joy in their eyes.

Unsure if he'd done the right thing by giving them something to make them feel useful, he concentrated on reattaching the gate.

Neve approached and smiled when she saw what the girls had in their hands. 'Looks like you've got two little helpers.'

He nodded without making eye contact. He couldn't risk her seeing how much he enjoyed her rare, full smile.

When he went to his ute to get some new tie wire, Maya and Kait followed. And when he returned to the fence, they remained by his side. He made sure he angled his body so they could see what he was doing. The more their attention was on the wire he twisted, the fewer questions he'd need to find answers for.

Once he'd checked the finished fence for any potential pony hazards, Maya handed him his phone, and Kait his hat.

'Thanks.'

Both girls grinned but didn't move away. He settled his hat on his head and pulled the brim low. He opened his mouth to say he'd see them on Monday, but Neve spoke first.

'Tanner ... the girls have made you some cupcakes. They were supposed to be for next week, but maybe you'd like to come inside for a cool drink or a cuppa and have one now?'

The word 'no' formed in his head, but there was something about the hope that lit up the sisters' faces and the way they jiggled from one foot to the other in their tiny cowgirl boots that held him quiet. The sun burned through the cotton of his blue shirt.

'A cool drink sounds ... good.'

Before he knew what Maya was doing, she slipped her hand in his and before he could recover, Kait took his other hand. The girls' fingers felt so delicate and fragile and yet their grip was surprisingly strong.

His eyes met Neve's. An emotion he couldn't define was quickly replaced by one of reassurance. She gave him a small nod.

He swallowed. 'Okay, then. Let's go inside.'

Careful not to walk too fast for the girls' little legs, Tanner followed Neve and Patch through the leafy garden. He was already regretting saying yes even before he climbed the veranda steps. The aroma of fresh baking greeted him along with the impression of warmth and cosiness. The white-painted hallway with its pale polished floorboards was decorated in pretty floral prints, and on a small table sat a cluster of candles.

His feet dragged as the girls led him into a kitchen that overlooked what had to be a small child's paradise. A large plush patterned rug was surrounded by boxes of toys and shelves of books. Even without a white picket fence outside, Neve had created a home that embraced whoever entered and reflected her own inner warmth. He focused on the blue cupcakes on the kitchen bench. He didn't need to notice any more details. He already admired her far too much.

The girls must have sensed his unease as their hold on his fingers tightened.

'Why don't you go and wash your hands with Tanner?' Neve said as she filled a jug with water.

When Tanner and the girls returned from the bathroom with their hands smelling of something fragrant, Neve had set a plate of cupcakes out on the veranda table. Tanner masked his sigh of relief as he walked out the front door. He still couldn't relax, but at least not being surrounded by walls meant that the pressure constricting his chest would ease. A light breeze carrying the fresh scent of eucalyptus played over his skin. The tense line of his shoulders lowered.

He'd always sought solace in the outdoors. When he'd discovered his biological father had come from the bush and had been a horseman, everything had made sense. But his adoptive father, who came from generations of lawyers, had never understood why Tanner had preferred to spend his school holidays on boarding friends' farms. As for his decision to not practise law and to work with horses, that had been the final disappointment.

'Take a seat,' Neve said over her shoulder before she disappeared inside.

Tanner sat at the table. Maya and Kait climbed into the seats on either side of him. Patch sank onto the floorboards by Tanner's boots, his tongue lolling. Needing to do something, Tanner poured water into the cups.

Neve returned with a plate of watermelon cut into stars and a bowl she placed in front of Patch. The girls looked under the table as the border collie played in the water with his paw before taking a drink.

Neve took the seat opposite Tanner and offered him a cupcake swirled in light-blue icing.

'Thanks.' He carefully placed a cupcake on his plate. 'I had no idea cakes could be blue.'

Both girls giggled as they too took a blue cake.

While he tried to think of a suitable conversation starter, Patch leapt to his feet and barked. A familiar white four-wheel drive barrelled through Rosewood's front gate. Tanner glanced at Neve. Her chin lifted. She too knew exactly who her unexpected visitor was.

Edna Galloway.

# CHAPTER
# 5

Tanner's distinctive blue ute would be his downfall. Neve snuck a sideways look at the drover as she came to her feet. He stared at Edna's vehicle, his tanned face settling into guarded lines as though he was weighing up his chances of making a fast getaway. The one time he didn't race off home was the one time Edna came to visit.

Beside him the girls sat as close as possible, both of their attention on him. As if conscious Edna's arrival could prove disruptive, he half smiled at each child to reassure them. He then took a bite of his cupcake. Maya and Kait copied.

Neve walked down the veranda steps to greet Edna before Tanner could notice her expression. He couldn't know how much his empathy towards the girls left her feeling both moved and unsettled. She still couldn't explain to herself why he affected her so much.

Edna left her four-wheel drive, her stride purposeful as she bustled through the narrow garden gate.

'Well, hello there,' she said, looking past Neve, her attention already on where Tanner sat.

Neve dutifully exchanged air kisses. 'This is a surprise.'

'I was just passing by.'

'Your timing's perfect.' Neve repressed a smile. They both knew she was the only person to live along this road. 'Would you like a cuppa and a cupcake?'

'That would be lovely. The first time I saw you I thought how much you were like your grandmother. She always had the kettle on.'

Before Neve could reply, Edna strode towards the veranda. Neve trailed behind, inhaling the overpowering scent of the older woman's perfume. Patch wagged his tail as they climbed the steps but didn't leave his position beside Tanner's boots.

Tanner stood and Edna enveloped him in a robust hug. '*So* wonderful to see you … it's been a while.'

'Yes, it has. I haven't been to town. What brings you out this way?'

'Do I need a reason to see the daughter of an old friend?'

Neve was sure Edna batted her eyelashes.

'Not at all.'

Neve waved a hand towards a spare seat on the other side of the table far away from Tanner. 'Cupcake, Edna?'

'I'd love one. Dr Fliss was so pleased with my last cholesterol results I'm allowed a treat every now and then.'

Neve didn't comment that every time she saw Edna in the Windmill Café she was having a piece of her favourite caramel slice.

Edna's smile contained none of her usual sharpness as she took her seat and looked across at Maya and Kait. 'These cupcakes look delicious. Did you make them?'

Mouths full, both girls nodded.

Neve poured Edna a glass of iced water.

'Thank you.' Edna took a sip, her attention again focusing on Tanner. 'Isn't this nice?'

He nodded.

Neve hovered in the doorway. She should make Edna's tea, but she wasn't sure about the wisdom of leaving without defusing Edna's curiosity. 'It is. Tanner doesn't usually stay.'

The narrowing of Edna's eyes was only subtle. 'Well then, my timing was impeccable.'

'It was.'

The dry note in Tanner's reply had Neve head inside before anyone saw her smile.

When she returned with Edna's tea the conversation had turned to the soon-to-be-finished adventure playground. After Kait grew restless Neve suggested that she and Maya play inside. The older woman watched as the girls waited for Tanner's slow smile before they left.

The front screen door hadn't clicked shut before Edna looked towards the orchard. 'So is that the pony and donkey?'

From her tone it was almost as though she expected Bassie and Dell to sport devil's horns.

Tanner nodded.

'They look so … sweet.'

Neve gave a short laugh. 'Don't let their looks fool you. Tanner's only back again this afternoon because Bassie got himself stuck in the fence.'

'Again? You've already been out today?'

Neve spoke quickly. There was a glint in Tanner's now steely gaze. 'Briefly this morning. Bassie was saddled for the first time. Another cake, Edna?'

Neve may as well have not spoken. Edna didn't look away from Tanner. 'I hope your work here will soon be done … the sooner the girls can ride that pony the better.' As if realising how insensitive her words sounded, she gave a saccharine smile. 'Of course ... after all they've been through they do need something fun to look forward to.'

Tanner folded his arms. 'Of course, but I'm not having the girls injured because I rushed through my work with Bassie.'

This time Neve had no doubt Edna's eyelashes batted. 'That's why you're so good at what you do. I know when you work with Bethany on this project horse she's picking up from the Hunter Valley this weekend that you'll stay until your work's done.'

Tanner came to his feet and so did Patch. 'I'm glad Bethany's found a project horse, but it's the first I've heard that I'll be working with her. I'll be off droving soon, but if she does need help tell her to give me a call.'

Edna also stood. 'She'll need help all right. She'll be giving you a call.'

To Tanner's credit his deadpan expression didn't change. 'Remember, until I'm finished with Dell and Bassie, I won't be available.' He looked at Neve as she left her seat. 'Thank the girls for the cupcakes. I'll see you all on Monday.'

Neve made sure she told herself that the soft light in his eyes was just his appreciation that when it came to Edna they continued to be a united front. His warmth towards her didn't mean anything more. 'Okay.'

The fixed intensity of Edna's stare towards Tanner left Neve in no doubt that Edna's reputation for being single-minded in a crisis hadn't been exaggerated. She also hadn't finished with the drover yet. 'Before you go, Tanner, a little birdy tells me your name wasn't on the small-hall festival's ticket list.'

His broad shoulders moved in a silent sigh. 'No, it wouldn't be.'

'That's too bad. I do understand though how busy you are. I'll tell Bethany she'll have plenty of time to catch up with you when you're working together.' Edna turned to Neve, her expression smug. 'Your name was on the list, so I'll look forward to seeing you tomorrow night. Now I believe you haven't met the Barton boys yet?'

'You're in trouble if Edna is intent on matchmaking you with Finn and Mac.' Ella cast Neve a serious look as she drove along Rosewood's driveway. 'Just what were you and Tanner doing when she visited?'

Neve could feel a blush coming on. 'Nothing.'

Ella arched a brow.

Neve laughed and then wished she hadn't when the sound emerged more hollow than amused. 'Do I have to state the obvious? We were with the girls.'

Ella's grin only widened.

Neve shook her head. 'Surely there have to be some other eligible bachelors Edna can obsess over besides poor Tanner? He can't seem to do anything or be seen with anybody. What about the Barton boys?'

'Edna has a longstanding feud with Clive Barton, so she won't be allowing Bethany anywhere near his sons. They're the only single blokes in the district who've never been invited to Sunday lunch at the Galloways'.'

Neve was yet to meet Bethany, but she already felt sorry for her. 'You're single and know Tanner. Edna leaves you alone.'

'She does, but I have a secret weapon—her husband. I was fair game until I helped Noel save his prize bull. He doesn't say much, but when he does, even Edna listens.' Ella paused to look past Neve out the passenger-side window. 'You don't know how happy it makes me to see Dell and Bassie doing so well.' Neve looked to where Dell stood in a blue hula hoop. The donkey used her teeth to pull it forwards and backwards as she played.

'You don't know how happy I am to see them still in their paddock.'

Ella's laughter sounded. 'How long have they stayed there now?'

'Eight days. And yes, I'm counting.'

'So another Tanner success story?'

'Yes. I've learned to lunge them both, Bassie has been saddled and next week Tanner will bring Arrow over to lead Bassie around.'

'Then the girls can have their first ride?'

'That's the plan.'

Neve let the conversation lull as, deep in thought, she looked out her window. Beyond the road, paddocks rolled in golden waves towards the distant ridge.

Geometric bands of red earth marked where cereal crops had been sown and awakened a memory of watching her grandfather plough on a rattling tractor. Whereas all her memories of her grandmother were clear and distinct, she had trouble picturing the gruff, angry man who'd smelled of beer and tobacco.

She looked back at Ella. She didn't want to sound too curious, especially after they'd already been talking about Tanner, but there was something she needed to know. 'Have there been many … Tanner success stories?'

'Let's just say it's not a coincidence how many single women have horses that need re-educating or breaking in, or who need campdrafting help. When he's home, Tanner's in demand.'

'I can only imagine. Edna personally delivered the news that Bethany will soon have a project horse.'

Ella shot her a quick look. 'Trust me, it wouldn't matter who Tanner helped; he's never going to breach his professional boundaries.' The vet pulled a face, half humorous and half sad. 'Tanner has the look of someone not interested in a relationship even if Edna refuses to see it … I know because I see such a look every day in the mirror.'

Neve touched Ella's arm. When she'd worked overseas, she'd had her heart broken. Much to the disappointment of the local men, she continued to be in no rush for a new relationship. 'There will come a time when you're ready.'

'We'll see.' Ella glanced over Neve's classic little black dress that over the years had only seen a handful of outings. 'That's a gorgeous dress,' she said, changing the subject.

'Thanks.'

Ella too wore a knee-length dress. Blue and fitted, the style showcased her long legs and honey-blonde hair. If Tanner had the district's single women calling on him to train their horses, Ella would have all the single farmers needing veterinarian attention for their animals.

'It will be a fun night.' This time Ella's smile contained its usual spark. 'You think Bassie and Dell got up to mischief in your garden, that's nothing compared to some of the things I saw when I lived in the Cotswolds.'

For the rest of the drive to the remote village of Reedy Creek, Ella kept Neve entertained with stories about sheep dogs herding sheep into their owner's kitchen and a pony escaping to participate in a local charity walk.

Ella joined the queue of cars turning off to visit the corrugated-iron hall nestled in a clearing on the outskirts of the tiny community. Behind the rustic building wound the creek and to the left were two symmetrical tennis courts. Dusk cloaked the scene, causing the strings of white lights laced between the box trees at the front of the hall to gleam.

Neve took a picture on her phone. 'Fliss was right. It looks beautiful.'

'It sure does. Wait until you hear the music and taste the mojitos, and as for the steak sandwiches ...'

Neve's mouth watered. She'd been so focused on organising her mother's collection of photographs she'd skipped lunch.

Ella parked at the end of the furthest row of cars and they walked across the slashed grass. The aroma of steak and onion wafted from the small room attached to the back of the hall. When they reached the front alcove, Neve snapped a photo of the bookshelf that housed a book exchange. She still had a much-loved copy of a horse book she'd once found there.

The hall that the community had worked together to build in the late 1920s had been a special place of her childhood. She'd spent many a summer's evening listening to the *thwack* of balls on string racquets and the lighthearted laughter that lasted long after the final ball had been hit. It was here that her grandmother had always seemed to be so carefree. For some reason her grandfather had refused to come with them. In the days after they'd visit, his mood would always deteriorate.

Neve followed Ella inside the bustling hall. Cressy waved from where she sat three rows from a makeshift stage. Music would soon replace the buzz of animated chatter. The small-hall festival was designed to bring folk and contemporary artists out to isolated rural communities. This year the international act was from Canada.

Fliss and Taylor, the petite platinum-blonde hairdresser, sat on Cressy's right while empty seats stretched to her left. Denham and Hewitt had to be outside enjoying the steak sandwiches. At least Tanner wouldn't be there so she could relax and not worry about his smile sabotaging her social skills. She still was at a loss as to why it mattered so much that she didn't make a fool of herself when around him.

After hugs were exchanged, Ella and Neve headed for the food area. Denham and Hewitt were deep in conversation with Drew Macgregor over near the bar. Beneath the white twinkling lights, Meredith and Phil spoke to Taylor's mother, Sue. Neve had only taken a bite of her steak sandwich when two men dressed in crisp cotton shirts, jeans and cowboy boots approached. From their similar broad grins and the twinkle in their blue eyes when they greeted Ella, Neve guessed they were the very single Barton twins.

Ella introduced them as Finn and Mac. The laughter and conversation flowed as they too enjoyed their steak sandwiches. To Neve's surprise, she found herself at ease and readily joining in with the jovial banter. As the group laughed at something she said, the suspicion grew that maybe it was only around a certain drover that she grew tongue-tied.

When a young vet nurse and her giggling friends joined them, Neve took her leave. Telling Ella she'd see her inside, Neve headed around the side of the corrugated-iron hall. Before it became too dark, she wanted to visit the tennis courts. Her grandmother used to tell a story about how at the beginning of the Second World War the courts hadn't been used and rabbits had burrowed beneath them. When they'd been repaired, hollows remained. A depression in the first court used to always form a large puddle when it rained.

After a quick search, she found the familiar indentation. Memories rushed through her, quickly followed by a tide of sadness. She was about to bend and place her palm in the rough hollow when the deep timbre of a masculine voice sounded from the shadows to her left. Even before she turned, the flip-flop in her stomach identified the man who was pacing and talking on his phone along the courtside fence.

Tanner had come to the small-hall festival after all.

The gleam of red-gold hair and the pale glow of skin warned Tanner he wasn't alone. He ended his tense call to his adoptive father. Of all the people privy to his uncomfortable conversation it had to be astute Neve.

He returned his phone to his jeans pocket. He'd left a message first thing wishing Stewart a happy birthday and it had taken all day for his father to call back. Every time he thought the conversation couldn't get any colder or any more brutal. Every time he'd been wrong.

He stepped out of the shadows and counted on the gathering dusk to hide his expression.

Neve walked across the court to meet him. The evening breeze tangled in the skirt of her sleeveless black dress and she lowered a hand to keep the material from lifting.

'Hi. You made it.'

'Yes. There's a reason Meredith organises the church fete and has an army of volunteers … she's impossible to say no to.'

'Tell me about it.' The warmth of Neve's smile soothed his battered emotions. 'When I arrived I was adamant I didn't want to impose, and yet a week's worth of dinners were already in my freezer.'

'That's Meredith.' He looked to where Neve had been standing at the end of the court. 'Reliving your tennis glory days?'

'Not exactly. I used to come here as a child with my mother and grandmother. The dip is still there and it just took me back … to a very happy time.'

'The same thing happens whenever I drive past the park near my childhood home.' He paused. When Neve's gaze searched his, he was even more appreciative of the poor light. 'My father used to push me so high on the swing, I'd feel like I was flying.'

'That was always such a great feeling.'

'It was. Neve ... I'm sorry about your mum. I didn't realise she'd grown up here.'

'Thanks.' Neve bowed her head as her fingers pleated the skirt of her dress.

'It will get better.'

She again met his eyes and he answered her unspoken question. 'My adoptive mother ... to endometrial cancer.'

'I'm so sorry.'

He nodded. Neve hadn't shown any surprise about his revelation that he'd been adopted. It was common knowledge around town that Meredith hadn't raised him.

Neve's phone rang from inside the black bag she carried. She checked her messages, her heavy hair falling over her bare shoulder as she looked down. In the gloom the glossy strands shimmered like the flicker of winter firelight.

'Ella texted to say the concert's starting.'

'We'd better head in.'

'We should.'

For a moment they stared at each other and then as one they turned. He hadn't imagined her hesitation or his own reluctance to return inside. Both weren't in the mood for festivities. If he was honest he'd enjoyed talking to Neve. There was something about her quiet strength that calmed and centred him.

He slowed his pace so that she could walk in front of him. She gave him a small smile before walking through the side entrance. Instead of following, he headed for the front door. Edna was already tracking his movements with the accuracy of a GPS. When he'd arrived, she'd been outside his driver's side door even before he'd turned off the engine. Just as well Bethany was away collecting her new horse, otherwise he knew whom he'd be sitting with.

He took his seat between Denham and Hewitt. Just like he knew who'd be sitting near Neve in the row behind him. As he'd left the hall to take his call, he'd heard Edna's voice organising for the Barton boys to sit with Ella and her. There was no reason to feel protective about whom Neve hung out with, even if Edna's fingerprints were all over the association. Neve deserved to find someone who could make her smile and who could help her find happiness in her new life. But as her soft laughter was followed by Finn's chuckle, he couldn't help shifting in his seat.

Denham threw him a swift sideways glance. 'All good?'

'Yeah.'

The first half of the small-hall concert proved engaging and entertaining, but Tanner couldn't relax. He joined in with the applause that exploded around him for the young local singer-songwriter. Normally, he would have appreciated the storytelling quality of the country songs, but now he only clapped out of politeness. All he wanted to do was turn to see just how close Neve and Finn were sitting.

After a supper break was announced, between Denham asking him a question, and Hewitt checking he'd still be around on Monday for their ride, when he did turn, the seats were empty. While the audience enjoyed the array of cakes, Tanner divided his time between avoiding Edna and scouring the hall for Neve. But when everyone resumed their seats, he still hadn't caught a glimpse of Neve's strawberry-blonde hair. The chair beside Finn remained vacant.

As the next act, a trio of folk singers, took the stage, Tanner gave in to his impulse to leave. He had a hunch where Neve might be. He left via the front door but turned left so he could access the tennis courts. In the weak moonlight the courts looked empty, but down the far end of the first court he could see a figure sitting on the ground. Before he could check himself, he walked into the court to join her.

When he sat beside Neve, she didn't immediately look up. When she did her cheeks were wet. He didn't say a word, just took her hand in his. Her warm fingers curled into his. The simple, trusting action hit him with the force of a Montana mountain wind. In that moment, self-reliant Neve needed him.

He squeezed her hand. 'I know it feels impossible right now, but you will find a sense of peace.'

'I hope so. My emotions and I are not going to have a very friendly relationship if they keep sabotaging me like this.' Bravado strengthened her muffled words.

'Things will get better ... not necessarily easier, just more manageable.'

'It's just ... I thought moving here would make me feel connected to my mother, and my grandmother, and it does ... it also makes me unbearably sad.' Neve reached out to touch the hard court surface. 'I spent my life caring for my mother, her health wasn't good, but it never felt like a burden. There was always so much fun, love and laughter. Now the world is just ... silent.'

Her deep sigh that seemed to come from a desperate place inside her moved him more than her husky words. He rubbed his thumb across the smooth skin of the back of her hand. 'It won't always be that way.'

She shivered. 'That's what I keep telling myself.'

He drew her to her feet. The melodic strains of music drifted on the cool night air. When she was standing, he let her hand slip free. He'd already forsaken all common sense by touching her.

A cold breeze engulfed them. Neve wrapped her arms around her waist but didn't make any move towards the sheltered hall.

He dug his hands into the pockets of his wheat-brown chinos to stop himself from acting on the urge to pull her close to warm her. 'I could take you home, if you'd like?'

She gazed at him, eyes dark and unreadable. He thought she'd say she was fine to stay, but she nodded. 'Yes, please.' She took her phone out of her handbag and he lost sight of her expression. 'I'll text Ella to let her know.'

It was only when Neve clicked in her seatbelt and the fragrance of flowers filled his ute cabin that he realised the enormity of his mistake. In the close confines he couldn't escape the way she made him feel or the insistent pull of attraction. His hold on the steering wheel tightened. Even with her makeup smudged and sadness dulling her gaze, she took his breath away.

As the lights from the hall disappeared and darkness cloaked the road, Neve broke the silence. 'I feel bad that you're missing the rest of the concert.'

'It's okay. I wasn't exactly in a ... festival mood.'

Neve didn't speak, just turned to look at him.

After her trusting him with her vulnerability, it seemed natural to explain his earlier phone call. 'Let's just say I understand donkeys and ponies much more than I do humans.'

'Luckily for me and the girls you do.'

'If my father shared your view then our call tonight might have been a bit easier.'

'He's not from the bush?'

'No, and has no interest in what happens beyond the city.'

'I can see why your conversation would have been ... difficult.'

Tanner slowed as he caught movement in the strong beam of his light bar. A grey kangaroo disappeared into the scrub on the right side of the road.

'Life out here couldn't be more different to that of a Queen's Counsel, even when retired. When my mother was alive, we at least had something in common. We loved her.'

Despite how hard he tried, he couldn't strip the rawness from his words.

'She must have been a wonderful woman.'

'She was.'

'Families can be complex. I never knew my father as he died when I was young, but I did know my grandfather. He refused to talk about what happened in the war, and while nothing was ever said I think that's why he was so ... difficult.'

Tanner nodded. 'My grandfather flew missions in France but never made it home, so my father's always been interested in military aviation. It's now become an obsession. I've taken him to the War Memorial in Canberra and to air shows to help find some common ground, but we still can't have a civil conversation.'

'I'm sure my grandmother mentioned something about there being a flying school around here during the war. Maybe there could be an old airfield he could visit?'

'Nothing will get my father past the Blue Mountains. He took my decision to not practise law personally and won't have anything to do with me or the bush. It's as though I've gone across to the dark side.'

'That's a shame.' Neve's voice grew soft. 'My mother always said time can bring about great change.'

'I hope so and that there'll be enough time. His health isn't what it used to be.'

'I've only just met you, but Tanner .... any father would be proud to call you his son.'

The honesty in Neve's words unlocked the tight hold he maintained on his emotions.

'Thank you.'

'There will be a way forward with your father.' Neve's smile shone in the dim light. 'You're welcome to borrow Bassie and Dell anytime you want to take the bush to him.'

Tanner chuckled. 'I don't think my father, let alone the city, would be ready for those two.'

'I don't know.' Neve smothered a yawn. 'When they aren't escaping or raiding my garden I must admit they are quite adorable.'

'They are.'

A comfortable silence settled between them. All too soon the front gate of Rosewood appeared in the headlights. Tanner parked close to the garden gate and looked across to the orchard to check on Dell and Bassie. In the pale wash of moonlight, he could only make out Dell standing near the lemon tree.

'What is it?' Neve moved to the edge of her seat to better look through the windscreen.

'Maybe nothing,' Tanner said, unclipping his seatbelt. 'I'll take a closer look at where Mr Bassie is.'

Neve joined him as he walked towards the pony paddock. When she tripped on the uneven gravel, he offered her his arm. She hesitated before curling her hand around his biceps to walk beside him. He blanked out the way even her light touch accelerated his heartbeat.

If their physical closeness also affected Neve, it didn't show in her even words as she peered around them. 'Where could he be?'

'Knowing Bassie, it will be somewhere only he would go.' Even to his own ears his voice sounded too deep.

When they reached the paddock gate, Neve let go of his arm but didn't move away. The wind eddied around them causing her long hair to brush the skin at his throat with silken fingers.

Shoulders rigid, he opened the gate for her to walk through. He'd never thought of himself as being ruled by his hormones, but at that moment all he could think about was the satin softness of Neve's lips.

He slowly followed her into the paddock and forced himself to focus on finding Bassie.

'There he is.' Tanner pointed to where he could make out a blurred, blue shape near the back fence. 'I have a feeling he's somehow got himself stuck in his rug.'

'I wouldn't be surprised. This morning he'd wriggled out of it. I did check on the internet to make sure the straps were the right length and done up properly.'

'Let's take a look.'

As he'd suspected, Bassie had his blue rug half off and the straps were tangled around his front legs, hampering all movement.

Tanner went to his aid. 'Mr Bassie, what are we going to do with you?'

Working fast, he set the pony free. Bassie sniffed his shirtsleeve before ambling over to Neve for a quick pat.

Tanner carried the damaged rug over to the gate. 'Bassie will be fine without this for a night. I'll take it home and make some adjustments to ensure it's Bassie-proof.'

'I hope there's such a thing.' Even the darkness couldn't dull the brilliance of her red-gold hair or the beauty of her smile as she stopped in front of him. 'Tell me what to do and I can fix it.'

Tanner firmed his grip on the rug. It was official. He had rocks in his head. He was a heartbeat away from dipping his head and seeking her mouth. All he could smell was the scent of flowers. All he could think about was kissing the woman before him.

'It's all good,' he said, jaw locked. 'I've another rug that needs repairing.'

'Okay. Thanks.'

To his relief, Neve turned to head through the gate. He made sure a body length opened up between them before he too left the pony paddock. After making sure Neve safely navigated the garden path until the sensor lights clicked on, he said a brief goodbye before his self-control deserted him.

He slid into the driver's seat and released a tense breath. He wasn't surprised to see the shake in his fingers as he reached for the keys. Tonight he'd almost crossed a line he shouldn't even be near.

It hadn't only been attraction weakening his resolve. Neve had a way of making him talk. She also made him feel and the combination was dangerous. He couldn't make the mistake of letting down his guard, especially for a woman who was trying to find her way in an unfamiliar world. He'd already paid the price for allowing a woman to use him when her life had become unsettled. When she'd found her way again, what he'd believed they shared, the promises and plans they'd made, had meant nothing.

He fired up the ute engine. Come Monday, he'd make sure his relationship with Neve was nothing but professional and at all times remained purely about Dell and Bassie.

# CHAPTER
## 6

'I'm sorry you didn't enjoy the festival more.' Fliss's serious tone matched the look she flicked Neve as she set the sponge cake she'd brought with her for afternoon tea on the kitchen bench.

Neve summoned a bright smile. 'You've got nothing to be sorry for. I had a great time.'

Which was true until her emotions had burst forth like storm water through floodgates. Heat warmed her cheeks. Of all the people to witness her loss of control it had to be Tanner.

Fliss's scrutiny didn't waver. 'I should have realised how hard it could be for you.'

This time Neve didn't have to force a smile. Fliss's friendship and empathy had wrapped around her from the first day they'd met and continued to warm her.

'It's fine. Really. I'm glad I went.'

The crease between Fliss's brows eased and she lifted the lid on the clear plastic container enclosing the sponge cake. 'I hope Tanner didn't leave early because of Edna? He has the patience of a saint, but these past months she's been unrelenting. There're only two things that rattle him—Edna's matchmaking and kids.'

Neve stilled as she set four plates on a wooden tray and glanced out the kitchen window to where Maya and Kait played in a tent made of a bedsheet. 'Why doesn't he like kids?'

Fliss came to stand beside her to also look at the sisters as they rearranged pink-and-green cushions around a small white table. The wedding glamping talk with Cressy had inspired Neve to make the girls their own pretty outdoor area. Yesterday they'd helped her sew some pink-and-white bunting flags that were now strung between the jacaranda tree and the tent. The cheerful triangles waved in the autumn breeze.

'It's not that he doesn't like them. He just isn't used to babies or little people. You only have to see him with a foal, or even Patch when he was a puppy, to know Tanner will be a great dad.'

Neve nodded and turned away from the window. The thought of him loving someone enough to have a family ushered in a sense of unease. If Fliss noticed her preoccupation with sorting through the cutlery drawer, she didn't say anything.

'Phew, it survived.' Fliss carefully lifted the sponge cake onto a large plate. 'I wasn't sure how it would go when I drove over the cattle grid.'

Neve passed Fliss the cake knife she'd been searching for. 'It looks delicious.'

'Believe me, it's taken many attempts at Meredith's never-fail recipe to get something that doesn't resemble a door stopper.'

'Even door stoppers taste good with strawberry jam and whipped cream.'

'Try telling that to the magpie that wouldn't eat my last attempt.'

Neve smiled as she cut rockmelon into thin wedges for the girls. 'That's the magpie's loss. Bassie and Dell would have eaten it.'

'I've no doubt they would have. When's Tanner coming? I want to see this angelic side of Bassie.'

'Soon.' Neve picked up the laden afternoon tea tray. 'We'd better eat before he does arrive. Once he's here, not even your sponge cake will keep the girls away from him.'

Neve walked through the door before Fliss could read her face. Fliss couldn't know that she was as bad as the girls. Once Tanner was here, she too wouldn't be able to think about anything else. It didn't matter how many times she saw him, each day he affected her just as much as he had the day before.

When he'd found her on the tennis courts, not once but twice, his empathy and decency had further stripped away another layer of her defences. It was no surprise she'd gone from being tongue-tied to divulging far too much personal information. Her grip on the tray handles tightened. Today was all about damage control. She'd make sure she didn't appear anything but composed and self-assured.

For the next fifteen minutes, Neve focused on the happiness in Maya and Kait's laughter and the melt-in-the-mouth sweetness of Fliss's cake. Then the rumble of a V8 ute and the rattle of steel sounded. All of Neve's best intentions dissolved. Powerless to look away, she could only watch as Tanner's blue ute pulled a silver horse float through the front gate.

Maya jumped off her cushion. Neve caught the plate resting on the five-year-old's lap just before her cake fell to the ground. Kait shoved her rockmelon in her mouth until her cheeks bulged. Both girls gave Neve a high-wattage smile before speeding through the garden to welcome Tanner.

Fliss chuckled. 'I see what you mean.'

'I don't even think a baby unicorn would keep them away.'

'It wouldn't.'

As Tanner left his ute he gave Maya and Kait his easy smile.

'Pinch me,' Fliss said, tone awed. 'Did Tanner just smile a real smile?'

'He's still not ready for the hug the girls are dying to give him, but he does seem more comfortable now.'

'I think they've been as good for him as he's been for Bassie and Dell.'

Maya and Kait giggled as Patch jumped out of the ute and bounded over to greet his favourite small humans.

Fliss cleared her throat as the girls hugged the exuberant border collie. 'I'm getting teary. If Cath were here she'd be so happy to see her girls surrounded by so much love.'

Hard hooves clattered as Tanner led Arrow out of the float. Sunlight glistened on the mustang's golden coat, and as he tossed his head, Neve could sense that his spirit remained untamed. When he thrust his nose into Tanner's hands demanding attention, Tanner grinned as he ran his palm over the gelding's glossy neck. It was only a moment of affection, but it was enough.

Neve repacked the afternoon tea tray. As powerful as the images had been on Tanner's website, seeing the deep love between a wild horse and the man he trusted hit her hard. Gorgeous, strong and compassionate Tanner was every single woman's dream. She picked up the tray to head inside.

But to her, he was the worst possible man that she could be around. She didn't have the capacity or resilience to cope with how he made her feel. His touch made her want things she'd never yearned for before. When they'd stood at the pony paddock gate the night he'd dropped her home, she could have sworn he'd stared at her mouth. The reality was it would have only been her wistful thinking.

'I'll just get the sunscreen,' she said over her shoulder to Fliss.

It wasn't long until she returned outside to join the girls and Fliss on the bench in the shade beside the round yard. While Neve reapplied the girls' sunscreen, Tanner led a saddled Arrow past.

Maya grabbed Neve's hand. 'Tanner said he'd take us for a ride.'

'Did he?' Neve glanced over at the drover, who nodded as he tied Arrow inside the yard. 'That sounds like fun. I'd better get your riding helmets.'

Too late Neve realised that Tanner walked through the gate at the same time as she came to her feet. As they were both heading to the pony paddock, it would seem odd if they didn't walk together. Conscious of Fliss watching them, Neve fell into step beside him.

They'd taken three paces when he spoke quietly. 'How are you doing?'

Knowing their backs were towards Fliss, she answered honestly. 'Much better than Saturday. How about you?'

'I've three missed calls from Edna.'

'Yikes. That many.' Neve scanned the drive into Rosewood, half expecting Edna's four-wheel drive to appear. 'I'm guessing she wants to talk to you about Bethany's project horse?'

'Maybe, but Bethany knows it will be at least a week until I can get there. No, it would be about something else.'

'Any ideas?'

A smile kindled in his eyes. 'Not a clue and I'm in no hurry to find out.'

Tanner stopped at the gate where Dell and Bassie waited for him. He stroked each of their noses before continuing with Neve to the tack shed.

To her relief, he waited until she'd collected the helmets and left the small space before stepping inside to get Bassie's bridle and saddle. In his ute she'd been acutely aware of the leather notes of his aftershave, the way his well-shaped hands rested on the steering wheel and the pull of his shirt across his biceps as he changed gears.

After they'd returned to the pony paddock, Tanner sat Bassie's saddle on top of the fence. As she turned to walk over to Fliss and the girls, the intense seriousness of Tanner's expression held her still.

'Neve ... thanks for ... the other night. I appreciated having someone to talk to.'

Warmth fired in her cheeks and she fought to stop her words from deserting her. When he looked at her like he did now, his gaze an intent, unfathomable blue, she felt as though she was freefalling. 'You're welcome. Thanks for ... listening to me too and for the lift home.'

Then before she could say anything foolish, she headed back over to the round yard. Tanner followed, leading Bassie.

In between putting on the girls' helmets and listening to their excited chatter, Neve had no opportunity to answer the questions in Fliss's eyes. But when the girls were again sitting between them, Fliss cast her a we'll-talk-later smile.

Tanner led Bassie into the yard and introduced him to the palomino gelding. When their noses touched, Bassie's big eyes blinked. The pony stood still while Tanner took hold of Arrow's reins and swung into the saddle. When the palomino walked forward, Bassie followed at a consistent pace.

Tanner sat in the saddle as if that was where he was born to belong. Relaxed and at ease, he was all hard, masculine angles and fluid, muscled strength. With his hat brim pulled low, his blue shirt, jeans and dusty boots, he appeared the epitome of a cowboy.

Except it wasn't what he wore, but the way he wore it that spoke of his bone-deep connection to the bush. This was where he was meant to be and where he felt at home. Her heart ached for what he must have endured trying to please his lawyer father at the expense of following his dreams and being true to himself.

Fliss chuckled softly. 'You know, Bassie almost had me fooled, but that look he just sent us as he walked by was far more sassy than angelic.'

'Tell me about it. Sometimes he even curls his top lip so it looks like he's laughing at me.'

After Tanner had ponied Bassie off Arrow for another circuit, Tanner dismounted and led Bassie through the gate to tie him up outside the round yard.

Tanner grinned across at the girls. 'Who's for a ride?'

The girls leapt off the bench. Neve made sure she kept a secure grasp on each little hand. She didn't want either girl to spook Arrow. As they entered the yard, the gelding lowered his head for the girls to pat him.

'He's so pretty,' Maya said, with no trace of nervousness.

'Would you like to go first?' Tanner asked.

Maya nodded so hard Neve checked that her riding helmet remained securely in place.

After Tanner had returned to Arrow's saddle, Neve examined his face. His hat shadowed his eyes, but his hold on the reins was relaxed. It was only a flicker of a muscle in his cheek that hinted that having Maya and Kait ride with him wasn't in his usual job description.

Fliss bent to pick up Maya. 'Okay, missy moo, let's get you into the saddle.'

Soon, the five-year-old was sitting on Arrow with Tanner's strong arms around her. The joy brightening her smile was enough to cause a lump in Neve's throat.

After Arrow had walked around the yard several times, it was Kait's turn. Neve tried not to notice the way Tanner held the delicate three-year-old with such care. She didn't need any more evidence of either his tenderness or his kind heart.

Beside her Fliss murmured, 'See, he'll make a great dad.'

Once Kait's booted feet were back on the ground, Maya tugged at Neve's sleeve. 'You too.'

She shook her head. 'It's been decades since I was this close to a horse as big as Arrow, let alone ridden one.'

Fliss took hold of Maya and Kait's hands. 'Which means you should make the most of having him here. You once said how much you enjoyed riding. I can look after the girls.'

Tanner watched her, his expression inscrutable.

Neve bit the inside of her cheek. As much as she would love a ride, she didn't want to make a fool of herself or take up any more of Tanner's time. 'My riding skills are almost non-existent.'

Fliss smiled. 'You should have seen mine when I came home.' She looked across at Tanner. 'You know … Cressy's Jazz would be perfect for Neve, wouldn't she?'

'She would be.'

Neve inwardly groaned. There was nothing she'd like more than to have a horse so she could ride out with the girls. But she'd need lessons and that could mean working even more closely with Tanner. 'I thought Ella was seeing Jazz for her sore knees?'

Fliss nodded. 'The new supplement has worked a treat. Cressy was only saying last week she wishes she had more time to ride her.'

The liveliness of Fliss's hazel eyes warned Neve that Fliss already knew it would only take one ride on Arrow for Neve to agree to Jazz coming to Rosewood.

Still unsure, she turned to Tanner. Apart from a subtle tensing of his mouth, his tanned features had settled into hard-to-read lines.

Arrow moved to sniff at her hair. The smell of horse surrounded her and took her back to her childhood, when she'd counted down the days until her horse-riding lessons. She touched the mustang's velvet-soft cheek, and as he nuzzled her hand, the decision to ride had already been made.

Neve's ride would either go very well or horribly wrong.

It wasn't Neve falling off that concerned him, or Arrow spooking, but how he'd react to being near her. If it wasn't enough that his self-control was already wire-tight, Fliss's all-seeing stare hadn't left them as they'd walked to the pony paddock together.

Keeping his tension carefully hidden, he blanked out the fact that Neve stood within kissing distance. Her large eyes were serious as he matched the stirrup leathers to the length of her arms. But as Arrow's ears flickered towards him, he knew he couldn't fool the mustang into thinking he was relaxed. He smoothed a hand over Arrow's shoulder to reassure himself as well as the perceptive gelding.

'Right,' he asked, tone businesslike as Neve made an adjustment to her helmet. 'Shall I give you a leg-up?'

He didn't miss her quick glance at the mounting block beyond the round yard fence or her slight hesitation before she said, 'Yes, please.'

Without looking at him, she bent her left leg and took hold of the reins above Arrow's withers.

He moved in close and placed his hands under her boot, losing the battle to ignore the way her heavy, loose hair fell down her back. Against the green of her shirt, the strawberry-blonde strands shimmered more gold than auburn.

'After three. One ... two ... three ...'

He hoisted her high, then had to grasp above her denim-clad knee to anchor her into the saddle. He hadn't meant to lift her with such force. Beneath his palm, he felt the strength of her fine muscles as she balanced herself. When he was sure she was okay, he lifted his hand.

Colour painted her cheeks as she slid the toe of her boots into the stirrups. Her eyes briefly met his as she showed him the reins threaded through her fingers. 'Is this right?'

Without thinking, just like he'd done with other clients, he covered her left hand to curl her fingers into a loose fist around the reins. Her knuckles felt so delicate against the width of his palm. 'Just shorten your reins and close your hand like this.'

It was no surprise his voice emerged husky. Touching Neve, even in a professional context, had started a pounding in his chest. He pulled his hand away and forced himself to concentrate on making sure she felt safe and comfortable. 'Feeling okay?'

This time her eyes met his for longer. In the sea-green depths he caught the glow of happiness. She leaned forward to rub Arrow's neck. 'I've forgotten how great it feels to be on horseback.'

He didn't reply, only nodded. Seeing Neve finding pleasure in something that brought him so much peace shouldn't steal his words.

He began walking and Arrow followed. By the time they'd completed a full circuit Neve smiled. By the second circuit Arrow no longer followed him as Neve was in control. By the third circuit Tanner remained by the gate to let Neve ride on her own. By the fourth circuit Tanner had his emotions locked down.

He'd earlier gone off plan when he'd asked her how she was doing when they'd walked to the shed. The hollows in her cheeks had made a mockery of his intention to not let things become personal between them. But now seeing her joy at riding and feeling the undertow of attraction whenever he touched her, he had to stick to his plan to put distance between them.

She rode Arrow over and he took hold of the gelding's reins while she slid her feet from the stirrups.

He risked a brief look at her radiant face. 'It didn't take long to remember what to do?'

'The basics didn't, but there's heaps I've forgotten. Arrow was so patient.'

She hugged the gelding's golden neck before swinging her right leg over and dismounting. Her boots hit the ground with a thud.

Tanner reached out to stop her from toppling backwards. Arrow stood over fifteen hands high and Neve wasn't very tall. His hand found the small of her back and even through the thick cotton of her green shirt he could feel the heat of her skin. The scent of summer flowers enveloped him.

For a moment she stayed still, his arm supporting her, then she moved away. 'That's quite a drop.'

Not looking at him, she gave Arrow a final pat before making her way out of the round yard.

Tanner followed with Arrow. His temples hammered and his mouth was as dry as a billabong in a summer drought. He pulled his hat brim lower. Neve's ride couldn't have gone more wrong than if Arrow had put his head between his knees and bucked.

Once out of the yard, Tanner vaulted into the mustang's saddle. Riding to the ridge with Hewitt tonight couldn't come soon enough.

He glanced to where Neve stood with Maya and Kait. 'I'll take Bassie for a longer run and see how he goes.' He looked across at Fliss before Neve could glimpse his tension. 'Tell Hewitt I'll drop by soon.'

'Great. He's got cattle to move before you head off. If you're feeling energetic, he's also making a new garden bed with some noisy, antiquated rotary hoe.'

'No worries.'

He whistled to Patch, who was off following a rabbit trail, before leading Bassie down to where the red river gums marked the meandering line of the river. White wings flashed as cockatoos protested at their presence. The raucous calls echoed across the water, fuelling his restlessness.

While out droving, often the low of cattle and the screech of cockatoos were the few sounds he heard. It would only be out on the long paddock that he could wrestle back the control he lost when around a woman whose smile caused his chest to tighten and whose touch awakened a loneliness so deep it was scored into his soul.

'Fliss said the girls really enjoyed their ride on Arrow.'

Tanner guided the palomino around the dark depths of a wombat's burrow before answering Hewitt. 'They did. It shouldn't be long until they can ride Bassie. I just want to make sure he's done testing Neve. The last thing she needs is for him to pull back while she's leading him on Jazz.'

'He sounds like my first pony. One minute Mum would be holding the lead while she rode her stock horse, and the next I'd be hanging on while Rocket took off home.'

'Give me a wild horse any day. Ponies might look cute and cuddly, but they are smart and crafty and know all the tricks.'

'So true. Lizzie's been asking for one since her birthday and it's taking a while to find a pony with the right temperament.'

'Good luck.' Lizzie was Hewitt's six-year-old niece and Tanner had no doubt whatever pony Lizzie ended up with it would be well loved. 'I know we ran out of time, but if you need help with the new garden bed let me know. Fliss said something about an old rotary hoe?'

'Thanks. I will.' Hewitt chuckled. 'I bet she did. It makes a racket … I love my toys, but it's even too noisy for me.'

Tanner halted Arrow while Hewitt opened the paddock gate on his blood-bay mare, Garnet. A series of scars marred her shoulder and chest from where she'd taken on a devil of a rodeo bull to protect Hewitt.

Tanner whistled to the two border collies investigating the nearby clumps of wiregrass. They raced each other to the horses. Patch wasn't yet the size of his father, Max, but he already showed that he shared his speed and agility.

As if sensing the task ahead, Arrow's steps quickened as they rode away from the open gate that the steers would soon flow through. The mustang wasn't the only one with excess energy and who was looking forward to pitting his wits against unpredictable cattle.

Garnet's pace also increased and Hewitt shot Tanner a grin. Now Hewitt no longer rode pickup in rodeos, the mare too yearned to be back amongst the action.

Three white-faced Herefords lifted their heads from where they grazed. When they caught sight of the border collies, they ambled towards a group of cows clustered around the dam edge. Two cows who stood knee-deep in the water waded to shore. Thanks to the wet spring, even though the summer had been hot and dry, dam levels remained high.

Max and Patch guided the cattle in the right direction and soon they'd bunched into a slow-moving mob. When one steer broke away heading for the gully, Tanner gave Arrow his head. The mustang cut off the Hereford, who turned to rejoin the herd.

The burst of speed, the rush of adrenaline and the wind rushing over his skin soothed Tanner's restlessness. He rolled his shoulders to disperse the last of his tension.

When another steer looked like he'd bolt, Arrow spun around, ready for the chase. But apart from two cows who tried to make a run past Garnet and Hewitt, the cattle cooperated and followed the fence line until they headed through the open gate.

With the cattle being where they were supposed to be, Hewitt and Tanner retraced their steps towards the dam. The horses had a drink while Patch and Max cooled off. The once black-and-white border collies were soon mud-brown as they chased each other through the shallows. A pair of galahs soared overhead, their pink-and-grey hues blending in with the blush of sunset that crept across the darkening sky.

Arrow and Garnet needed no excuse to power their way across the open grazing country towards the rolling timbered hills that rose into a granite-hewn ridge. By the time they reached the top, both horses were breathing hard but remained reluctant to stop. Tanner didn't know whose grin was wider, his or Hewitt's. They'd all needed to take such a ride.

Tanner left his saddle and Hewitt followed. They took a seat on the smooth grey wood of a fallen tree to watch the sun's descent. To their left, the horses lowered their heads to graze. Tanner didn't break the silence that settled around them. He'd made this sunset trip before. This small clearing was Hewitt's special place that allowed him to feel close to the brother he'd lost.

When the sun hovered at the edge of the horizon, Hewitt briefly closed his eyes. Once the shards of burnt orange could no longer be seen, he turned to Tanner. Peace lightened the clear grey of his gaze. 'Do you remember the first time we sat on a log?'

'I do. The trail ride.'

'You sure grilled me about Fliss that day.'

Tanner chuckled. Hewitt possessed an understated and steady strength that ensured he'd be the last man standing in any situation. There was nothing that rattled him except the loss of his twin and Dr Fliss when he'd first met her. 'I didn't give you that much of a hard time. Besides, I seem to remember being concerned for you too.'

'You were right to be concerned. Everything I'd ever wanted was right there in front of me ... well, across the garden ... and I was too stubborn and pig-headed to see it.'

'It all worked out.'

'It did.' Hewitt paused and the intensity of his stare warned Tanner about what was to come. He'd been right in thinking Hewitt had sensed his awareness of Neve. 'I just don't want you to ... be in a similar situation.'

'I won't be.'

'That's the thing ... you will be unless you're prepared to take down that wall of yours.'

Tanner didn't speak, just stared at the horizon as darkness eclipsed the last of the life from the sky.

Hewitt continued, his voice low. 'Take it from me. I thought I didn't need anyone, but Tanner ... even guys like us aren't meant to be alone.'

Tanner stood and kept his reply casual. 'I hear you ... but this is the only way I know how to be.'

Hewitt too came to his feet. He clasped Tanner's shoulder. 'Even when we think we have everything figured out, sometimes it turns out we have no idea at all.' Hewitt moved away. 'We'd better get home. Fliss doesn't think I know, but she hid a pavlova in the spare fridge, which means she's already planned for you to stay for dinner.'

Tanner took his time to walk over to Arrow. Behind him the sky was now sombre and bleak, stripped of all light. He couldn't risk trusting and letting anyone into his life again, especially Neve, no matter how much a part of him wanted Hewitt's words to be true.

# CHAPTER

# 7

'Are we there yet?' Neve smiled as Maya asked the age-old question of any child who'd been in the car longer than half an hour.

'Almost.' Neve pointed to the corrugated-iron tank sitting on a wooden stand that tilted at an alarming angle. Every trip to Woodlea she expected to see the tank on the ground, but the stalwart posts refused to collapse. 'See, there's the wobbly tank. Town's over the next hill. How about we count the windmills?'

There was a reason why Woodlea was known as the town of windmills. Maya and Kait's childish voices counted as they passed windmills with their blades twirling or windmills dressed in the woollen creations of the yarn bombers. Neve was yet to work out who the members of the underground knitting club were. Not once had she seen anyone around town with even a pair of knitting needles.

When the girls were up to eight, the *Welcome to Woodlea* sign flashed by. But instead of taking the road into town, Neve turned left to drive past the rodeo ground.

She slowed to join a queue turning right.

Today was the final working bee for the adventure playground that had been Hewitt's brainchild. His niece Lizzie and nephew Quinn were frequent visitors to town to see Fliss and him, and while there was a playground near the sportsground, it was limited in its size and variety of play equipment. Hewitt had joined forces with Edna and the result was a new play area of custom-designed equipment that would appeal to children of all ages. The playground, bike track and barbeque areas would also encourage travelling families to spend time in Woodlea.

Even though it was a weekday, many locals would be helping, from the State Emergency Service volunteers to the members of the Woodlea Wallaroos rugby club. Neve had spent the morning baking and she and the girls were delivering morning smoko. The girls had made Tanner a special blueberry muffin.

'Where's Tanner?' Maya leaned forward to look through the side window.

'He'll be there somewhere. See, there's his ute.'

Tanner had let them know yesterday he wouldn't be coming to work with Dell and Bassie today as he'd be here helping Hewitt. The girls' bottom lips had dropped. As much as they'd enjoyed their first ride on Bassie yesterday, not seeing Tanner had made their smiles fade. So Neve had suggested they leave early to go to the library and to drop off their baking.

Neve parked alongside a Hilux that sported twin aerials. Beyond the rows of cars, the castle-themed wooden equipment almost appeared finished. The names of businesses and individuals who had helped make the playground a reality had been carved into the posts on the front fence. Today the trees were to be planted and the painting completed. All that then would be needed were some large shade sails.

With her arms filled with containers of brownies and banana bread, Neve accompanied Maya and Kait along the paved path. The trick would be to keep the girls away from Tanner while he worked, as well as off the bridges and ladders that would tempt even an adult.

As they drew near to the entrance, and the volume of the laughter and conversation increased, the girls moved closer to Neve. She handed Maya the white noodle box they'd decorated to hold Tanner's muffin to distract her. She then took hold of Kait's hand.

When they walked into the playground, Denham left the tree he'd been planting to come over. His Woodlea rodeo cap, jeans and cherry-red work shirt were streaked with mud.

'I hope all that food's for me,' he said with a wink.

The girls giggled and nodded.

Neve returned his smile. The once world-champion bull rider never failed to make her feel at ease. 'Cressy here?'

He shook his head and Neve glimpsed concern in his blue gaze. 'She wanted to be, but she had to head to Dubbo to finalise some honeymoon stuff. Which is just as well as she's done something to her side and it seems to be taking a while to heal.'

'She wasn't right when I saw her last week. Let me know if she needs any help with anything.'

'Thanks. I will. I think all she really needs is to rest. We both know that's the last thing she'll do.'

Denham's attention strayed to the containers Neve held. She let go of Kait's hand to prise open the top lid before offering him a brownie. 'I didn't see a thing.'

Denham chuckled as he snuck two brownies. 'A man has to eat even if he has a wedding suit to fit into.'

Neve again took hold of Kait's hand. They strolled over to the covered barbeque area where a table was laden with food and eskies.

She added their brownies and banana bread to the feast and looked around. She told herself she was only checking where Tanner was for the girls' sake.

But when she caught sight of a familiar pair of broad shoulders dressed in blue, the flutter in her midriff called her bluff. It was bad enough Tanner occupied her thoughts as much as he did, but now, ever since her ride on Arrow, her senses craved his touch. It didn't matter that all he'd done was help her into the saddle and show her how to hold the reins, she now knew how right it felt to have him physically near.

Taylor, who was standing next to Finn Barton, gave her a wave from high on a platform where they applied red paint to a castle turret. Preoccupied, Mac Barton didn't notice her or the girls as he painted the posts of a nearby walkway. She hoped Finn didn't think her rude for suddenly leaving last Saturday night. She'd enjoyed his and Mac's company.

Kait tugged at her hand to lead her over to where Tanner had his back to them as he dug a hole in a garden bed. Maya grabbed Neve's other hand and they followed the path that would take them past the tyre swings to where Tanner worked. They hadn't even made it to the first swing when a strident voice called Neve's name.

Neve stopped and slowly turned to see Edna bearing down on them. Dressed in her trademark pearls and immaculate town clothes, she brandished a clipboard.

'Neve … how wonderful you're here and that you brought the girls.'

'We thought we'd deliver our baking early.'

Edna crossed off something on her clipboard. Her gaze sharpened as she stared at the noodle box Maya held.

'Sorry, this wasn't on your food list. It's a special delivery,' Neve said.

Edna arched a pencilled brow. 'Let me guess. Whatever's in the box is blue?'

'Tanner likes blue,' Maya said, her attention not leaving the drover.

Edna's smile softened. 'You're right, he does.'

Tanner straightened and half turned. Instead of his wide-brimmed felt hat today, he wore a navy Woodlea rodeo cap similar to Denham's.

Neve kept a firm hold on each of the girls' hands. 'Remember Tanner's busy. We won't stay long.'

She may as well have not spoken. When Tanner passed the shovel to an older farmer beside him and headed towards them, both girls pulled their hands free and ran to meet him.

Neve bit her lip to stop herself calling them back. She could feel inquisitive eyes on them. Even though it would be common knowledge that Tanner wasn't comfortable around kids, she hoped people knew that he'd been a recent visitor to Rosewood. The girls being excited to see him shouldn't prove newsworthy.

But instead of stopping a body's length away like she usually did, Kait ran right up to him. Neve held her breath. This could get awkward very soon. Without hesitating, Tanner bent to scoop Kait up in his arms. She tucked her head into his shoulder and snuggled against him. Before Tanner could react, Maya threw her arms around his leg and hugged him tight. His hand lowered, hovered above her head and then curled around her shoulders.

Edna's shocked gasp was clearly audible.

From the corner of her eye Neve could see Hewitt heading towards Tanner as well as Denham. But Tanner gave no sign that he needed rescuing or was uncomfortable. When Maya eased away from his leg to pass him the noodle box, his slow grin flashed white.

Denham and Hewitt shared a look before leaving to return to what they'd been doing. Neve didn't dare glance at Edna. She'd either be pleased Tanner would indeed make a loving father or be horrified that his affection for the girls would distract him from the plans she had for Bethany.

Tanner and the girls walked towards them. Neve blinked to hide her misty happiness. Fliss had been right. The girls had been good for Tanner.

His gaze flickered over her face before he gave her a nod. 'Neve.'

'Hi. Sorry about the enthusiastic … greeting.'

'It's okay.' He looked down at Kait and Maya, whose brilliant smiles hadn't dimmed. 'It's time I had a break.'

Edna tapped her pen on her clipboard. 'Maya, why don't you take Tanner over to the tables so he can eat his surprise. Neve, there's tea or coffee if you'd like one.'

If Tanner was stunned at Edna's suggestion it didn't register on his face. Neve wasn't quite so successful. She snapped her open mouth shut. Was Edna pushing them together instead of prying them apart? She threw her a quick look, but Edna had turned away.

Realising she was standing on the path by herself, Neve followed Tanner and the girls over to the covered barbeque area. Tanner sat Kait on the bench seat and then opened a nearby esky to take out some water bottles. His gaze caught Neve's and she nodded. A cold drink was what she needed, not hot tea. Her skin already felt too warm. Being around Tanner made it impossible to stay calm and unaffected.

He passed her a water bottle. The condensation cooled her palms and she resisted the urge to press the bottle against her heated cheeks.

'What's up with Edna?' she said in a voice only he could hear. 'Did you find out why she called?'

The corner of his mouth kicked into a grin. 'No, when she saw me earlier she said she'd talk to me later. But I'm calling in to meet Bethany's new horse when I finish here. Only because Bethany asked me, not because Edna engineered it. I guess she's in a good mood.'

Neve dashed an unexpected twinge of jealousy. She didn't have a monopoly on Tanner's time or whom he saw. 'She must be.'

Tanner took a seat between Maya and Kait, and as soon as he sat, Maya passed him his muffin. Neve sat on the opposite side of the table.

The girls' baking efforts were rewarded when Tanner opened the noodle box and whistled in appreciation. As he took a huge bite of the jumbo blueberry muffin Neve wished she hadn't left her phone in the car. Graham would have enjoyed seeing the joy and delight on his daughters' faces. He worried about them so much.

Neve briefly left the table to get the girls a piece of banana bread. With Tanner eating, they'd want some morning smoko too. She wasn't sure, but she thought she saw Edna surveying them over the top of her clipboard.

She returned to the table, and as the girls enjoyed the banana bread she unscrewed the lid of her water bottle.

'Have you heard from Fliss?' Tanner asked. 'She's been trying to reach you.'

'I thought so. I had a missed call last night and keep getting her voicemail this morning.'

'I have no idea what time she and Hewitt got here but it would have been early. She's out with Ella picking up the last load of trees in Hewitt's ute. She said if I saw you to ask if you'd like to come to Bundara tonight for a barbeque.'

Neve took her time to answer. She loved visiting her mother's childhood home, but on the previous occasions it had just been Fliss, Hewitt and her. After the way she'd reacted at the small-hall festival, she wasn't sure attending another social function would be a wise move. 'I'll have the girls until Graham finishes work so will see how I go. I'll try to pop around, but it could be late.'

'I'll let Fliss know.' Tanner's blue gaze studied her. 'Cressy and Denham can't make it, Ella's hosting book club and Taylor's heading to Orange. So it will just be the four of us.'

'Okay.' Neve couldn't hide the relief in her voice. 'I should be there. I'll text Fliss about what I can bring.'

Tanner nodded as he finished his muffin. He smiled at Maya and then at Kait. 'Thanks.'

Maya nodded, her mouth full of banana bread. Kait leaned over to give him a hug. Tanner stiffened and then put his arm around her. Not to be outdone, Maya hugged his other arm until he also drew her close. Tanner sent Neve an uncertain look. She only hoped her smile gave him the reassurance he needed.

She reached for Maya and Kait's water bottles. As great as Tanner was doing, she didn't want the girls to overload him. 'We'd better get going.' The girls' expressions grew crestfallen. 'We have the library to visit … and as a special treat for helping with the baking, also the lolly shop.'

Maya and Kait wriggled out of Tanner's embrace and climbed off the bench as fast as they could.

Laughter twitched on his lips. 'Have I just been ditched?'

'Sorry, you have.' Neve stood. 'The power of visiting the lolly shop can't be underestimated.'

Tanner came to his feet as well. He pushed back the brim of his cap, the corners of his light-blue eyes crinkling with amusement. 'I'll try not to be too crushed.'

Neve didn't temper her own laughter. For once she wasn't worried she'd say something ridiculous or appear awkward. 'You've got broad shoulders. You'll survive.'

An indefinable emotion replaced the mirth in his eyes, an emotion that triggered a flurry of awareness in her stomach. His attention dipped to her mouth and her breath caught. Then Maya grabbed her hand and the intensity between them was broken.

It was only the husky edge to his quiet 'see you tonight' that proved she hadn't imagined the spark that had flared between them.

Foolish didn't even come close to describing what he was.

Tanner rammed the crowbar into the red earth to deepen the hole he had dug. Afternoon shadows blanketed the playground and the car park was now almost empty. Even though his muscles ached with fatigue, he refused to stop. There was one more tree to be planted, but most of all his thoughts still raced.

So much for hiding the way Neve made him feel. When she'd met his gaze, with no trace of wariness, and teased him about surviving being ditched, something had unlocked within him. It didn't matter if they were in a public place. It didn't matter if he wasn't supposed to feel this way. He couldn't have made it any more obvious he was attracted to her than if he'd given in to the deep need to kiss her.

He again rammed the crowbar into the hard-packed earth. He didn't know if it was Hewitt's words the other day, or if the loneliness he repressed was hellbent on vengeance. All he knew was that the self-control he'd always relied on had failed.

He stopped to pass the back of his gloved hand over his forehead and saw Denham looking his way. He hadn't missed how his cousin and Hewitt had come to his aid when the girls had run to him. He also hadn't missed Denham's blue stare tracking his movements for the rest of the day.

He didn't know what he'd been thinking when the girls had raced towards him. When the anxiety on Maya's face had transformed into a smile and when Kait's little arms had reached for him, all his reservations had fled. It seemed the most natural thing to do to pick her up.

When she'd snuggled against him he'd be lying if he hadn't felt a gut-deep response to her trust and fragility. He'd also be lying if he didn't admit that holding Kait, and Maya hugging him, had kick-started yearnings he thought he'd never have. He could now understand the look Denham wore when he saw Cressy cradling a baby.

Footsteps sounded as his cousin headed his way.

'Hit any water yet?' Denham said as he inspected the hole.

'I wish. Is it just me or is the day getting hotter?'

'Just you. You've been working up a sweat for hours.' Denham took hold of the crowbar. 'Why don't you head home? You've done the work of two men.'

'It's fine.'

'I'll finish up here.' Denham's firm tone said the offer wasn't negotiable. 'Aren't you supposed to be calling in at Edna's before you go to Fliss and Hewitt's?'

Tanner sighed. 'Yes.' He checked the position of the sun. 'I'd better have a shower, otherwise Fliss won't let me in the door.'

Denham grinned. 'Wise move.'

Tanner went to turn away when Denham asked, 'Neve going tonight?'

He forced himself to face Denham. He'd been deluding himself if he thought his cousin wouldn't comment on what had happened earlier. 'Yes.'

'Graham's two little redheads sure do like you.'

'I've no idea why.'

'Because they're smart; they've worked out you're not as tough as you look.' Denham's voice lowered. 'The bad news is Neve has too.'

Tanner didn't answer, just peeled off his gloves.

'If you go off droving again you've got rocks in your head.'

'The thought has crossed my mind.'

Denham's eyes narrowed. 'About droving or the rocks.'

Tanner spoke honestly. 'Both.'

His answer seemed to satisfy Denham. He nodded before swapping the crowbar for a shovel. 'I'm here anytime you need that cold beer.'

After a quick trip back to Claremont to shower, feed Arrow and collect Patch, Tanner took the bitumen road that would lead him to the Galloways' farm. When he came to a front entrance with ornate scrolled gates, he slowed and drove along the gum-tree-lined driveway. Edna's husband, Noel, was a respected farmer. The straight fence lines and neat, organised sheds were a testament to how little time he spent in town, unlike his social wife.

The road forked and Tanner headed to the right to where the stables stood next to a rubber-lined round yard. Throughout the years of pony club, pony camps and equestrian expos, Bethany had retained her love of horses. Even the time away at Sydney completing an exercise physiology degree hadn't dampened her enthusiasm. Now at home on the farm and in between jobs, Tanner could understand why she filled her life with her horses. It was either that or be at the beck and call of her mother.

Bethany had heard his ute and came to the door of the stable complex to wave. Tall and blonde like her father, Bethany had no shortage of male admirers. He was sure her tendency to go out with smooth-talking city boys was a reflection of her mother's pressure to settle down with a suitable country boy.

He was also sure her reputation as sometimes being difficult and moody was a result of having Edna micro-manage her life. Whenever he'd worked with her, Bethany had always been pleasant and cooperative. Early on in their friendship, she'd also reassured him she didn't share her mother's matchmaking plans.

He left his ute and Bethany gave him a hug. He resisted the urge to turn towards the house to see if Edna had the front window curtains back, watching them.

Bethany pulled away with a smile. 'It's okay, Mum's still in town. She had a meeting about the picnic races and they always go for ages.'

'So there's a reason why you said I needed to come around late afternoon?'

Bethany's smile widened. 'You bet. Come and meet my new horse. All will be revealed.'

Intrigued, Tanner followed her into the stables. There was something about the spring in Bethany's step that warned him there was a little of Edna in Bethany after all. Bethany was also very good at getting her own way.

'So ... this project horse will need a lot of work?' he said as they passed several empty stalls. There had to be a reason why Bethany's project horse was stabled so far away from the doorway.

Bethany led him to the very last stall. She turned to face him, her expression surprisingly serious. 'Yes ... I hope so.'

Tanner stepped forward to look over the half-door. He didn't know what he expected—an unbroken brumby, a fresh-from-racing thoroughbred or a horse no one could handle. Instead, all he saw was a black Shetland pony who stared at him with large eyes. Even from such a brief look, Tanner knew this open and relaxed horse was no Bassie and would be easy to work with.

'Yep. He's a real troublemaker.'

Bethany gave a quick laugh. 'That's all Mum needs to hear.' Bethany dug into her jeans pocket. 'Plus, I've shown her this.'

She held up her phone for Tanner to see a close-up picture of the pony, ears pinned back and the whites of his eyes showing while he reared. 'He doesn't like drones.'

'And that's all he doesn't like?'

'Yes, otherwise he's bombproof.'

Tanner looked at the pony again who'd come over to the stable door to greet them. He stroked his nose. 'So … I'm to come and *work* with him as much as I can?'

Uncertainty tempered the light in Bethany's grey eyes. 'Yes … if that's all right. Mum thinks all ponies are trouble. She also never comes to the stables so won't know he isn't as he seems.'

Tanner nodded, letting Bethany keep speaking. 'I've always wanted a pony like him … his home wasn't great. And …'

'And …?'

Bethany scrolled through the pictures on her phone. 'And this happened.'

She held up a picture of her with her arm around a man, and not just any man, but Mac Barton.

'Ah, I see.'

She sighed. 'I knew you would. Thanks to Mum's family feud with Clive, she would have kittens knowing Mac and I are seeing each other.'

'So with me being here she'll be busy thinking something might happen between us and not wondering what else you're up to.'

Bethany crossed her fingers.

Tanner spoke again. 'Does your dad know?'

Bethany and her father were close.

'Of course. He said if it was okay with you, it was okay with him.'

Tanner searched Bethany's pretty face. This was the most earnest he'd ever seen her. She'd also picked some less-than-worthy city blokes to torment her mother with. Mac Barton was a good guy, even if his father was as hard as nails.

Bethany continued. 'Tanner … I really like him. He's so good to me.'

Tanner looked at the placid pony. 'I might need to head off for a week droving, it depends on whether it rains out west, but otherwise this little fella and I can get to know each other. There're some tricks I could teach him and we can work on his fear of drones.'

Bethany's hug was tight. 'I owe you.'

'Just don't ask me to come to Sunday lunch.'

'That's a given.' She looked at the time on her phone. 'We have about an hour if you want to come and have a coffee with Dad. He's missed all of your chats.'

Forty-five minutes later Tanner drove past the ornate front gate and onto the bitumen road. He lifted a hand in greeting as a strange car travelled in the opposite direction. The driver returned his wave.

Spending time with Bethany's father made him think of his own. If only his father would come to the bush to see the camaraderie, the wide-open spaces and the sheer natural beauty. Once he did perhaps he'd understand why Tanner had made the choices he had. He hadn't rejected his father, or his city world, he'd just listened to his heart.

He took the turn onto the red dirt road that led to Bundara and slowed as a wallaby sat poised by the roadside. Dusk always saw wildlife on the move as they went in search of food. Even though he knew Graham wouldn't have collected the girls so Neve wouldn't be on her way, he scanned the road ahead for signs of dust.

The moment of intensity they'd shared at the playground couldn't happen again. He had no right to complicate Neve's life any more than it was. He rolled his shoulders as the ute rattled over the old white wooden bridge. As for his haemorrhaging self-control, tonight he could only hope his common sense also didn't abandon him.

Patch's loud barking announced their arrival as Tanner parked outside the bluestone stables that had been converted into living quarters.

Max, accompanied by Molly, raced across the velvety lawn and through the open garden gate. Their fluffy black-and-white tails wagged in welcome. As soon as Patch was unclipped the trio sprinted into the large garden. Over near the cedar tree, freshly turned earth marked the site of the new garden bed. A rusted orange rotary hoe was parked beneath the tree.

Dressed in a long-sleeved white dress, Fliss walked down the veranda steps of the bluestone homestead. The restored farmhouse barely resembled the derelict eyesore the doctor had purchased when she'd needed an isolated sanctuary to deal with the loss of a patient.

'That's what I call good timing.' Fliss kissed his cheek. 'Hewitt just cracked open a beer.'

Tanner grinned and passed her a bottle of red wine. 'So much for waiting?'

'As if I couldn't hear you coming,' Hewitt said as he walked through the front door with two beers in his hand. 'No wonder Edna always knows where you are. It's not just the colour of your ute, everyone knows the sound of your V8.'

'I swear she's put a GPS tracker on it somewhere,' Tanner said with a grimace as he accepted a beer and followed Hewitt to the outdoor table in the barbeque area.

After Tanner had taken a seat, Hewitt clinked his bottle against his. 'Thanks for your help today. To the new adventure playground.'

'I'll drink to that and also to having some Edna-free days.'

Their beers were only half finished when the dogs barked as Neve's white sedan negotiated the dip in the road and then parked beside his ute. Tanner took a swig of beer to hide his tension. Tonight his self-control had to be watertight.

The three border collies rushed to welcome Neve. Dressed in a fitted floral dress that showed off her slender waist and the curve of her hips, she patted each dog before walking through the garden gate. Her hair was pulled into a high ponytail, leaving the delicate, pale curve of her neck bare.

At the wisteria-covered tank stand, she slowed to examine the corrugated-iron tank. As she drew closer to the bluestone homestead she studied the front façade, a half-smile curving her lips. It was as though with every step the green light in her eyes softened and her shoulders relaxed.

'I see what you mean,' he said in a low voice to Hewitt.

'Coming here just seems to lift a weight off her.'

They both stood to meet her.

'I'm glad you could make it,' Hewitt said as he gave Neve a hug.

'So am I.'

'Tanner.' She gave him a friendly smile, but her eyes didn't hold his for long.

'Neve.'

'Your timing's perfect too,' Fliss said as she joined them to set a cheese-and-cracker platter on the table. 'The usual to drink?'

'That would be lovely.'

Fliss disappeared inside, taking with her the pink box of chocolates and green leafy salad Neve had brought.

Neve took a chair beside Hewitt and passed him an envelope. 'I found some more old garden photos in Mum's albums.'

'Great. It's been interesting seeing what the garden used to look like.'

He opened the envelope and took out a black-and-white photo of a woman and a child sitting on a rug on the lawn.

Neve leaned over to point to a garden bed filled with flowers that lay beyond the cedar tree. 'Look how far back the fence used to be.'

Hewitt groaned. 'Don't let Fliss see this. She'll want new beds over there too. I thought the old rotary hoe had finally called it quits yesterday, but I'd only run over a metal box. Actually ... I wonder if you recognise it. It might have been your mother's or grandmother's?'

Hewitt headed inside and Tanner became acutely aware that he and Neve were alone. A faint blush coloured her cheeks and wariness had returned to cloud her gaze. The moment between them that morning had affected her too.

He made sure his words sounded casual. 'How was the lolly shop?'

'Fun ... except Graham mightn't agree thanks to the sugar high the girls were on when he collected them.'

Tanner smiled. 'If it's okay, I'll be out mid-morning tomorrow.'

She nodded, her attention on Hewitt as he walked across the lawn carrying a brown metal box. He placed the box on the table in front of Neve. 'Look familiar?'

She shook her head, her brow creasing as she ran a finger along the battered edge. 'I haven't seen anything similar in any photo either.' She tilted the box to look at the keyhole at the front. Something inside rattled.

Hewitt returned to his seat. 'I thought there might have been a key buried too, so did some digging with the shovel, but there was nothing.'

Neve looked at the house and then back to the box. 'I wonder ...' She stood. 'There was an old key hidden on the veranda rafters. Mum found it once when she was using the broom to get rid of wasps' nests. I remember when she put it back she was stung.'

Tanner followed Neve and Hewitt to the northern side of the veranda. Neve pursed her lips as she looked around and then pointed at a section of the old roof line that sloped downwards. 'It was about here, I think. I watched Mum through this window as she made me go inside away from the wasps.'

Hewitt stretched to run his hand along the dusty rafters. Tanner did the same on the other side.

'Got it,' Hewitt said as he lowered his arm. In his palm lay a rusty, old-fashioned key. 'It looks the right shape.' He handed Neve the key and dusted off his palms. 'We'll soon find out.'

Once back at the table Neve appeared to hold her breath as she inserted the key. Delight and hope brightened her eyes even before she uttered an awed, 'It fits.'

She turned the key and opened the box, making sure she angled it so Tanner and Hewitt could see the contents. There looked to be a dried posy of faded flowers, a gold-embossed invitation, a metal plaque of some sort and a wartime wedding photograph.

When the smile died on Neve's lips, Tanner forgot all about what was in the box.

'Neve?'

She didn't appear to hear him. Then she shot him a confused, wide-eyed look. 'This is my grandmother ...' She carefully took out the wedding photograph. 'But I have no idea who ... this man is.'

# CHAPTER

# 8

'Who was he? Why didn't we know?'

In the days since the discovery that her grandmother had had another husband, Neve's questions had only increased. She finished the last spoonful of her breakfast cereal and ran her finger over her favourite picture of her grandmother. Taken when she was in her twenties, Netta looked serene, an expression Neve didn't always remember.

She'd been through the family photo albums and grainy old film-reel footage she'd put onto discs for her mother to watch when her mobility wasn't good. It was as though the man in the photograph, and her grandmother's secret marriage, never existed. Today was Saturday, and apart from Cressy delivering Jazz, Neve could devote the whole day to delving deeper into the past.

She was sure her mother hadn't known of her grandmother's other marriage. No mention was ever made of her grandmother even having another suitor. Neve had always understood that her grandmother and grandfather had been family friends and married after the war. They'd only had the one child, and while her grandfather had been difficult to live with, her grandmother had never mentioned having had a life with someone else.

Neve stretched in the kitchen chair and rubbed at her lower back. Shock had given way to a burning need to know more about the man in the picture and why he'd been erased from her grandmother's life. As a child she'd accepted her grandfather's black moods and her grandmother's explanation that he'd be back to his old self soon.

But as an adult she questioned what type of marriage her gentle and loving grandmother had really had. She owed it to her to now piece together the fragments of her life. A life that the wedding photo proved had brought her great joy. A life that the buried and much-treasured mementoes said was one she'd wanted to hold on to.

Neve stared at the wedding photo that had been hidden in the box. While she hadn't found any marriage certificates on the internet for her grandmother at all, she had dated the cash box to around the 1940s. She'd also discovered the metal plaque was an engine plate from an aircraft. The gold-embossed invitation for a Grand RAAF ball held at the Air School Ballroom, Narromine on 21 March 1945, further gave her a wartime context.

She examined her grandmother's photo again. 'What happened? Is this why you would sometimes look so sad when you stared out the window?'

Only the sound of tyres on gravel and the rattle of a horse float answered her.

A cool breeze greeted Neve as she left the farmhouse. It wouldn't be long until the cicadas carolling in the trees would quieten. Over on the trellis that shaded the western side of the house, the green ornamental grape sported a single burgundy leaf. Soon the other leaves would also change colour and the Virginia creeper entwined around the gum tree would burst into rich red hues.

Cressy waved as she left her silver ute. In the back of the horse float Neve could see Jazz's grey-dappled rump.

'Morning.' Cressy's cheerful greeting was at odds with the stiff way she moved.

'Morning.'

Neve took a closer look at her visitor. The cowgirl's pink work shirt hung off her and failed to impart colour into her cheeks. Weddings could be stressful and she'd known university friends who'd lost weight before their big day. But Cressy wasn't one to worry about whether or not she'd fit into her bridal gown.

When Neve went to help the cowgirl take Jazz's gear from the back of the ute, Cressy's smile contained its usual sunshine. 'Jazz's so excited.'

Bassie's high-pitched neigh was followed by Jazz's whicker.

'She's not the only one.' Neve made sure she took hold of the heavy saddle before Cressy could reach for it. 'How's that side of yours?'

Cressy shrugged as she collected the saddle cloth and bridle. 'Doing okay.'

After they'd stored Jazz's gear in the tack shed, Cressy unloaded the mare. Neve moved to pat the gentle grey who'd always come to the fence to say hello whenever she'd visited. Jazz had been rescued by Cressy when she'd been injured in a horse-truck accident and her owner had been intent on calling the doggers.

'She's going to love being here,' Cressy said as Jazz nuzzled Neve's hand. 'I also appreciate her coming to stay. I feel guilty enough having Phil check on our place every second day while we're in Europe.'

Cressy had explained when she'd called to arrange a drop-off time that Jazz needed to be fed her nutritional supplements for her arthritis daily.

'It's no trouble to feed her every afternoon. I just hope she doesn't mind me having my learner plates on.'

Cressy stroked Jazz's grey neck. 'She'll be more than happy poking around. The easy exercise will do her good.'

Neve walked alongside Jazz as Cressy led the mare over to a gate behind the round yard. A cow mooed. Hewitt and Fliss's breeding herd grazed down on the alluvial flats kept green and lush by irrigation pivots. Jazz would be living in the undulating hills that overlooked the river.

Cressy nodded at the mass of golden mini-tumbleweeds caught against the fence. 'It's going to be a bad year for hairy panic grass. It took me an hour yesterday to clear the stable path.'

'Tell me about it. I don't know how, but they ended up filling the girls' play tent.'

A cow mooed for a second time. Cressy stopped Jazz to look across the paddock. Black cows were clustered beneath trees and it was impossible to determine where the noise had come from.

When there was no further sound, Cressy walked Jazz into her new home. Neve rested her arms on the steel gate. She couldn't stop smiling. This beautiful grey mare would be hers to ride whenever she wanted. Cressy unclipped the lead rope and after gazing around, Jazz lowered her head to graze.

'See, she's happy already,' Cressy said, heading back through the gate.

When another loud moo disturbed the silence, Cressy took her phone out of her jeans pocket. 'Something's up. I've got to meet the horse chiropractor, Denham and Hewitt are out of town, Fliss is at the hospital, but I know Tanner's not far away at Bethany's.'

Neve kept her expression from changing. She had no right to feel anything at the news that Tanner was helping Bethany on his weekend off from working with Dell and Bassie.

Cressy briefly spoke to Tanner. After the call ended she looked out over the distant cattle with a frown. 'It might be nothing, but other farmers have been having problems with wild dogs attacking their calves. Tanner will check everything's okay.' Cressy's hazel gaze met hers. 'He has Arrow so suggested we saddle Jazz and that you might like to ride around with him?'

Neve took her time to reply. At the adventure playground she hadn't imagined Tanner's attention focus on her mouth or her instant response. To her relief, at Fliss's barbeque it was as though they'd made the unspoken decision that no further moments could happen between them. Neither had looked at each other for very long. But the trip in her pulse at possibly seeing him again was a giveaway that she'd be asking for trouble being alone with him.

She bit the inside of her cheek. Going for a ride on Jazz was so tempting, and having Tanner with her when she did take her first ride was also the only sensible thing to do.

She nodded slowly. 'That sounds a good idea. I'm right to saddle Jazz, though.' She reached for the lead rope Cressy held. 'You get going so you aren't late for the horse chiro.'

Cressy didn't immediately relinquish the rope. 'Are you sure?'

'Yes. I'm a pro at saddling Bassie now, even if he does blow up like a helium balloon when I tighten the girth.'

'Thanks, Hugh does always run on time. See you Friday for coffee?'

'I'll look forward to it. Graham has a day off so I won't have the girls.'

Neve gave the cowgirl a final wave before opening the paddock gate and walking over to the grey mare. 'I'm sorry, Jazz. I know you just got here, but you'll have plenty of time to eat after our ride.'

Neve led the mare into the round yard and busied herself with brushing and saddling her. She pulled the saddle cloth high into the saddle pommel like Tanner had showed her. She also walked Jazz around in small circles to ensure that the girth wouldn't pinch. When Jazz was ready, Neve made sure she carried the mounting block into the yard. There'd be no more up-close-and-personal contact with Tanner while he gave her a leg-up into the saddle.

Tanner arrived and parked in his usual place under the cedar tree. He gave her a wave, which she returned, and soon joined her with a saddled Arrow and an energetic Patch.

'Rosewood seems to be the place where it all happens,' he said, stopping in front of her. He smiled, his dimple appearing briefly.

Neve took his lead to keep things friendly but impersonal between them. 'I know. If it isn't Bassie getting stuck, it's a cow who doesn't sound happy.'

As if on cue, the cow mooed. Both he and Arrow looked out over the paddock and she sensed their mood shift from casualness into a need for action.

Tanner glanced back at her. 'How about you get to know Jazz before we head into the paddock?'

'Okay.' Neve checked her helmet was securely in place before she entered the round yard.

With the mounting block in position and her stirrup leathers measured, hoping she didn't look as ungainly as she felt, she climbed into Jazz's saddle.

Tanner gave her a thumbs-up sign. She headed Jazz to the edge of the round yard and hadn't completed two circuits before Tanner opened the gate wide. Jazz's grey ears flickered in happiness as Neve rode her out of the yard. Neve patted her neck. She already enjoyed riding the responsive, soft-mouthed mare.

Tanner swung into Arrow's saddle, and with Patch running alongside the horses, they rode into the cattle paddock. She didn't miss the way Tanner looked across at her every so often to make sure she was going okay. Today he wore a faded blue work shirt and stubble blurred the firm line of his jaw. She curled her fingers tighter around her reins. She had the insane urge to lean over to feel the rasp of his whiskers against her fingertips.

Tanner initiated the small talk. 'How are the girls?'

'Going well. Graham's taken them to the movies in Dubbo.'

'They'd like that. They were talking about some snowman from some movie?'

'This is the movie sequel to the snowman one.' She paused. There was only one thing that they talked about more than their favourite movie character. 'Their rides on Bassie are the highlight of their day. Thanks for all that you've done for them … they can be a little overwhelming at times.'

Tanner rubbed at his chin. 'They can, but … they've grown on me.'

Neve smiled. Since the working bee, if Tanner wasn't carrying Kait he was swinging Maya around, making her laugh her uncontrollable belly-chuckles. Every day his confidence grew. 'Considering they love hanging off you, that's a good thing.'

Tanner returned her smile and she wished his sunglasses didn't shade his eyes. 'I was worried about dropping them, but they have a grip any bull rider would be proud of.'

'I bet they do.'

'Any luck discovering anything about your grandmother's wedding photo?'

'Not yet. I'll do some more online research to see if I can find out about the ball.'

'There didn't seem to be anything on the man's uniform to say what he did during the war.'

'There wasn't.'

Tanner didn't immediately reply. 'If you like I could send the photo to my father. He might know something.'

The wave of warmth that rushed through her had nothing to do with the sun on her skin. Tanner was willing to reach out to the father he barely spoke to in order to help her. 'Thanks, but only if you're sure.'

The corner of his mouth quirked. 'I'm sure.' A drawn-out moo sounded to their left. 'Cressy was right. Someone isn't happy.'

Tanner changed course to head Arrow along a gully. Neve followed in single file as the ground became uneven and rocky.

Tanner stopped Arrow as a lone black cow lifted her head and gave a loud, plaintive moo. 'She's calling for her calf.'

Neve halted Jazz beside the palomino. Tanner's stillness confirmed he was listening as he scanned the paddock to his left. Then she heard it too, a faint and thin moo.

She frowned. 'The calf almost sounds like it's … underground.'

'It most likely is, in a wombat burrow.'

They rode closer. The distressed cow retreated a few paces then swung around to watch them.

Tanner dipped his head towards a series of large cavernous openings burrowed into the bank of an old creek bed. 'The calf will be in one of these.'

He dismounted, small puffs of dust rising from where his boots hit the dry ground. Patch ran to his side. Tanner tickled behind his ears. 'You stay here with Neve and the horses.' He glanced across at her. 'I'll take a look.'

She rubbed Jazz's neck to distract herself from noticing the masculine grace with which he walked. There was no swagger, no arrogance or ego, just an inbuilt confidence that conveyed that whatever trouble the calf had got itself into Tanner would handle.

He looked in the first two holes and then drew back from the third. He turned to nod at her, expression grave. He'd found the calf.

∝

Tanner took a closer look at the small black bundle wedged deep into the wombat burrow. The calf gazed at him with big, anxious eyes.

'I have no idea how you got yourself in there, buddy,' he said softly, 'but it's going to be a job getting you out.'

Footsteps sounded behind him before Neve came to his side. 'The poor thing. He's well and truly stuck.'

'He?'

'No self-respecting girl calf would get herself so stuck that she needed rescuing.'

Tanner silenced his laughter to a quiet chuckle. 'We're just lucky *he* called for his mum and that we can see him. Denham and I had a calf in a burrow over at Claremont.' He met Neve's gaze with a grin. 'Yes, he was a he. Not only was he at least a metre deep, he wasn't even visible.'

'How did you get him out?'

'I held onto Denham's legs while he pulled the calf free.'

Neve's eyes widened. 'Is now a good time to tell you I don't like confined spaces?'

'It's fine. This calf isn't in as far.'

'At least he's in the shade; it sure is warming up.'

Neve removed her black riding helmet. She ran her fingers through her loose hair and lifted it off her neck. The sweet scent of flowers drifted to him.

'We should be able to get him out without having to go back for a shovel. But we'll be here for a while. So …' He took off his hat and placed it on her head. 'This is better on you than me.'

As she settled the oversized hat in place, her sunny smile made him forget all about why he had to keep his distance.

He turned and stepped away. It would be so easy to dip his head and brush his mouth over hers. 'I'll make the hole bigger.'

Using a sturdy stick like a crowbar, he worked at the side of the hole furthest away from the calf's head. When he bent to scoop out the dirt he'd loosened, Neve came to help. It wasn't his imagination that she made sure their hands didn't touch.

The mother cow called and the calf gave a weak response. Tanner broke away more of the creek bank. When the soil had been removed, he straightened. 'Okay. Fingers crossed.'

He knelt beside the calf and bent to wrap his arms around the tiny body. The enlarged burrow entrance gave him just enough room to manoeuvre his hands beneath the calf. It took two goes to lift him. As young as the calf was it still weighed enough to make his muscles protest.

As soon as the calf's black front hooves were free, Neve helped to lift out his back end. They carefully lowered him to the ground. As Neve had predicted it was a bull calf. He lay there, sides heaving, before he struggled to his feet. Legs wobbly, he made his way over to his mother, who'd rushed closer. As he sought her udder, his tail wriggled.

'Well done.' Neve's voice was breathless with relief.

'It was a team effort.'

She looked at her dirt-covered hands. 'My digging was pretty spectacular, if I do say so myself.'

'It was.'

His attention was caught by a smudge across her jaw. Against her white skin the mark looked like a bruise. 'Did you get kicked?'

'I don't think so. It's probably dust.' She touched her face. 'Here?'

'No.' He smoothed a thumb over her chin. 'Here.'

Her skin felt warm and petal soft. The breeze tangled in her hair and before he could lower his hand silken tendrils wound around his fingers.

'Sorry.' Neve turned her head to free his hand, but the strands only tightened. 'My hair comes from my grandmother ... hers was just better behaved.'

He stared at the way the strawberry-blonde colour caught the sunlight. If he looked into Neve's green eyes he'd be lost. He'd never wanted to kiss a woman as much as he did the one standing so still before him.

He straightened his fingers and her hair unravelled, sliding over his skin in a whisper-soft caress. He took a step backwards and worked hard to keep his voice even. 'We'd better make tracks.'

'We should ... Thanks for this.' She removed his hat and passed it to him without making eye contact.

'No worries.'

Using a fallen log to give herself height, Neve didn't need help reaching Jazz's saddle.

The ride home passed in silence and occasional small talk as they rode past a mob of kangaroos lounging beneath the box trees. It was only after the horses were unsaddled and Tanner walked with Neve from the tack shed that he spoke the words that had been on his mind since he'd seen the girls yesterday.

'Neve ... this will be my last week.'

Her only reaction seemed to be a slowing of her steps as she walked beside him. 'I thought it might be. Bassie's been going so well.'

Tanner went over to where the taffy pony poked his nose through the gaps in the fence panel and rubbed his neck. 'I've enjoyed getting to know you, Mr Bassie ... and you too, Miss Dell.' Not wanting to miss out on anything, the donkey had approached. He stroked her grey-and-white forehead.

Neve's lips curved, but he couldn't quite see if her smile reached her eyes. 'They're going to miss you, and so are the girls. Tanner ... maybe when you're not busy ... you could still give them a lesson every now and then?'

'I was thinking the same thing. I might even know of another pony I could bring out so we could all go for a ride.'

'That sounds wonderful. I wasn't looking forward to telling the girls that they wouldn't see you again.' There was no mistaking the warmth and thanks in her words. 'Saving calves is thirsty work. Arrow also seems happy in the shade. Would you like a cool drink or a coffee? I promise I won't make you eat anything blue.'

'A cold drink sounds good, and while I'm there I'll take a photo of your grandmother's wedding picture.'

He took a last long look at Dell as she walked away before falling into step beside Neve. From somewhere in the garden Patch barked. Tanner stopped to study a perfect donkey hoof print in a soft section of the gravel driveway.

Neve sighed. 'Yes, the unbroken record of Bassie and Dell staying in their paddock ended yesterday afternoon. After Maya and Kait took them their dinner the gate somehow wasn't shut properly. But instead of raiding the garden, Dell and Bassie made themselves at home on the veranda. I swear when Kait held the screen door open to show me they were there, they would have walked inside if they'd had the chance.'

Tanner chuckled. 'How did you go putting them back?'

'Dell was a sweetheart and Bassie ... well, he gave me that look. So Maya marched up to him and told him you said he had to behave. And guess what? He was an angel.'

Knowing that anxious Maya was more confident thanks to something he'd worked on with her made him feel humble and honoured. 'Bassie knows he's met his match.'

Neve didn't reply; she veered towards where Patch sat on the lawn near the bird bath, staring at a football-sized mound of red earth.

'That's strange, that pile of dirt wasn't there earlier.'

'I'm sure it wasn't.'

Neve's brow creased. 'Is it something I should be worried about?'

'Only if you're an ant or a termite.'

Neve's expression cleared. Tanner didn't look back at the cream spikes attached to a dark body visible at the edge of the hole beneath the dirt. He could never get tired of watching the green hue of Neve's eyes change as they reflected her emotions.

'Ah, it's an echidna. The girls said they saw one the other day.'

'Patch must have given him a fright so he's dug himself in.' Tanner whistled for the border collie to follow. 'We'll leave him alone and tonight he'll continue on his way.'

'Inside or outside?' Neve asked when they reached the bottom veranda step.

'Outside. We can make sure Patch won't try to play with his new friend. Do you need a hand with anything?' At her smile and head shake he headed for the outdoor table that would give them a good view of the garden.

It wasn't long until Neve returned with a water jug filled with ice and slices of lemon. On a plate sat a pile of white chocolate-chip cookies. Neve disappeared again to return with glasses, plates and a water bowl for Patch.

She offered Tanner a biscuit. 'They're not blue ... but I must confess the girls have discovered where I put the food colouring so there's a very blue cake in the freezer for when you visit on Monday.'

He filled the water glasses. 'Just remind me next shirt order to get some different colours.'

Neve returned inside and this time came out with an envelope and the metal box Hewitt had dug out of Bundara's garden. Her expression sobered as she sat and passed him the wedding photograph. 'What do you see? Honestly.'

'I'm no body-language expert, but from the way your grandmother and this man look at each other and are holding hands so tightly, they are happy being together.'

Neve's fingertips touched the photo. 'I think so too, but that's all it tells us. There're no clues about when or where this was taken. Grandma's dress is simple and her bouquet small, which suggests it was a whirlwind wedding.'

'Which fits in with it being wartime. Theirs wouldn't have been the only marriage to have taken place in haste.'

Neve took out a photo from the envelope and laid it beside the first photo. 'What do you see in this one?'

Tanner chose his words carefully. The second photo also captured the wedding day of a bride and groom. The woman was the same, but that was the only similarity. Her wedding dress was intricate and the bouquet she held large. Instead of gazing into each other's eyes, the bride and groom stood in a church doorway looking at the camera. The woman's hand was clasped in the crook of the man's elbow and her body held slightly away. But it was the expressions that were the most telling.

'Well … this looks more formal. Your grandmother's smiling, but her eyes are almost … sad. As for your grandfather, he perhaps looks more pleased with himself than happy.'

Neve sighed. 'He does and yes, Netta doesn't look at all like how she does in the other photo. She's also lost weight. I don't ever remember her being so thin.'

Neve opened the box and took out the metal plaque.

'I've seen something similar before,' Tanner said, taking his phone out of his shirt pocket to snap a picture. 'Maybe on an airplane? My father will be most interested to see this.'

'I'm sure he will be as it is an aircraft engine plate.' Neve shot him a quick look. 'Are you sure about contacting him? It's more than okay if you have second thoughts.'

'If anyone knows their wartime aircraft, my father does.'

'Thank you.'

'Don't thank me yet, he mightn't pick up the phone.'

Even though humour edged his tone, Neve didn't smile. 'He will.'

Tanner masked his doubt by taking a photo of the wedding picture as well as the ball invitation. If he had to he'd drive to Sydney and knock on his father's door. The years of following leads and grasping at hope when searching for his birth mother made him aware of the importance of Neve finding out as much as she could about her grandmother and her secret groom.

When the water glasses were empty and Patch had enjoyed the cookie Tanner had snuck under the table, there was no more reason to stay. He helped Neve to carry the jug and glasses inside. Just like when with the girls, she waited on the front steps and waved to him until he'd driven through the front gate. Long after she'd stopped waving, he checked in his rear-view mirror until she'd headed inside.

He blew out a deep breath. Somehow, he'd held himself together while alone with Neve. Today there'd been no further intense, out-of-control moments, even when he'd touched her face. Instead, a companionship and sense of peace had evolved while they'd worked to rescue the calf and then sat on the veranda. For the first time the lure of the long paddock didn't beckon. In that moment there was nowhere he'd rather be than riding by Neve's side.

Once back at Claremont, he unloaded Arrow and headed to his flat. He'd call his father before he went in search of Meredith in the main part of the house for their daily cuppa. It was his choice he lived where he did. Not only did he have his own space, but he had the freedom he needed to leave at any time.

He took a seat at the small kitchen table. Beyond the window the midday sun warmed the undulating summer-gold hills. Now the days were growing shorter, the rural landscape would soon lose its bleached hue. Fingers cold, he dialled his father's number. The ringtone echoed in his ear as no one answered. He was just about to lower his mobile when his father's well-educated voice sounded. 'Stewart Callahan speaking.'

Tanner swallowed. His father still didn't recognise his number.

'Hi, Dad, it's me.'

He could picture his father's lips pressing together at the news.

'Dad, you still there?'

'Yes. You only just called for my birthday. Are you in trouble?'

He briefly closed his eyes. He'd always been the model son. Never once had he called his father for help, even when he'd needed it. 'No.'

'Right.'

He wasn't sure, but there could have been relief in his father's clipped reply. More likely it was a crackle in the phone line.

His father spoke again. 'Are you coming back to practise law?'

Tanner ground his teeth. 'No. I'm calling because I have a friend who needs someone knowledgeable in Second World War aviation history.'

'Is this friend a woman?'

'Yes, but she's just a friend.'

'Where's she from? Not America again?'

Tanner repressed a sigh. His father wasn't going to let him forget every poor choice he'd ever made. 'No. Here.'

'Was she born … *out there*?'

'No, she's moved here from the city.'

'So she's a city girl?'

Tanner took a silent breath and strove for calm. Even in his seventies his father would still slay an opposing counsel. 'Technically, yes. But she's a girl who can live anywhere she wants and at the moment she chooses to live *out here*.'

To his surprise his father gave a dry laugh. 'I like her.'

'You don't know her.'

'I don't need to. You're calling because you want to help her, which means she's more than a friend, and if she's a city girl it also means you still have something in common with the world you left behind.'

'Dad …' As much as he tried, he couldn't stop the warning rasp in his voice. A bout of his father's coughing silenced the rest of his reply. They hadn't even spoken for five minutes this time before his coughing had started.

'Have you been to the doctor like you were supposed to?'

'I don't need to.' His father coughed again. 'What does your city friend want to know?'

'There's a good doctor here you could see.'

'I'm fine.'

Tanner sighed. Bassie's stubbornness was nothing compared to his father's. 'I'll send two photos to your email. Neve's trying to identify the man in the picture. The woman is her grandmother.'

'Okay, I'll make no promises about helping, but I'll take a look.'

Then his father hung up without another word.

# CHAPTER

# 9

Autumn had officially arrived.

Neve tugged at the sleeves of the denim jacket she wore with a white shirt and black jeans. The cold air contained the bite of winter and the flawless sky had turned a dull grey. She sipped at her breakfast cup of tea that she always enjoyed on the veranda. Tomorrow might be a morning to stay inside.

A stiff breeze swayed the treetops and a flurry of raindrops drummed on the tin roof. She'd woken to the sound of rain and thunder last night. Now the garden glistened and the fresh scent of wet soil mingled with the perfume of the yellow roses. She was surprised how little she missed the cityscape with its hard concrete angles and pungent fumes.

A tiny blue-and-black wren hopped across the lawn to perch on the rustic bird bath. As Tanner had predicted, the echidna had vacated its nearby hidey-hole by the following morning. The girls had helped her fill in the indent and after the night's storm the grass would soon cover the bare dirt. Every day now Maya and Kait continued to search the garden to see if their spiny visitor had returned.

Neve stared into her tea, the warmth of the mug seeping into her palms. With Graham having the girls today, Tanner's last week of coming to Rosewood had ended a day early. The girls' sadness had been eased by his promise that he'd give them a riding lesson whenever he could.

They'd also been buoyed by the knowledge that next Friday was the first day of the Mudgee small-farm field days and they would see him there. Tanner was booked to do a horse-training demonstration. Neve would drive the girls over to the neighbouring town—she'd never been to a field day—then Graham would arrive to take them to a friend's house for the weekend.

A magpie carolled, but Neve didn't look away from her tea. All week she'd been dreading Friday arriving and now it was here, she wasn't sure how she felt. No longer would there be a blue ute parked beneath the cedar tree every weekday. No longer would the sight of Tanner striding across the garden fill her with equal parts nervousness and happiness.

The day they'd rescued the calf had reminded her of all the reasons why she hadn't managed to stop thinking about him. Tanner, with his integrity, strength and unselfishness, was a forever man. She frowned at her tea. But it had also highlighted her vulnerability. He triggered emotions and longings that she wasn't currently equipped to deal with.

When his thumb had smoothed across her chin she had been gripped by a need so strong she was surprised he didn't feel the trembling of her knees. If she'd been a more confident person she'd have stood on tiptoes and kissed him. But she wasn't. Tanner was no more looking for any complications, let alone a relationship, than she was. She also hadn't wanted to end their time together on any awkwardness.

It took a second to register her mobile ringing from where it lay on the table beside her. Ella's face filled the screen.

Neve answered, hoping her words didn't sound distracted. 'Morning.'

'Morning. How about this weather?'

'I know. It feels like we've fast-forwarded into winter.'

'Don't worry. By lunch the humidity will kick in and it'll be back to feeling like summer. Are you still coming to town?'

'Yes, but not to see Cressy. She couldn't make coffee. But Meredith called and invited me to lunch. She has some old wartime scrapbooks and photographs she thought I might like to look at.'

Tanner had asked if he could also show the wedding photograph to Meredith as she had a keen interest in local history.

'I'm heading out your way to see a horse with ringworms and would like to take a look at Miss Dell.'

'Not Bassie?'

'No ... Tanner called to ask if there was a chance Dell might be in foal. I said I didn't think so but would look into it.'

'No way.' Neve looked across to where Dell and Bassie had sought shelter from the wind behind a dense orange tree. She'd noticed Dell's stomach had grown a little rounder but had assumed it was the lack of exercise now that she remained in her paddock.

'Yes way. It turns out where Bassie and Dell went after they were rescued, Dell used her Houdini skills to open stable doors and gates. She apparently had a special friend, a donkey called Bolt.'

'Why doesn't that surprise me? When will we know for sure?'

'I trust Tanner's hunch but will check her over to make sure she's going okay.'

'The girls will be so excited. Do you want me here? I can stay.'

'No, it's fine. And yes they will be, but it will still be a while until they'll have a baby Dell to cuddle.' What sounded like a big breed of dog barked in the background. 'I'd best get back to work but will call you tonight.'

'Okay. Talk soon.'

As Neve ended the call she realised she was smiling. A baby donkey. She couldn't think of anything more adorable.

Heart now light, she headed into town. Apart from small puddles on the side of the road, the overnight rain had drained away. Once in Woodlea she replenished her grocery supplies, returned the girls' books to the library and visited Sally for her regular latte.

As much as she didn't want to admit it, she kept a close eye out for Tanner's blue ute. She also kept watch for Edna's white four-wheel drive. But apart from seeing Hewitt in the post office, she didn't stop to talk to anyone else.

When it was close to lunchtime, Neve took the road out of town that would deliver her to Claremont. Ella had been right. The cloud cover had dispersed and now bright sunshine bathed the bitumen road. The car's air conditioning hummed and her jacket lay discarded on the back seat. She'd also twisted her hair into a messy bun. The humidity had rendered her curls more rebellious than usual.

At a drystone-wall entrance she turned to enter a poplar-tree-lined driveway. She slowed to enjoy the journey. She'd never been to Meredith's home before. The aged trees on either side of her would have witnessed the progression of time as horse-drawn vehicles had given way to motorised cars. Just like in years gone by, the poplars continued to mark the ending of summer with a hint of yellow shimmering amongst the green. By the middle of autumn they'd glimmer like living flames.

Through the tree trunks she glimpsed the impressive veranda-wrapped historic homestead. She could only imagine Tanner's reaction to discovering this was where generations of his mother's family had carved out a life in the Bell River Valley. Unpretentious and humble, Tanner never talked about where he lived. She wondered if he didn't have Rigby blood in his veins if Edna would consider him such a worthy future son-in-law.

Neve parked in the shade cast by a towering jacaranda tree. To her right stood a modern stable complex complete with a round yard. Down by the creek gold glistened as Arrow rested beneath a tree, his tail swishing. To her left a sandstone path led past manicured beds filled with cheerful flowers and a last flush of white iceberg rose blooms.

As she passed the corner of the house she stepped off the path to touch the glossy deep-green leaves of a sheltered pale-pink camellia. Her mother had loved camellias and had grown an assortment of varieties.

A door opened and closed, before light footsteps sounded on the veranda floorboards. Meredith appeared and walked down the wide front steps between two sandstone urns filled with white alyssum.

'I thought I heard a car,' she said with a welcoming smile. 'Patch usually barks, but he's over at the shed with Phil and Tanner getting ready for sowing.'

Neve smiled, hoping her expression didn't reveal it had been on her mind whether or not Tanner would be home. 'They would have welcomed this rain.'

'They did.' Dressed in simple white pants and an orange linen shirt, Meredith gave her a hug. The older woman's subtle and delicate perfume completed the impression of grace and elegance.

'Thanks for lunch and letting me look through the scrapbooks,' Neve said as their embrace ended.

'My pleasure. I was hoping to eat outside, but it's a little too wet so we'll have to make do inside.'

Meredith's version of making do involved a gourmet quiche, avocado salad and homemade bread, all set out on a lace tablecloth in a dining room flooded with natural light. Neve's mouth watered and her senses rejoiced at such a beautiful room. Despite its formality, the silver-framed photographs on a side board and the vase of purple salvia and gum leaves made the room feel welcoming and lived in.

She bent to look closer at the photographs. The largest frame held a picture of Tanner and Meredith standing side by side. Tanner's relaxed smile, and the arm he had around his mother's shoulders, communicated the love he had for the woman who had been missing from his life for so long. Another photo held an image of Tanner next to Meredith and Phil that had to be taken at their garden wedding. Other photos contained Denham and his family, Denham with Cressy, while black-and-white pictures paid tribute to past Rigby descendants.

'They're lovely photographs, Meredith.'

Meredith came to stand beside her. 'Even before I lost Tanner, family had always been important to me. I think it was because, to be honest, I never felt like I had one as a child.' She picked up a picture of an elderly couple in which each adult wore a severe expression. 'I loved my parents, but ours wasn't a house full of affection. My brother and I weren't raised to express our emotions.'

'I understand. My grandfather was a cold and distant man. My mother never said anything, but I think she made sure she broke the cycle. She was always hugging me and telling me she loved me, so much so I used to catch the bus to school so she wouldn't embarrass me in front of my friends.'

Meredith laughed softly. 'I would have liked your mother. Poor Tanner ... I know he's a grown man, but a day doesn't pass without me kissing or hugging him too.'

'He wouldn't mind. Deep down, I didn't either.'

Meredith passed Neve a grainy photograph of a smiling man holding the reins of a horse. 'This was Simon, Tanner's father.'

Neve studied the image. Even with the poor photo quality she could see the resemblance to Tanner in the similar face shape and the way his father held his shoulders. 'They're very alike.'

'They are and not just physically. Simon was a jackeroo and loved his horses.' After Neve handed the frame to Meredith, the older woman took a last look before returning it to the side board.

They made their way to the dining table and were soon enjoying the delicious lunch.

Meredith looked up as she buttered a piece of crusty bread. 'Tanner mentioned Maya and Kait have been baking for him.'

Neve nodded before she finished a mouthful of creamy quiche. 'He's been such a good sport. Did he tell you everything they make for him is blue?'

Meredith's eyes rounded. Neve wasn't sure if it was because she'd called Tanner a good sport when it came to interacting with children or if it was because of all the baking being blue. 'He didn't. Why blue?'

'They think it's his favourite colour because of his ute and work shirts.'

'You know ... I'm not actually sure what his favourite colour is. I'll have to ask him.'

Neve smiled. 'It would be helpful if it was red or yellow. Do you know how hard it is to find blue food?'

Meredith's answering smile revealed a faint dimple. 'It would be. I'm curious now, I'll be looking for blue food recipes.'

'Lucky for Tanner and his tastebuds there won't be any more blue treats as we won't be seeing him for a little while.'

Meredith's fork stopped halfway to her mouth. 'Has he said he's going off droving again?'

'No, not that I've heard. It's just his work's done with Bassie and Dell, and Bethany has a new horse she needs help with. We'll still see him, at the field day and then the following week when he'll give the girls another riding lesson.'

Meredith's slender shoulders relaxed.

While they ate and discussed growing camellias in a hot climate, Neve couldn't help but sneak glances at the scrapbooks and photo albums at the far end of the mahogany table. Maybe they contained the clues she needed.

Once lunch had been cleared away and a fresh pot of tea sat in front of them, Meredith moved the scrapbooks and albums closer. 'So what are we looking for?'

Neve scrolled through her phone to find her grandmother's wedding photo and the ball invitation. 'Any pictures of this couple or anything about this ball.'

Meredith's attention lingered on the wedding photograph. 'You take after your grandmother and I'm guessing your mother?'

'I do. Even if I didn't share their hair colour, our similar smiles make it obvious that we're related.'

Neve opened a photo album thick with black-and-white images.

Meredith leaned over to look at the pictures. 'These are all my mother's. It's funny to think of her as being a social butterfly; my memory of her is not having a vast circle of friends.'

Neve examined the images of smiling young men in uniform and their fresh-faced female companions. Some photographs were of couples dancing, and others of groups of friends having a picnic. 'They all look so young.'

'They do. They all would have been about nineteen or twenty. I can only imagine the excitement of my mother and her friends after the flying training school opened and there was an influx of young men into the district.'

Neve turned another page to study the picture of an open-air pool that was dated 1944. 'They certainly looked to have made the most of their time off.'

'Even though it was wartime, there was also a strong sense of community spirit.' Meredith pointed to a photo of a weatherboard building. 'This was a house set up as a club where students could play table tennis, darts and chess and relax. Locals would drop around with home-cooked meals.'

Meredith flicked back a page to where two young men stood near a tractor. 'This was taken here. My grandparents often invited students to come to Claremont for the weekend to join in with farm activities or to play tennis. Some other local properties were also used as satellite airfields.'

'I wonder if that's how my grandmother met whoever is in the photo? Students could have stayed at Bundara?'

'The ball ticket does suggest it was a wartime romance. There are still families around here whose grandparents met in such a way.'

Neve examined the wedding photo on her phone. 'After seeing all of these pictures … I'm thinking that my grandmother's mystery man looks a little older?'

Meredith also looked at Neve's phone. 'I agree. He does.'

Neve thought hard. As a teenager she hadn't paid as much attention as she should have to her mother's family stories. 'If I have this right, my grandmother was going out with my grandfather before he left for the war and when he returned they were married. I need to track down his war record to find out what the exact dates were.'

Meredith nodded as a loud splash sounded from outside. 'I wondered how long Phil and Tanner would last in the shed now it has warmed up. Come and meet Phil. They'll both be cooling off in the pool.'

Cold water on his hot skin had never felt so good. Tanner swam underwater until his lungs protested. He surfaced to the sight of Meredith wearing an unreadable smile. Air again left his lungs. She wasn't alone.

He wiped water from his eyes and dragged both hands through his hair. He had no idea Neve would even be here. If he had he'd have taken a shower instead of a swim. Just as well he hadn't totally stripped off like he did on a summer's night when he worked late and the house lay quiet and dark.

He swam closer and stood, water lapping around his waist.

'Phil not here, darling?'

'He's gone to get air-seeder parts in town.' He nodded at Neve. 'Hi.'

'Hi.'

He couldn't work out from her voice, or her expression, if she was pleased to see him. Instead, she appeared intent on lavishing attention on a wriggling Patch.

Tanner looked at the large striped towel draped over a poolside chair. Meredith heeded his silent request and moved forward but stopped just short of the towel. 'What are you doing while Phil's away?'

'What would you like me to do?'

Her instant smile warned him he should have given more thought to his answer. 'Show Neve around and then load the scrapbooks and albums into her car. We won't get through them today.'

He didn't miss Neve's quick glance at Meredith. But Meredith's gaze didn't leave him. He had the distinct impression that unless he agreed, his towel would stay on the chair. While her expression remained innocent, her blue eyes contained an ominous twinkle. He mustn't have been as convincing as he'd hoped that Neve was just another client.

'No problem.'

'Great.' She handed him his towel, seemingly oblivious to his narrow-eyed stare. 'We'll keep going through the album we were looking at until you're ready.'

He thought Neve wasn't going to look at him again, but as she turned to follow Meredith she gave him a brief smile.

He didn't rush as he dried himself off, collected his clothes and headed to his flat. He needed time before facing Neve again.

Neve in loose cotton shirts and faded jeans proved enough of a distraction. Neve in black jeans that fitted like a second skin and a white T-shirt that clung in all the right places would be lethal to his concentration. He couldn't give Meredith any more reason to suspect that he was far from immune to her lunchtime guest.

Once dressed in clean clothes he headed for the dining room. At the closed door he stopped to listen to the sound of Meredith and Neve's laughter. Meredith was always helping others, but she seemed to have taken a special interest in Neve. From the way they were getting on, Neve obviously enjoyed Meredith's company. He'd be lying if he said that it didn't make him feel content that the two of them had such a strong connection.

As he entered the room both women glanced up, their faces alight with amusement.

Meredith gave him another quick smile. 'Darling, I spoke to Phil and he'll be ages so you'll have time for the grand tour. No skimping like you did when my second cousin called in.'

'I didn't … skimp. I'd already heard the life story of her very eligible daughter … twice.'

Meredith closed the photo album that sat before Neve and her. 'Denham and I keep telling you the longer you remain single the more you'll be a marked man. Wedding fever's highly contagious, you know.'

He didn't dare glance at Neve for her reaction.

Meredith rose from her chair. 'Now before you go, I'll get some carrots for Reggie. Who knows, today might be your lucky day?'

At Neve's curious look he shrugged. She didn't need to know about him failing the Reggie test. Denham and Hewitt continued to give him enough grief about the bull refusing to accept his beloved carrots from him.

When they were seated in his ute, a container of carrots balanced on Neve's knees, he held onto the hope that Neve wasn't fully on board with Meredith's tour plans. Even before he started the engine, he knew that a tour of any length was a bad idea. Neve sat so near he could see her chest rise and fall with every breath she took, and with every breath he took he inhaled her light floral fragrance.

He cleared his throat. 'Are you sure about having the grand tour? Not everyone finds Claremont interesting.'

'If you have time, I'd love to have a good look around.'

'Okay, then. To our left we have …'

For the next fifteen minutes he pointed out features of the house, garden, stables and outbuildings. At a corrugated circular shed they left the ute to take a closer look. Patch didn't stray from Neve's side. The border collie was missing his daily visits to see Neve and the girls.

'I've never seen a roof like this before,' she said, stopping in front of the tin structure. 'It looks like a pixie cap.'

Tanner didn't let on he had no idea what a pixie hat was. 'This was once an enclosed round yard where horses were broken in. The original timber roof's beneath the flattened tin of old kerosene cans.'

Neve walked to the door and peered inside. As she looked up, her heavy hair unravelled from its high knot. She slid out the clip and her hair fell down her back. Against the white of her shirt, it shone more red than gold. 'I can see the shingles. If only the roof could talk.'

He didn't reply; he'd already taken two steps back to his ute. He was having trouble thinking about anything but tangling his hands in her silken hair and kissing her until they were both breathless.

They continued on towards the custom-built rodeo yards. It was from here Denham ran his rodeo cattle side of their business. The first lot of calves from the cows he'd bought with bucking blood were showing promise as future rodeo bulls. Not that Cressy saw Reggie's genetics as contributing to such a potential. The cowgirl still swore good-natured Reggie wasn't capable of siring feisty progeny.

Neve turned to look through the back window to where Patch wore a doggy grin. 'He loves riding in the ute.'

'He does. When he was a pup he used to wait for me by the driver's side door.'

'He would have been adorable as a puppy.'

'He was, too adorable, even when burying Meredith's gardening clogs, one of which has never been found.'

Neve laughed softly. 'I can only imagine how besotted I'll be with Dell's baby.'

Tanner briefly glanced at her. 'I didn't say anything about her being in foal in case it couldn't be true. You're okay about it all? A young donkey can be a big commitment.'

'Yes. I took Dell and Bassie on to give them a proper home. When life … settles down … I'll look for my own small farm. I'm sure I'll find something to keep me busy when Graham no longer needs me to look after the girls.'

Tanner nodded and stared through the dusty windscreen at the dirt road that followed the fence line. Not only was this the first indication Neve was planning to stay, but her words hit a scarred, broken place inside him with the precision of an arrow.

He had no doubt, with what he knew about her, she'd honour her pledge to Dell and Bassie. Neve was genuine. She was a woman who meant what she said and who wouldn't take advantage of a situation. Unlike Genevieve, who'd had no more use for him after he'd served his purpose.

Neve's voice sounded again. 'How's Bethany's new horse going?'

'Really well.' Which was the truth. Skittles was a dream to work with and would make a perfect second pony for the girls.

'That's great. You shouldn't be there too long, then?'

The serious edge to Neve's question had him looking at her again. 'Maybe.' Which also was the truth. Bethany couldn't hide that she was with Mac from Edna forever. But he could understand her wanting a chance for her new relationship to strengthen before Edna took to it with her sledgehammer of choice.

'Are you planning on going droving anytime soon?'

'Not in the next fortnight. But I will need to take some cattle down south before the wedding.'

But even as he said the words the urgency that had hounded him over the past weeks to head out to the long paddock didn't hammer as hard as it had.

'It must be very peaceful when you're on the road?'

'It can be, but between trucks that don't heed cattle signs, or irresponsible recreational users of the stock routes, things can get hairy. That's how I met Denham. Arrow and I had to find some of Cressy's cattle that jumped the fence after motorbike riders had spooked them.'

'Doesn't Reggie jump fences too?'

'He does if he doesn't get his daily carrot fix. Speaking of Reggie ... you're about to meet him.'

He slowed as Reggie lumbered over to the fence that ran along beside them. The massive rodeo bull stopped to paw the ground before shaking his head.

Neve stared out the side window with a slight frown. 'He looks ... bigger than I expected. The way Cressy and Fliss talk about him I thought he'd be ... I don't know ... smaller.'

Tanner turned off the engine. 'Maybe the words you're looking for are *less intimidating*.'

'Maybe. Cressy always says he's as sweet as a lamb.'

'He is, when around Fliss and her. He tolerates Denham and Hewitt, but he hates me.'

Neve turned to him with a laugh. 'No animal hates you. It's impossible.'

Tanner unclipped his seatbelt. 'I've been bringing him carrots for over a year and every time this happens.'

He headed for the fence, the bucket of carrots in his hand. When he reached the rodeo bull, he held out a chunk of carrot. 'Prove me wrong, Reg. Eat a carrot out of my hand.'

The bull glared at him, bellowed and moved backwards.

Tanner sighed. 'At least that's an improvement. I'm still looking at your front end.'

'Maybe he's not hungry?' Neve said from behind him, amusement in her voice.

Tanner spun around. He'd assumed she would have stayed in the ute. Even Patch didn't jump out like he usually did. His senses sharpened. There was a secure wire fence between the bull and Neve, but the thought of what could go wrong chilled the blood in his veins.

He stepped in between Reggie and her. 'I'll toss him his carrots and we'll keep moving.'

Before he knew what Neve was doing, she thrust her hand into the carrot bucket and moved around him. 'I still can't believe any animal could hate you.'

'Neve ... not so close.' Tanner couldn't keep the tension from his words.

'Does Cressy get close?'

'Yes, but she hand-raised him.' Tanner didn't take his attention off the bull.

Neve held out her hand, a carrot in her palm. 'He's just standing there quietly waiting. I trust Cressy when she says he's harmless and that people misjudge him.'

Tanner didn't answer. Muscles flickered beneath the bull's grey-mottled coat. Tanner transferred his weight, ready to reach for Neve if Reggie showed any sign of aggression. But all the bull did was to slowly walk forward to eat the carrot Neve held over the fence.

She fed him another carrot. When she turned to look for more carrots, surprise widened her eyes when she realised Tanner stood close.

Her gaze dipped to his mouth before she reached for the bucket. 'Sorry, I'm on team Cressy. Reggie's a sweetheart. He couldn't be any gentler when he takes the carrots.'

Tanner didn't reply. Reggie had eyeballed him while Neve's back was turned.

Once the bucket was empty, they returned to the ute to drive the short distance to the rodeo yards. Tanner looked in the rear-view mirror to see Reggie watching them.

They hadn't spent long at the rodeo yards when he suggested they head back to the homestead. Even though Neve had been more than fine when feeding the rodeo bull, Tanner's nerves remained rope-tight. He could almost hear the rip in his self-control as it started to fray. The thought of anything happening to her continued to make his adrenaline spike.

To his relief, Neve agreed. He parked at the side of the house close to the entrance of his flat. Out of habit he opened the sliding door. There was a shortcut through his small kitchen to the main house. He ruffled Patch's neck as Neve walked through the open door. Meredith had a no-dogs-inside rule.

Tanner stepped into his minimalistic flat. His rolled-up swag was where it usually was, beside the door ready to be thrown in his ute. Mounted on the wall above the swag was a wooden coat rack on which his oilskin, good hat and Woodlea rodeo cap hung.

Neve studied the coat rack. 'Is this where you live?'

'When I'm not droving, yes.'

After a long look at his ready-to-go swag, she followed him into the kitchen of the main homestead.

Meredith greeted them with a wide smile. 'How was your tour? Shall I put the kettle on?'

He hadn't realised Neve had shaken her head at the same time he did until Meredith's gaze travelled between the two of them.

Neve spoke first. 'The grand tour was great, thanks. I met Reggie. But I'd better say no to a cuppa. I'll head home so I can keep looking through the albums and scrapbooks.'

Meredith nodded before moving to give Neve a hug. 'Good luck. I'm happy to answer any questions or help look up anything you need to know.'

'Thank you.'

Tanner wasted no time heading to the dining room to collect the albums and scrapbooks. Meredith would see through any reason he gave for not wanting to linger over a cuppa with Neve. He just needed a moment.

Meredith gave them both a wave from the kitchen window as he carried the albums and scrapbooks outside. After Neve's car was loaded, she opened her driver's side door with a sunny smile. 'Thanks again for showing me around.'

'Anytime.' He hesitated. He should step away and let her leave. But Patch wasn't the only one missing seeing her every day.

It was just a subtle gesture, but when her lips parted and her tongue touched her bottom lip, need uncoiled deep inside. Whatever reply he was going to make disintegrated.

The urge to kiss her was so strong he swayed forward. She held his gaze, eyes wide, but didn't move away.

'Neve …' His voice was nothing more than a hoarse groan.

She half lifted a hand as if to touch him.

Patch's loud bark sounded from somewhere in the front garden, before Phil's diesel engine chugged.

Neve blinked. Even as her hand lowered, she was turning away. She slid into the driver's seat as Phil's white farm ute came into sight.

Tanner cleared his throat. 'See you Friday at the field day.'

Her only response was a hasty nod, before he carefully closed her car door.

# CHAPTER
# 10

'I'm glad we've got our walking boots on,' Neve said to the girls as she followed the instructions of the field-day parking attendant to pull in beside the vehicle ahead of them.

It was only mid-morning and already lines of dusty cars were parked in ordered rows. The farm field-day site was situated on the other side of the local airstrip and would require a reasonable walk. She was also glad she'd brought Kait's lightweight stroller.

'Can we see Tanner now?' Kait asked, her voice high-pitched with eagerness.

Neve hoped the noise of the dual-cab ute parking beside her drowned out her sigh. Kait had only put into words what Neve's subconscious had been thinking. It had been a week since she'd seen Tanner in the pool, all tanned, sculptured muscle and toned, water-beaded hollows. The memory of him dragging his hands through his wet hair, making his biceps curl, still stole her breath.

But more than that, it had been a week since she'd almost given in to her fascination and kissed him. Her cheeks warmed. She'd lost count of how many times she'd relived what had happened. With each recollection the situation didn't become any less mortifying. Moments didn't get any more awkward than a near kiss. At least today when she saw him, the girls would provide a welcome distraction.

She unclipped her seatbelt and turned to Kait with what she hoped appeared a normal smile. 'We'll see him soon. Remember he'll be working, so we can't spend as much time with him as we usually do.'

Both girls nodded, but their eyes remained excitement-bright.

When everything they'd need for a day away from the car was packed into a backpack and hung on the stroller handle, Neve joined the procession of field-day visitors making the scenic trek past the airstrip. At least she'd have no trouble spotting her car when she returned. It was almost the only one without either a bull bar or a light bar.

She stopped to read the yellow sign to the girls that warned people to check for approaching planes as they flew low over the road. But apart from a helicopter giving joy rides, the blue sky was as free from aircraft as it was of clouds.

Beyond the entryway, flags fluttered and colour blurred as crowds milled amongst the stalls and exhibits. Neve already knew she'd have to return next year. There were too many demonstrations and talks to fit into one day.

She'd aim to see Tanner's event, the working sheep dogs, the after-lunch fashion parade and an afternoon gardening session if Graham arrived in time to pick up the girls. There also was a scarecrow-making competition that would be fun to see. She had making a scarecrow for the vegetable garden on her to-do list.

A school-aged girl with her face painted as a black-and-white Dalmatian ran past. Neve consulted her map to find the quickest way to the face-painting stall located in the centre of the site.

As she pushed Kait in the stroller, she scanned the people around her. But while a multitude of men wore shirts in every possible shade of blue, none were Tanner. She checked her map again and made a slight detour to dawdle through the farm-animal nursery.

'I can't wait for Dell to have her baby,' Maya said, holding her hand out for a young donkey to sniff.

'I can't either,' Neve said, before pushing the empty stroller after an excited Kait who raced towards a tiny cream alpaca in the next pen.

Once they'd had their cute-and-cuddly animal fix, they walked out of the shed into the bright sunshine. There was still a block to go to reach the face painting. They'd only made it halfway when Maya suddenly stopped and let go of the pram. Smile beaming, she dashed to her left.

Neve went to call her back when she saw two blue-shirted arms catch the five-year-old and swing her into the air.

'Tanner.' Kait kicked her small cowgirl boots against the stroller and tried to undo the straps. Neve helped her out and soon the three-year-old was also in Tanner's arms. He walked over with each little redhead balanced on his hip.

Neve tried not to be impressed. Maya might be fine-boned, but she still made Neve's muscles work hard when she lifted her into Bassie's saddle.

Tanner's dimple flickered. 'Neve.'

If he felt the same awkwardness at seeing each other again, it didn't show in his smile. 'Hi, how did Arrow travel?'

'Any trip over half an hour makes him grumpy. He's happy now he's here and being treated like a celebrity.'

Neve nodded as she glanced away. She'd forgotten she wasn't supposed to look into Tanner's eyes for too long. Just being near him made her skin heat and her heart drum.

He half turned. 'I'm heading to the horse arena. Did you want to see him before our demonstration?'

Neve didn't need to answer. Maya and Kait had nodded before Tanner had finished speaking. As she'd hoped, the girls gave them something else to focus on besides what had happened the last time they were together.

Still carrying the girls, Tanner walked beside her as she pushed the empty pram. Maya kept up a constant stream of chatter and questions. They arrived at the fenced-in horse arena to the sound of clapping as a white pony was being lunged by a small boy. His grandfather talked on the microphone as the pony kicked a large green ball with his front feet.

To the side of the arena, Arrow stood in a portable yard filled with straw. A cluster of cowgirls made a fuss over him. Sunlight glanced off the bling on their belts and the rhinestones on their back jeans pockets. Their laughter carried as they threw bright-eyed looks in Tanner's direction.

He led the way behind the arena to where a collection of horse floats was parked. Camping chairs and trestle tables had been set up ready for morning smoko. A black fluffy dog wagged his tail from where he lay in the shade beneath a table.

Tanner sat Maya and Kait in the chairs by his ute before reaching into a nearby esky. While they all enjoyed Meredith's jam drops, they watched the pony in the arena place his front feet on a podium before doing a farewell lap. The applause continued as the little owner led his pony out of the gate.

'Well done, buddy,' Tanner said as they passed by.

The boy sent him a toothy grin.

Neve checked the time on her phone. 'Okay, girls, it's Tanner and Arrow's turn now. Let's go find a seat in the stands to watch.'

As they left, she gave Tanner a smile. This would probably be the only time she saw him today. 'Hope your demo goes well.'

His answering grin stayed with her until she and the girls were seated on the bottom row in the middle of the tiered seats. The audience for the previous demonstration had been a mixture of ages. Now there seemed to be a predominance of pretty young cowgirls. Meredith and Denham were right. Unattached Tanner was a marked man, even when he wasn't in Woodlea.

But as he entered the arena with a saddled Arrow and gave the crowd his easy smile, Neve couldn't blame the cowgirls for their interest. Today Tanner wore a monogrammed silver belt buckle with his usual blue shirt, jeans and boots. He'd left his hat in his ute, giving the audience an unrestricted view of his face.

She thought he was looking at her, and then was sure as he approached. He adjusted the microphone headpiece beside his mouth before turning to ask over his shoulder, 'Can you please clip this on?'

She stood and reached through the fence to secure the black clip to the back of his shirt. It was just a small gesture him asking for help, but as assessing and hostile stares turned her way she realised it had established her as more than a spectator.

'Thanks.' He gave her and the girls a wink before returning to the centre of the arena.

Tanner introduced himself, the microphone carrying his deep voice and magnifying his appeal. As he made a joke and the audience laughed, Neve could almost hear hearts breaking.

Every so often, as he talked, and demonstrated how to build trust between a rider and a horse, he'd glance at her and the girls. Each time Maya and Kait giggled and once Maya held up her hand in a thumbs-up sign. Neve relaxed on the wooden seat. This was a rare time when she could look at and listen to him simply as an observer.

All too soon the demonstration ended. Even before the applause had faded, cowgirls left their seats to crowd the arena fence.

As Neve helped Kait into the stroller, she looked across at Maya. 'What shall we do now? Face painting?'

The five-year-old didn't answer. Instead, she frowned across at the jostling cowgirls. 'They'll give Tanner a headache.'

'Don't worry, he'll be okay.' Neve reached for her phone in her handbag. It didn't seem right just walking off and leaving. She typed a quick text.

*Great demo. Heading to face painting.*

She'd only pushed the pram two steps when her phone *whoosh*ed. *Meet for lunch?*

She looked across to the arena. Tanner remained surrounded by his fan club and yet he'd texted her. She capped a quick rush of pleasure. *Sounds good.*

She again pushed the stroller, resisting the urge to look over to see if he read her message.

When they drew near to the face-painting area, loud whip cracking cut through the field-day chatter. As they walked closer they discovered that the whip cracker standing in the centre of a grassed area was a child no older than Maya. Dressed in a wide-brimmed hat, boots and jeans and red shirt, the little boy handled the kid-sized leather stockwhip with ease.

When he'd finished, and was replaced by a girl holding two stock whips, Neve took the girls away from the noise. She caught sight of a familiar face as Taylor strode by, her light dancer steps hurried and brow furrowed. The Woodlea hairdresser had mentioned that she would be doing the makeup and hair for the festival's fashion parades.

When she saw Neve, she stopped, her expression clearing. 'I was hoping you'd make it.' She bent to grin at the girls. 'Having fun?'

'I saw Tanner,' Maya said with a big smile.

Kait nodded. 'Me too.'

'You know ...' Taylor straightened, lips pursed. 'Tanner's just who I need. I'd forgotten he'd be here. I wonder what time his demonstration's on?'

'He's just finished,' Neve said.

'Perfect.' The hairdresser took out her phone from her jeans pocket. She dialled, then held her mobile to her ear.

From the length of time until Tanner answered, Neve guessed he was still surrounded by cowgirls.

'Hi, Tanner, are you busy? I need a favour.' Taylor looked at the watch she wore while he answered. 'Great. Can you come to the pavilion ASAP? Thanks to food poisoning, we're one model down for the next fashion parade.'

Whatever Tanner said caused Taylor to laugh. 'As much as it would fill the seats, no, you don't have to take your shirt off ... you will ... fabulous ... see you soon.' She ended the call. 'Phew. That saves me from approaching some poor random farmer. Have you seen the parade yet? I can save you front-row seats.'

'Thanks, but we'll keep moving.'

Neve had already tempted fate by indulging her need to see Tanner. She'd spent far too much time staring at his mouth during his talk. The girls had also sat still for long enough.

'If you change your mind you know where I'll be.' With a cheery wave to the girls, Taylor headed back the way she'd walked.

Neve hesitated and then texted Tanner. His good heart again had him helping someone out. She could be wrong, but modelling wouldn't exactly be a cowboy's forte.

*Good luck.*

His reply was almost instant. *Thanks. Will need it. Lunch after?*
*If you survive.*

Tanner's crying-with-laughter emoji made her smile and her
happiness hum.

She joined the face-painting queue with the girls and people-
watched until it was their turn. After their faces were decorated as
a white unicorn and a rainbow butterfly, they went in search of the
scarecrow-making competition.

Neve took some pictures of the various shapes, sizes and designs
for inspiration. When still no text from Tanner had come through,
she found a quiet corner in the food area for a picnic lunch and
some down time.

While Kait slept in her stroller, Maya snuggled against Neve's
side playing with her toy horse. When Neve's phone *whoosh*ed she
didn't immediately check her messages. Instead, she let the sudden
flurry in her nerves subside before she reached into her handbag.
Her teenage days were long behind her. No good would come of
her heart flying into her throat when all Tanner had done was send
a text.

But when she read the message it wasn't from Tanner. Dread
caused her stomach to pitch. Their missed lunch was now the least
of her worries. Graham had arrived early to spend time with the
girls.

A potential hour alone had now turned into a whole afternoon
with only herself for company.

There was no risk of him giving up his day job to become a model.

Tanner shrugged on his regular shirt and collected his mobile
from the plastic tub Taylor had given him for his clothes. After

seeing how the parade wouldn't work without a fourth male model, he'd agreed to stay for the final parade. Thanks to the lunchtime show starting late, there hadn't been time to return to his phone to message Neve before he'd needed to get dressed for the next parade. He fired off a belated text.

*Sorry. Just done.*

He buttoned his shirt, relieved to be wearing his familiar work clothes, and waited for an answer. While the outfits he'd modelled were mostly classic country wear, the suit and tie he'd worn for the last catwalk run had made him feel claustrophobic. No wonder Denham had something urgent to do in the shed whenever he was needed for his next wedding-suit fitting.

Tanner checked his phone, even though he knew there'd be no message, and headed for the pavilion exit. Taylor blew him a kiss of thanks before he walked into the afternoon sun. Thankfully, all he'd needed to do was to give her a look when she'd mentioned hair and makeup and she'd left him alone. Arrow wouldn't appreciate him smelling like a hair salon.

Giggling sounded to his left and when he heard his name, he turned a sharp right. He didn't mind the harmless lash fluttering and head tossing of the cowgirls. After his demonstration there'd been some serious and insightful questions amongst all the flirting. The country girls loved their horses as much as their bling.

But he'd reached his threshold for the day. Suddenly, he was envious of the ring that would soon be on Denham's left hand. He really did need to change his ute to a less conspicuous colour, or after the wedding head off for an extended droving trip. For now, he'd settle for some serious caffeine.

As he made a beeline for the nearest coffee truck his mobile pinged.

*Hope you survived. Girls with Graham. They said to say bye.*

He took a step forward in the queue and stared at the message. Neve's noncommittal words were exactly what he'd needed after the day's constant attention. She hadn't made any reference to their missed lunch or any suggestion that they catch up anyway. But instead of feeling relieved, he felt … disappointed. Before he could fully analyse his feelings, he typed a reply.

*In coffee queue. Like anything?*

Telling himself he was a grown man and it didn't matter whether Neve replied, he returned his phone to his shirt pocket. At the first vibration he reached for it again.

*You read my mind. Latte pls.*

*Meet at ute?*

*On way.*

As he neared the horse arena and saw Neve sitting in a camp chair by his ute, he slowed his pace. Even though he wasn't in Woodlea, he had to be careful about how he interacted with her in public. He'd stopped being surprised at how small the world was when he'd walked down the main street of an isolated North Dakota town and met the woman he'd once been prepared to sacrifice everything for.

'One latte.' He handed Neve her coffee.

'Thanks. I feel like I've hiked a mountain and I've only covered half the site.'

He sat in the seat beside her. 'I hear you. I'll never think of a catwalk as being a short walk again.'

'Was being in the fashion parade that bad?'

'Not bad, just not my thing.' A text came through on his phone. As he looked at the accompanying picture, he groaned. 'And something I won't be living down for a while.' He showed Neve the picture Denham had sent. In the photo Tanner was wearing the parade suit and Denham had then added some large red emoji hearts.

Neve laughed softly. 'I thought he was up north looking at cattle and the phone reception was going to be patchy?'

'Knowing Denham, he would have been on the back of his ute with his arm in the air to find some.'

'I hate to say this, but if Denham has such a photo Edna will too.'

'Tell me about it. Just as well I did a grocery shop yesterday. Town will be off limits again.'

Neve studied him over the top of her takeaway cup. 'But if you're at Bethany's, won't Edna see you there?'

'Touch wood, no. Edna never comes to the stables.'

He didn't add that Bethany made sure Edna wasn't home, especially on the days when Mac joined them. Edna's only concern seemed to be the date Tanner would finish, which was at least a week away. So far he'd fielded two phone calls about the topic. Now he'd seen Bethany with Mac, he could understand why she'd gone to such lengths to distract her mother. They were good together.

'Has Edna let on what she needed you for?'

'Not yet. Odd's on I'll find out when Bethany no longer needs my help with Skittles.' He paused. 'I'm sorry too my father hasn't been in contact. I'm guessing he hasn't found anything.'

He hoped Neve didn't hear the disappointment he did his best to strip from his tone.

'It's fine. Thanks again for asking him.'

'Any luck with Meredith's scrapbooks and albums?'

'No, but I still have two more to go. I did finally find my grandmother's marriage certificates though.' Satisfaction infused Neve's words. 'I'd assumed Netta was short for Annette. But on her birth certificate I discovered her proper name was Pauline Loretta. Netta was her shortened middle name.'

He glanced at the silver STC on his belt buckle. 'If ever anyone tried to track me down, not that there'll be any marriage certificate to help, they'll have trouble too. My real name's Simon Tanner. Simon after my father.'

'I thought that's what the S stood for.' She pulled a face. 'There's zero chance of me ever going by my middle name; it's Bertha. I don't know what my parents were thinking.'

Tanner fought a grin. 'Did you find a name for the man in the picture?'

'I did. His name is ... drum roll, Edward Lance Jones and he was born in the United Kingdom.' Neve's smile dimmed. 'But my poor grandmother ... it turns out he died five months into their marriage. I'm not sure how; there's nothing I can find on what he did during the war or why he was here. He also isn't listed as being buried in the local war cemetery.'

Sadness for what Neve's grandmother must have endured losing her new husband so soon filled him. There'd been no mistaking their love and the joy on their wedding day. 'What was the timeframe between your grandmother's marriages?'

'Eighteen months.'

'That's why she looks about the same age in the wedding photos. It does seem strange there isn't any information about Edward. I'll pass the name on to my father.'

'Thanks, but only if things are okay between you.'

Tanner shrugged. 'What's another uncomfortable phone call.'

Applause signalled the end of the heavy horse talk, which was the final arena event for the day. Soon Arrow would be the only horse left in the portable yards.

Neve glanced at the dispersing crowd and smothered a yawn. 'It didn't seem to take long to get here, but I have a feeling the drive back will feel a whole lot longer.'

'You'll also have to watch out for roos.' He paused as Neve chewed on her lip. 'I'm leaving soon … we could travel in convoy.'

She studied him, expression guarded. 'That would be the sensible thing to do.'

He came to his feet and offered to take her empty coffee cup. 'How about I meet you at the main road in twenty minutes?'

She passed him her cup, stood and folded the chair she'd been sitting in. 'Okay. Thanks. I'll be there.'

Tanner wasted no time loading the ute and making sure Arrow was comfortable in the float. For once the gelding didn't fuss. He too had reached his attention threshold and wanted to go home.

Tanner joined the throng of traffic leaving the field-day site, and when he reached the main road out of town, Neve's white sedan was parked well off the bitumen. Soon she was driving behind him, her lights already on. His reasons for travelling together might be based on safety, but he'd found a way to spend a couple more hours with her even if they were in separate vehicles. After the first glance, he had to stop himself from looking in the rear-view mirror to make sure she was still there.

Today had confirmed his worst fears. A week apart hadn't diluted the pull she wielded on him. When he'd glimpsed her pushing the stroller with Maya by her side, he'd been hit by the same emotion and need as when he'd almost kissed her. He was just thankful that, apart from an initial wariness, what had happened between them at Claremont hadn't resulted in her acting any differently. He valued their friendship and couldn't again allow testosterone to overrule all common sense.

His phone rang and he touched the screen on the dashboard to answer. Distracted by his thoughts, too late he registered it was his father's number. 'Tann—hi, Dad.'

'Where are you? This line is atrocious.'

'Driving. I'm coming up to a hill so it should improve.'

'Your friend with you?'

'No ... she's behind me. Her car doesn't have a bull bar so we're in convoy.'

'She has a city car?'

Even the echo from the hands-free phone line couldn't disguise the approval in his reply.

'Yes, but she's not like the type of city girl you're picturing. She rides horses, wears boots and is planning to stay here.'

'But she was a city girl?'

Tanner sighed. 'Yes ... the signal could drop out soon ... did you take a look at the pictures?'

'I did ... but some more information would be useful.'

'The man in the wedding picture now has a name—Edward Lance Jones. He was born in the United Kingdom.'

'Jones, you say?'

'Yes. Sorry, there'll be a ton.'

His father gave a chortle of laughter. 'It could have been worse. I could be looking for a Smith.'

The phone line crackled. Tanner's grip tightened on the steering wheel. He needed the line to hold. His father had actually made a joke, let alone laughed. Apart from on his birthday, this was also the first time his father had called in a very long time.

His father continued talking. 'The man in the photo was most likely an instructor at the elementary flying school that was set up out there in 1940 as part of the Empire Air Training Scheme. It's interesting he's from the United Kingdom. He must have had some sort of expertise.'

His father coughed and Tanner forced himself to wait in silence for the spasm to pass. Any further mention of him needing to see a doctor could end their phone call.

His father gave a last small cough before speaking again. 'I'll see what I can find out.'

'Thanks. Anything you discover will be great.'

'Did this Neve of yours find a personnel war-service record?'

'She says there isn't any information about his time in Australia.'

'That does complicate things, but it's not unusual.' His father sounded intrigued more than disgruntled. There also was a new vitality to his tone. His clever brain loved a mystery. 'Thanks to non-standardised data collection, military records can sometimes be incomplete or inaccurate.'

The line crackled again. 'Dad, I'll go now as my phone will soon drop out.'

'That wouldn't happen in the cit—'

Tanner ended the call as his father's voice faded. No matter what his father said, he'd never swap patchy phone reception for any city comfort.

After checking on where Neve was, Tanner concentrated on the drive home. The late-afternoon shadows gave way to the gloom of dusk. The last flare of orange across the horizon ebbed and lights of approaching cars threw pools of white light across the bitumen.

Tanner slowed as a large grey kangaroo bounded out of the scrub and along the gravel verge. The kangaroo veered sideways before jumping into the bush. Where there was one kangaroo there could be more. Movement flickered as a second smaller kangaroo popped its head up from where it had been grazing near a wattle tree a safe distance away.

They'd soon clear the dense scrub and reach the white wooden bridge where Neve would turn to travel home on her familiar red dirt road. He drove over the crest of the hill, and as the bridge came into sight, he flicked on his blinker. It mightn't be his smartest decision, but he'd say a quick goodbye in person. Next time he saw her she'd have the girls.

He parked in a wide, grassed section of a track that led to a reserve that was part of a travelling stock route and popular for fishing. Amber flashed as Neve followed. He let the ute engine idle as he left the driver's seat. Neve too kept her engine running as she exited her car.

Both sets of headlights shone across the water that rippled as it flowed by. Overhead pinpricks of starlight cast tiny slivers of light. Somewhere far off an owl hooted, while close by crickets sang. A stiff breeze rushed past, its icy fingers delving beneath the collar of his shirt.

Neve rubbed at her upper arms. 'How can it be this cold when it was so hot earlier?'

'After spending a Rocky Mountain winter in a log cabin, this temperature's warm.'

Neve's smile flashed in the gloom. 'At least I'm awake now. I must admit I was getting tired. How big was that roo? I thought he was going to jump in front of you.'

'He was thinking about it.'

The wind toyed with her hair, suddenly whipping it into her face. He half lifted a hand to smooth away the windblown strands before his fingers clenched and his arm lowered.

Neve brushed the hair out of her eyes, and when her serious, intent gaze met his he couldn't have moved even if he'd wanted to.

'Tanner ...'

He had to bend to catch her quiet voice.

'I know you won't want to hear this ... but ... I've missed you.'

Not stopping to think, he threaded his fingers into her silken hair and placed a kiss on the top of her head. He didn't know if it was the cold or her admission that was causing her to shake. 'You probably don't want to hear this either ... this past week of hardly seeing you has been ... hell.'

Her only reaction was to tilt her head against his palm. He'd never seen her eyes so large or so dark.

'Which means ...' He pressed his mouth to her temple. 'Next week will be too.'

She lifted her chin to grant him access to the delicate satin hollows of her neck. 'And the week after?'

'More hell.' He slid his other hand into her hair and kissed the point of her jaw. 'But ... there's one thing I didn't miss.'

She turned her head so he could brush the corner of her lips. Her hands lifted to warm his chest before her palms curled over his shoulders. 'What's that?'

Her question was little more than a whisper.

'I didn't miss ...' He lowered his head. Her shallow breaths feathered over his skin. 'The constant battle to not do this.'

He covered her mouth and kissed her with a restraint and a care that contained none of the hunger that erupted inside. But as her body aligned with his, and she dragged him closer, the latch securing all common sense slipped. She filled his arms like no other woman ever had. He deepened their kiss and lifted her off her feet so not even gravity could separate them.

It was only the smash of an impatient hoof against metal that brought reality back into focus. They broke apart to breathe. His wrists were locked behind her waist. Her hands were tangled in his hair. Every ragged breath they drew was as if they were one.

He loosened his grip just enough for Neve's boot heels to touch the ground. Struggling to think, he rested his forehead against hers. She placed a hand against his cheek. In her trembling he could feel his own instability. For him everything, and yet nothing, had changed.

He covered her fingers with his and turned her hand to kiss her palm. Despite things already being out of control, he sought her mouth. He couldn't get enough of her. She stood on tiptoes to meet him. Her lips didn't just touch him physically. Their softness and sweetness reached a place deep inside that had never felt the sun's warmth.

Arrow's hoof smashed against the horse float.

Neve smiled against his mouth. 'I think that's our cue to keep moving.'

He eased himself away to tuck her tousled hair behind her ear. His fingers were unsteady. 'I'll call tomorrow.'

'You'd better …' Her fingertips traced the stubbled line of his jaw. 'Because like Edna, I know what colour ute you drive.'

# CHAPTER

# 11

In the clear unforgiving light of day, regret bit deep.

Neve stared unseeingly at the black-and-white photographs in the last wartime photo album. Her breakfast cup of tea sat cold and untouched beside her. Today she'd stayed inside instead of starting her day by sitting out on the veranda.

Kissing Tanner hadn't only made her senses rejoice, but also her heart. When his arms had anchored her to him like he'd never let her go, she'd felt as though something she'd been searching forever for had been gifted to her. She'd driven home on an emotional high, relieved that her admission about missing him hadn't sent him running or led to any awkwardness.

But if she could, she'd have unsaid her words. If she could rewind time, she'd have done anything to ensure there'd been no physical contact between them.

She forced herself to focus on the photographs in front of her capturing the swirls of a summer dust storm. She turned the page to see pictures of locusts and the bare soil of ravaged paddocks. Wartime hadn't only fractured families and brought personal hardship, it had also delivered challenges from nature.

After three more page turns she reached the end of the album. Thanks to the photographs and the newspaper clippings in the scrapbooks, she had a much better understanding of the era despite not discovering any new information. She added the album to the pile beside her. But not finding any clues to her grandmother's hidden life wasn't the reason why this morning it felt as if a light had switched off inside her.

When she'd arrived home from Mudgee last night, Graham had called to let her know at the end of the week he was having a fortnight off work to take the girls to the Sunshine Coast. Now the world spun around her. Now she questioned everything she felt towards Tanner.

As she'd lain awake reliving the urgency and possessiveness in his touch, and all had seemed complete in her world, she realised a damning truth. She herself wasn't complete.

Yesterday at the field day after Graham had collected the girls, despite being surrounded by people, she'd never felt so lonely or displaced. Everywhere she looked there were families enjoying a day out, couples who shared intimate smiles and mothers and daughters whose laughter spoke of their close bond.

Then Tanner had texted. When he did that, it was as if she mattered, as though she was a part of the world she'd been looking in on. He'd thrown her a lifeline and she'd latched onto it with a desperate grip. She hadn't hesitated before she accepted his coffee offer, or agreed to his suggestion that they travel home together.

She came to her feet to tidy the already spotless kitchen. The thought of being on her own for two weeks without the girls terrified her. She couldn't remember a day, even while at school, when she wasn't filling the cupboard with food, paying bills or dispensing medicine. Every minute had been accounted for and had had purpose. She didn't know what to do with her spare time, let alone how to live a life that wasn't centred around the needs of someone else.

The sick, uncertain feeling that had gripped her after Graham's phone call refused to leave. Were her fears of being alone pushing her towards Tanner? Was her need for stability and routine why she wanted him in her life? She didn't think so, but what if that was the reason behind the intense pull she felt? A pull she'd never felt for any other man.

Yes, she was attracted to him. Yes, he was a decent, good man who'd proved he'd be there for those who needed him. But she didn't want to lead him on or to hurt him if her feelings didn't stem from any genuine emotion.

She stopped wiping the bench to frown through the kitchen window to where Bassie and Dell grazed. If her feelings were legitimate, then there was also the very real issue of how Tanner felt. He'd made it clear through his comment about there never being a marriage certificate with his name on it that he wouldn't be looking for any long-term commitment. Finding a new direction in life couldn't involve falling for a man who only did casual relationships. If she wasn't careful, Tanner would break her heart.

She finished cleaning the bench. As much as she would continue to miss him, her priority over the next two weeks had to be to solve her family mystery and to learn to live life by herself. There could be no more heady starlight kisses. It would only be when she was content with her company that she'd know for sure she wasn't seeking Tanner out to make herself feel complete or to avoid being on her own. She'd then just have to deal with the issue of what they'd each want from a relationship when, and if, such a time ever came.

She took a notebook out of the desk drawer in the play corner and started a list of things she could do on her own. It took five minutes and much pen tapping to come up with three things. When she'd got to her fifth activity, the mobile beside her rang. She dismissed the pang of nerves in her stomach that this could be Tanner calling.

When she reached for her phone it was Fliss's face that smiled out from the screen.

Neve took a moment to make sure her voice would come across as cheerful. 'Morning.'

'Morning. You sound tired. Big day yesterday?'

Neve briefly closed her eyes. So much for hiding anything from Fliss. 'You could say that.'

'There's always so much to see. I heard Tanner's missed his true calling.'

'Has he?'

'Yes, Taylor said he stole the show in the fashion parade.'

'He didn't say a word.'

'He wouldn't.' Fliss chuckled. 'He's as humble as he is heartbreakingly handsome.'

Neve didn't quite know how to answer without incriminating herself so settled for a casual laugh.

Fliss spoke again. 'Are you busy? If I didn't know better I'd say Cressy was avoiding me, so I've pulled rank as bossy big sister and said we're going out for morning tea. I thought you might like to come?'

'I'd love to. Where are we going?'

'There's a café in an old rail carriage on an alpaca farm not far from Reedy Creek. Yes, there will be alpacas.'

'I'm in.'

'Wonderful. We'll pick you up in about an hour.'

'Thanks.'

Beeps from her phone distracted her from replying to Fliss's, 'See you soon.'

When she checked her screen, she discovered she had a missed call from Tanner. Mouth dry, she listened to his voicemail message. The deep timbre of his voice stirred her senses and made her yearn to see him. She replayed the message again.

'Hi. Got roped into doing a shift on the tractor. When I'm done I was hoping I could call round. I think it's best if we talk … in person.'

Neve listened to the message for a third time but still couldn't gauge his frame of mind. The content of his words did suggest that he too was having second thoughts about what had burned between them, even if his tone contained its usual warmth. If he was, then she should be feeling relief, not even more uncertain.

She texted a reply. As he had farm work to do she didn't want to distract him.

*Sorry missed call. Good idea. Home after lunch.*

After three checks of her phone to see if Tanner had answered, she turned off her mobile and stashed it in her handbag. At this rate she wouldn't be out of her pyjamas by the time Fliss and Cressy arrived.

When a car engine sounded, Neve collected her bag and headed out the front door. Cloud cover hung heavy overhead, but she wasn't fooled. At the moment it was like having four seasons in one day. Beneath her warm denim jacket she wore a short-sleeved white dress. She'd also piled her hair into a cool and practical up-do.

'You look nice,' Cressy said as Neve sat in the back seat behind her.

'Thanks. I wasn't sure if a dress was okay.'

Fliss smiled over her shoulder from where she occupied the driver's seat. 'It's definitely a dress kind of day.'

Cressy too wore a dress in a simple floral fabric, while Fliss had chosen a stylish black sleeveless design that left her toned arms bare.

Talk soon turned to the wedding plans and glamping village. Neve didn't miss Fliss's sideways glances at her sister whenever Cressy shifted in her seat as if to get comfortable.

When they reached the small village of Reedy Creek, instead of taking the road that wound past the corrugated-iron hall, Fliss turned right and then left.

'You weren't joking when you said there were alpacas,' Neve said as the café came into view. In front of a row of silver train carriages was a small paddock filled with big-eyed, long-necked, fluffy cuteness. 'The girls would love this. I'll have to bring them for a milkshake.'

Cressy carefully turned to smile at Neve. 'They'd be in alpaca heaven. But watch out, you might come home with more than you bargained for. The café sells far more than milkshakes.'

Fliss parked in the car park, and as they walked into the café garden, alpacas came over to the fence to welcome them.

Neve ruffled the topknot of a cream alpaca with large liquid-dark eyes. 'Sorry, I don't have anything for you to eat.' She looked to where a group of young alpacas were being handfed through the fence by three small children. 'But there has to be some food around here somewhere.'

Cressy arrived carrying small containers she'd filled with chaff from a nearby feeding bin. Alpacas surged towards them. Neve made sure she fed the quieter ones that didn't push to the front. When a car load of visitors arrived with school-aged children, they offered the group the now empty food buckets.

Neve walked with Fliss and Cressy over to the train carriages. Pepper trees shaded a cluster of white tables and chairs that provided outdoor seating options.

Neve stopped at the café door. She'd spent her city life catching a train like this one to school, university and then her North Shore occupational therapy practice. 'I feel like I'm in a twilight zone. I'm in the country, but ...'

Fliss grinned. 'I felt the same way when Meredith first brought me here.'

They entered the carriage. A blonde teenager carrying a jug of water smiled and told them to take a seat and that she'd be right over. While Cressy and Fliss moved along the carriage, Neve stopped at a display of alpaca items. She chose two small knitted alpacas for the girls and a soft-touch grey-and-white scarf. She'd need an extra layer for when she fed Jazz, Dell and Bassie in the winter.

When she joined Fliss and Cressy at a bench seat and table, the sisters were engrossed in a serious conversation. Cressy had her arms folded, while Fliss's hazel stare held an intent sharpness.

Fliss glanced at Neve. 'Cressy and I are ... discussing why she's moving like she was a bull rider in another life.'

'I'm fine,' Cressy said with a sigh. 'As I told Neve, I did something to my side in the hay shed.'

Neve nodded. 'She did. When we had coffee.'

Fliss's eyes narrowed. 'That was weeks ago.'

Cressy's fingers played with the stand that held their table number. 'I might have broken some ribs, even though I didn't have any bruises.'

Fliss briefly closed her eyes. 'Might have ... please don't tell me you consulted Dr Google and not your sister.'

'Dr Google's very informative. It happened on your day off and I didn't want to call you. I also couldn't be bothered driving into the hospital. Besides, even if they are broken nothing can be done, they just need time to heal.'

Fliss stared at her sister. 'Cressy Knight, soon to be Rigby ... what are you not telling me?'

'What makes you say that?' Cressy's tone was all innocence.

'Because you've somehow hidden how badly you were hurt from Denham. If he knew he'd have told Hewitt, who would have told me. There's more to the story.'

Cressy lifted her hands. 'Oh all right. I almost got bitten by a snake. That's why I fell.'

Colour drained from Fliss's face. 'Almost?'

'It bit my boot.'

'It was a western brown, wasn't it?'

Cressy nodded.

Fliss took a moment to speak. 'If that was your ankle or your hand ...'

'I know. You and Denham already tell me I take too many risks. All I was doing was climbing the hay bales ...'

'*Why?*'

Cressy's smile grew sheepish. 'I thought it would be quicker to get the top one down. Otherwise I'd have to get the tractor out.'

Fliss looked at Neve and shook her head. Neve just smiled. She'd been privy to banter before about Cressy's risk-taking and Fliss's non-risk-taking.

Fliss turned her attention to her sister again. 'I'm going to want to take a look at those ribs.'

Cressy picked up the menu. 'Sure. But first I'm going to eat. For some reason I haven't been hungry lately.'

The approach of the cheerful blonde waitress silenced Fliss's reply but not her exasperated sigh.

Once their orders were taken, Neve changed the subject to the upcoming picnic races on the weekend before the wedding. She'd thought it would be a safe topic until Cressy mentioned Tanner's name.

'Somehow we have to make sure Tanner goes. Edna tells me he's been spending lots of time working with Bethany and her project horse.'

'Yes, he has.' Neve did her best to stop the telltale colour from flooding her face. The strength and feel of Tanner's arms holding her were imprinted on her senses. 'The horse's name is Skittles.'

'That's an odd name,' Fliss said, expression speculative.

Cressy nodded. 'It doesn't exactly sound like a project horse Bethany would buy. Her days of having a pony are long gone. She's up to something.'

Concern for Tanner had Neve ask, 'I thought only Edna had a hidden agenda?'

Cressy grinned. 'Bethany's her mother's daughter even if she doesn't look like her … Skittles … now I'm curious. I hope for Tanner's sake she hasn't decided to go along with Edna's matchmaking after all.'

'I agree,' Fliss said, smiling her thanks at the waitress as she placed scones and small dishes of jam and cream on their table. 'Tanner's the brother Cressy and I never had … he deserves more than a mother-in-law who has a different definition of personal space than the rest of us.'

Neve didn't answer as she pretended to focus on selecting a scone. Unlike Cressy who already had slathered cream over her scone, her appetite had deserted her.

Even though it was doubtful Tanner would be looking for a relationship, when she told him that what had happened between them was a mistake, would Bethany be the person he'd turn to?

It was going to be one of those days.

Tanner stretched after tightening a bolt on the air seeder to iron out the kinks in his back. He'd taken over from Phil in the direct drilling of the winter wheat crop into the unploughed paddock. But so far, the alarm had already gone off twice to tell him to clear the stubble from the sowing tubes and from beneath the air-seeder frame.

To his left Patch sniffed the back tractor tyre. He usually didn't have the young border collie with him as he became too restless in the tractor cabin. But he'd come to the end of a run and Patch had been sitting in the gateway waiting for him. So Tanner had opened the tractor door and the border collie had joined him. Tanner had let Phil know over the UHF radio where Patch was in case he was looking for him.

Tanner walked around the air seeder to check no other bolts needed adjusting. He'd received Neve's message and had until after lunch to work out how to tell her that they needed to put the brakes on what had ignited between them. From her text he had a hunch that they shared the same thoughts. She wouldn't have said it was a good idea to talk face to face unless she too had reservations.

He sighed and bent to tighten another bolt. He'd learned long ago not to question life's logic. Last night when he'd held Neve all he'd ever wanted was within his grasp, but never had it been so far out of reach. It was too early to appreciate the irony. Neve was a woman he could make a home with, raise a family with. But he only ever got involved with women who had casual at the top of their relationship requirements.

Despite Neve's strength and self-containment, she was vulnerable. He now understood the wariness he'd sensed about her and the reason behind the soft colour that could wash her cheeks. After caring for her mother, Neve wouldn't have had many opportunities for a social life.

She also needed to get her life back on track. He couldn't cause her pain or start a relationship that could only end in one way. As much as the thought made his stomach roil, she deserved to be with someone who could give her a lifetime of laughter.

Preoccupied, he hadn't noticed where Patch was. A sharp bark to his left had him turn. Patch had found a mob of black feral pigs. Even as he watched, the border collie sprinted across the stubble to head off a large male boar. It was too late to whistle him back. The boar suddenly changed direction, charging at Patch. The young border collie slowed, then spun around to race back towards Tanner. The boar set off after him.

Tanner stayed where he was. Luckily for Patch, the heavy boar would soon give up. When he did, Patch continued at a frantic pace until, sides heaving, he reached Tanner.

He rubbed behind Patch's ears as the border collie leaned against his legs. 'I know, it seemed like a good idea at the time.'

He opened the tractor door for Patch to jump in. His new water cooler would be safe. The border collie wouldn't have any energy to chew on anything. All he'd do was sleep for the rest of the shift.

When the sun had reached its zenith, Phil's farm Hilux drove through the paddock gate. At the end of the run, Tanner stopped.

Phil greeted him with a grin as he and Patch climbed out of the tractor cabin. 'Had some excitement, I hear?'

Tanner had spoken to Meredith over the UHF. 'Let's just say Patch's pig-dog career was over before it started.'

Phil ruffled Patch's head. 'Very sensible. Ella's had a new case of brucellosis.'

Tanner nodded as Phil disappeared into the tractor cabin. Swine brucellosis didn't just infect pig-dogs, but also humans. It had been a problem when he'd been droving in Queensland, but now dogs down south were showing signs of infection.

Phil gave him a wave before the tractor commenced another arrow-straight line.

With Patch close by his side, Tanner strode towards his ute. He'd have a shower and quick lunch before seeing Neve.

He still wasn't quite sure what to say. He'd take his lead from her about how to approach their conversation. That way he wouldn't put his boot in it and make a potentially uncomfortable situation worse. Give him a rogue stallion to deal with any day. When it came to emotions he either avoided or buried them. Life was far simpler and safer that way.

As he was driving past the machinery shed, his mobile rang. He sighed and took the call. The number displayed on the touch screen of the ute dashboard was Edna's.

'Hi, Tanner. I'm so glad I caught you.'

'You were lucky. I've been on the tractor.'

'Yes, it seems to be my lucky day.'

It definitely wasn't his. Now that Edna had called he was certain a black cat must have crossed his path while he wasn't watching.

'What can I do for you?'

'I'm calling for two reasons. One, to thank you for helping Bethany with her new horse. She's very happy with how things are going. I've never seen her smile so much.'

'No problem.'

'Which leads me to the second reason. I've been wanting to talk to you about a fundraising idea I've had. I've been holding off on mentioning it as you've been so busy with Bethany.'

'Thanks.'

If Edna registered his dry comment it didn't show in her too-cheerful reply.

'My Bethany enjoys working with you so much, it made me think of a way to raise money for the shade sails for the new playground. The pony club doing a cattle drive isn't going to happen anytime soon.'

He rubbed at his chin. It was a given he wasn't going to like Edna's plan. 'What's your idea?'

'A weekend horsemanship clinic. We keep it small, no more than eight, but price it high. I've already checked and the rodeo ground is free the weekend after next. When people know you're running it, spaces will fill in no time. Look how many people you had for your demonstration yesterday.'

His shoulders moved in a sigh. He'd been right to watch his interactions with Neve at the field day. Resourceful Edna had information sources everywhere.

When he didn't speak, Edna filled the silence. 'Of course, you'll need someone to help and the best person to do so is my Bethany.'

'Of course.'

'So what do you say? It's for a good cause.'

That was the trouble, it was. Even though the official opening of the adventure playground was next week, the playground needed shade sails to be fully complete. He also didn't mind donating his time and expertise. Hewitt had spent far more than one weekend making sure his playground vision became a reality.

The clinic would also give him something to focus on besides Neve. If it was Bethany helping, and not Edna herself, everything would be fine. What Edna needed to talk to him about could have been much worse; she might have wanted him to enter the best-dressed-man category at the picnic races. It was bad enough having to wear a tie for the race day, let alone a flower on his coat lapel.

'I'm in.'

'Bethany will be so thrilled. I've already drafted an ad for tomorrow's *Woodlea News*, but from here on in Bethany's your go-to person. She'll give you a call today to discuss the finer details.'

'It's okay, I'll talk to her tomorrow when I see her.'

Even down the phone line Edna's trill of laughter could be described as smug. 'Silly me, of course you'll be seeing her tomorrow. Now I'd better get that ad sent in. Hooroo.'

It wasn't long until a text from Bethany came in.

*SORRY.*

He parked near the back garden gate before he sent a reply.

*It's a good idea. Tell Mac he can bring that green broke horse of his.*

Bethany's reply was instant. Three emojis blowing kisses were followed by the words, *You're a legend. Didn't think of that.*

His lips twisted into a smile that if anyone saw they would have called bittersweet. His own love-life might be in the trenches, but at least Bethany and Mac's relationship was being given a chance.

Patch followed him over from the ute before heading off to check on Meredith's chickens in the chook pen. He wasn't sure Meredith's plan for them to free range would be a success until Patch grew older. Unlike the boar, the Rhode Island Red hens wouldn't chase him back.

He made a point of avoiding the main house as he returned to his flat for a shower and lunch. Meredith had come to his small kitchen last night for a cuppa to see how his demonstration had gone. Neve was only mentioned in passing, but there was something about the way Meredith's blue gaze rested on him that tripped his suspicions that she knew something had happened between them.

The closer he drove to Rosewood, the more his restlessness caused his nerves to tighten and his jaw to ache. He knew what he had to do, and why he had to do it, but that didn't stop the rush of loss when he drove through the front gate and saw Neve in the round yard with Jazz. In a perfect world he'd be here to pick up where they'd left off last night.

Dell and Bassie met him at the pony paddock gate. He gave each a neck scratch before going to meet Neve as she walked over carrying Jazz's saddle and bridle.

'Hey,' he said, noting the purple shadows beneath her eyes. The single, tight braid that fell from below her black riding helmet gave him all the answers he needed. She was taking no chances her hair would be anything but well-behaved. Just like her curls, her emotions too would be tightly controlled.

'Hey.'

He reached for the heavy stock saddle even knowing she'd refuse. She gave a too-brief smile. 'Thanks. I've got it.'

He fell into step beside her.

'No Patch today?' she asked after a quick sideways glance.

'I left him asleep on the veranda. He thought he'd chase a feral pig but ended up being chased himself.'

'No wonder he's worn out.'

Tanner opened the tack shed door. 'How was your ride?'

'Really good. Jazz is such a joy to ride.'

Neve joined him outside the shed. She'd removed her helmet and her thick braid hung over her right shoulder. Against the apple green of her shirt, the red-gold strands shone rich and vibrant.

A strained silence stretched between them. Until they had their talk, neither of them would relax. He also wasn't a coward, even if he was so far out of his comfort zone his heart slammed against his ribs.

Giving in to the longing to touch her, he ran his finger down the smooth indents of her braid while he searched for the right way to start. 'Neve ... what happened between us last night wasn't normal for me. I usually stay in control.'

As his arm lowered she caught his hand and laced her fingers with his as if she too needed to be physically connected. 'We both got a bit ... carried away.'

He stared at their joined hands before he replied. Against his tanned skin, her fingers appeared fragile and delicate, an impression that didn't match the quiet, dignified strength in her eyes.

'Neve ... I'm not in the right place to start anything ... The last thing I'd want to do is to ... hurt you.'

'I understand and I'm glad you're having second thoughts too. It's no secret I'm not in the best spot either ... so from here on in ...' Her attention drifted to his mouth. 'We need to make sure we don't put ourselves in any situation where we ... lose control again.'

He took a second to answer. His testosterone was staging a last-minute revolt. 'Agreed.'

The tension ebbed from her expression. She squeezed his hand before easing her fingers free.

When she turned towards the house, he walked beside her.

She looked at him with a half-smile. 'All I can say is thank goodness Edna hadn't driven past last night. It wouldn't have mattered if our families had been friends, I wouldn't be on her Christmas-card list.'

He gave what he hoped passed as a chuckle and dug his hand into his jeans pocket to hide how empty he felt now that her hand was no linger linked with his. In his pocket he felt the crisp edge of folded paper. Glad of a distraction, he withdrew his hand and passed her the note.

'Before I forget, my father emailed through this list of all the known aircraft crashes at the training school. Even though none of the dates line up with when Edward passed away, he suggested you do some digging as sometimes dates and information can be wrong. He also suggested looking to see if there were any other aircraft accidents, even minor ones, as well as non-aircraft fatalities.'

Neve unfolded the paper. 'Please pass on my thanks. I'll definitely do some digging. Maybe I could give you Meredith's family albums to take back? I'll keep the scrapbooks a little longer as some of the newspaper articles did mention road accidents. It's so sad, I didn't realise so many young pilots lost their lives while training.'

Tanner nodded as he looked at the list that contained at least eleven fatal crashes. In most cases two men had been in each plane. Families had lost loved ones even before they'd made it to the frontline.

When they reached the veranda he hovered on the bottom step. Leafy vegetables again grew in the raised garden beds, wood smoke tinged the air and soft cushions invited him to sit on the church pew to the left of the outdoor table. Neve had a gift for turning a blank space into one that welcomed and beckoned.

He couldn't heed such a call. Since he'd met her his loneliness had already given him nothing but grief. He'd come today to make sure nothing further happened between them. For her, and for him.

He didn't realise he was frowning until Neve's quiet voice sounded from where she held the door open. 'Everything okay?'

He nodded, not trusting himself to speak.

'Have you got time for a cuppa?' she asked, her grip on the doorhandle tightening until her knuckles whitened.

Despite their open conversation about what had happened by the river, a clear way forward hadn't yet been established fully. He needed to show her they could still have an easy and companionable friendship, even if they couldn't act on what simmered between them.

'I'd love one.'

She gave him a sweet smile.

When inside he offered to help, but she waved him over to the kitchen table. He looked through a photo album until she joined him at the table.

He pointed to a photograph of a couple on the dancefloor. 'Call me paranoid, but doesn't this woman look like Edna?'

'She does. It would have to be her grandmother.' Neve looked at him from over the rim of her mug. 'Any news on what Edna wanted? Maybe she has a surprise planned for Friday's adventure playground opening?'

'I wouldn't put it past her, but she wanted to talk to me because she's come up with an idea for a weekend horsemanship clinic to raise money for the shade sails.'

'Let me guess, Bethany has a role somewhere?'

It was just subtle, but Neve's question had sounded clipped.

'Yes, as chief organiser and my right-hand person.'

She stared out the window before replying. 'So how many people will go?'

'We're hoping for eight. It will be at the rodeo ground, which is where the trail ride's usually held. It's all set up for horses and camping.'

'What do you do in such a clinic?'

'It depends, but generally it's things like ground work, confidence building, re-education.'

'So people ... like me could go?'

'Absolutely.' He took a swallow of too-hot coffee to hide his hope that she was thinking of signing up.

'Would you mind if I went?'

'Of course not. It would be perfect for you and Jazz and it's also for a worthy cause.' He hesitated. They'd agreed to draw a line between them and to keep to their respective sides. But he was powerless to silence his words. 'I'd really like to have you there.'

Her soft green eyes met his. 'Okay. Count me in. Jazz and I'll be there.'

# CHAPTER

## 12

The day of the official opening of the new adventure playground promised to be a clear and sunny afternoon, even if the morning proved crisp and cold.

Neve walked faster to keep up with Maya and Kait as they skipped beside her on the paved path. As promised, the girls were going to be the first children to play on the equipment. That afternoon, about the same time as the playground ribbon-cutting ceremony, she'd say goodbye to them for the fortnight. She curled her fingers a little tighter around the two warm hands nestled in hers. Until then she was determined to make the most of their time together.

Hewitt greeted them at the playground entrance. 'Morning.'

'Morning. Sorry we're early. I don't know why, but for some reason we were ready in record time.'

The girls giggled. They'd had their boots and jumpers on before Neve had even picked up her car keys off the bench.

'No worries.' Hewitt stepped away from the entryway and gave a small bow. 'Maya and Kait, welcome … the playground is all yours.'

Both girls gave Neve a quick hug before beaming high-wattage smiles at Hewitt as they tore past. They made a beeline for the bridge that led to the red-topped castle turret. Squeals and laughter sounded from inside.

Neve's eyes misted. Beside her Hewitt cleared his throat.

She knew he understood how the loss of a parent could strip the joy from young lives. After the death of his brother he'd stepped in to help raise Quinn and Lizzie.

Neve spoke softly. 'If that isn't a reward for all you've done, nothing is.'

He nodded as Maya and Kait ran along a suspended walkway. 'It's the only reward I need.'

Neve followed Hewitt over to where the morning sun warmed a wooden bench.

'I hear you've signed up for Tanner's horsemanship weekend,' Hewitt said as he sat and stretched his jean-clad legs out in front of him.

'I did.' Neve slid the backpack that held the girls' water bottles and snacks off her shoulder, before also sitting. 'Jazz is such a sweetheart. I'm sure I'm not asking her to do things the right way.'

'She's such a gentle soul, she wouldn't mind. Is Tanner picking her up or do you need a hand to get her to the rodeo ground?'

'Actually …' She was reluctant to ask for help, but the alternative was Tanner collecting Jazz. Despite his reassurance, she wasn't sure she'd done the right thing by signing up for the weekend. She shouldn't have let the thought of Edna and Bethany taking advantage of Tanner's kind heart get to her. The sensible thing would have been to stay away. 'Would that be okay? I'm sure Tanner will be flat out.'

A smile lightened Hewitt's grey eyes. 'It's no problem.'

'Do you know who else is going? When I spoke to Bethany four spots had been filled.'

'All eight spots have gone now. There's Mac Barton, two city friends of Bethany's who'll ride her horses, Freya George, who teaches at the Reedy Creek school, you, Sibylla Elliott, who apparently has returned to town, and a husband and wife who saw Tanner's demonstration at Mudgee.'

'He's certainly in demand.'

'He is. There're another eight names on the waiting list.'

'Poor Tanner … Edna will be booking him in for another fundraising weekend. Freya's a redhead, isn't she?'

'She is and she's also from Sydney. You'll have fun together.'

'I'm sure we will. Cressy, Fliss and Ella speak highly of her.'

The conversation paused as Maya and Kait waved from over at the swings.

Hewitt chuckled. 'I think that's our signal to push.'

Neve stood with a smile. 'Something tells me we'll be pushing for a while.'

Her prediction proved true. After a lengthy time on the swings, the girls took only a short morning-tea break. Looking like they'd never stop, they continued to explore. Hewitt went back to the last-minute jobs he needed to complete before the afternoon opening while Neve moved to a bench that was in the shade. The girls had already discarded their jumpers.

The next fortnight would seem too quiet without their energy and constant supply of hugs. But at the end she hoped being alone and at a loose end wouldn't fill her with the dread it did now. Her list of things to do to help her face her fears had grown. From taking a solo day trip to Dubbo, to reading books from the Reedy Creek Hall bookshelf, to cooking a recipe her mother had loved, however she filled her day, she'd make sure she had no time to feel lonely or lost.

When the girls appeared from out of a purple tunnel, their cheeks pink and their run having slowed to a walk, Neve called out, 'Five more minutes.'

Kait pouted. Maya tugged at her hand. 'Let's go to the castle again.'

Kait's displeasure changed to a laugh as they raced away. When they peered out of the turret windows, Neve returned their two-handed waves.

The plan for when the girls were away was to also stop thinking about Tanner. Even with him sharing her view that nothing could again burn between them, she'd been surprised at how unsettled she continued to feel. It didn't matter how many times she'd reminded herself she'd done the right thing, her heart and her hormones refused to listen.

On the day he'd come to talk to her, she'd appreciated his honesty and directness. But she'd never been more relieved than when he'd agreed to come in for a cuppa. When he'd hesitated on the bottom veranda step, she hadn't been able to shake the feeling that if he'd turned to go it would have been her life he'd been walking out of.

She pushed to her feet and looped the backpack over her shoulder. Even with the five-minute warning, it took another ten minutes to have a last swing, say goodbye to Hewitt and walk back to the car.

The girls were silent as they drove along Main Street. Even when they passed the turn-off to the lolly shop there were no requests to visit. White yarn bombing decorated the bench outside the Royal Arms, while a nearby lamp post sported the beginning of the race-day-themed woollen creations. She pointed out the horseshoes and colourful tiny jockey hats to the girls. When she didn't receive a response she glanced in the rear-view mirror. Both Maya and Kait were asleep.

That afternoon, knowing she'd feel emotional when she stood on the veranda to wave the girls off, Neve made sure she had a contingency plan in place. She'd visit the library to take a look at their family-history resources. As soon as Graham's white four-wheel drive disappeared, she turned to head inside to collect her keys and handbag.

But instead of reaching for the screen doorhandle, she stopped. On the handle rested a pale-brown locust. She looked around for others, but no small bodies clung to any leaves or plants. When she glanced back, the winged insect was gone. She'd seen the advertisements on the television asking for landholders to report mass hatchings, but as time had passed she'd thought the locust threat hadn't eventuated.

She glanced over at her vegetable garden that now was home to a large scarecrow with straw plaits and an oversized hat. She could only hope Dell and Bassie were the worst things to have happened to her carrots and corn.

She continued inside for her keys and handbag, and on the way past the coat stand she grabbed her denim jacket. With her hands full, when her mobile rang from inside her cherry-red tote, she fumbled to find it. Breathless, she finally answered the call.

'Hi.' Tanner's deep voice kick-started a chain reaction in her senses.

She made a conscious effort to slow her breathing and to ignore the goosebumps rippling over her arms. 'Hi. Sorry, I couldn't find my phone.'

'It's just a quick call. The girls gone?'

'Yes.' As she talked she walked through the front door before locking it. 'It's far too quiet already.'

'I bet it is.'

'How was the playground opening?'

'Busy. Hewitt and I are just about done cleaning up. My father called. Good news. He's found where Edward's buried and it is here. He's in the general Woodlea cemetery and not the war one.'

Neve stopped on the top veranda step.

'Neve?'

'I'm still here, I'm just … processing. I go there every weekend to put flowers on my family's graves. Odds on, I've walked straight past Edward's headstone.'

This time it was Tanner who was silent.

'Tanner?'

'Sorry … I didn't think. I should have known your mother's buried here.'

'She is, she's beside my grandmother. I'm heading to town now and will see if I can find Edward's grave.'

'I can meet you there … if you like?'

She didn't know if it was his earnest tone or the calm cadence of his words, all she knew was that it felt right to have him with her while she searched for Edward's headstone.

'If that's okay? It will be easier to find with the two of us.'

'See you soon.'

Neve unlocked the front door and returned inside. After she'd picked some bunches of yellow roses and wrapped the stems in wet newspaper, she again headed for her car.

On the drive to the historic cemetery she worked hard to make sure her feelings were buttoned down tight. There'd be no repeat of the emotional instability Tanner had witnessed at the tennis courts. Even when she placed flowers on her mother's and grandparents' graves.

Once she neared town she turned north. When she crossed the cattle grid that marked the cemetery entrance, she saw a blue ute parked to the left. She pulled in beside Tanner. Before she left the driver's seat she tugged on her jacket.

The cemetery was situated on the side of a hill, which guaranteed crisp winds as well as a rural view. In spring the vivid yellow of canola crops would be interspersed amongst swathes of deep green. Today the warm brown ploughed paddocks were patchworked alongside the lighter green of emerging wheat crops.

Tanner met her as she stepped out into the wind. His head was bare and his dark-blond hair sat in tousled spikes as though he'd run his hand through the front.

Now that she knew the feel of what lay beneath his blue shirts, she couldn't look at him without wanting to run her hands over his muscled strength. Now that she knew how it felt to have his arms anchor her against him, she couldn't be near him without longing for his touch.

'Thanks for coming with me,' she said, making sure she didn't stare at him for too long. 'I hope you haven't been waiting.'

'No, I only just got here.'

She thought his gaze searched her face before she secured her loose hair in a high ponytail using the hairband she'd worn around her wrist.

'Shall we start in the middle?' she asked as she lowered her arms.

'Sounds good to me.'

Before they moved away, she collected a bunch of roses from her car. She still didn't know anything about Edward Jones, but she did know her grandmother had loved him and cherished their life together. She'd do all that she could to honour his memory.

When they reached the ordered rows in the midsection, Tanner walked one over to start his search. At the end of each row they moved further apart as Tanner checked the graves on the high side. Every so often they'd exchange head shakes.

At the top of the hill weathered statues kept watch over loved ones while rusted wrought-iron fences enclosed the memories of precious tiny pioneer lives. Further down the hillside, headstone edges became sharp and polished and colour bloomed as living relatives paid tribute to beloved family members.

The roar of a lawnmower disturbed the quiet as an elderly man on a ride-on mowed the grass at the cemetery entrance.

She didn't realise Tanner was waving at her until her phone beeped and she read the text message.

*Found him.*

Neve walked as fast as she could up the slope to where Tanner stood in front of a dark headstone. As she drew near, her pace slowed. Sadness held her silent as she stared at where the man her grandmother had married lay buried. The details on the headstone listed Edward Jones's name and relevant dates, but otherwise didn't give any other information.

She bent to rest the delicate yellow roses beside the black granite. As she straightened she was conscious of Tanner standing close beside her.

'Five months was all they had,' she whispered.

The warm weight of his arm settled around her shoulders. 'Let's just hope they fitted a lifetime's worth of living into those months.'

The lawnmower noise increased as the elderly man drove to the end of their row. Silence descended as he turned off the motor. Legs bowed, and hair silver white, he approached. 'Afternoon. I'm Bill.'

Tanner shook his outstretched hand. 'Tanner.'

Neve also shook Bill's gnarled hand. 'Neve.'

His faded blue gaze briefly rested on her hair before he looked at the headstone. 'Family?'

'He is now,' Neve said.

The old man rubbed the side of his jaw. 'I've been taking care of things around here for a while.' He dipped his head towards a section of headstones lower down the hill. 'My Eileen and baby son are here.'

Neve could only imagine Bill's heartache at losing not only his wife but also his child. 'I'm so sorry.'

He nodded. 'I've got nowhere else to be so I've seen generations of family members come and go.' Bill studied Edward's headstone. 'But I've never seen anyone visit this grave ... even though for many years there were always flowers here. Fresh ones too.'

'There were?' Neve turned to face him. 'Who left them?'

'I don't know. One day they just stopped. But ...' Bill again glanced at her hair. 'I did see a woman with the same colour hair as you near here. There'd been a storm and the ground was wet. She slipped and when I went to help her she couldn't get away fast enough. I'd also have said that she'd been crying.'

Tanner's hand brushed hers. It was just a whisper of a touch, but it comforted her.

She swallowed past the lump in her throat. 'That had to be my grandmother.'

'Thought so.' Bill looked at the bunch of yellow roses Neve had left. 'It's good to see flowers here again.'

With a nod, he returned to his mowing.

Neve stared at the headstone in front of her. Neither she nor Tanner spoke. The need to find out more about her grandmother's first husband beat inside her with a renewed urgency. Who was he? What brought him here? Why did her grandmother have to hide her marriage?

She touched the smooth, cold granite before turning to leave. Her attention flew to where her grandparents' graves lay side by side. And why did her grandmother marry another man so soon after she'd lost the man she'd truly loved?

'Watch out.'

Tanner was already jumping out of the way as Denham's shout rang out. He'd seen the young bull in the cattle race eyeball him before his back leg lashed out.

'Remind me again why I help you with these rodeo cattle of yours?' he said with a grimace.

Denham grinned as he opened the gate at the front of the race. The cattle jostled and pushed along the narrow space until they spilled into the adjacent yard. 'Because we're partners.'

Tanner moved to the back of the cattle left in the holding yard. He guided them into the race. Even with low-stress handling, the young bulls were fractious. There was no doubt Reggie bred feisty offspring.

When the last Brahman-cross had been doused in the pour-on drench, Denham opened the yard gate. Tanner swung into Arrow's saddle, while Denham started his ag bike. Together they moved the herd through the paddock near the yards and towards the creek. Patch and Juno, Denham's poodle-kelpie cross, kept the testy cattle in a bunched and workable mob.

Once the young bulls surged through the gate, some bucking and kicking, Denham left his bike to shut the steel gate.

'Want to toss a coin to see who goes after the runaways?' he asked as he came over to where Tanner sat on Arrow.

Before Tanner's time, a bushfire had torn through this part of Claremont and the Rural Fire Service had needed to cut the boundary fence. The wire had been rejoined, but Reggie's offspring had also inherited his ability to jump. When Tanner had mustered the paddock earlier that day, the weakened fence was just a few defiant wire strands. Denham was lucky to only be missing three bulls.

Tanner scanned the paddock beyond the fence line. 'I'll go. Arrow will enjoy the ride.'

The neighbouring property was owned by a Sydney financier who only used the farmhouse on weekends. According to the farm manager, the owner was planning some fancy house renovations.

'Okay.' Denham whistled for Juno to follow him. 'I'll tackle the fence.'

Tanner turned Arrow, and with Patch running alongside them, they headed along the boundary. Since the fire, a gate had been cut into the fence to allow easier access between the two farms. Tanner texted the farm manager to let him know he'd be scouting around for the missing cattle. Instead of returning his phone to his pocket, he checked to make sure there hadn't been a message from Neve.

Being around her yesterday while they looked for Edward's headstone had been like riding one of Denham's rodeo bulls. One lapse of concentration, one error in judgement, and life could change in a split second. Despite their mutual decision to cool things, the pull between them remained. It had been there when sadness had drawn her cheeks and he'd felt as though he too was suffering. It had also been there in her quick glances at his mouth and in the shortness of his breath when their eyes met.

He slid his phone into his pocket and rolled his shoulders. No good would come of checking whether or not she'd been in touch. Just like no good would come of his wondering how she was going not having the girls around.

He headed through the gate. The last time it had been opened was during the wet spring when he'd had to drive a tractor next door to pull the farm manager's tractor out of the mud.

Just like on his previous visit, the beauty of the timbered hills and elevated grazing plateaus spoke to him.

He reined in Arrow at the top of a high hill. At the other side of the valley floor the distant ridge was tinged blue by the eucalyptus oil in the air. He smoothed a hand over Arrow's neck as the gelding quivered. The palomino felt it too.

Something about where they were reminded the mustang of the Montana valley where he'd been born. A valley that had also been where Tanner had found peace. He'd arrived bitter at how he'd allowed the woman he'd believed he'd loved to use him, and feeling guilty over how he'd disappointed his father. He'd left secure in who he was and the path he'd chosen in life.

He stifled a surge of restlessness and doubt. Since he'd met Neve it was as though his emotions had come out of the shadows, and it was now a battle to subdue them. He was certain that the decision he'd made in that faraway Montana valley to value his freedom over commitment remained the right one for him.

A breeze tugged at his hat and rippled in the silver-tipped gum leaves beside him. To his left a hawk glided on the airstream. If it were up to him he wouldn't renovate the weatherboard farmhouse set in close to the valley floor. Instead, he'd build a home right here where he could soak in this view every single day.

With still no sign of the cattle, Tanner followed a gully to his right. There was a nearby dam where they might head to water. If the escapees weren't there, they could be over near the Herefords in the next paddock. He whistled for Patch to stay close as a stubby-legged goanna emerged from the rocks to clamber up a tree.

At the dam there were cattle tracks but nothing else. Beyond the dam wall, Tanner spotted a car parked on the gravel road that ran along the front of the neighbour's farm. The road surface was rocky and notorious for flat tyres. From the way the boot was open and the mother and daughter were unloading the contents, he didn't have to be a betting man to guess they'd had a puncture.

When he rode up to the fence, the relief on the woman's face thanked him even before he'd introduced himself and offered to help. With Arrow tied in the shade and Patch lolling beside him, Tanner vaulted over the fence. The dark-haired teenage daughter gave him a shy smile.

'Where are you headed?' he asked as he hefted a large suitcase out of the car boot.

'Out west to Nyngan. We thought we'd take the scenic route.' The mother pulled an embarrassed face. 'Does it sound bad that I've never changed a tyre before?'

Tanner shook his head as he placed the spare tyre next to the flat back one. The sleek-lined city car wouldn't have seen many country roads. 'Hopefully, it will be a while before you have to change one again.'

'I hope so. My husband tried to explain what to do over the phone, but we were about to look on the internet for a how-to video.'

'You're lucky there's a signal.'

Tanner glanced at the teenager, whom the mother, Amy, had introduced as Ruby, as the brunette snapped a picture of the flat tyre. Ruby gave him another shy smile. 'Can I take a picture of your horse and dog to show my friends?'

'Sure. The horse's name is Arrow and the dog's called Patch.'

As the teenager moved away, Amy said quietly, 'Thank you for helping us. We would have been here for hours. My sister has enough to worry about without us being late.'

Tanner picked up the jack. 'How about I explain what I'm doing so if you get a flat again, you'll be all set.'

As he jacked up the car and replaced the punctured tyre with the spare, Amy listened carefully. Ruby too asked questions as she snapped photos and filmed what Tanner was doing.

When the boot was again loaded, Amy gave him a warm hug. 'Thanks so much.'

Ruby stared at him, then cheeks pink, she spoke in a rush. 'Can I have a photo?'

'Sure.'

He stood beside her and draped his arm loosely around her shoulders while her mother took pictures on the teenager's phone. He waved them off as the car's tyres kicked up red dust.

He returned to searching for the missing young bulls. As he'd suspected, he found them hanging out near the neighbour's Herefords. After heading them home to Claremont's cattle yards, he drenched the trio before returning them to their paddock. The section of fence where the hole had been was now fixed. Not even Reggie would get through Denham's repair.

Back at the homestead, Denham's ute was parked near the jacaranda tree. After Tanner had unsaddled Arrow, instead of going around to his flat, he headed up the front steps. Denham most likely would be chatting to Meredith. Sure enough, he heard voices as he walked along the polished hallway floorboards.

When he entered the kitchen, the grin Denham cast him was predictably a little too wide. His cousin was still ribbing him over his field-day modelling. Meredith gave him her usual serene smile.

'You were gone a while. Cattle give you any trouble?' Denham asked as Tanner switched on the electric kettle.

'No. I wasn't away that long.'

'You sure?'

Tanner finished making himself a coffee and sat at the table opposite his cousin. 'Yep.'

Denham passed him his phone. 'You were gone long enough for this …'

Tanner frowned but didn't look at the screen. Anything to do with social media couldn't be good. 'You didn't post my modelling picture somewhere, did you?'

'No.' Denham placed his hand on his heart. 'I swear I had nothing to do with you becoming a "hot hero".'

'A what?' Tanner glanced at Meredith. She slowly nodded. He reached for the phone. Ruby had posted the picture of them together online with the words, *So this happened. Tanner helped us change our flat tyre. I love the country!*

She'd also tagged him using the name of his horse-training business, which she would have seen on his shirt.

He looked at Denham. 'That's not too bad. She was a nice kid.'

Denham chuckled. 'Scroll down. Your nice kid has an army of followers.'

Dismay filled him as comment after comment lay beneath the picture. Somewhere someone must have called him a 'hot hero' because the phrase suddenly kept appearing and now had a hashtag.

He groaned. 'How did you find this?'

'It wasn't me. Fliss is at the hospital and Christi showed it to her.'

Christi was the young hospital receptionist and he could see how she'd have been in the circles where he'd guessed the photo had been shared.

'It gets worse, keep scrolling,' Denham said.

Tanner did as Denham suggested and soon photos from his website were popping up along with a photo of him modelling in a different outfit than in the photo Denham had somehow got hold of.

A series of comments then discussed the upcoming picnic races and whether Tanner would be there and if he had any friends.

'Look on the bright side,' Meredith said, touching his arm. 'Think of how many people now know the Woodlea Picnic Races are on.'

He dragged a hand over his face. 'This is a nightmare.'

Denham stood. 'You know that talk we had about you having rocks in your head … if there ever was a time not to have them it's now.'

Tanner didn't answer. He just stared at the comments that still hadn't ended as he scrolled. The lipstick target on his bachelor back already felt like a brand. Surely people wouldn't come to the races expecting to see him? But as he read the comments definite plans were being made.

Denham clasped his shoulder. 'I'm ready for that cold beer whenever you are.'

Tanner handed him his phone. 'Thanks, but I'm becoming a hermit.'

'Hermits can still drink cold beer.'

'They're going to have to.'

As Denham left to head home, Tanner looked across at Meredith.

'Sweetheart, it will be okay. A handful of extra people might come. You won't be mobbed.'

At his I-won't-be-because-I'm-not-going look, she smiled. 'Of course you'll go. Even hermits have to accompany their aged mother to the races.' Meredith stood, looking nothing but sprightly. 'If Edna suspects you'll be a no-show she'll be around with Bethany, engineering some more one-on-one time.'

Tanner sighed and took a gulp of hot coffee. Until Bethany told her mother the truth about Mac and her, there'd be no respite from Edna's attention. Meredith placed a slice of his favourite lemon-and-poppy-seed cake in front of him. She patted his arm before collecting the bucket of food scraps and leaving to make a trip to the chook pen.

His phone vibrated in his pocket and he checked his screen. Neve had texted.

*Heard you had a busy afternoon. Are u ok?*

He hesitated. Then, succumbing to the need to talk to her, he called instead of texting a reply.

She answered after only two rings. 'Hi.'

He glanced around to make sure Meredith wasn't nearby. Hearing the softness of Neve's voice was enough to stir his emotions. How much he missed seeing her would be stamped all over his face.

'Hi. News travels fast.'

'Unfortunately, social media travels faster.'

'You can say that again.' Even to his own ears his tone sounded grim.

'You did a nice thing for the mother and daughter. Just forget about everything else. Tomorrow the social networks will be buzzing with something new.'

Neve's sincerity and the humour infusing her words soothed him. He smiled into the phone. 'So I'll just be yesterday's news.'

She laughed and the sound had the same effect as if she'd touched him. Hunger and need uncoiled deep inside. 'Yes, sorry, even hot heroes only have fifteen seconds of fame.'

He chuckled, hoping the phone line would disguise the huskiness of his laughter. 'How's your Edward search going? I'm sorry there's been no more word from my father.'

'That's okay. I really appreciate all the help he's already given me. I'm ignoring the wartime angle for the moment and instead looking into Edward's family. If he has any brothers or sisters who are still alive, they might have the answers we're looking for.'

'Good luck.'

'Thanks. I'd better go. Bassie's kicking the gate with his front foot and I'm only five minutes late with his dinner.'

'Give him and Dell a pat from me.'

'I will. Bye.'

'See you.'

Tanner gazed out the kitchen window to where Patch followed Meredith back from the chook pen. He didn't need to physically be near Neve for her to decimate his defences. When it came to attention spans he could only wish his was fifteen seconds long. He'd now be thinking about her until the grey of dawn pushed through his bedroom curtains and the birdsong chorus welcomed in the new day.

'Do I need to keep my eyes closed?' Neve said as she walked beside Cressy along the driveway of a brick house on a back street in Woodlea.

Cressy had called earlier to say she had a special surprise and to meet her at this address after lunch.

The call couldn't have come at a better time. Despite the books she'd read, the rides she'd taken, the research she'd done about Edward, and her lounge room being rearranged, her keeping-busy list was looking sparse. It was only Friday morning. She hadn't yet reached the end of the first week of the girls being gone. Two weeks on her own already felt like a life sentence.

'Not yet …' Cressy changed her grip on the basket Neve had offered to carry. 'But you will.'

The cowgirl still moved carefully, but the bruises beneath her eyes had disappeared and her skin glowed with health. She would make such a beautiful bride in two weeks. The enforced rest, insisted on by Fliss and Denham, had been what her body needed.

Neve looked around. Apart from her sedan and Cressy's silver ute, the only other nearby vehicle was an unfamiliar car parked across the road. It almost seemed as though the house was empty. When they reached the back door, Cressy didn't knock, just twisted the handle.

She gave Neve a cheery wave. 'In you go.'

Neve walked into a neat kitchen. Apart from canisters filled with tea and coffee beside an electric kettle, the house didn't look inhabited. There was no fruit bowl. No cooking utensils or toaster on the bench. She was sure if she opened the fridge the shelves would be bare.

Curious, she glanced at Cressy.

Cressy only grinned and then held up a hand to cover her eyes as she guided her towards a closed door. 'No peeking.'

The door squeaked open. Cressy lowered her hand. 'You said you wanted to learn to knit while the girls were away.'

Neve stared. She didn't know what to look at first, Edna sitting in an armchair knitting something white, or the plastic tubs filled with a rainbow array of wool that lined the back wall. On a small table stood jars containing knitting needles and scissors, while on another table was a pile of completed horse shoes similar to the ones she'd admired on the day the girls had played in the new playground. Cressy had brought her to a guerrilla knitter's paradise.

The clicking of Edna's knitting needles stopped before she rested her hands on her lap. 'Now, Neve, there's only one golden rule … remember what happens in our underground knitting club stays in our underground knitting club.'

'I'll remember.'

She sat in the seat that Edna patted beside her. From the number of chairs, there were far more guerrilla-knitting members than Cressy and Edna.

The cowgirl spoke from the doorway. 'Cuppa, Edna?'

'Yes please, and just a small piece of whatever you have in that basket of yours. I've been so good only having a special treat every now and then.'

Neve swapped looks with Cressy. Edna was the queen of understatements. She'd love to be in the room when Dr Fliss next received Edna's cholesterol results.

Edna left her seat to collect Neve a pair of thick red needles and a ball of green wool. 'I'm sure you'll be a fast learner. Your grandmother was quite the knitting legend. She holds the wartime record for the most number of socks knitted for the overseas troops. She also knitted me Rodger's cardigan for his christening day. If Netta was still with us she'd love what we do here.'

Neve took hold of the wool and needles. She couldn't ever remember seeing either her mother or grandmother knitting. But there were photos of her as a child in some pretty hand-knitted jumpers. 'I'd love to hear more about my grandmother.'

As Edna explained the basics of casting on and casting off, she also recounted childhood memories of Neve's family. In the stories there was nothing to change Neve's perceptions or any new information that would help fill in the blanks of her grandmother's life.

Cressy placed two cups of tea and a plate of vanilla slice on the small table in between Neve and Edna. From a set of drawers she removed a bag, made herself comfortable in an armchair, took off her boots and started knitting. She too was working on something white. No wonder she'd had a twinkle in her eye when Neve had commented the day they'd had coffee in town that the recent yarn bombing could be themed white for a wedding.

When Neve had completed two uneven rows, Edna steered the conversation towards Tanner. Neve hoped Edna didn't notice how the wool slipped off the end of her knitting needle at the topic change.

'It's most concerning Tanner becoming such a social media star.' Edna's frown would have even stopped Bassie from doing the wrong thing. 'His popularity has race-day ticket sales soaring, but we all know that Tanner hates female attention and being pursued.'

Neve stopped knitting. She didn't dare look at Cressy. Surely Edna could see how ironical her words were? She thought she heard Cressy stifle a laugh.

'Yes, he does,' Neve managed.

'A local girl would have his best interests at heart. An out-of-towner won't see past his country-boy good looks … they'll be falling for an image not for him as a person.'

Neve nodded. Edna's words actually made sense.

'Which is why I need your help, Neve. On race day, when you see him surrounded by girls, go over and run interference. Unfortunately, Bethany won't be there until the last race and she can take over then.'

'Okay.' Neve wound green wool around her knitting needle. 'It will be Operation Save Tanner.' She glanced at Cressy. 'Between all of us, he'll be fine.'

This time Edna's frown was fully directed at Neve. 'No, it can't be a group effort, it has to be just one of you. The only way to signal he's unavailable is if he's regularly seen with the same person. By the time Bethany arrives his fan club would have moved on, hopefully to those Barton boys.'

Neve held Edna's stare. 'Edna … I'm not pretending to be a couple with Tanner just so he will stay available for a local girl, even if perhaps her motives are more genuine.'

Edna stopped knitting. 'Why not? Have I missed something? There's a rumour that Mac Barton is seeing someone. Even though it was Finn you were getting on so well with at the small-hall festival.'

Neve ground her teeth. 'With respect, my love-life's no one's business but mine. I'm not being a fake couple with Tanner for Tanner's sake. He just might find somebody different and interesting. He deserves to have some fun. *If* he looks uncomfortable of course I'll help him out, just like any of us will.'

To her surprise Edna merely nodded. 'Fair enough. Be careful or you'll drop another stitch.'

For the rest of the afternoon the topic of Tanner was never again mentioned. When the natural light in the lounge room dulled, Neve helped Cressy and Edna tidy what turned out to be Meredith's house. As she now lived at Claremont, she'd made the building available for the underground knitting club. Which meant Meredith would be involved.

After Neve had waved farewell to Cressy she drove towards Main Street.

She slowed as she passed the historic church where her mother had been christened and her grandmother married for what she now knew was the second time. Usually, the sight of the picturesque stone building with its bell tower brought her a sense of belonging.

Today it just magnified the reality that she was going home to a silent and empty house. As if echoing her thoughts, she drove by the old fire station that had its windows boarded up. The double-storey brick building had been superseded by a new Rural Fire Service site on the outskirts of town.

Not far along, other buildings that once would have housed bustling shops also stood vacant. While the yarn bombers and events such as the markets, annual rodeo and campdraft and the races brought tourists to town, Woodlea still was a shadow of what it had been in her mother's day. Between the younger generations heading to the mines or the city, and shrinking services, what Woodlea needed were some new businesses to regenerate the streetscape.

In the rear-view mirror she glanced back at the large wooden doors of the disused fire station. It wasn't only the Woodlea locals that would benefit from new skills and expertise, outlying rural and remote families would too. The concerns she'd seen city children for in her occupational therapy practice would also affect many country children.

She passed the Windmill Café. Through the front window, tables appeared unoccupied and no cars were parked outside. On impulse she pulled over. Woodlea also needed residents to shop local and to support locally owned businesses. She'd grab a quick coffee and one of the caramel slices Edna loved so much. Fallen leaves crunched beneath her boots as she left her car. Beside her a plane tree dressed in pale yellow rustled and she pulled her denim jacket closed against the stiff breeze.

When she pushed open the café door Sally greeted her with a huge smile. 'Long time no see. The usual?'

'Yes please, and a piece of caramel slice. I'll take them with me though.'

A prickle at her nape had her half turn. The blue shirt warned her who else was in the café even before she identified the male customer as Tanner. He sat at a corner table reading the paper, an empty mug in front of him.

Their eyes connected and then the corner of his mouth curved. 'Hi.'

'Hi.'

She'd walked over to him even before her mind had made a decision about what she should do.

He stood and pulled out the seat opposite him. She glanced to where Sally was frothing milk behind the counter before sitting. 'I won't stay long. Dell, Bassie and Jazz will want their dinner.'

His gaze skimmed her face and she resisted the urge to smooth her hair and to wet her dry lips. She couldn't remember when she'd last slicked on lip balm.

She broke eye contact to look out the front window. He couldn't know how good it was to see him. 'Your ute isn't in town?'

'Phil's away so I've been using his. I'm parked in front of the post office.'

'Let me guess, you haven't seen much of Edna lately.'

Tanner's smile gleamed white. 'It's been at least a week.'

Neve couldn't think of a single thing to say. She'd missed him and his easy grin so much. With perfect timing, Sally brought over her latte and caramel slice. 'Here you go.'

'Thanks, Sal. Now the weather's turning cold, I'll be seeing more of you.'

'I'll look forward to it. I might need some help with my science assessments.'

'Anytime.'

As the university student headed back to the counter, Tanner's phone rang.

'Sorry, I'd better take this. Meredith was calling if she needed anything.'

Neve took a sip of her latte while Tanner answered. 'Yes, I'm still here. I had to wait for the part. Do you need anything? Okay, I'll

swing by the grocery store. I'm at the café.' He glanced at Neve.
'I was, but Neve's here now … I'll ask … Meredith wants to know
if you'll come for dinner? Apparently I'm on barbeque duty.'

Neve didn't miss the way he sat very still while he waited for her
reply.

'Thanks.' She didn't have the heart to refuse generous Meredith's
hospitality. 'That sounds lovely.'

Tanner relayed her acceptance. 'Yes. Right. Will do.' He ended
the call.

Neve picked up the paper bag containing her slice and got to
her feet. 'I'll duck home first to feed everyone and to get Meredith's
scrapbooks.'

Tanner stood too. 'Was there anything useful?'

'Interesting, yes. There was a crash where no one was injured
when a pilot landed and ran into a queue of planes on his first
night-time solo flight.'

'I bet he wasn't popular.'

'I think the term used in the newspaper was he was "scrubbed"
from the programme. But unfortunately no, there wasn't anything
to help with finding out who Edward Jones was.'

They both gave Sally a smile as they walked towards the door.
Once outside Tanner turned to her. 'Fliss or Hewitt wouldn't mind
feeding Dell, Bassie and Jazz.'

Indecision held her quiet. She hated asking people to do things
for her, but it would be an hour round trip home and then out to
Claremont. Knowing Meredith, she'd already be prepared for Neve
to arrive when Tanner did.

'There's also no rush to return the scrapbooks,' Tanner added
quietly.

'Okay. I'll call Fliss and drink my latte, while you get whatever
Meredith needs.'

After Neve had spoken to Fliss, she returned to the warmth of her car. Tanner had disappeared inside the grocery store and hadn't again emerged. As she finished her coffee and ate the caramel slice, she did an internet search for the local service she needed. When she found the number, she hesitated before making the call.

The image of the derelict fire station refused to leave her. Just like the half-thought that had formed and she'd expected to dim and fade.

When Neve walked beside Tanner through Claremont's garden and Meredith greeted them at the front steps, Neve was glad she hadn't delayed her arrival. Meredith's smile was as welcoming as her embrace.

After Meredith had bustled Tanner off to cook the marinated chicken, she poured Neve a glass of red wine. They went to sit on a sheltered side veranda that overlooked the pool and barbeque area, where a cheese-and-dip platter sat on the wrought-iron table.

Neve settled into a chair and used the toe of her boot to scratch Patch's stomach as he lay near her feet. This was the first time she'd spent any length of time with Meredith and Tanner together. Their banter and quick smiles while Tanner cooked the barbeque conveyed their closeness. Despite the years apart, they appeared to have forged a connection out of the complexity and heartache of their separation.

But as Neve stayed impartial about their discussion as to whether or not brown dress boots were an acceptable footwear to wear with formal wedding attire, she noticed Tanner kept a part of himself back. It wasn't anything he said, or did—his laughter was unrestrained, his tone engaged—it was just a micro-expression that dulled his eyes when he thought no one was looking.

Once the chicken was ready, and a Greek salad and fresh rolls were placed on the table, Tanner sat in the seat opposite her. His gaze didn't hold hers for long as usual. She could understand why. She was having difficulty not staring when his smile crinkled the corners of his eyes. Every time he reached for something it was a struggle to then not glance at his strong, tanned hands. Her skin still remembered the heat of his touch.

She focused on buttering a roll and on answering Meredith's question about what she was doing without the girls around. 'I've been working through a long to-do list and riding as much as I can.'

'Anytime you want a cuppa you know where I am.'

'I do. Thank you.'

The conversation then revolved around theories about who Edward Jones could have been and why he'd been stationed here during the war.

After they finished with apple pie and cream for dessert, Meredith took a phone call from Phil. When she went into the kitchen to talk, Neve shifted in her seat. She shouldn't feel so vulnerable when alone with Tanner. She should have faith that her self-control would hold.

Tanner's eyes met hers. She hadn't realised she'd locked her fingers around the stem of her wineglass until he glanced at her clamped grip.

'Neve … it's okay. We both agreed nothing should happen.'

She swallowed. She hated that he could read her so well and that her feelings were so transparent. 'It's … harder than I thought.'

A smile tugged at his lips before his gaze lowered to her mouth. 'Tell me about it.'

Her breathing quickened as her hormones stirred. 'It will be easier on your horsemanship weekend won't it? We'll both be busy.'

'I'm sure it will be.'

His hand moved on the table. All she had to do was inch hers forward and their fingers would connect.

'You don't sound confident.'

His gaze flicked to hers. No longer clear and pure, his irises were an intense, brilliant blue. 'I'd be lying if I said I was. Neve ... you make me feel things ...'

Needing to touch him, because words wouldn't be enough to convey she too felt overwhelmed, she straightened her fingers so their fingertips could meet.

Meredith's footsteps sounded.

Neve pulled her hand away after only the briefest of touches.

'Who's for coffee,' Meredith asked, voice cheerful as she appeared in the doorway.

Tanner shook his head as he came to his feet. 'Not me. Patch and I have a river pump to turn off.'

Neve also stood. She collected the dessert bowls. 'I'm fine too, but will help with these dishes before I head off.'

Tanner filled his hands with the empty wineglasses. 'If I don't see you before, I'll see you Saturday week, bright and early.'

From his casual expression and smooth words, she'd never have guessed they'd just had a conversation like they'd had. 'Jazz and I'll be there, even if we're not fully awake.'

'Do you need a swag?'

'Cressy said she has a spare.'

'How about I come and get Jazz Friday night? She can stay here and I'll take her with Arrow on Saturday?'

'Thanks, but I'm sure you'll have heaps of things to do. Hewitt's offered to float her.'

'Okay. No worries.'

Tanner's gaze briefly met hers as he waited for her to precede him through the doorway.

It was only when she walked along the hallway into the kitchen that she realised Meredith hadn't joined in the conversation. Instead she'd stood by the table, silently studying them.

Rain splattered on the tractor cabin roof and turned the dust on the windscreen into a filmy red sludge. Tanner activated the windscreen wiper. He needed the rain to hold off. Today was supposed to be the last day of sowing Claremont's winter wheat. Other farms had sown earlier and their wheat was already visible green shoots. But thanks to the threat of the locust swarms, Phil had held off on sowing for as long as possible. If the locusts did arrive their crop would hopefully still be in the ground.

The rain flurry stopped, but the lack of blue sky didn't fill him with confidence. It was mid-afternoon yet felt like early evening. It wasn't a coincidence that since Neve had come for dinner on Friday night, he'd spent the weekend obsessively sowing. It was the only way to escape the way she made him feel. He could only hope Phil put the long hours he'd spent in the tractor down to the forecasted rain.

As for Meredith, he'd abandoned all hope she'd missed the intensity between Neve and him. She hadn't said a word. She didn't have to. Instead, there was a new watchfulness in her eyes. He didn't know how, but he needed to have a conversation to dispel any expectation she had that he and Neve were a couple. As hard as it was, they were adhering to their agreement to cool the chemistry between them.

The UHF crackled to life and when he heard his name he took hold of the handset. Denham too was sowing.

He pushed the talk button to answer Denham's query as to whether or not he was on channel. 'Yes, here. Had any rain?'

'A few spots. How about you?'

'The same.'

'How's Cressy?'

'Resting.'

'Really?'

'No, but she's sitting in the office doing book work.'

'That's resting for Cressy. She still in Fliss's bad books?'

'Yes, and mine. I knew something wasn't right, but she kept saying she was fine.'

Another crackle sounded and then a voice came on as old Will spoke. The UHF channel wasn't private. 'She's still in my bad books too. If anything happened to her …'

With Cressy and Fliss's mother and father no longer with them, Will would be walking Cressy down the aisle.

'Will,' Denham answered, 'I'm watching her closely. Fliss has also set some very strict rest guidelines which she regularly makes sure are being followed.'

Will's chuckle sounded. 'I wouldn't want Fliss checking up on me.'

'Or me,' Tanner added. 'Will, you still making those kids' whips?'

'Yup. Want two for those little redheads Neve looks after?'

Tanner clenched his jaw. Not that he'd admit this to his father, but as much as he loved the cohesiveness of small-town life there were times when he did appreciate the anonymity of city living.

'Maybe. They liked the whip cracking at the field day.'

Denham's voice sounded. 'Cressy's turned up in the ute. She must have had enough of desk duties. Wish me luck telling her she shouldn't be driving the tractor.'

Will chuckled again. 'Rather you than me. Over and out.'

Tanner hung up the handpiece with a smile. He already knew how Denham and Cressy's conversation would go. His cousin would still drive the tractor, but Cressy would end up in the second seat despite the fact it would be uncomfortable for her broken ribs. They'd then spend the rest of Denham's shift not wanting to be anywhere else but with each other.

It wasn't easy to elbow aside the loneliness that filled him.

Rain again splashed his windscreen and he again flicked on the windscreen wiper. An alarm sounded and he slowed to a stop. Time to clear more stubble. As he left the tractor rain dotted his forearms below his rolled-up shirtsleeves. He stretched to ease the strain in his lower back before climbing onto the air-seeder frame.

He'd do another couple of runs and then let Toby, who helped out at busy times, take over. Meredith would soon call on the UHF to remind him to take a break and have a late lunch. He walked along the metal frame checking the heads, something he'd done countless times before.

He didn't know if it was fatigue, the rain on the metal making it slick, or just bad luck. All he knew was that his boot slipped, before a sharp blow landed on the front of his head and he tasted dirt.

Dazed, he pushed himself into a sitting position and spat red earth out of his mouth. The metallic smell of blood tainted the air as liquid warmth ran past his left eye, over his cheek to his jaw. He pulled off his shirt, bunched a clean section and pressed it against his forehead. He waited a moment until the world stopped swaying before coming to his feet.

Hand still holding his shirt against his head, he climbed into the tractor. After calling Toby on the radio to take over from him early, he drove to his ute. Blood now oozed over his shoulder and trickled down his chest. Careful to not transfer any blood to his ute seat, he maintained the pressure on his head and made his way home. When he passed Toby on the track, he briefly lowered his shirt to give him a wave. No one needed to know he'd lost focus.

He'd thought he'd achieved the impossible when he reached the front door of his flat without Patch barking or there being any sign of Meredith. Except he soon discovered where she was. She sat at his kitchen table, mouth tight and a first-aid kit beside her. He caught sight of his reflection in the glass door as he walked by. He shouldn't have bothered to lower his shirt when he'd passed Toby. The side of his face, neck and chest glistened with blood.

'What am I going to do with you?' Meredith came to her feet and pulled out a chair for him to sit in.

He gave a sheepish shrug. 'Nothing. I'm fine.'

Meredith only shook her head. Beneath her tan her skin was pale. He reached for her hand and gave it a squeeze. 'I didn't knock myself out. I'm okay.'

'I'll let Fliss be the judge of that.'

He groaned as he lowered himself into a chair. 'You didn't.'

'I did.'

'Meredith?' Phil's worried voice echoed through the flat.

'Darling, in here.' Meredith's attention didn't leave Tanner as she opened a sterile wad of white gauze. 'A certain someone was trying to sneak in.'

'I wasn't. I was just going … to get cleaned up.'

Phil stopped in the doorway. Tall and lean, a frown drew his grey brows together. 'Whatever you've done, you've done a good job.'

'I slipped off the frame. It's just a cut. Head wounds always bleed.'

Meredith eased away his shirt to press the gauze in its place. The once faded blue cotton of his shirt was now dark. His chest itched where blood had dried in crusty streaks.

Gravel crunched under car tyres before Patch barked.

'Fliss must have broken a land-speed record to get here,' Phil said, heading towards the front door.

Tanner took over holding the gauze in place and then went to stand. Fliss didn't need to check him over. He just needed a shower. Meredith gave him her don't-even-think-about-it look.

As he sighed and sat back in his chair, her expression softened. 'Let Fliss take a look ... please.'

Except when Phil returned, the woman with him wasn't Fliss. Tanner's jaw hardened to the consistency of concrete. Neve stood beside Phil, who was now holding the pile of scrapbooks she'd come to return.

She stared at him, her lips pressed together, before she glanced at Meredith. 'Let me guess, he was sneaking in.'

She nodded. 'He was.'

'I was not.'

But no one appeared to listen. Neve walked towards him, her gaze assessing as though he was one of her occupational therapist clients. 'Any dizziness, nausea or blurred vision?'

Even her voice sounded different, crisp and no-nonsense.

'No. As I said to Meredith, I didn't knock myself out.'

When Neve's attention turned to the blood on his chest a flicker of worry passed across her face. He fisted his hand on his thigh as he weathered the need to reach out and ease her concern. He vaguely registered Patch barking and Phil again leaving the kitchen.

Neve moved in closer and bent to look at the side of his head.

'I'm fine,' he said, voice low and husky.

She stilled.

'I might sneak but I don't lie,' he added so only she could hear.

Her gaze met his. Her eyes were so dark they resembled the bruised hue of a storm-tossed sea. The intensity of what passed between them made him shake.

Fliss's voice sounded. 'Where's my patient?'

Neve straightened and moved away as Fliss entered and headed straight for him. She didn't say a word, just placed a hand on his clean shoulder before turning to the others.

'Meredith,' Fliss said with a smile, 'seeing as Tanner decided to injure himself right when I was enjoying my afternoon sugar fix, I'd love one of your hot chocolates.'

'Coming right up. Neve, would you like a tea?'

The room emptied as Phil followed Meredith and Neve into the main house.

'Thanks,' Tanner said, well aware Fliss had cleared the room on purpose.

She opened the bag she'd brought with her. 'Anytime. It's not every day I see you looking this tense. Let's get you cleaned up so I know what I'm dealing with.'

He lowered the white gauze and remained immobile while Fliss examined his wound. After he'd answered some questions to confirm he wasn't concussed, she stepped back. 'Don't be surprised if you end up with a black eye, but after a couple of stitches, you'll be as fine as you would have said you were.'

At his quick glance, she grinned. 'Don't forget how many times I've patched Denham up, not to mention when I met Hewitt his favourite word was "fine", yet he couldn't lift a puppy with that bad shoulder of his.'

Fliss's light tone didn't match the seriousness of her expression. 'But … as for the real reason why you're so on edge, that isn't my area of expertise. I still don't know how I've ended up with someone as wonderful as Hewitt. All I can say is, Tanner, you deserve to be happy.'

He just stared at her. The truth was he didn't so much feel tense as trapped. He couldn't reassure Neve he was okay or act on the feelings that hadn't diminished despite being away from her. As for being happy, he'd once thought that retaining his freedom to safeguard his heart was the answer.

'Tanner?' Concern furrowed Fliss's brow.

'I'm—'

'If you say you're fine I'm not ignoring Edna's pointed suggestions that you sit next to Bethany at the wedding.'

He forced a smile. 'I was going to say … I'm working on it.'

'Now that I believe.' Her voice softened. 'Good luck.' She again looked at his wound. 'Let's get this sorted.'

'Fliss … thanks.'

'You're welcome.'

When the cut on his forehead, which was close to his hairline, had been sutured, Fliss gave him the usual spiel about stitches. After she left to have her hot chocolate, Tanner went to have a shower. While the hot water eased the physical aches of his body, the chill that gripped him from within refused to thaw. After he'd showered, he made a call before throwing clothes into a duffle bag. It was time. He'd delayed going droving long enough.

He sent Bethany a text saying he'd be away for the week. With sowing finished, he had a small window of opportunity before the horsemanship weekend. He'd use the space, simplicity and clarity of the long paddock to get his life, and himself, back in order. He rolled his shoulders that felt as though they'd hardened into granite. When he returned he could only hope he'd rediscovered the contentment that he'd once carved out.

He sat his duffle near his swag. Feet leaden, he went to find Meredith. He didn't need to check the front driveway as he walked past the wide dining-room window. There wouldn't be any cars parked on the gravel or near the jacaranda tree. Three messages had been left on his mobile while he'd been in the shower. One was from Fliss to remind him to take it easy, another was from Denham checking in on him, and the other was from Neve saying she hoped he was okay.

Glass clinked and he turned towards the kitchen. As much as Meredith expected him to come and go, each time he said he was leaving he had to be hurting her. He braced himself as he walked through the doorway. On the kitchen table sat the large blue esky he always took away.

Meredith slowly turned from where she loaded the dishwasher. Though she smiled, it didn't ease the sadness in her eyes. He didn't know how she always knew when he'd leave, but she did.

He didn't say anything, just walked over to hug her. They stayed that way in silence, then he said, 'I'm sorry. I just … need to go.'

'I understand.' Meredith moved away. 'Please tell me you're not going tonight with your head how it is.'

'No, at first light.'

Avoiding his gaze, she brushed something off the front of his shirt. 'I'll be here, my son, and waiting … however many times you have to leave.'

The second week of the girls being away proved easier. Neve smiled as she packed a hand-knitted woolly red scarf into an overnight bag. She'd finished her first knitting project and was on her way to embracing solitude and learning to just be. Sitting in front of the fire, with only the crackle and flicker of flames for company, now made her feel peaceful instead of unsettled.

She added a book and reading light to her bag. She'd also read her target number of books even if, despite her extensive research, she was no nearer to finding answers to her questions involving Edward. While nothing concrete had eventuated, the half-idea Neve had had about the empty fire station was now fully formed. The only thing she couldn't bring herself to do was to cook one of her mother's favourite recipes.

Neve zipped her bag closed and carried it to the front door. Hewitt would soon arrive to take her and Jazz to Tanner's horsemanship weekend. Her sigh echoed along the quiet hallway. While being on her own hadn't filled her with the same anxiety and uncertainty as it had when the girls left, her thoughts had still been preoccupied.

Whenever Tanner's week away droving had been mentioned, there'd been a gravity about everyone's words that fuelled her suspicions that something wasn't right. Even though there'd been talk about how dry it was out west and that his skills would be in demand, the timing of his leaving the day after he'd hit his head seemed off. The deep concern on Meredith's face the afternoon it happened hadn't eased when Neve had called in for a cuppa midweek.

The rumble of an engine disturbed the early-morning stillness. Neve checked she hadn't left anything behind before heading out to help Hewitt load Jazz. Eyes bright, Jazz walked straight onto the float.

'Someone's excited,' Neve said, lifting Jazz's saddle into the back of the four-wheel drive.

Hewitt closed the horse float tailgate. 'I wish all horses self-loaded. Don't get me started on how hard it is to load that bad-tempered buckskin of Denham's.'

After they drove through the front gate Neve glanced at Hewitt. She had a project she hoped he'd be on board with.

'Hewitt … you know how the Reedy Creek Hall has a place to exchange books?'

He nodded.

'Well, I was wondering about setting up a community street library at the adventure playground. Kids could swap books and parents could also grab something to read while their kids played.'

'That's a great idea. My home town has one outside the local church. It looks like a wooden bird house on a pole with a glass door.'

'I've also seen them made out of metal.' She grinned. She wasn't the only one Hewitt had made a garden item for out of old plough discs. 'I don't suppose you know of a handy welder …'

'I might do.' His smiling grey eyes met hers. 'I like the way you think, Neve Fitzpatrick.'

'Thank you.'

The discussion about potential designs continued until they reached the outskirts of Woodlea.

'It looks like half the town's awake and here,' Neve said as they turned into the rodeo ground.

The pale light of a new day fell over a scene that bustled with movement and colour. To the left of the rodeo arena, horses were being unloaded from horse floats and riders were setting up portable yards. Behind the arena people were congregated around a barbeque or sitting on benches eating what looked like bacon-and-egg rolls. Dew lay heavy on the grass where boot prints crisscrossed in curved lines.

Hewitt chuckled. 'There sure are a lot of people for an eight-person clinic. It didn't take long for Edna to charge a fee for fence sitters to watch and also to camp.'

'Hopefully, the playground committee will get close to what they need for the shade sails.'

'I'm sure they will.'

Neve continued to scan the rodeo ground, hoping it wouldn't be obvious she was searching for Arrow and Tanner. Behind all the horse floats and horses, she caught a glimpse of gold.

Hewitt parked alongside a white four-wheel drive. He waved at a redhead who brushed a bay mare tied to the side of a horse float.

'That's Freya. Drew, her fiancé, will be around here somewhere. Until he met Freya, he was a loner and we'd never have seen him at an event like this.'

Even as Hewitt spoke, a tall man strode around the back of the float carrying a stock saddle as though it were no heavier than Bassie's kid-sized one.

Neve followed Hewitt over to the couple. Freya turned to them with a pretty smile. Her shoulder-length hair was a true shade of red and her eyes were a soft grey-blue that communicated a quiet composure. No wonder Neve had heard that even the farm boys who'd rather be in the paddock were happy to attend the one-teacher school at Reedy Creek.

'Hi, Neve,' Freya said, her tone warm, 'Cressy mentioned you'd be here. It's really nice to meet you.'

'Lovely to meet you too.'

From where he stood beside Freya, Drew dipped his dark head towards Neve. 'Hi.'

Without hesitation, Neve smiled at the cattleman. 'Hi.'

Since moving to the bush, she was getting better at meeting people. But out of everyone she'd met, it was only Tanner who'd made her feel self-conscious and caused her words to stall.

'Are you camping or heading home?' Freya asked as Hewitt and Drew moved away to look at a dent on the bonnet of Hewitt's black ute. While following a truck to town last week, a piece of wood had fallen off and hit his vehicle.

'Staying here. How about you?'

'Camping too. Maybe we could be swag buddies? Bethany and her friends have put their swags over near the campfire ready for a late night. After a full day in the saddle I won't be able to walk let alone stay awake.'

Neve glanced over to the large pile of wood a safe distance away from the kitchen and amenity block. From the number of green canvas swags, Bethany and her city friends weren't the only ones planning to make the most of the weekend. The last place Neve would feel comfortable would be in such a large group. She would also be saddle sore and tired after riding all day.

'I'd love to be swag buddies.'

As Hewitt and Drew went around to the back of the horse float, Neve gave Freya a farewell smile before helping to unload Jazz. While she saddled the grey mare, Hewitt unhitched the float from his ute so it could stay at the rodeo ground for the weekend.

He came over as Neve walked Jazz in a small circle. 'Fliss finishes her night shift soon, so I'll head off. We're meeting in town for breakfast.'

'Tell her hi. Thanks again for chauffeuring us here.'

'You're welcome. Have fun. There's no better person with horses than Tanner.'

After she waved goodbye to Hewitt, she collected her helmet from the horse float. She led Jazz over to Freya and her bay mare. The two horses touched noses. When a car door slammed the two quiet mares didn't flinch. Unlike the chestnut that Mac was saddling at a nearby float. The gelding surged sideways, his snorts loud and agitated.

Neve exchanged a look with Freya. 'Dealing with a spooked horse is a little above my pay grade. I'm just getting used to being around horses again.'

'Me too,' Freya said. 'It's been a long time since my pony-camp days. Liberty's also coming off a tendon injury. She loves Tanner. He's already helped us so much.'

Liberty sniffed at Neve's shirtsleeve and Neve rubbed the mare's forehead. 'Everyone loves Tanner. He worked wonders with my donkey and my pony, whose attitude is bigger than he is.'

Freya laughed. 'I believe Reggie's the only non-member of the Tanner fan club. But he'll come around.'

Neve was only half listening. She'd seen a familiar set of broad shoulders in an oilskin vest and blue shirt.

Her preoccupation must have shown on her face as Freya reached for Jazz's reins and Neve's helmet. 'I've already said hi. If you want to as well now's a good time. It's obvious Bethany's friends are more interested in Tanner than they are in their horses.'

Neve hesitated. 'I just need a quick word.'

'Go,' Freya said softly.

Neve went. As Tanner disappeared amongst the horse yards heading for Arrow, she walked faster. She wanted to see how his head was. If that wasn't enough of a reason to talk to him, there also was her visceral response to catching sight of him. The too-fast beating of her heart had nothing to do with how quickly she walked. She just plain missed him.

Tanner came into view again as he reached Arrow's yard, which was away from all the other horses and floats. He vanished into the horse float.

When the palomino mustang saw her, he came over to the fence, hung his head over the top and whickered.

Neve ran a hand over his golden nose. 'Good to see you too.'

Metal clinked and she swung around to see Tanner holding Arrow's saddle and bridle. For a long second he stared, then he said, 'Morning.'

'Morning.'

Neve didn't buy his casual greeting. Just like the first day she'd seen him, reserve cast his face in tanned, carved lines. The grooves beside his mouth were deeply etched. Her gaze flew to his forehead despite his injury not being visible beneath his dark-blond hair.

'Fliss took the stitches out last night,' he said, resting the saddle on the ground before going into Arrow's yard. 'Girls back soon?'

'Monday. I can't wait.'

A too-brief smile shaped his lips as he slid on Arrow's bridle. 'I bet they can't either.'

'Your week away went well?' Neve passed him the saddle blanket. His serious eyes met hers. 'Yes … and no.'

'Are you going away … again?'

When his gaze flicked to her mouth she felt a rush of relief. The time apart hadn't defused the chemistry between them.

He turned to place the saddle blanket on Arrow's back and she lost sight of his expression. 'No. I'm here until the wedding. Denham needs me.'

She hefted the heavy saddle over the fence. 'So you'll be here for the races?'

He grimaced as he took hold of the saddle. 'Yes, even though becoming a hermit's still looking good. My photo's still apparently being shared.'

'You'll be fine, even if all the girls who say they're going to go do attend. We'll have your back.'

Tanner didn't reply as he lifted the saddle flap to do up the gelding's girth. He led Arrow out of the yard and stopped beside her. She breathed in the scent of leather and oilskin mingled with the fresh morning air. He was so close she could see the whiskers softening the firm line of his jaw. So close she could see the darker flecks in the pure blue of his eyes.

'I'd better get this clinic underway,' he said, voice low.

'Okay.'

She slid her hands into the pockets of her black coat and waited for him to lead Arrow away. With the new strain between them, she was back to feeling awkward and over-analysing everything she said.

She just needed a moment to collect herself and she'd head over to Freya and the horses.

But instead of moving, Tanner caught her chin and brushed his mouth over hers. His thumb caressed her jaw as his touch lingered. 'Everything's okay. It's just been another long week.'

She simply nodded. A reply of any sort wasn't possible. They weren't supposed to be acting on whatever this was between them. But it mattered, and mattered a lot, that he'd missed her and things were okay between them. She fell into step beside him. Even though she wasn't yet sure if the joy that unfurled within her could be trusted, she savoured the feeling that for a very brief moment all was complete in her world.

When they reached Freya, Tanner gave them each a nod before heading over to the arena.

Neve and Freya soon followed. As they joined the other riders in the arena, she glanced across at Freya. 'I see what you mean.'

'I know. Poor Tanner.'

Two willowy blondes, who looked like they'd stepped out of a glossy magazine with their immaculate cream jodhpurs and long black boots, were positioned on either side of him. One rode a white horse, the other a long-legged bay. Beside the girl on the left, Bethany sat on another well-groomed bay.

When Neve had briefly met Bethany in town with Edna, she hadn't smiled once. Now it was as though she was viewing a different person. Bethany's smile lit up her face and her laugh sounded loud and often.

Next to Bethany were a husband and wife dressed in country shirts, jeans and cowboy boots. Beside them Mac was still having trouble with his young chestnut, who couldn't seem to stand still. After a large gap, Sibylla Elliott, who had long ebony hair, stood in front of her Appaloosa. Even though her horse stayed still and didn't fuss, Sibylla's expression remained apprehensive.

Tanner wore a microphone, and as the group introduced themselves, Neve noticed Tanner ride around to stand beside Sibylla and her Appaloosa. His calm tone and humour soon had her relax. Neve focused on what he was saying as he outlined how the weekend would run and not on reliving when his mouth had covered hers.

As the morning progressed, Tanner spent time with each rider to assess their needs as well as those of their horses. By the end of the weekend they'd all have a toolbox of practical techniques, whatever stage they or their horses were at.

While Tanner worked with Freya, Neve talked to Sibylla. Across from them, Bethany chatted with her city friends in a tight-knit group. But when Bethany slightly turned to the right, the reason for her high spirits became obvious. It had just been a look, but when Mac's green horse had stood still for long enough, he and Bethany had swapped glances.

Even without knowing the rumour that Mac was seeing someone, Neve would have recognised the delight in Bethany's eyes. It was how she too felt when Tanner smiled at her. The million-dollar question was, did Edna know?

Tanner rode over to Neve. He'd left her and Jazz until last. She made sure she stayed relaxed in the saddle and her expression didn't change. Not only would Jazz sense any reaction she had to Tanner, half of Woodlea was watching from around the arena. Not to mention so too were the two blondes who hadn't made any effort to socialise with Freya, Sibylla or her.

Neve matched Tanner's professionalism as he went through what had brought her to the clinic and what she hoped to achieve out of the weekend. When they'd finished, he suggested they break for morning tea. As the other riders headed for the arena's exit, he remained next to her.

'Going okay?' he asked, his gaze holding hers.

'Yes. Really well. I have a question.'

He nodded.

'Bethany's Skittles ... there's a story there, isn't there?'

As she spoke she looked over to where Mac was talking to Freya, except his young horse wasn't happy at being left behind by the others.

Tanner followed the direction of her gaze. 'There is ... I think you've guessed the gist of it. Skittles is as sweet as his name. He can now bow, doesn't mind the noise of a drone and will be a perfect second pony for the girls.'

'You're a good man, Tanner Callahan.'

'I don't know about that. Bethany and Mac deserve to have a chance to be together.'

'Edna knows Mac's seeing someone.'

'Does she?' Tanner walked Arrow forward and Jazz followed. 'I'll give Bethany the heads-up.'

Freya waited for them, and once out of the arena gate, Neve and Freya rode over to their horse floats. After they'd made sure Jazz and Liberty had water and their girths were loosened, they went to collect Sibylla.

Sibylla was a coastal audiologist who'd returned home to help out on the family farm after her father had had a stroke. A bad fall when mustering cattle had left her terrified. Now that she knew she'd only be doing ground work and wouldn't have to ride, colour had returned to her face.

'You know,' she said, studying the crowd as they walked over for morning tea. 'Is it just me or is there a high percentage of female spectators.'

Freya smiled. 'This is nothing ... wait until the picnic races.'

Tanner had never been so glad to have a day at one of his clinics end. Tension burned across his shoulders and down his side. His body hadn't forgiven him for his lapse in concentration when walking on the air-seeder frame, even if he hadn't ended up with a black eye. He made no move to follow the others as they left the arena to unsaddle and shower before the campfire dinner.

He rubbed Arrow's neck and let out a slow breath. 'Sorry, buddy. I was a little distracted today.'

When he was sure he'd be clear to leave without being intercepted by the two city blondes, he too made his way through the arena gate. He'd had a quiet word to Mac at lunch and could now see Finn's Land Cruiser ute parked near his brother's float. There'd been a need to balance the male–female ratio. With any luck, Finn's country-boy charm and outgoing personality would keep Bethany's friends entertained.

Tanner headed Arrow away from the rodeo ground. As usual, he'd enjoyed working with his clients to help them connect with their horses in a respectful and positive way. As usual, he'd made sure he invested the same amount of time with each rider. Except unlike other clinics, there'd been a constant pull to be with Neve.

He'd deliberately left her until last whenever he could, but that hadn't stopped him from being distracted. He'd always prided himself on his single-mindedness. Today he'd only been focused on one thing: a woman with changeable green eyes and a sweet, soft mouth.

Once at Arrow's yard he unsaddled the mustang, rugged him and fed him his nightly biscuit of hay. He'd made sure he parked away from the main hub of horse floats. Even then the activity and noise made him yearn for the peace of the travelling stock routes. Except this trip away even the long paddock hadn't settled him, or led to any clarity or contentment. It had taken all of his willpower not to call Neve just to hear her voice.

Now he was home, his resolve to honour their agreement had lasted all of three minutes. When vulnerability had rounded her eyes and her tone had flattened, he'd been lost. He'd gone from keeping his distance to kissing her in a matter of heartbeats. He couldn't make the same mistake a second time.

The breeze carried the scent of steak and onion and the sound of feminine laughter. With a deep sigh he removed his hat and tunnelled a hand through his hair. Give him Denham's testy rodeo cattle any day over having to socialise with a crowd that whichever way he turned seemed intent on ending his bachelor status. At least after today's turnout, the shade sails for the playground would become a reality.

When he drew near to the barbeque area, the last of the sunlight was draining from the sky. Over near the campfire, Sibylla, Freya and Neve were deep in conversation. Bethany helped Mac over on the barbeque, while Finn sat in between the two blonde city girls. As he'd hoped, they didn't look his way as he walked past to see what he could do to help the dinner volunteers.

As darkness blanketed the rodeo ground, he managed to keep any conversation that involved hair twirling to a minimum. Over dinner he joined the husband and wife from Mudgee and their group of friends. For dessert he wasn't so lucky. Two cowgirls slipped into the spare chairs near him. When there wasn't room for a third girl, she sat on her friend's knee. While they'd chatted about horses, he stayed. But once the conversation turned to the races and meeting up with him at the bar, he came to his feet.

Neve had spent most of the night on the other side of the fire with Freya and Sibylla. She'd returned his smile when they'd stood in the steak-and-salad queue, but otherwise there'd been no contact between them. The breathing space had allowed him to regroup and his tension to defuse. Tomorrow was a new day and he'd handle being around her much better.

When the fire died to an orange glow and sparks no longer lit up the night sky, chairs emptied as people drifted off to bed. Bethany, Mac, Finn, the city blondes and a collection of others showed no signs of calling it a night. Laughter grew louder and stories more animated as the beer esky beside them emptied. After double-checking Neve's chair now sat empty, he too headed to his swag.

The squeal of a horse drew him to the centre of the yards. After spending time with Mac's young chestnut to reassure him, he ducked past Hewitt's float to make sure Jazz and Liberty weren't restless. In the moonlight he made out three swags. Neve, Freya and Sibylla looked to be asleep. But as he walked by a white light shone as someone read a book. Neve's red-gold hair glimmered.

The light moved as she sat up. 'Tanner?' she whispered.

He moved closer and kept his voice low. 'Can't sleep?'

'Not a wink. What are you doing?'

'Checking the horses.'

Canvas rustled as Freya rolled over.

'I'll come with you.' Neve flipped open her swag and stood.

In the pool of reading light he glimpsed pale, shapely legs as she pulled on jeans to wear with her long grey T-shirt.

After flicking off the reading light, she grabbed her boots and a jacket from the open horse float before coming over to him. They didn't speak as they walked. A horse stamped to their left and they changed direction to take a look. In the dim light the white splotches of Sibylla's Appaloosa gleamed as the gelding shuffled over to see them.

'We all had a great day today,' Neve said as she stroked the Appaloosa's neck.

'I hope so.'

'Sibylla was so worried she'd only last until lunchtime. I know you said you don't understand humans as much as you do horses, but you know, you're just as good with people.'

He was glad the poor light masked his expression. The sincerity and honesty in Neve's words moved him. He didn't think he could handle people well at all. Look at the mess he was in with his father. 'Thanks.'

He moved away to put distance between them. He'd already pushed the boundaries enough by giving in to his need to comfort her earlier.

They walked towards his float. Over in his yard, Arrow paced around the small space, his pale mane shimmering.

'I thought I wasn't sleepy,' Neve said as the mustang flung his head up high.

Tanner ran his palm over the palomino's warm neck. 'He'll settle when I'm in my swag.'

Arrow's ears flickered before he pushed his nose into Neve's hand. Her smile flashed as she stroked his cheek.

Tanner stayed quiet. Just like that morning when he'd come out of his float to the sight of Neve and Arrow together, another chunk of his defences fell away. The aloof mustang hadn't ever taken to another person the way he'd taken to Neve. Tanner wasn't the only one to recognise that she was special.

She stopped patting Arrow to smother a yawn.

'How about I walk you back?' he asked.

'Thanks, but I know the way. See you tomorrow.'

'You will. Sleep well.'

With a light touch to his hand, she slipped into the darkness.

Long after Neve had left and Arrow had settled, Tanner lay in his swag and stared at the jagged void of the distant ridge. Just like the granite landscape etched against the night sky, he had to stay resolute. He couldn't listen to the whispers of his loneliness that just maybe he could trust Neve to stay in his life.

He was glad the moonlight masked his expression. The sincerity and honesty he pictured would rob him of his right. He didn't need a handsome profile. All he offered Neve was a steady hand to hold.

It was no surprise that when Tanner saw Neve the following morning at breakfast his eyes were gritty and his jaw tight. He made himself an extra-strong coffee. He'd only taken a mouthful when an exuberant voice called out, 'Why there you are, Tanner.'

It wasn't his imagination that the people around him suddenly needed to be somewhere else. Edna sailed over to him, her smile too bright for that time of the day. He hoped Mac and Bethany realised she was there.

'Morning, Edna.'

'Good morning to you too, Tanner. And what a fine morning it is.'

He hoped his stiff nod passed as an agreement.

Edna barely drew a breath before she continued. 'Bethany tells me everything's going well.'

'Thanks to Bethany, it is. All I've had to do is turn up.'

Edna's smile beamed. 'I'll be sure to pass on your kind words. The two of you make the perfect team.' She paused, her eyes narrowing as she stared past his shoulder. 'I didn't realise the Barton boys would be here.'

Tanner took another swallow of coffee. 'Mac brought his green broke horse to the clinic. Finn came for the barbeque and camped.'

Edna didn't reply, just continued to stare in the direction of the horse floats behind him. He casually turned to see which Barton boy had caught Edna's attention. If it was Mac, chances were Bethany was with him. But it was Finn who sauntered over to breakfast, flanked by the two city blondes.

'Edna … Clive might be known around the district as a tough man to deal with, but Mac and Finn are decent blokes.'

'That's a matter of opinion.' Edna glanced back at him, her gaze having lost none of its sharpness. 'Now where do you think I'd find Bethany?'

The appearance of Neve, Freya and Sibylla saved him from answering.

'Morning, Edna,' Freya said, her voice sunny.

'Good morning, Freya.' Edna gave Neve a quick glance. 'Neve.' Her attention then homed in on Sibylla. 'Nice to see you again, Sibylla. How's your father doing?'

'Good, thanks.'

Edna seemed to have forgotten all about finding Bethany. She linked her arm with Sibylla's. 'How about you and I get a nice cup of tea and you fill me in on what you've been doing since you've been home. I believe you've been over at Hugh's helping out with little Riley …'

Neve and Freya exchanged glances before they set off to save Sibylla from one of Edna's interrogations that could last far longer than one cup of tea.

Hair wet, Bethany emerged from the shower block. At Tanner's pointed nod towards her mother, she hurried over to her float.

Tanner finished his coffee.

By the time Edna had left and the second day of his clinic was underway, the double hit of caffeine had cleared the fog from his head. Just like on the previous day, he worked with each rider and their horse in a combination of ground skills and riding exercises. In Sibylla's case he kept to ground work to restore her confidence and to rebuild the trust between her Appaloosa and her.

Just like the day before, he also remained hyper aware of Neve. But unlike yesterday, Bethany's two friends concentrated on their horses instead of on monopolising his attention. And luckily, Mac's young horse also stood still.

After an early lunch, he took everyone out on the nearby travelling stock route to have a break from the intensity of the arena activities. To his delight, Sibylla asked if she could ride beside him.

By the time they'd reached the creek and the horses' hooves clattered on the rounded pebbles, Sibylla rode in between Freya and Neve. The tension that had stiffened her spine had given way to a more natural posture. But every so often, especially when her horse stumbled, she'd chew on her bottom lip.

They continued along the stock route and at a clearing dismounted for a break. From his saddlebag he took out apples and shortbread biscuits. Bethany handed out the bottles of water that had filled her saddlebag. While the group relaxed on the tree trunks that framed the grassed area, Tanner's phone beeped. The horses had needed to climb to reach the elevated clearing which now provided a few bars of phone signal.

When he saw two messages from his father he opened the first one. He ground his teeth. No wonder his father hadn't been in touch with Neve. He'd been hospitalised with pneumonia. The concise wording of his message indicated that any inquiries about his health wouldn't be appreciated. The second message related to information he'd found out about the aircraft engine plate.

Feeling Neve's eyes on him, Tanner looked across to where she sat with Freya and Sibylla.

'Everything okay?' she asked, her apple halfway to her mouth.

He nodded. As terse as his father could be, the hospital wouldn't have let him home if his health hadn't improved. He'd earlier heard Neve filling Freya and Sibylla in on her family mystery so knew it was okay to pass on what his father had discovered.

'He has some news on the engine plate ...' Tanner read out the message. 'The engine plaque is from a de Havilland plane, but it isn't a match to the de Havilland Tiger Moths that were used at the flying school.' Tanner glanced at Neve. 'He also can't think of a reason why a different wartime aircraft would have been out this way in 1945.'

'So here's another thing that doesn't add up.' A small frown creased Neve's brow. 'The engine plate would have to have belonged to Edward's plane. There's no other reason why my grandmother would have kept it.'

'That's right.' Tanner checked his phone as another text came in. 'He's looking into the possibility that your grandmother's Edward Jones was involved in some sort of secret mission.'

'See, I said there was something top secret going on,' Sibylla said with a knowing nod.

Neve's frown cleared. 'That would explain why there's nothing about what he did during the war or why he was here from the United Kingdom.'

'I love mysteries. Maybe it's because I can get a little obsessive.' Freya stood to dust off her jeans. 'I'm pretty sure one of the boys at school said after the spring floods he and his father fished an old aircraft wing out of a creek somewhere near Shingle Bend.'

Tanner sent a reply to his father before returning his phone to his shirt pocket. 'Shingle Bend's a reserve on another travelling stock route. There's also what's left of some Second World War hideaways where wartime planes were hidden. I keep meaning to take a closer look and send photos to my father.'

Neve came to her feet, having saved her apple core to feed to Jazz. 'Imagine if that was where Edward's plane was hidden.'

Freya's eyes shone. 'I'm free either Saturday or Sunday. We could take the horses.'

Sibylla sighed. 'Count me out. My nerves wouldn't survive. But I hope it's not too long until we can go on some trail rides together.'

Neve's gaze rested on him. 'No one knows the stock routes like you do …'

He took his time to answer to fool himself that he hadn't already made the decision to go. He was powerless to pass up an opportunity to spend time with her, even if it was only for a day and even if it was the last thing he should be doing. At least if Freya came, there'd be three of them.

'Okay. I'll drive. We can take my horse truck.'

CHAPTER

15

'Have a great weekend. See you Monday.' Neve hugged Maya, savouring the tightness of her embrace. The first week of Maya and Kait being back had passed in a flurry of pink glitter, cake baking and pony rides.

'Me too.' Kait jumped up and down. Her tiny boots thumped on the veranda floorboards. 'I want a hug.'

The fortnight away had been kind to the girls and to Graham. Building sandcastles, swimming in the waves and strolling along the beach had added a healthy glow to their skin. Maya and Kait even seemed to have grown. Graham's smile still could appear strained, but the weariness that had lined and thinned his face had diminished.

Neve loosened her hold on Maya, who moved to take her father's hand where he stood on the top step. Kait launched herself into Neve's arms. She bent to hold the three-year-old close. The girls used a berry kids' shampoo and they always smelled of fruity sweetness.

'I'll see you Monday too,' Neve said against Kait's ear.

The softness of Kait's red curls tickled Neve's cheek as the little girl nodded.

'Enjoy your ride out at Shingle Bend,' Graham said before he turned with the girls to walk along the garden path.

Neve blew each little redhead a kiss as they looked back at her. 'I will.'

When all that remained visible of Graham's four-wheel drive was the faint glow of tail-lights, she returned inside. The days were getting shorter and the evenings possessed a distinct winter chill. The forecasted weather now contained more references to cloud and rain than sunshine and clear skies. The broad leaves of the ornamental grape alongside the house were no longer a summer green but instead a deep purple and russet red.

Over in the orchard Dell and Bassie stood together near the lemon tree. In the paddock behind the round yard, Neve could make out Jazz's grey shape near the fence line. The girls had helped to feed the two horses and donkey and to put on their rugs. Bassie continued to behave beautifully around Maya and Kait. It was only when Neve put on his rug that he would think about walking off mid-buckle.

As she entered the farm house, the heat from the fire in the living room warmed her. She made her way to the toy corner where she scooped up the picture books that had fallen off the bookshelf and returned the plastic tea set to the container shaped like a teapot. After two weeks of having a too-tidy home, the farmhouse again felt lived in.

But after a fortnight of silence she also now looked forward to a quiet evening after the girls had gone. No longer did she fill every moment of her alone time to make it go faster. Now she appreciated having nothing planned and no urgent to-do list. She was learning to let life happen and to value her own company.

She was now onto her second scarf and Fliss had given her some tips to help her trace Edward Jones's family tree. She'd discovered one of his younger sisters was alive and living in the United Kingdom. The next step was to confirm her address.

She placed another log on the fire and was turning on her laptop when her mobile rang. She answered the call and settled herself on the lounge. It was Ella and she hadn't spoken to the vet for a week.

'Hi, stranger.'

'Hi. How's our donkey mother-to-be?'

'Going well. Are you sure she isn't having twins?'

Ella laughed. 'I'm sure. She would have had a foal before, that's why she's not as trim, taut and terrific as she was. How's Bassie?'

'He's been very well-behaved, which makes me suspicious. We've been riding every day, except this week when we lost a couple of days thanks to the rain.'

'Tanner still giving the girls lessons?'

Neve wasn't sure, but there could have been curiosity in Ella's question.

'Not since he went droving as he's been busy helping Denham get ready for the wedding. He's hoping to fit one in next week.'

'It's good he's back. Even though with all the social media fuss I bet he wishes he wasn't. Yes, I think they've been stick picking and slashing. Getting married in a paddock isn't as fuss-free as it sounds.'

'I'm sure it isn't. Glamping will be so much fun though.'

'It will be. Before I forget, there's plenty of room for Sibylla to sit with us at the picnic races.'

Ella had booked a track-side private table that came with a gourmet lunchtime hamper.

'Wonderful. I'll let her know. When I moved here, I had no idea my social life would be so hectic.'

'It will quieten down over winter so that's even more of a reason to make the most of what's on now. What are you doing this weekend?'

'Tomorrow Freya and I are going with Tanner to somewhere called Shingle Bend.'

'Are you now?'

This time Neve had no trouble hearing the curiosity in Ella's words.

'We're taking the horses and looking at the aircraft hideaways. Would you like to come?'

'I would, but I'm on call so will be working. Have a lovely day out.'

'Will do. Are we still meeting at your place before the races?'

'Yes. I hope you're not allergic to hairspray? Taylor's offered to do our hair. Needless to say, Fliss said she'd think about it.'

Neve smiled. Fliss and Taylor had a long-running joke about what Fliss saw as the hairdresser's hairspray obsession. 'Taylor styling our hair will be a treat. I'd better let you go. You could be in for a busy weekend.'

'Yes, I'd best have an early night. There's a mare due to foal and no doubt I'll get a pre-dawn phone call.'

'Hope you're not up too early. See you next Saturday.'

Neve ended the call. She should have an early night too as Tanner would be there first thing to pick up Jazz. But the flutter in her stomach and the kick in her pulse at the thought of seeing him tomorrow didn't give her any hope that sleep would be easy to come by.

As arranged, Tanner arrived while the dew was still wet and Neve's breaths formed delicate white clouds. The garden kookaburras gave a sleepy cackle and the seed pods on the golden robinia rattled in the stiff breeze as she led Jazz from her paddock to the horse truck. Bassie trotted along the fence line to check out what was happening. Dell stayed near the lemon tree, and after an inquisitive look went back to sleeping.

Neve waved at Freya, who sat in the passenger seat. Tanner greeted Neve with a smile before he reached for Jazz's lead rope. The mare nuzzled his sleeve.

This morning he wore a heavy navy jacket with his usual jeans and boots and his head was bare.

'Cold enough for you?' he asked, his breaths turning white.

Neve rubbed her icy hands together to give herself something to do besides staring. It had been another week since she'd seen him and missing him had become an almost physical ache.

'It is. Jack Frost will have to be visiting soon. I'll grab my backpack and will be right to go. Patch not coming with us today?'

'No, he's stayed behind to help Phil move cattle.'

She should turn to leave but instead she stayed still. This perhaps would be the only time they'd be alone. 'Thanks for doing this.'

'No worries. How was your week with the girls being back?'

'Busy but fun. How was yours?'

'Busy but not always so fun … Denham and I had our last suit fitting and Fliss handed us a colour-coded five-page to-do list.'

Neve smiled. 'I can only imagine. I can't believe that the wedding is only two weeks away. I told Fliss to make sure she gave me some jobs to do too.'

He nodded, his gaze holding hers. 'She said you offered to help and has us working together on a few things … if this isn't okay let me know.'

She searched his features for a sign as to whether this was good or bad, but his expression revealed nothing.

'I don't mind … if you don't.'

Something flared in his eyes but was quickly doused. 'I don't.'

'Great.' Then knowing that her own face would reveal just how much she didn't mind, she turned away. 'I'd better get my backpack before frostbite sets in.'

With her bag stowed and the heat of the horse truck cabin thawing her fingers and toes, Neve sat back and relaxed for the drive to the reserve. The early-morning shadows gave way to clear daylight as the clouds lifted and the day warmed.

Tanner caught up to an old Hilux, not quite doing the speed limit. In the back rode a gold-and-white border collie. The dog, chained in the middle, went from one side of the trayback to the other. His doggy grin widened as he barked at a passing car.

'Someone's enjoying the ride,' Freya said, a smile in her voice.

The Hilux put on its blinker to turn into a farm gateway. A second dog popped up its head.

'There can't be any more in there.' Neve hadn't finished speaking when a third dog, a kelpie, appeared. All three dogs barked as Tanner drove by.

The road ahead again stretched in an empty ribbon-straight line.

Tanner slowed before turning to follow a dirt track that led towards the river. When the bush opened up into a large clearing, Tanner continued along to a second smaller clearing. Red, blue and yellow flashed as eastern rosellas left the fence they'd been perched on.

'Shingle Bend's popular for swimming and fishing, but not as many people drive this far in so we should have this place to ourselves,' Tanner said as he parked in the shade of a grey box tree.

'I can see why it's popular.' Neve stared out the window at the sandy curve of the riverbank that resembled a beach. With its unhurried flow and deep waterholes, this section of the river was scenic as well as accessible. High on the opposite steep bank, a line of sticks and debris marked the level of the spring floodwater that had revealed the aircraft wing.

They left the horse truck to unload the horses. Jazz and Liberty strolled down the ramp, their ears flickering and eyes curious. Arrow pranced out, unimpressed he'd been inside for so long.

The horses were soon saddled and saddlebags filled. By now the sun had chased away the winter chill and jackets had been discarded.

'It's going to be such a nice day,' Freya said as she settled into Liberty's saddle.

Neve only nodded. She'd led Jazz over to a rock that was the right height to help her get onto the mare. In the grass beside her, she heard a click before something small and brown hit the side of her boot.

As she stared, another locust flitted from one grass clump to another. Across the clearing, she caught more movement as tiny bodies flew out of Tanner and Arrow's way. While she wouldn't call this a swarm, there were enough locusts to make her worry about her garden if they migrated her way. She climbed into the saddle and headed Jazz over to where Tanner and Freya waited for her.

She snuck a sideways glance at Tanner. She'd never get tired of seeing him on a horse. Even with his shoulders relaxed and his forearms resting on the front of his stock saddle, he projected an impression of power and capability. It would only take a split second for him and Arrow to explode into action. No wonder Cressy said they were campdrafting champions.

Tanner led the way along the shaded track that followed the river and then veered inland. Neve caught the scent of honey and heard the buzz of bees. There had to be a nearby beehive in a tree hollow.

She patted Jazz's neck as some swamp wallabies bounded through the wattle trees to their left. But the mare wasn't concerned. Her stride had a youthful swing and her grey ears were relaxed and forward. Tanner wasn't the only one to enjoy being out on the long paddock.

After riding deeper into the bush, Tanner stopped at what looked like a pair of post stumps. 'There's not much left of this first hideaway.' He snapped some pictures on his phone. 'These posts supported a camouflage canopy that would have concealed the planes from the air.'

Neve also took some pictures. 'I wouldn't have given these stumps a second look.'

'I wouldn't have either.' Freya rode closer to study the post near her.

They continued on and this time Neve would have mistaken the hideaway for a tangled disused fence. Bundles of rusted wire were coiled in a pile and choked with hairy panic grass.

Tanner nodded towards a tree to the left. 'Here the wire mesh supporting the camouflage netting would have been strung between the tree and the post. The plane would have been parked on this horseshoe-shaped patch of gravel.'

Neve studied Tanner as he dismounted to take photos. The fact that he was so knowledgeable about the hideaways proved how much he'd tried to find common ground with his father. She hoped through their conversations about Edward Jones that a new beginning could be brokered between them.

She too left the saddle. Jazz followed her as she walked over to the post in line with the tree. Neve pressed her fingertips against the rough, weathered wood. The post had been buried deep in the red earth at a time of profound turmoil and unrest. How many young men had stood where she was and, stomach tight, scanned the sky. Had Edward been here while her grandmother had waited for him at their home?

She closed her eyes. So many lives lost. So many families fractured. So many relationships ripped apart just like her beloved grandmother's.

'Neve?' Tanner's deep voice sounded close by.

She opened her eyes. 'It feels so real.'

'It does.' His arm lifted. She thought he was going to cover her hand that rested on the post with his, but then he stepped away. 'The day's heating up. It might be an idea to head to the river for an early lunch?'

She nodded and with a last look at the hideaway returned to Jazz's saddle. Tanner rode alongside her. When the conversation turned from the sadness of war to the promise of weddings, he and Arrow continued on ahead.

The closer they rode to the river the louder the screech of the cockatoos congregated in the treetops. The hot sun on her shoulders was soon replaced by the cool of shade as they wound their way through the red river gums.

Just like where they'd left the horse truck, the riverbank gave way to a thin sandy beach. Arrow had already negotiated the steep slope and had his head down drinking in the shallows. Neve reined in Jazz to let Liberty and Freya go first. She waited until they'd reached the water's edge before following. One minute Jazz was picking her way down the bank. The next minute she'd stumbled and Neve was falling.

She hit rock-hard earth. Pain vibrated through her hip before momentum flung her onto coarse sand. Stunned, she lay still, gravel biting into her cheek. Then strong, gentle hands helped her into a sitting position.

'Jazz ...' she managed. All the breath had been slammed from her lungs.

Tanner's arms encircled her. 'She's over with Freya and is fine. Are you okay?'

She gave in to the need to rest her head against the solid wall of his chest. The steady thud of his heart drowned out the ringing in her ears.

'Neve?'

She didn't realise she hadn't spoken until his hoarse voice rasped her name.

She eased herself away. His eyes were so grave it was as though she were staring at a sky devoid of all light.

'I'm ... okay.'

Her words didn't relax the grooves slashed beside his mouth.

He brushed the sand from her cheek, his thumb caressing her skin. 'It doesn't hurt anywhere?'

She shook her head. She was sure her hip soon would, but with Tanner holding her as though she was both precious and rare she felt no pain. He smelled of leather and sunshine, and she'd never wanted anything more than to stay within the circle of his arms.

His intent gaze raked over her face. 'Can you stand?'

She nodded.

He eased her to her feet, and even when she was standing, he supported her. It was only when she dusted off the dirt from the front of her shirt that his arms dropped away. Without the warmth of his embrace she shivered.

Needing to check on Jazz, she hobbled over to where the mare stood beside Freya and Liberty.

'What were we saying about not being able to walk after the clinic?' she said with a grimace as the school teacher passed her Jazz's reins.

Freya gave her a concerned look. 'Are you really okay? You hit the ground pretty hard.'

Neve stroked Jazz's neck to reassure herself that the mare was fine. 'I will be once I've soaked in a hot bath.'

From the corner of her eye she saw Tanner swing into Arrow's saddle. As okay as she was, she wasn't so sure about him. She'd never seen his face so grim, his shoulders so rigid or the line of his jaw so taut.

Tanner stared at the long afternoon shadows draped over the bitumen. His thoughts were chaotic and his body felt like he'd been the one to smash into the riverbank. It was a relief to finally have the horse-truck cabin to himself.

He'd made sure he'd delivered Neve and Jazz home first. It didn't matter how cheerful her conversation was, the liveliness in her green eyes had dimmed. Her smile also hadn't shone as bright when she'd refused his help to leave the passenger seat. The way she'd held herself as she'd then stood in front of him suggested her right hip had been giving her problems.

But no matter how much pain she'd been in, her voice had remained steady. 'Thanks again for today. I really enjoyed the ride and seeing the hideaways.'

'You're welcome. I hope you're not too sore tomorrow.'

'I'll be fine.'

Her use of Fliss's least favourite word hadn't generated any amusement. Uncaring that Freya was nearby, he'd pressed a kiss to her forehead. 'If you need anything, call.'

'I will.'

When Freya had then walked with Neve over to the farm-house, he'd taken Jazz past the round yard and over to her paddock. After he'd dropped off Freya and Liberty at Drew's, he'd made a call to Dr Fliss. On her way back from town, Fliss would swing past Rosewood to check on Neve.

He eased his clamped grip on the steering wheel and sat back in his seat. But even with such physical cues to relax, his emotions remained as tightly strung as new fence wire. The memory of Jazz tripping and the horror of knowing that Neve would fall was only matched by his feelings of powerlessness. He couldn't get to her in time.

As if in slow motion he'd seen her slam into the bank before tumbling down the slope to land in the river sand. His heartbeat had amplified in his ears and his mouth had become parched. He'd witnessed horse-riding accidents before, but never had the sight of a rider being thrown from the saddle filled him with such deep-seated fear.

On autopilot, he turned onto the back road that would lead to Claremont. He scraped a hand over his aching jaw. This time he really was going to have to sneak into his flat. Meredith would sense he was rattled the second he stepped out of his ute.

The answer as to why he felt so out of control slipped into his subconscious with the silence of a winter snow fall.

It mattered so much that Neve could have been hurt because there was a name for the emotion that consumed and rocked him.

Love.

As hard as he'd fought, and as much as he'd kept his distance, the end result had been inevitable. The love he'd believed he'd felt once before was nothing compared to the depth of what he felt for Neve. From the outset, she'd drawn him to her with her sweetness, compassion and warmth. He didn't think there'd ever be a time when he'd look into her green eyes and not feel as though he'd forgotten to draw breath.

His sigh was part groan. The battle to keep his emotional distance had been lost. Now his self-preservation and emotions were locked in a war over a way forward.

Heart heavy, he turned past the drystone wall of Claremont's front gate. The tips of the poplars along the driveway were now winter bare and golden leaves carpeted the ground.

Meredith waved at him from over near the rose garden. He forced his shoulders to lower as he waved in return. After he'd unloaded Arrow, he took his time to unpack and clean the truck.

As he walked over from the stables, Meredith came to meet him.

'How was your day?' She sat the basket she carried on the ground. To his relief, her attention didn't linger on his face.

'Neve had a fall but says she's okay.'

Concern furrowed Meredith's brow. 'What do you think?'

'She will be sore, but nothing's broken. I still gave Fliss a call.'

'I would have too.' Meredith glanced at where he'd hit his head. 'Dr Fliss's been in demand.'

'She has.' He half turned. He needed a shower, a cold beer and space to sort out his thoughts.

'Tanner ...' He stiffened at the seriousness in Meredith's voice. 'That would have been hard, seeing Neve hurt.'

He went to shrug, but that was the coward's way to answer. He faced Meredith again. 'It was ... I couldn't stop it from happening.'

Meredith bent to pick up the basket that was full of carrots from the vegetable garden. It was as though she sensed the more she looked at him the less he'd talk. 'That's not a very nice feeling.'

'It isn't.'

'Tanner ... you're just like your father. You're one of the strongest men I know, both physically and mentally. But ... at the end of the day we're all human.'

Even though her words related to not being able to stop Neve falling, they were now on a different topic.

Meredith adjusted her hold on her basket. 'And that isn't a bad thing. Being vulnerable, doubting ourselves, being uncertain all lead to growth and empathy. They also lead to ... connection.'

Tanner nodded. Anything he said would only emerge as a rasp. His emotions remained too raw.

'It's okay you didn't get to Neve in time. You didn't fail her ... or yourself.' Meredith's earnest gaze held his. 'I'm saying this out of love ... but you will fail her ... and you ... if you keep on leaving. As much as you've both been fighting it, there's something real and special between you ... something I thought I'd never find again.'

Sadness deepened the lines in Meredith's face, making her appear years older. There was no doubt about how much she'd loved his birth father.

'I hear what you're saying.'

'I hope you do, sweetheart because as difficult as it might seem I've no doubt you have the strength ... to stay.' She gave a small smile as she moved forward to pat his chest. 'Right, maternal talk's over, you can relax.'

He gave a hoarse laugh. 'I wish.'

Sympathy softened her mouth. 'Keep busy, that's what your father used to do when he had things to think over.' She glanced at the sky that was now more grey than blue. 'It's getting late. Reggie will want his carrots.'

'Here, I'll take them. I need hay out of the shed anyway.' Tanner reached for the basket. 'Is it Reggie's birthday?'

Meredith's light laughter took the edge off his strain. 'Reggie wishes. They're not all for him, some are for dinner and a carrot cake.'

'Okay.' Tanner paused. 'Thanks for … the talk.'

'You know I'm always here for you.'

He gave her a kiss on her cheek before heading inside. Once he'd cut up some carrots, he made his way through the house to where his ute was parked out the back.

Meredith's wisdom had helped make sense of his emotions. His thoughts no longer raced in top gear. He hadn't failed Neve or let her down. He passed a hand around the back of his neck. But as for Meredith's faith that he had the strength to stay, he wasn't so sure he shared her optimism. The only way he knew to keep himself safe was to make sure he had his freedom. Also, Neve might not feel the same deep emotions as he did. After their kiss she'd been open in saying now wasn't a good time for anything to start between them.

He'd just reached his ute when his phone chimed in quick succession. The first text was from Fliss confirming that Neve hadn't done any serious damage. He texted a reply. The second message was from Neve.

*When Fliss has her doctor hat on she isn't to be messed with.*

He replied: *She isn't. How's the hip?*

*Unimpressed my knees didn't hold on tighter.*

He typed again: *Need help feeding the troops?*

*All sorted.*

He hesitated. Meredith's words echoed in his head. He texted a quick reply. *See you at races?*

*Yes. Looking forward to it.*

This time there was no hesitation. He sent an emoji of a thumbs up, which didn't fully represent the degree of his happiness at her answer. After there were no further texts he opened the ute door.

When he reached Reggie's paddock the rodeo bull was pacing along the fence line. The Brahman-cross speared him a glare as he approached.

'I know, Reg. Your carrots are late.'

The bull pawed the ground.

'Don't worry, I'm not even going to try to feed you today.' He tossed a chunk of carrot behind Reggie, anticipating the bull would swing around as usual. The carrot landed with a dull thud. Reggie shook his massive head.

'Right ... you mustn't have seen me throw that one.'

He held up a piece of carrot for Reggie to see and then threw it more slowly. Still Reggie didn't turn to eat the carrots.

'Okaaay.'

Tanner took another carrot out of the bucket. Reggie shifted closer to the fence and hung his head over.

'You're kidding.' He moved forward to offer Reggie the carrot. '*Now* you want to be fed?'

The bull ate the carrot out of his hand. He fed him another and another. By the time the bucket was empty, he was rubbing the whorl high on Reggie's grey forehead. 'So you accept me now, do you? Go figure.'

Reggie blew into his empty palm before leaning closer to have his neck scratched.

Tanner smiled, both at the bull's blissful expression and at the thought that Denham and Hewitt could no longer rib him about not passing the Reggie test. He was man enough for any relationship.

His heart thundered against his chest. Now he just had to silence his fears and go after the woman he loved.

'I don't even think a cyclone will move my hair.' Neve raised a hand to touch her low, messy bun.

Despite the persistence of the midday breeze and the walk into the Woodlea racecourse, there wasn't a hair out of place.

'Mine either.' Ella smoothed the casual French twist below her powder-blue fascinator. 'I'm starting to understand about Taylor's hairspray obsession.'

Beside them Fliss ran her hand through her glossy hair that Taylor had styled into loose, soft waves. Her race-day fascinator featured a white orchid on a small bone-coloured hat. 'And you wondered why I left my chair as soon as Taylor reached for the can.'

Neve laughed and adjusted her headband that sported delicate silk flowers in a creamy beige. 'All jokes aside, Taylor does do the most incredible job.'

'She does.' Fliss paused to wave at Cressy. 'Wait until you see our hair at the wedding.'

Cressy turned to smile at them from where she stood beside Denham over near the racetrack fence. Today the cowgirl wore a classic black-and-white dress and fuss-free fascinator. The side fishtail braid Taylor had completed with quick and efficient fingers lay draped over Cressy's left shoulder.

Ella scanned the brooding, gunmetal-grey sky. 'I hope it's not like this next weekend for Cressy's big day. I also hope this weather holds today, otherwise not even Taylor's hairspray will help if it rains.'

Neve nodded. 'I was thinking the same thing.'

The wind collected beneath the skirt of her A-line teal dress and rushed over the skin of her shoulders, which were left bare by the low back. It wouldn't be long before she'd be wearing the black jacket she was glad she'd brought.

Fliss studied a nearby crowd of girls, who all sported a fluorescent-blue wristband that confirmed they were over eighteen. Most were dressed in short jumpsuits, brown ankle boots and wore floppy felt hats over their straightened hair. 'I know this makes me sound old—they all look so beautiful—but if this weather changes they'll freeze.'

Ella sighed. 'Oh to be young again.'

Neve swapped a look with Fliss. Sadness had crept into Ella's usually upbeat voice. They both looped their arms through the vet's.

'I for one am quite happy being the age I am,' Fliss said. 'All that self-consciousness and doubt. No thank you.'

Neve and Ella both stopped to stare at Fliss. Headstrong and assertive, Fliss gave the impression she'd never had a day of uncertainty in her life.

'What?' she said, looking between the two of them. 'Ask Cressy. I was a complete nerd with my head in a book, oblivious to any signals from the opposite sex. I'd wonder why at a college social function guys would ask if I wanted a drink after only one dance together. I used to think they lacked stamina and were definitely not boyfriend material.'

Neve joined in with Ella's burst of laughter as the vet hugged Fliss. 'Fliss, you're priceless. Lucky for Hewitt you got up to speed on those male signals.'

Their arms again linked, they continued towards the distant marquee.

'Speaking of Hewitt …' Neve said, looking over to where Hewitt stood with Mac Barton and the horse chiropractor, Hugh. All wore wheat-coloured chinos, boots and various shades of crisp cotton dress shirts with ties.

'He wasn't too late after all.'

Hewitt had called while Taylor had been styling their hair to say he'd hoped to get there by mid-afternoon as a water pipe had broken.

Fliss nodded. 'He wasn't, thanks to Denham dropping round to help him.'

Feminine laughter sounded and Neve glanced at four women as they exchanged hugs. This sophisticated collection of racegoers possessed a city polish and confidence. All were tanned, athletic and gorgeous. Despite the height of their heels, their shoes wouldn't be off by the end of the night like some of the local cowgirls.

Ella whistled softly. 'They aren't from around here. Look at those clothes, they're high-end designer labels. Tanner might not like being the race-day drawcard, but every single guy here today will be buying him a beer.'

Neve frowned as she looked past the glamorous women. She tried not to make it obvious that she was looking for someone. Ever since they'd left Ella's four-wheel drive, she'd been keeping a careful watch for Tanner.

The past week of taking it easy to allow her bruised hip to heal had clarified one thing. She wasn't the same person she'd been when she'd arrived. Having time on her hands no longer filled her with dread. Her newfound peace proved that her feelings for Tanner weren't a response to any fear of being alone or need for stability. The knowledge legitimised the pull she felt towards him and reassured her that her emotions were genuine. She was complete without him.

Fliss led the way past the bookmakers, where hopeful punters were placing their bets, and then past the bar that already had drawn a sizeable clientele. Neve again searched the crowd. There remained no sign of Tanner.

Now that she had no doubt that what she felt was real, her regret grew over their agreement to not act upon their chemistry. But, despite the way he touched her and his concerned tenderness, she couldn't assume that he too felt the same. There also remained the very real issue that, even if he had changed his mind, he wouldn't be looking for anything permanent or serious.

Ahead of them, a white marquee gleamed against the red dirt of the racetrack. Tables and chairs dotted the section of lawn in front of the marquee that was enclosed by a picket fence. Crisp white tablecloths rippled in the wind. Leafy greenery in stylish pots prevented the tablecloths from taking flight.

Freya waved from where she sat with Drew at a table that overlooked the racetrack. While Drew and Ella went to the marquee bar in search of drinks, Fliss and Neve sat opposite Freya.

Fliss took out a selection of cheese and dips from their gourmet table hamper. 'These all look delicious.'

'I know, I've been eyeing off those baguettes.' Freya peered into the basket. 'Although now those wraps also look mouth-watering.'

While they enjoyed the cheese and dips, talk turned to who was still to arrive. Neve kept her expression neutral when Fliss mentioned there'd been no sign of Tanner yet. Thankfully, Ella and Drew returned with bottles of wine and champagne and the conversation lapsed as drinks were poured.

Neve's phone chimed as a text came through. Sibylla had arrived after taking her father to Dubbo for an early medical appointment. Neve excused herself before she went to meet the audiologist at the entry gate.

A crowd now congregated around a makeshift stage that featured a line of well-dressed girls and boys. All had tags pinned to the front of their dresses or small suit coats as the winners of the children's section of the fashions on the field were announced.

She could only imagine the competition for the Fashionable Filly section. She scanned the sizeable throng of racegoers.

For every pair of masculine shoulders there were at least three well-groomed young women. She couldn't blame Tanner if he'd decided not to come after all.

Then she saw him. No wonder she hadn't caught sight of him earlier. Today he wore a fawn wide-brimmed hat that she hadn't seen before. He stood alongside Finn and both men were partially obscured by a bevy of women. Even as she watched, a striking brunette ran her hands through her long hair and laughed at something he'd said. Her body was angled towards him, making it clear she liked what she saw. She wasn't the only one. A petite blonde leaned in close to adjust the navy tie he wore.

Neve's steps slowed. She'd told Edna that she'd have Tanner's back, but by anyone's definition he didn't look like he needed saving. The brunette again lifted an arm and this time curled her fingers around Tanner's left biceps with a teasing pout. He gave her the same easy grin that had moved Neve on the first day she'd seen him in Woodlea.

Something inside her shrivelled and died. Tanner was so out of her league. She forced her feet to move. He could have any woman he wanted. What had she been thinking? With every step the heartbreaking answer became clear. She hadn't been thinking, she'd just been hoping, because … she loved him.

From the beginning Tanner had unsettled her and skewed her judgement. All along she'd known someone like him wasn't meant for someone like her. But she'd ignored reason and common sense to invest in their friendship and connection. Now she hadn't just lost her way, but also her heart.

Her hands curled into fists as she walked. The colours on the racing silks of the jockeys near the stables didn't seem as bright. The laughter of the children blowing bubbles nearby didn't seem as musical.

A familiar heavy fragrance scented the breeze before Edna called out her name. She slowly turned, hoping the makeup she wore would conceal her distress. 'Hi, Edna, I was just thinking about you.'

'Were you now?' Edna stopped in front of her. She was wearing an eye-catching purple outfit with a matching oversized feathered hat.

'Yes. I've seen Tanner and he seems fine, even though he does have quite an audience.'

Neve expected Edna to frown and look around, or at the least ask where the drover was. Instead, the older woman's attention swept over her hair and face. 'Don't you look nice. I see so much of your grandmother in you.'

'Thank you.' Neve touched her floral headband. 'Ella found the dress online and Taylor did my hair.'

'So Tanner's not looking like he'd rather be anywhere else but here?'

'Not that I could see.'

'Well, it isn't even lunchtime so keep a close watch on him. Bethany should make it here for the last race.'

Neve excused herself with what she hoped passed as a normal smile. Her facial muscles felt far too stiff. 'I'd better keep moving. I have to meet Sibylla.'

'Yes, off you go. I've just seen Mrs Knox. I must see how she's going. Harriet has broken off her engagement.'

As Neve continued towards the entrance she drew a deep breath and squared her shoulders. It was inevitable she'd see Tanner. When she did, she'd have to hide how she felt and that things had changed between them. Somehow, she'd have to get through the day with her composure and dignity intact. It would be the only way to protect her secret that she loved him.

Sibylla stood by the entry gate. When she saw Neve she gave her a warm smile. Her ebony hair curled around her shoulders, adding to her fresh, natural look. She wore a black floral knee-length dress that tied at the waist.

'Sorry for the wait,' Neve said, giving her a quick hug.

Sibylla's reply was drowned out by the thunder of hooves and the cheers of the crowd as horses crossed the finishing line behind them. Red dust filtered through the air.

'How was Dubbo?' Neve asked as they wove their way through the spectators towards the marquee.

'Busy. It also seemed to take forever to get there. I'm out of practice driving long distances.'

'You'll soon get used to being out here again.'

'I'm sure I will. Dad's making good progress, but there'll be a few more specialist trips to Dubbo.'

Neve didn't answer. They were drawing near to where Tanner and Finn still stood surrounded by women. The brunette now appeared to stand even closer to Tanner, as though staking her claim.

Sibylla shook her head. 'Looks like Tanner's fears have come true.'

'Maybe. He doesn't look too out of his depth.'

As if knowing he was under discussion, Tanner turned his head and looked straight at them. Whatever he said caused the brunette to frown in their direction before he strode towards them.

'Hey,' he said, giving them both a smile. 'May I escort you two lovely ladies to lunch?' He offered each of them his arm. 'I have a sudden need to smell fresh air and to talk about farm machinery.'

Sibylla giggled. 'That bad, huh?'

'Let's just say right after lunch, I'm leaving.'

Relief coursed through Neve, quickly followed by guilt. Tanner hadn't been as relaxed as he'd appeared. Now she could see him up close, she recognised lines of strain bracketing his mouth. She shouldn't have let emotion blind her to how he'd really been feeling. Next time, she'd make sure she did have his back.

She looked to where Finn still held court with his admirers. The brunette was giving Sibylla and her a death stare. 'Do we need to wait for Finn?'

'No. Trust me, he's enjoying himself.'

As they walked away, Sibylla gave Tanner an update on how she was going getting her confidence back when riding. Conscious of the warmth and strength of Tanner's arm beneath her hand, Neve stayed quiet. All she could smell was the leather-toned scent of his aftershave. All she could hear was the husky rumble of his voice.

When three young children ran in front of them in pursuit of a bubble trail, she wasn't prepared to stop. As she cannoned into Tanner, his arm caught her. His hand lay splayed against the sensitive skin of her bare lower back. She held herself stiff to hide the instant tremors that rippled through her.

'Sorry,' the eldest child said, a gap where his bottom tooth was, before he dashed away.

In her peripheral vision, Neve caught Tanner's sideways glance at her before his hand left her skin. Cool air replaced the warmth of his touch. When he again offered her his arm, she took hold with a light clasp.

Sibylla smiled as the children blew more bubbles in between gasps of laughter. 'It's always the simple things, isn't it?'

'It is,' Tanner replied.

Neve's gaze flew to his face. But as he looked ahead all she could see beneath the brim of his hat was the carved line of his profile. She hoped it was only her heightened emotions that made her think his voice had been too deep and too grave.

Something wasn't right between Neve and him. When he'd steadied her, unmistakable tension had vibrated in the fine muscles of her bare back. Over lunch, his suspicions crystallised into certainty. Even though she sat across from him, she barely looked his way. From the texts they'd exchanged during the week, she'd said her hip no longer troubled her, so she wasn't in pain. Her texts had also been her usual warm and witty responses. Had the race day brought back family memories like when she'd visited the small-hall festival?

He took a slow swig of beer to cover his appraisal as she chatted with Sibylla. Neve's swept-up hair revealed the pale, porcelain-smooth line of her neck. Silver hung from her ears and sparkled every time she moved. The rich colour of her dress made her eyes appear a startling green, except there was a new brittleness to their expression. The satin sheen of her pink lips caused his jaw to clench in need. She was so beautiful.

The only reason he was at the races was to see her and to engineer some alone time so they could talk. The way she'd rested her head against him when she'd fallen off Jazz gave him hope she'd be open to revisiting their friends-only discussion.

If Meredith had noticed his preoccupation with scanning the crowd when they'd arrived, she hadn't made any comment. All she'd said when she'd left to talk to Taylor about secret wedding business was for him to enjoy himself. He and Denham were expecting an ultimatum from the hairdresser about getting a haircut, but to their surprise, so far they'd been left in peace.

He felt Neve's attention on him and looked up to meet her gaze. His grip on his beer bottle tightened. Her eyes only held his for a too-brief time. As if from a distance, he heard Sibylla ask him about which horse he'd pick in the next race.

He stared at the race programme. He didn't even know what horses were running. Three seats down from him Hewitt mentioned a potential winner and the conversation shifted away. Then as colour flashed and hooves pounded, everyone turned to watch as the horses sped past. Everyone but him. He didn't look away from Neve.

Meredith hadn't even been gone for ten seconds before he'd been engulfed in a cloud of perfume as women surrounded him. He owed Finn not just a drink but a slab of beer for coming to his aid. As much as Finn had enjoyed the attention, it'd taken all of Tanner's willpower to stay.

His adoptive mother hadn't raised him to be rude or churlish. Meredith also wouldn't expect anything less than good manners. Some of the women, like the touchy-feely brunette, had driven six hours to attend the races. When he'd finally seen Neve, emotion had overridden any sense of social duty. And now here he sat a body length away, desperate to touch her and talk with her.

A raindrop splashed on his chin and then the back of his hand. Even though weak streams of sunlight held their own against the incoming rain, it wouldn't be long until the first cloudburst hit. Denham came to his feet and Tanner followed.

'It might be time to head to the grandstand or marquee,' Denham said as he caught a paper napkin dancing across the table.

'I second that,' Fliss said as she joined the others in packing away the remnants of their lunch.

They'd only made it to the tiered grandstand steps when raindrops pelted on the tin roof. Squeals sounded as spectators dashed for shelter. Tanner kept close to Neve to make sure she wasn't crushed as the grandstand filled. She gave him a small smile of thanks, before turning to talk with Cressy. Above the noise of the rain, a woman's voice called his name. With the flirtatious brunette in the lead, a group of the women he'd been talking to earlier pushed their way towards him.

Neve was suddenly by his side, her arm around his waist. The press of the crowd had to be making her feel claustrophobic. He pulled her close, savouring the contact and the way she tucked herself against him. Her hand lifted to rest on his chest.

When the approaching brunette stopped three people away and the girls behind her did too, he realised Neve was staring in their direction. He couldn't see her exact expression, but from the tilt to her head he guessed she wasn't smiling. Whatever message was exchanged between the brunette and her, it caused the brunette to toss her hair before weaving her way through the crowd in a different direction. The other women followed.

'Neve?' he said, voice low.

'Your fifteen seconds of fame had expired. She wasn't right for you.' Colour flared on her cheekbones as she went to pull away. 'Unless, sorry, you thought she was … and I just ruined everything.'

The only person who was right for him was the woman whose softness and warmth fitted so perfectly against him. But with half of Woodlea jam-packed into the grandstand, now wasn't the time to start such a conversation.

He tightened his hold to reassure her that he hadn't been interested in the brunette. 'She wasn't right.'

The furrow between Neve's brows cleared, but the indecision tensing her lips remained. On his chest, he could feel her fingers curl into his shirt. 'Not even a little?'

'Not one bit.'

Intent on their discussion, he hadn't realised the rain had stopped. People drifted out of the grandstand and space opened up around them. Curious eyes turned their way. He lowered his arm.

Cressy looked over her shoulder with a grin. 'Come on, you two, chop chop. You'll miss the next race.'

Neve preceded him down the stairs and fell into step alongside Ella as they headed for the marquee. The vet said something he couldn't hear and Neve nodded.

Sunshine again filtered through the clouds, but the horizon remained an ominous grey. The main rain squall would soon arrive. He hesitated. Lunch was over and he should leave. But until he had more of a talk with Neve, he wasn't going anywhere.

The crowd dispersed, the majority heading for the bar and the racetrack. In the distance thunder rumbled. Tanner listened to Hewitt and Denham's banter as they tried to persuade each other to enter the men's section of the fashions on the field.

'Don't look at me,' he said when they both stared at him. 'I'm becoming a hermit, remember.'

He barely registered their laughter as Neve left Ella's side and headed in the direction of the exit. Her shoulders were hunched and she walked with a fast-paced urgency. He turned to follow, when purple feathers bobbed in front of his face.

Denham and Hewitt gave him wide grins as they made drinking gestures before hightailing it to the bar. He bit back a sigh. So much for mateship and blood ties.

'Hello, Edna.'

'Well hello, Tanner. What a great turnout it's been today, thanks to you.'

He didn't immediately answer. Instead, he looked over the older woman's shoulder to track where Neve walked. When he saw her talking to old Will, he refocused on Edna. 'I'm not so sure I'm the reason why so many are here.'

'Of course you are, you don't need to be modest … yours is the only name I've heard all day.' Her smile grew. 'But don't worry, Bethany will be here soon and will keep you company in case things get out of hand with any of these city girls.'

Neve had started walking again and would soon disappear from sight.

'I'll look out for her.' Tanner touched the brim of his hat. 'Sorry, I must go.'

Without waiting for Edna's reaction, he strode away. A raindrop wet his shoulder and then his cheek.

As he cleared the race ground gates, all he saw were rows upon rows of parked cars. A glimpse of green had him jogging to his left.

When he drew near to where Neve walked, she must have heard him as she swung around to face him. Her large eyes filled her face. Even as he watched, her lashes lowered to hide her emotions.

He stopped before her, curbing the longing to take her into his arms. 'Doing an umbrella run?'

His light tone failed to relax her strained expression. He didn't need to be a betting man to know she didn't have the key to Ella's four-wheel drive in the small black bag she carried.

'No ... just having some time out.'

The gathering breeze rippled through the silk flowers on top of her head. The temperature had dropped and the sky would soon rip open.

'Are you remembering coming here with your family?'

As the silence lengthened he thought she wouldn't respond. Then she folded her arms and slowly shook her head. 'Tanner ... it's no secret there's ... something between us. But I think we need to revisit our discussion about not giving in to our chemistry.'

He nodded, digging his hands into his pockets. Her solemn tone indicated she wasn't quite on the same page as he was when it came to revising their agreement terms.

She continued, her eyes searching his. 'The same goes for our ... emotional connection.'

He weathered the stab of rejection and the hot flare of pain. He had to retain perspective and not let his emotions blindside him. Neve wasn't abandoning him, she was just renegotiating the terms of their relationship. Something had upset her and he needed to find out what it was.

'Is it possible we don't need to do such a thing?'

Her chin lifted. 'You sound like you're in a courtroom.'

'Do I? I don't want to lose this ... discussion ... or you. The last thing we need to do is to walk away from what we have.'

She blinked. 'But ... you don't want marriage ... or I'm guessing a family? I want both of those things. I can't do casual, which is why I'm so bad at all this relationship stuff.'

He lost the fight to not touch her. He slid his hands out of his pockets to cup her jaw, ignoring the splatter of raindrops on the brim of his hat.

'I thought I had everything figured out and knew what I did and didn't want … but I was wrong.'

'Wrong?'

The wind swept away her breathless word.

'Dead wrong. And you're not ba—'

Neve's lips silenced him. His hat fell to the ground. Her hands were in his hair and her body pressed against his. He sought the skin of her lower back beneath her jacket and she shuddered as he mapped the smooth, bare contours.

Kissing Neve was like seeing the glow of a sunrise after an endless night. Having the woman he loved in his arms was like finding the part of him that he'd always denied existed. This was what he'd longed for but had fought against. This was what he'd dreamed of but hadn't been strong enough to admit he wanted.

He didn't know when the heavens tore apart and the deluge started. All he knew was that icy water streaked over his heated skin and soaked his shirt. When thunder cracked he lifted his head and sought Neve's hand. She bent to scoop up his hat before following him at a half-run over to where his ute was parked several rows away.

Water saturated his hair and dripped into his eyes. The wind stripped warmth from wherever it touched. He held Neve close to shelter her from the gusts that hit them from an oblique angle. Through the grey wall of water he saw the blue of his ute. For once the distinctive colour wasn't a liability.

Lights flashed as he unlocked the doors using the key in his chinos pocket. He battled against the wind to hold the passenger door open so Neve could disappear inside. Finally, he too was in the dry ute cabin. Rivulets trailed frozen fingers down the back of his neck and over his chest. His boots were heavy and sodden.

The noise of the rain hammering on the windscreen made speaking impossible. Lightning flickered before thunder rolled.

Neve gave him a smile as she removed her headband and dragged wet hair off her face. He reached behind the seat for the towel he kept there. When he passed it to her, her hands shook.

He leaned over to kiss her lips. No longer soft and warm, they were as cold as a winter snowfall. He pointed in the direction of home. She nodded and took her phone out of her bag to send a text. He guessed it was Ella that she was letting know where she was. He started the ute engine. The windscreen wipers worked hard to keep the downpour at bay.

He reached out to link his fingers with hers. Her teeth chattered as she dried her hair and then mopped up the water around her. He didn't try to make conversation, just concentrated on driving through the storm. Whenever his thumb moved over the back of her hand she'd look at him, eyes bright, and squeeze his fingers.

When they reached Claremont, rain still fell in thick wet lines. He parked as close to the front steps as he could before dashing inside to grab an umbrella from the hallway hat stand. But when he returned Neve was already on the veranda.

Arms wrapped around her torso, she attempted a smile. 'I c-couldn't get any w-wetter.'

He tucked her against his side and guided her up the wooden staircase at the end of the hallway. She shook so much he could almost hear her bones rattling. Once on the landing, he opened the door to the light and airy guest room Meredith kept prepared. Plush towels were folded in a pile on the end of the white bedspread that covered the dark wood four-poster bed. He collected the robe that hung behind the door and draped it over her shoulder.

'En suite is on your right. There's plenty of hot water so take your time.' He smoothed the wet hair from her cheek, not surprised his own fingers shook. His unsteadiness had nothing to do with how cold he too was and everything to do with the depth of his feelings. 'I'll be in the kitchen when you're done.'

Her smile was as sweet as it was shaky.

He went downstairs to his flat. After he too had showered, he returned to the kitchen in jeans and a grey T-shirt. His feet were bare as he hadn't wanted to waste time finding a dry pair of boots.

He went through the fridge. Yesterday Meredith had made a pot of minestrone soup. When the hallway floorboards creaked he set out two bowls. Neve appeared, fresh colour in her face, hair wrapped in a white towel and the thick robe swamping her. Her pink toes peered from beneath the robe's hem.

He smiled and before he could ask if she wanted tea or coffee she'd crossed the kitchen to wind her arms around his neck. He pulled her against him, feeling the slide of the robe over the bare skin at her waist. She smelled of vanilla soap and summer flowers.

'Yes,' she said, her eyes and tone serious. 'Yes, it is possible we don't need to keep our emotional distance.' Her fingers toyed with the shower-damp hair at his nape. 'But you asked the question in such a way that you knew that was the only answer I could give.'

'True ... I had my lawyer hat on. I wasn't accepting any other response.' He paused as a rush of need consumed him when she brushed her lips across his throat. 'Do we need to continue our ... discussion?'

Her answer was to stand on tiptoes and kiss him. The towel around her hair unravelled, and without breaking contact with her mouth he tossed it onto a chair. He buried his hands in her wet hair and angled her head to find the soft skin below her ear. Her hands delved beneath his T-shirt, and as her palms pressed heat into his skin he shuddered. The oversized robe slipped off her right shoulder, confirming she wore nothing below.

He stopped to drag in a ragged breath. Lips swollen, cheeks flushed and eyes heavy-lidded, Neve appeared as lost as he was. His self-control held by a thin strip of leather. But he had to make sure things weren't moving too fast. He went to speak when Neve pressed a steady finger against his lips.

She stared at him. Her irises were a shade of green he hadn't ever seen before. Pure and vibrant, they shone with a shy promise. There was no more need to keep either their emotional or physical distance. They were on the same page. A smile curved her lips as she took his hand to lead him upstairs. His feet didn't move. Instead, he snagged her waist and swung her into his arms. Walking would take too long.

# CHAPTER
# 17

Cressy and Denham's special day had arrived. Overnight Woodlea had been yarn-bombed in a final display of white. Neve was proud to say her first attempts at crocheting now decorated the town post box. She could add Sue, old Will and Judith to her known list of members of the underground knitting club. She had a feeling that not even the members knew who all the guerrilla knitters were.

She leaned closer to the bathroom mirror to apply light colour to her complexion with a soft oversized brush. Last Saturday she'd been getting ready for the races and this Saturday she was again putting on makeup. Her hand lowered and her reflection smiled back at her. The difference was last weekend her stomach was in knots, and while this weekend her midriff wasn't exactly a place of peace, she knew exactly what would happen when she saw Tanner.

Still smiling, she applied a few last touches of makeup. The same thing that had happened the past seven days. When he kissed her she'd take a second to remind herself that she was the woman

Tanner wanted. While he hadn't said the words, the tenderness of his touch reassured her he had no regrets about what had happened after the races. Heat filled her cheeks and she was glad she hadn't added too much colour. She certainly didn't regret a thing.

All the embarrassment and awkwardness that had sent her running after what had happened in the grandstand no longer haunted her. She still chose what she said carefully, so as to not rush or overwhelm him, but when they were together there often wasn't any need for words. She'd never have thought she'd ever feel so comfortable around him.

During the days, she looked after the girls and helped Tanner where she could with wedding jobs. Fliss's to-do list was down to a single page. Every night he stayed with her and by morning he was gone when the girls arrived. She wasn't sure what Meredith thought. But when Tanner came bearing a lasagne one night and a lemon meringue pie another night, she hoped it was a sign of approval.

She added her makeup bag to the clothes filling the duffle on her bed. Today would be their first social event together and the plan was to stay under the public radar, especially when it came to Edna. They'd, of course, let their close friends know. Ella had been first to call, followed by Cressy and Fliss, who were in the car together and had put her on speaker.

Neve zipped up her bag and reached for her dress covered in thin plastic. There were still several hours until the ceremony, but she was heading out to help with the last-minute jobs. Sibylla was looking after Maya and Kait while Graham attended the wedding. She'd also kindly offered to come around with the girls to feed Dell, Bassie and Jazz and to put on their rugs. As planned, Neve was still sharing a glamping tent with Ella. But before Tanner had left this morning he'd made sure she knew what his tent number was.

The closer Neve drove to Glenmore the more cars she encountered. She hadn't seen this much traffic since she'd left the city. Many guests would be arriving early to settle into the glamping village. Thankfully, the autumn sun shone and unlike last weekend, the skies were a blissful and clear blue.

She slowed to join the convoy crossing the cattle grid. The car behind had what looked like a fine black mesh stretched over the front. Tanner had explained when she'd seen a ute in town with a similar thing that locals were protecting their radiators from overheating should the locust swarms fly in.

When the road forked Neve followed the other vehicles to the left past the machinery sheds. A cockatoo screeched as it flew to the top of a gum tree. This wasn't any ordinary wild cockatoo. Cressy had nursed a young Kevin back to health and the opinionated cockatoo refused to leave. Loyal and affectionate, he proved more of a watchdog than Tippy and Juno. No one could arrive without Kevin announcing their arrival. Neve was now used to him landing on her shoulder whenever she visited.

To the right stood the historic Glenmore homestead with its four chimneys and shady wraparound veranda. The bridal party would be getting ready inside. Fliss had already sent a photo of herself with a hand over her mouth as Taylor brandished a can of hairspray. Ella too was in the bridal party, along with Tanner as best man and Saul, a friend of Denham's from his bull-riding days on the American pro-rodeo circuit.

The glamping village appeared ahead. A sea of cream bell-tents stretched far across the paddock. The wedding was to take place on a small plateau that overlooked the river. The picturesque spot was where Denham had proposed and was a section of the land that had once been an issue of contention between the two neighbouring families.

A large marquee had been constructed and as Neve drove by she could make out a square wooden dancefloor beside the bar. Lights had been strung between trees and a short walk away, ordered rows of white chairs overlooked the river. Beyond the chairs curved Cressy's bespoke wedding arch that Hewitt had designed. It was Neve and Freya's job to adorn the scrolled ironwork with greenery and swags of flowers.

She examined the numbers on the pegs outside the tents. Tanner's tent number fifteen wasn't far away from where she and Ella would be sleeping. She unloaded the car and hung her dress on the hook on the centre pole, before going in search of Freya.

After they'd completed the first of their jobs, Neve left the marquee to check that flowers had been put in the ladies' portable amenity block. She hadn't made it two steps when a hand caught hers and pulled her around the side of the tent. She was kissing Tanner even before they'd disappeared from sight.

Her arms curled around his neck and she stretched to slide her fingers into his shortened hair. After a midweek negotiation that involved Meredith's baked cheesecake, Tanner and Denham had sat still long enough for Taylor and her scissors to make them wedding ready.

They broke apart to breathe. She took in his dusty work clothes and stubbled jaw. 'Please don't tell me Denham looks like you do? He's supposed to be married in an hour.'

Tanner grinned, his dimple flicking. 'He's worse, but he's gone to take a shower. I needed to see you.'

Another thorough kiss left her in no doubt he'd been missing her as much as she had him, even though they'd seen each other that morning.

'Fifteen,' he murmured against her lips.

'How could I forget … but I'll make sure Ella's okay before I desert her.'

Tanner's eyes twinkled. 'Have you met Saul?'

'Is he the American bull rider?'

'Yes. It might be nothing, but Fliss was so busy watching the two of them together, Taylor was able to get close enough to use her hairspray.'

'For Ella's sake I hope it's something.' She rubbed dust off the edge of his whiskered jaw. 'You really do need to get back to the house for a shower.'

He sighed. 'I know.'

He snuck a final kiss before leaving. She waited a moment for her breathing to settle before walking around the side of the marquee. In the middle of each table dusky-pink-and-white flowers sat in handmade rustic wooden boxes.

Freya grinned at her from where she was checking seating names on the round tables against a list on a clipboard. 'I take it Tanner found you?'

Neve smoothed her hair, hoping it wasn't too tousled. 'That obvious?'

'Sorry, yes … and to be honest it was even at the horsemanship clinic.'

'I thought I did so well hiding how I felt.'

Freya laughed quietly. 'I once thought the same thing whenever I was around Drew. Speaking of which, he's bringing the last of the flowers from the house.'

Neve reached for the clipboard. 'I'll finish up here if you like.'

'Thanks. I'll help Drew carry the boxes to the arch and meet you there.'

Neve continued over to check on the flowers in the amenity block. When she returned Edna, dressed in a peacock-blue outfit, was perusing the corner tables of the marquee. Neve frowned as Edna subtly swapped two name tags.

When the older woman glanced up and saw her approaching, Neve was surprised to see the indomitable gossip blush.

'Edna, what are you doing? Fliss won't be happy at any seating changes.'

'I'm sure she wouldn't be.' Edna looked down at the name tags she'd swapped. 'In my defence, these two would have changed seats anyway.'

Neve followed her gaze. The tags she'd swapped were Bethany's and Mac's and she'd seated them together. 'You know?'

Edna looked around and lowered her voice. 'Of course I know. Clive and I have been planning this for years.'

Neve just stared. Although no one seemed to know how Clive and Edna's family feud had started, even Neve knew they couldn't be in the same room together.

Edna bent to straighten Bethany's name tag. 'The only person to know Clive and I don't really hate each other was your grandmother. She caught us ...' Edna looked out at the sky with a faraway expression. 'On a moonlit night like it will be tonight.'

'That's just a little too much information.'

Edna laughed. 'It was just a kiss, but with our families having fallen out over the supreme cattle trophy at the Royal Easter Show, it was all that it could be. And I'm glad. Clive's father was a difficult man and he's turned out the same way.'

'But you approve of Mac and Finn?'

'Yes, they're fine young men. They have much of their mother in them. I always thought that quieter Mac would be best suited to Bethany and I was right.'

'So you went to a great effort to keep them apart because ...?'

'Bethany needed to go out with a few frogs to appreciate Mac. I couldn't also be seen to approve as she'd never go near him. For some reason she goes out of her way to date men I don't approve of.'

Neve smiled. 'So a little reverse psychology was in order?'

'Absolutely.' Edna's eyes softened. 'It also worked for you and Tanner.'

'You didn't ...'

'I did. You're the only woman Tanner's ever really looked at and not through. As for dear little Skittles ... I knew Bethany was serious about Mac when she went to such lengths to hide they were going out.' Edna touched her nose. 'It's our secret that I go to the stables every night to give Skittles an apple. He'll be a perfect pony for my grandchildren one day.'

Neve grinned. 'It can be our little secret.' She glanced at the name tags. 'And this can be too.'

'Thank you. Bethany's getting close to telling me ... Mac spoke to Clive this morning.'

'They are a lovely couple. It was obvious they were together at Tanner's horse-training weekend.'

Edna nodded and went to take the clipboard out of Neve's grasp. 'Now, you'd better get those flowers on the arch. Drew and Freya will be too busy distracting each other. He used to be so focused when he was single.'

When Neve didn't relinquish the clipboard, Edna pursed her lips. 'You are just like your grandmother when you look at me like that. Okay, I won't change any more places.'

Satisfied Edna wouldn't meddle any further, Neve went to help Freya and Drew. When the delicate floral swags were in place on the arch, and the white rose petals strewn along the aisle, they headed to their tents to get dressed.

Neve slid into her long coral-coloured dress and freshened up her hair and makeup. Cressy had added a personal note to the wedding invitation for women to wear sensible shoes as heels would sink into the paddock. As Neve slipped on the bone-coloured wedges she'd found in Woodlea's one dress shop, her phone chimed. Freya and Drew were ready. Before she left the tent to walk over with them, she put on the crystal hoop earrings that had belonged to her mother.

A crowd had already congregated around the rows of white seats. As Neve drew near she realised it wasn't just the marriage celebrant standing beside the arch. Denham, Tanner and Saul were too. All three men stood silent and tall, their feet apart and hands clasped in front of them. Their charcoal-grey wedding suits fitted to perfection. Tanner half turned. Clean-shaven and polished, no one would have known that less than an hour ago he'd looked like he'd ridden in from the long paddock.

Neve moved to stand on the right side of the crowd with Freya, Drew and Taylor. Taylor was only halfway through her story about Denham and hair gel when a convoy of utes pulled up behind the guests. Everyone turned. An expectant hush settled over the scene before the slow and soft strains of a country love song lilted on the air.

Ella was the first to glide down the aisle. Tall and elegant, her sleeveless, dusky-pink dress featured a flowing chiffon skirt. Taylor had styled her honey-blonde hair in a sleek bun. The tails of the ivory ribbons wrapped around the pink roses she carried fluttered as she passed.

Fliss followed at a sedate distance. The dusky palette of her dress and flowers also showcased her brunette beauty. Practical Cressy had chosen classical bridesmaids' dresses that Ella and Fliss could wear again.

Then Cressy appeared holding old Will's arm and carrying a large silvery-green-and-pink bouquet. The proud angle of Will's chin conveyed what an honour it was to walk Cressy down the aisle.

The cowgirl looked radiant in her off-the-shoulder lace gown that flared into a full skirt. She wore no veil; instead, her glossy dark hair was caught at the side and fell in natural, loose curls. The only ornamentation was a simple braid at the front and dusky-pink flowers tucked behind her ear. As she walked the toes of her white cowgirl boots appeared from beneath her long dress hem.

Neve darted a quick glance at Denham. If Cressy took the crowd's breath away, what did she do to the man who loved her? The intensity of his blue gaze and the stillness of his expression said it all.

Neve's eyes misted and she glanced at Tanner. Her breath caught. He was looking straight at her.

As stunning as Cressy looked, Tanner only had eyes for one woman. Neve stood at the side of the wedding guests. She wore a long dress that left her creamy shoulders bare and he hoped wouldn't take long for him to later unzip. Her long red-gold hair lifted in the breeze. As their gazes connected, he gave her a wink before looking back at Cressy.

He had no words to describe what the past week had been like waking up beside Neve. All he could do was feel … elation, contentment, love. Hewitt had spoken the truth. Even guys like them were not meant to be alone.

He turned as Cressy reached Denham and old Will moved away. As the wedding ceremony got underway, he concentrated on what was happening in front of him. When he leaned forward to give

Denham the ring, emotion ached in his throat. It meant so much that the cousin he'd never known had become a best mate who'd asked him to be his best man.

After their vows had been exchanged, Denham and Cressy shared a tender kiss. Tanner didn't dare look at Neve. What he felt for her would be written all over his face for the guests to decipher.

With the ceremony over, wellwishers came to congratulate the bride and groom. Tanner used the brief respite to find Neve. Soon he'd be looking into a camera lens trying to appear as though he wore a suit every day. He tugged at the stiff shirt collar as he made his way to where Neve stood with Taylor.

Neve greeted him with a dreamy smile. 'That was such a gorgeous ceremony.'

'It was and I didn't lose the ring ...' He paused as Taylor frowned at him. Her delicate dancer body masked a will of iron. It had taken a combined effort between Denham, Saul and him to make sure there hadn't been any product slicked through their cowboy hair.

Taylor moved forward to brush hair off his forehead. 'What have you done?'

'Nothing. It's been windy.'

Taylor's steady gaze held his.

He sighed. 'After we were dressed we might have walked to the shed to show Saul the new boom spray and to have a cold beer.'

Taylor's only reply was to arch a fine brow.

He spoke again. 'We also might have been good country boys and put on our hats.'

By now Neve had her hand over her mouth to hide her amusement.

Taylor looked skywards. 'And you wonder why I wanted to use a styling product.' She again flicked her fingers through his hair. 'No more being country boys until after the photos.'

'Okay.'

Taylor marched over to where Denham and Saul were laughing with Mac and Finn. Denham sent Tanner a this-is-worse-than-a-suit-fitting look while Taylor tidied his hair.

'I thought Fliss was scary when she was in work mode,' he said with a chuckle.

Neve laughed quietly. 'I think even Fliss finds Taylor scary when she has a can of hairspray in her hands.'

Tanner nodded before saying the words burning inside of him. 'You look beautiful.'

Colour washed her cheeks. 'Thank you. You don't look so bad yourself.'

Feeling someone watching him, he glanced sideways and saw Edna dressed in vivid blue staring across at them. Realising it could look like he stood too close to Neve, he went to take a step backwards.

'It's okay. She knows,' Neve said, so only he could hear.

'No way. How?'

'Superpowers. She knows about Bethany and Mac too and approves. She also wasn't serious about pushing you and Bethany together.'

'You mean I've been considering swapping to a white ute for no reason?'

'I'll fill you in later, but basically part of her plan was ...' The heat in Neve's eyes warmed him as if she'd touched him. 'For us to end up the way we have.'

Her grip tightened on the silver bag she held, suggesting she shared his battle to keep his hands to himself.

He cleared his throat. 'Remind me never to get on Edna's bad side ... the way her brain works terrifies me.'

Fliss's wave caught his attention. It was time to leave for the photographs. 'See you on the dancefloor?'

'Count on it.'

The beauty of Neve's smile stayed with him as the wedding party drove down to where the mottled trucks of the majestic gums lined the river. When Cressy and Denham had a photo with Will and Judith, emotion watered in Will's faded blue eyes.

It had never crossed Tanner's mind that one day his father might have stood beside him on such a day. But now that Neve was in his life, it was as though anything could be possible. Except last night, he'd made the mistake of calling his father. If his father had asked after Neve he'd been prepared to tell him they were together.

Instead, the phone call had been terse and brutal. It had started with the usual city-versus-country undertones, but when a crash had sounded and Tanner asked if everything was all right things had disintegrated. Curt and abrupt, his father had told him not to ring again. If he discovered something more about Edward Jones, then he'd call.

With the photographs over, and their hair officially able to be windswept, the bridal party relaxed and socialised. He'd caught Neve's eye several times while the smiling waitstaff carried around trays of canapés. But he hadn't sought her out. In between introducing Saul to the locals and making sure Ella's champagne glass remained full, he mentally ran through his best-man speech.

When dusk descended and the fairy lights emitted a gentle glow, he saw Bethany take her mother's hand and lead Edna off somewhere quiet. From over at the bar, Mac downed a beer, his attention never leaving the direction Edna and Bethany had taken.

It was soon time for seats to be taken in the marquee, and as Tanner sat beside Denham at the bridal table he looked over to where Neve sat across from Drew and Freya. Neve mouthed the words 'good luck'.

The entrée was followed by the first of the toasts and then it was Tanner's turn to speak. He kept his speech simple but heartfelt, and when he sat down Denham clasped his shoulder as if unable to speak. Meredith wiped tears from her eyes with a white handkerchief. With his best-man duties over, Tanner sat back to enjoy his succulent rack of lamb.

Despite the cool evening temperature, he took off his suit jacket hoping he'd feel less suffocated and restricted. He'd only had a few beers, so being on edge wasn't related to how much he'd had to drink. Even without his coat, his skin heated and prickled. He eased his top button open and dragged a hand through his hair. He just couldn't seem to relax. By the time Cressy and Denham cut the wedding cake, the clink of glass and the high-octane laughter from the rowdy corner tables grated.

He expelled a silent breath of relief when the music started, signalling the upcoming bridal waltz. He wouldn't have to keep sitting still. The guests left the marquee to surround the dancefloor as Denham and Cressy took their first dance as husband and wife.

Fliss touched Tanner's arm. 'Showtime.' Her voice lowered as he led her out to join the bride and groom. 'You know, the sooner you make it public you and Neve are together the better. Once Woodlea knows their "hot hero" can waltz you're going to be in even more trouble.'

Tanner swept Fliss around the dancefloor. It had been important to his adoptive mother that he knew how to dance and one summer they'd attended lessons. The memory of his mother's laughter as they'd trodden on each other's toes eased his agitation. He smiled across to where Denham and Cressy only had eyes for each other. Who knew Denham could be so light on his feet?

But with every swirl and twirl he and Fliss made, the light around him seemed to fade and the darkness pressed in on him. An unrelenting beat of restlessness pushed aside all contentment and happiness.

Hewitt appeared by his side and on autopilot he released Fliss into the pickup rider's embrace. Without looking at anyone, he slipped through the crowd. Moonlight guided him over to the empty white chairs. He sat and stared unseeingly at the flower-covered arch that symbolised the future home of a bride and groom.

All evening his subconscious had been trying to tell him something. He now knew what it was. Emotion constricted his chest with the force of a zip tie. Every moment with Neve, where he'd felt a deep, pure joy, a different feeling had been evolving. Fear.

As a child he'd been confused and hurt by the suspicion that his birth mother hadn't loved him enough to keep him. As an adult he'd been devastated when his adoptive father had rejected him over his career choices. He'd also been destroyed when the woman he'd believed he'd loved had manipulated and used him. But instinct told him if he ever lost Neve the pain and anguish would be incomparable.

He felt rather than heard her approach. Then the swish of fabric was followed by the feel of her gentle hand on his shoulder. 'Hey.'

'Hey.' His reply was little more than a low rasp.

She sat in the chair next to him and touched his face. 'Doing some thinking?'

He nodded and took his time to answer. He needed to be honest and to have the right words. Even if saying them would carve off pieces of his soul. 'Neve ... this past week ... what I thought I wanted seemed so clear.'

'Seemed?' Her hand slowly lowered to her lap.

'Yes.' He covered her fingers with his. 'Now ... I just don't know. I only know how to be alone. It's the only way I can be.'

She turned her hand over and linked her fingers with his as though she was never letting him go.

'So who was she?'

Tanner stiffened. So far, his father was the only one to know what a fool he'd been to follow a woman to the other side of the world. 'Genevieve.'

Neve waited for him to keep talking.

'She was a cowgirl who'd come to Sydney on a university exchange from Colorado. When she had a hard time settling in, I looked out for her. Before I knew it we were inseparable. I really did believe what we had was special and real.'

'What happened?'

'I turned my back on law to follow what I thought were two of my dreams. I went with her to work with horses on her family ranch.'

'And everything changed?'

'Yes.' He didn't hide the self-disgust hardening his tone. 'I should have realised sooner that her feelings hadn't been genuine. I was a convenient distraction, a crutch, to help her through a difficult time. When she was back in her familiar surroundings and around her usual friends, I wasn't needed anymore.'

'Tanner ... even though we both know I've been going through a difficult time too, I'm not using you. When life settles down, I'll still need you. The last thing I'd ever do is to abandon you.'

At the hurt in her voice he lifted their hands and brushed his lips across her smooth skin.

'My head tells me the exact same thing, but my self-preservation—'

He stopped. There was nothing he could say to explain the chaotic, convoluted mess of his emotions.

She spoke into the strain. 'What you're feeling is natural and understandable. You just need time ... time to process and to think.' She paused, her grip on his hand tightening. 'When are you leaving? Where will you go?'

He failed to hide his flinch. She'd already guessed he'd run. 'Tomorrow after I take Cressy and Denham to the airport ... I'll camp out on the long paddock somewhere.'

'Okay. You have a week.'

'A week?'

She placed the palm of her other hand against his cheek. 'Yes, because then I'm coming to find you. We can work through this together.'

He had no words. The woman he loved hadn't given up on him even if he'd given into his fears.

'Give me five days. If I'm not back, I'll text where I am.'

'Deal.'

She pressed a kiss to his lips and was gone. He stared after her, forcing his mouth to remain closed so he wouldn't call out her name.

He knew he was alive, blood pumped through his veins. But the ache where his heart lay made him feel as though his chest was nothing but a hollow void.

He had five days to make sense of his emotions. Five days to find a way to silence his deepest doubts. He rubbed his forehead with unsteady fingers. Five days to justify Meredith's faith that he had the strength to stay.

Beyond the symbolic wedding arch, just like his hope, the river flowed dark and sombre.

# CHAPTER
# 18

Somewhere between the wedding music ending and the rustle of Ella's blankets as she came to bed in their glamping tent, Neve fell asleep. The respite from her thoughts didn't last long. She awoke to the over-loud whispers of a couple walking past who were convinced they were being quiet.

As soon as her heavy eyelids lifted, emotion coursed through her. Last night there hadn't been a continuation of the magic between Tanner and her. Instead, their relationship had been put on pause. She swallowed past her dry throat. She could only hope it also hadn't ended. The moonlight couldn't hide the stark pain that had hollowed Tanner cheeks. She'd never heard his voice so taut or hoarse.

She'd sensed by the end of dinner that he was on edge. His ready laughter and quick jokes made him appear relaxed. Even when he'd waltzed with Fliss there'd been little indication he wasn't enjoying himself. But the reality was evident in the subtle tension that corded the muscles beneath the fine cotton of his white shirt and in the hard line of his jaw when he'd left the dancefloor.

She'd been bracing herself for the moment when the intensity of what lay between them tripped his internal alarm. The emotions that bound them were far from casual. She just hadn't expected it to be so soon. She'd suspected, but now knew, that to Tanner any relationship was synonymous with vulnerability. To protect himself he chose solitude and, even with Meredith, held a part of himself back.

Despite Neve's best intentions a deep sigh escaped. If the time alone didn't help him to gain clarity, she'd do all that she could to ease his fears. But as desperate as she was to convince him she'd never abandon him, this was a conclusion he had to reach by himself. Otherwise, he'd never truly believe she wouldn't reject him.

The blankets on the mattress on the other side of the tent again rustled before Ella's sleepy voice sounded. 'Everything okay?'

'Sorry, did I wake you?'

'I was already awake but must have drifted off.' Light flared as Ella used her phone to check the time. 'The birds will soon be sounding way too cheerful for all those with hangovers or who've just gone to bed.' The vet stretched. 'I did tell you I didn't snore, but I probably should have mentioned I'm an early riser.'

'That's okay. That makes two of us.'

'Coffee? Tea?'

Despite the luxuries of the fine linen and the indoor and outdoor mats, the glamorous tent lacked power so they'd each brought a thermos of hot water.

'Tea's just what I need.' She flipped back the bed covers and reached for a jacket.

Ella too left her bed. Dressed in an oversized T-shirt, she moved to turn on the LED lantern that sat on a small wooden table. The strong pool of light chased the darkness from the tent and revealed a sizeable scar high on Ella's thigh.

Neve's attention flew to Ella's face. Such a scar hadn't been the result of a simple accident and would be why the vet always wore running shorts over her swimmers. Ella turned away to pull her T-shirt hem lower. Neve busied herself with finding the tea and coffee to allow Ella the space to slip on a pair of black leggings. The vet's secrets were not yet ready to come out of the shadows.

With steam curling from their mugs, they unzipped the tent door and went to sit outside in the chairs positioned on the outdoor mat. Neve returned inside to get two blankets to tuck around their knees. To her relief, Ella hadn't again asked if everything was okay. She wasn't sure if she could discuss Tanner without her emotions overwhelming her.

Over at the marquee the fairy lights continued to glow. Black-and-white figures still dressed in their dinner suits sat on the large hay bales that formed a wall between the dancefloor and amenities block, beers in hand, waiting to welcome in the new day.

Neve had trouble focusing on anything but tent number fifteen. Even though all the tents were dark and silent, she was sure Tanner's would be unoccupied.

Ella's grave words validated her suspicions. 'Before the music stopped I saw Tanner get his swag and head towards the river.'

Neve cupped her cold hands around her mug, wishing the chill inside her could so easily be warmed. 'I thought he might have slept elsewhere. We hit a little ... road bump last night.'

'I guessed so.'

'He's having some time away ... to think.'

Ella looked across at her and even in the grey gloom Neve could see her concern. 'He's leaving?'

'For five days and then I'm going to wherever he is if he's not back.'

Ella's frown eased. 'It's not good he's going, but that length of time is okay.'

'It is?'

'Yes. Five days isn't anything compared to how long he's been gone in the past. I have a good feeling that after this trip there'll be no more road bumps.'

'I hope so.'

Ella leaned over to adjust the blanket on Neve's knees that was in danger of falling. 'I know I once said Tanner wasn't looking for a relationship, but since he's met you I can honestly say I've seen him change.' She paused as a kookaburra chuckled and a faint glow lightened the horizon to the east. 'If he hasn't listened to his heart in five days I'm coming with you.'

Neve's spirits lifted at the fierceness in Ella's tone. 'Thank you, but one female talking about how he's feeling might be enough.'

'Very true. I'm sure he, Denham and Hewitt have a code for any conversation that doesn't involve rodeos, cattle prices or bull bars as they suddenly seem to have something urgent to do over in the shed.'

'I'm sure they do.'

In silence they sipped their tea and watched the colour burst across the sky in brilliant pink-and-gold streaks. By now the dawn birdsong had reached its crescendo and murmured voices could be heard inside nearby tents.

'It's a new day,' Ella said in a solemn tone that made Neve think the vet said this as an affirmation every morning.

The sunrise faded and a mob of kangaroos came out of the trees to the left of the marquee. Two young joeys stood on their hind legs and wrestled while the adults grazed on the dew-soaked grass. In the distance dust lifted on the road out of Glenmore.

Tanner was taking Cressy and Denham to catch the red-eye flight from Dubbo. They'd fly to Sydney and then on to London and Europe. Neve stared at the dust as it settled. The dawn chill seeped through the layers of her jacket and she shivered. She could only hope that whatever roads Tanner then travelled, they brought him back to her.

Ella came to her feet. 'Staying for breakfast?'

'I don't think I can stomach any food.'

'Hang in there.' Ella rubbed her back. 'I've money on Tanner returning before the five days are up. How about I help you load your car so you can get home before too many roos are out?'

After Neve had had a hot shower and visited Jazz, Bassie and Dell, she'd managed to eat half a piece of toast. She wished she shared Ella's faith and positivity. The bleakness in Tanner's eyes and the emptiness in his voice continued to steal her appetite.

She was fooling herself that she was making progress on her latest knitting project when car tyres sounded on the gravel driveway. Through the living-room window she saw Meredith's grey sedan pull up outside.

Neve pressed a hand to her stomach. Meredith coming to visit highlighted how serious it was that Tanner had left. She went to open the front door.

Meredith greeted her with a strained smile. For the first time since she'd met her, Meredith appeared fragile. 'Sorry, Neve, the last thing you'd want this morning is a visitor … but I thought it could be good if we talked.'

'Of course. I'm glad you came.' Neve led the way inside. 'Cuppa?'

Meredith glanced at Neve's unfinished breakfast on the kitchen bench. Compassion filled her blue eyes. 'Only if you're having one.'

She nodded. Not because she wanted one but because it would give her something to do.

Meredith took a seat at the kitchen table. 'Tanner called about an hour ago. I thought he was ringing to say Cressy and Denham caught their plane okay, but he was really calling to fill me in on what happened last night and where Arrow and Patch were.'

Neve concentrated on adding boiling water to the teapot before looking across at Meredith. 'I'm hoping it's a good sign he called.'

'It is.'

Neve placed the teapot and mugs on the table. Neither said anything while she poured their tea.

Then Meredith spoke as she drew her mug towards her. 'Tanner hasn't ever said anything, but I know how hard it's been for him to feel settled here. I'd hoped with time ... and love ... he'd feel like Claremont is his home and this is where he belongs.' A small smile relaxed Meredith's face. 'Then he came to help you with Bassie and Dell and the light that I'd longed to see in his eyes was there.'

Neve took a mouthful of tea to hide her despair. Whatever he felt for her it also hadn't been enough to make him feel settled or to stay.

Meredith reached across the table to squeeze her hand. 'He loves you, Neve, even if he hasn't said so. This past week he actually used the word "home" and talked about the future with a new joy and certainty. I also think ... hope ... you feel the same way about him?'

'I do ... but what happens if he doesn't come back or when I go to him love isn't enough?'

'You'll know what to do and what to say. You can reach him when no one else can.'

This time Neve covered Meredith's hand with her own. 'Meredith, he loves you too ... so much. Please don't ever doubt it.'

'I just want him to be happy ... to feel like he belongs somewhere.'

'You and I both want the same things for him ... together we can help each other to help him.'

'We can.'

Meredith sipped at her tea and the high emotion between them eased as they each took a moment to collect themselves.

When Meredith was carrying the empty mugs into the kitchen, Neve's mobile rang. The caller was Graham. 'Hi, sorry to call on a Sunday, but Maya and Kait woke up with colds so I'll keep them home until they're well.'

'Are you sure? I don't mind them coming.'

'You do so much for us I don't want you to get sick too. I also could do with a few days here. Cath's garden's a mess.'

Happiness for Graham slid through her. This was the first time she'd heard him mention his wife's name. Sibylla had also texted that she'd had fun with the girls and that they'd had the sniffles but otherwise were okay. Graham just wanted to spend time with his daughters.

'If you need anything let me know. Please say hi to the girls.'

'I will.'

Neve ended the call and turned to see Meredith watching her from over near the sink. 'Come and stay with me,' the older woman said, voice gentle. 'The next few days will be tough on your own.'

'Thanks, but I've a letter to write to Edward Jones's sister and also need to go through my bookshelf. I want to take some more books to the new street library at the adventure playground.'

'Okay, but if you change your mind there'll be a room made up for you.' Meredith gave her a tight hug. 'Ring me at any time.'

Despite their solidarity, as she waved Meredith off Neve knew the fear that lingered in Meredith's eyes was mirrored in her own. As much as they would do all that they could to help Tanner, the decision to stay could only be made by the man who was somewhere out on the long paddock alone except for his horse and his dog.

Day one of Tanner's quest for peace passed in a numb, fog-like haze.

Even when at the wedding he'd taken his swag down to the river to be near the sound of running water, he'd failed to sleep. He'd kept up the act of everything being okay as he drove Cressy and Denham to Dubbo airport. It was when he'd returned to Claremont to load Arrow and to get his gear that his mask had slipped. When he'd called Meredith he hadn't tried to hide where, or why, he was going. She'd have sensed his torment, even though they'd only been talking by phone.

Not having a plan about where he'd go, he headed for the reserve he and Neve had visited to look at the wartime hideaways. At least there he'd feel as though she was with him. Her compassion and empathy still humbled him. He didn't deserve her understanding or her patience in giving him time. That night, even with Patch snoring at the foot of his swag, the sorrow widening her eyes haunted his dreams.

Day two of his time away to think involved a long ride on Arrow. But as much as he allowed the serenity and silence to soak into his soul, his thoughts refused to cooperate. They thrashed and tangled until they resembled the thickets of spiny box thorn that choked the base of the gum trees.

To his heart the way forward was clear. He needed to be with Neve. The feeling was growing that perhaps he'd pushed her away to test her or to force her to reject him. Except she hadn't. She'd stuck by him. But just when he thought everything made sense, the arguments of his self-preservation failed to give ground. He couldn't risk that she wouldn't then walk away when her life was back on track.

By that night the only decision he'd reached was that he had to see her. He also wasn't waiting five days. It was as though a part of him couldn't breathe when away from her. It would only be through talking to Neve that he would make sense of the noise in his head. So he'd packed up camp and slept in the horse truck ready for an early start. He had a small window in which to see her before Graham dropped off the girls.

Day three of Tanner being away, the fly-in locusts arrived.

He awoke to an eerie silence. When he looked out the truck window, a golden glow shrouded the bush. Tiny bodies and wings filled the sky, creating constant movement and absorbing all the blue. The abundance of feed after the wet spring meant the second generation of locusts had thrived. Ravenous, they travelled together in dense migrating bands towards areas of autumn-sown wheat.

He texted to let everyone know where the locusts were, then went to check on Arrow in his portable yard. The gelding gave him a long-suffering look and stamped his foot to dislodge the locusts climbing on his leg. Last night's lucerne hay had been stripped and all that was left were thick stalks. Bumps peppered his back as miniature bodies collided with him. Patch went to chase a locust that flew too close to his nose, but as locusts engulfed him, he retreated to the horse truck.

Tanner loaded Arrow. After checking the fly netting he'd covered the truck radiator in last week was secure, he left the reserve.

It was as though he was in the middle of a locust storm. Sandy-brown bodies flew straight towards him or lay across the dirt road in drifts. Driving slowly, he made sure his headlights stayed on so oncoming traffic would know he was approaching.

By the time he hit the bitumen the density of the winged insects had thinned. By the time he was halfway home, he drove at a normal speed with only a handful of locusts pelting the windscreen. Meredith's garden and Neve's vegetables would be safe for the moment, along with Phil's winter wheat crop.

Once at Claremont he unloaded Arrow and gave the front of the truck a quick pressure-wash. Patch disappeared in the direction of the chook pen. The border collie would be happy to stay while he went to see Neve.

Meredith's car wasn't in the garage, and when he went to the house for a shower she also hadn't been inside. He left her a note saying he was back and he'd talk to her soon. He'd deliberated about saying more, but until he talked to Neve he was no closer to finding a way through his emotional chaos.

He made sure netting covered his ute radiator, and that he had a spare piece for Neve's car, before taking the shortcut to Rosewood. Even with the locusts adding time to his journey, he'd arrive before the girls were dropped off. As he drove through the front gate smoke spiralled from the chimney, and Dell and Bassie were munching on their morning hay. He parked in his usual place beneath the cedar tree. As he walked towards the front veranda he rolled his shoulders and strove for calm. He had no idea what to say when he saw Neve, but he'd come too far to now run again.

Palms cold and heart hammering, he knocked on the front door. Nothing. No footsteps. No sound. He waited and then knocked again. Still nothing. He turned to study the garage. The closed door gave no clue as to whether or not Neve's car was inside. He followed the veranda around to the back of the house and peered through the kitchen window. No lights were on, but the small black rectangle on the bench appeared to be Neve's phone. When he dialled her number, lights flashed from inside as her mobile rang.

He headed to the garage to open the side door. The interior was empty. He dialled Meredith. Perhaps Neve didn't have the girls today and had gone out, leaving her phone behind.

'Hi, darling ...' Relief quickened Meredith's words. 'Where are you?'

'At Neve's, but she isn't here. Are you in town?'

'Yes, at the café. I would have thought she'd have been there. She didn't say she was going anywhere when we spoke last night.'

Guilt twisted inside. He would have been the reason Meredith and Neve had needed to speak. 'There's no sign of her car anywhere, is there?'

'No. I'm with Edna and we'll both keep an eye out.'

Meredith's mention of Edna had been natural, but it also had let him know Meredith would be careful about what she said.

'Neve's phone's still here so she can't have gone far.'

'She wouldn't have. Last night she'd almost finished the book she'd been reading, so she might be on her way to the library. She also was going to take some books to the adventure playground. I'll let you know if I see her.'

'Thanks. I will too. Love you.'

'Love you too, son.'

He tapped his phone against his leg. The library in the old train station didn't open until eleven, which was hours away. Neve's left-behind phone also suggested she'd been distracted. On a hunch he jogged to his ute. There was another place Neve went to find books, a place she'd already visited when troubled: the Reedy Creek Hall.

When the first locust hit his windscreen, he didn't give his worry full rein. But when one turned into twenty and there was no doubt the wind currents had swept the locusts towards Reedy Creek, dread settled deep into his gut.

Neve's sedan wasn't equipped to drive through a dense locust swarm. Insect-cleaning agent wouldn't have been added to her windscreen washer system and it was unlikely she'd have anything with which to clean locusts off her car. Her radiator air inlet also wasn't covered, which left her car at risk of overheating.

With his speed reduced to a crawl and locusts hampering his visibility, it felt like a lifetime until he saw the sign saying the village of Reedy Creek lay ahead. He hadn't passed Neve's car on the road, which gave him hope she either had made it here before the locusts hit or hadn't come this way after all.

Through the swarm he could just make out the corrugated line of the hall and the fence of the adjacent tennis courts. As he drove closer he saw the blurred shape of a white sedan. Tension drained from his body to be replaced by a sense of sheer relief. Neve was here and not stranded by the roadside anywhere. He parked beside her car and texted Meredith a quick message.

Then, not sparing any time to collect himself, he ran through the locusts to the front alcove of the hall. The slam of insects against his skin stopped as his boots rang on the wooden floorboards. At first all he registered was the bookshelf in front of him. Then movement to his left had him swing around. Neve looked up from where she sat in a sheltered corner, legs crossed, reading.

He wasn't sure who moved first. All he knew was that Neve's book thudded to the floor and he'd only taken a few strides when she was in his arms. He didn't have time to think, all he could do was feel. The steady pounding of his heart gave him the answers he'd been searching for and had been afraid to heed. Loving Neve and making a future together was worth every risk he had to take. Without her, he had no life. Without her, his world had no substance.

He framed her face with his hands.

'It hasn't been five days?' Her words were rushed and breathless.

'It shouldn't have even been one day. I love you, Neve and should never have left.'

She didn't reply, just kissed him. Her tight hold on his shoulders and the beat of her heart against his left him in no doubt that she'd meant every word about working through things together.

He lifted his head to brush tousled hair from her face. A day wasn't going to pass without him sliding his fingers through the vibrant, red-gold strands. He'd wasted so much time.

He spoke, uncaring that emotion would thicken his words. 'I don't just love you, I want to grow old with you and have our own little redheads that ask a million questions.'

'I want that too. So very much.' The radiance of her smile matched the luminous light in her eyes. 'I love you, Tanner and there's no other place I want to be but by your side.'

This time their kiss was a promise and a declaration, a resolution and a commitment.

It took a locust flailing in Neve's hair and another crawling over his cheek to break them apart. She touched his jaw as if proving to herself he was really there.

'Tanner … I just want you to know that you'll always be safe with me. I'm not going anywhere.'

He laced his fingers with hers and kissed the back of her hand. 'I know that … now.' He grinned and bent to pick up her forgotten book. 'I also know somewhere else I'd rather be.'

Together they turned towards the hall steps. Beyond the alcove the world was a seething, flickering locust cloud as thick as any snowstorm.

She brushed a locust from off his shirtsleeve. 'I was waiting for them to fly over so I could get home. I need to put some of that netting on my car.'

He stole another kiss before he answered. 'I have some for you, but I think that can wait until we come back for your car.'

'I think so too. There's no need to drive two cars back.' Eyes filled with light and laughter, she took hold of his hand, ready to make a run for his ute. 'Our time would be much better spent making the most of my empty house before the girls return tomorrow.'

If Neve never saw a locust again, it would be too soon.

Even though the swarm never made it to Woodlea, the damage to the crops, pastures and gardens around Reedy Creek had broken her heart. Just like the locusts in the black-and-white photographs in Meredith's family albums, they'd left behind nothing but bare earth and deep despair.

The emotional and financial damage inflicted by the tiny winged insects had been substantial. Farmers were having to re-sow crops, gardens were having to be started all over again and places like the Alpaca Café were in need of feed for their animals.

Edna and Meredith had organised a plant-and-hay donation day at the Reedy Creek Hall. Today Neve was over at Claremont helping Meredith pot up cuttings. She pressed a geranium shoot into a terracotta pot. The truth was she didn't need any excuse to spend the weekend at Claremont.

During the weekdays Tanner lived at Rosewood, and on the days she didn't have the girls she stayed over in Tanner's flat. They often ate dinner with Meredith and Phil in the main house and the kitchen would echo with their merriment. No longer was Tanner's swag permanently positioned at the flat door.

Ever since his trip away it had been as Ella had predicted: there'd been no more road bumps between them. Instead there'd been commitment, laughter and in-depth conversations, but most of all love. Now all she needed were some answers about Edward Jones and for Tanner to again talk to his father. But so far there'd been no reply to the letter she'd sent to the United Kingdom and there'd been no more contact between Tanner and Stewart.

As she added the pot to the collection filling the box beside her, Meredith smiled from where she was digging up clumps of leafy violets. 'I'm sure Reggie won't mind if we donate some of his carrot seedlings.'

'I won't tell him if you don't.'

Meredith laughed and moved to dig around another violet clump.

A car engine sounded. Meredith straightened and shaded her eyes against the morning sunlight. 'Where's Tanner?'

'At the rodeo yards.' Neve paused to examine the luxury vehicle that slowly made its way to the end of the poplar-lined driveway. 'Why?'

Meredith lowered her hand and took off her pink gardening gloves. 'That's a city car with a city driver. I hope ... Tanner might have a visitor.'

Neve pulled out her phone.

Tanner answered after one ring. 'Hey, finished with Meredith yet?'

His husky tone made her cheeks blush. 'No. I thought you said you had a ton of work to do this morning.' Neve paused as

Meredith approached the unfamiliar car and spoke to the elderly gentleman behind the wheel. Meredith glanced over at her and nodded. 'Tanner …'

'Yeah … you really do want me to come home?'

'I do, but not for the reason you're hoping for. I think … your father's here.'

Silence.

'Tanner?'

'I'm on my way. Neve … don't take anything he says personally … he's gruff and opinionated, but he's a good man.'

'Okay.'

She brushed off her hands and went over to where Tanner's father stood beside his car with the aid of a cane. Tall and thin, he once would have been a physically powerful man as well as an important one. His formal fawn trousers and blazer now hung off him, but there was no mistaking the hard line of his chin or air of self-assurance. It wasn't any wonder Tanner and his father's estrangement had endured. Both were strong-willed.

Bushy grey eyebrows drew together as Neve stopped in front of him.

'Hi, I'm Neve.' She offered him her hand, which he didn't shake.

When she saw his white-knuckled grip on his cane she understood why. He was working hard to maintain his balance.

'Good morning, I'm Stewart. I take it you're the city girl my son's been helping?'

She smiled, conscious she was in dirt-covered farm clothes and that Tanner's father's voice was modulated and highly educated.

'I think the politically correct term is I'm a ring-in, which means I get to enjoy the best of both worlds.'

Stewart's forbidding expression didn't change. She was also conscious he'd called Tanner his son. As hostile as their relationship was, he loved the child he'd adopted. He'd also ventured out to the bush to see him, which wouldn't have been a decision he'd have made lightly.

Meredith stood quietly watching the two of them.

Neve offered Stewart her arm. 'How about we go inside for a cuppa. I'll make yours Earl Grey so you too can have the best of both worlds ... city refinement and country hospitality.'

For a long second she thought he wouldn't accept her offer, then his lips twisted in what she hoped was a smile.

He took her arm. 'Thank you. A proper cup of tea would be appreciated. I don't know what I drank at that hotel I stayed in last night.'

She matched her pace to his. He looked around as he walked. 'Your photographs don't do your home justice, Meredith.'

'Thank you. I'm glad you've decided to see it for yourself. I've a large ground-floor guest room that I believe you'll find very comfortable.'

'We'll see,' was all Stewart said.

Neve had only helped him negotiate the bottom veranda step when the engine of Tanner's ute roared. Gravel skittered as he braked to a stop. Shoulders braced and stride long, he headed their way. His gaze skimmed her face before he greeted his father.

'Dad.'

From the grim cast of Tanner's profile, he hadn't expected his father to be so frail.

'Tanner.'

He moved forward to take his father's arm. Neve released her hold and went to stand beside Meredith at the base of the steps.

'You've met him before?' she asked quietly.

'No. We've only sent an occasional email since Tanner found me. I just wanted him to know that my door's always open. This is significant that Stewart's come today. I hope for Tanner's sake it isn't to deliver bad news.'

'Walking stick new?' Tanner asked when he and his father took a rest on the middle step.

'No.'

'Did you have a fall when we spoke last? Is that what that crash was?'

Stewart didn't answer until he reached the top step. Once on the veranda, he pulled his arm free from Tanner's grasp and looked around for Neve. She scaled the steps and again offered him her arm.

'Yes,' he said without looking at Tanner. His blunt tone indicated that this was the end of their conversation.

A muscle worked in Tanner's jaw.

When Stewart's arm trembled, Neve knew why he'd appeared to reject Tanner's assistance. He didn't want his son to know how exhausted and physically weak he was.

While Meredith prepared the tea, Neve made sure she sat between Tanner and his father. She was also careful to not make it obvious that she and Tanner were a couple. But when Tanner plucked a leaf out of her hair, his father's shrewd gaze narrowed.

After Stewart had enjoyed two cups of Earl Grey tea and a slice of Meredith's show-winning sponge cake, colour had replaced his ashen tone. Meredith and Neve worked hard to steer the small talk onto safe topics, but once Stewart had declined a second piece of cake, he turned to Tanner. 'I'm guessing you want to know why I'm here?'

Tanner nodded, his mouth a tense, serious line.

'I'm not sick, just old, so you can stop looking so worried. You'll have to put up with me for a while longer yet.' He glanced at Neve. 'I wanted to meet you and tell you in person why your grandmother's Mr Jones was such a mystery.'

Stewart reached into his coat pocket for a folded piece of paper. He placed it on the table, but before he opened it, he looked at Tanner. 'I also came because I owe you an apology. I shouldn't have snapped at you when you last called. Yes, I lost my balance and knocked over a small table, but that was no excuse for taking out my frustration on you.'

Father and son looked at each other, both of their gazes steely and their jaws jutted. Tanner mightn't be Stewart's biological child, but their similar mannerisms said they'd grown up as a close-knit family unit.

'Apology accepted,' Tanner said, tone gruff.

'While we're clearing the air … seeing as you finally would have made your mother proud and happy …' When Stewart looked at Neve she was surprised to see his grey eyes well with emotion. 'Cynthia would have liked you, Neve. I know she wasn't well, but she never went much on that American Genevieve.' Stewart looked back at Tanner. 'I also need to say I'm proud of you too … for being true to who you are.'

'Dad …'

Neve eased her seat backwards to give Tanner room to reach past to grasp his father's hand.

The intensity of emotion in the kitchen was almost palpable. She didn't dare look at Meredith because if her eyes watered, Neve's would too.

Stewart spoke again. 'I know you think I disapproved of you for not choosing law over the bush, but the truth is I was jealous of the blood that flows through your veins. Your passion for horses is a constant reminder that you aren't really my son. When your mother died … I was so scared I'd lose you too … I said things I shouldn't have.'

'You're the man who raised me. I'll always be your son.'

'I hope so ...' Stewart settled his other hand on the top of Tanner's. 'Son.'

Meredith briefly left the table to touch the corner of her eyes with a handkerchief. Neve blinked to hold back her own tears.

Father and son smiled at each other before Tanner settled back in his chair. His hand sought Neve's and she entwined her fingers with his.

Stewart sat straighter, before opening the folded piece of paper in front of him. 'Now, Neve ... why it's been such a challenge to find anything out about this first husband of your grandmother's is because ... he was a member of a top-secret United Kingdom squadron called the 618.'

'Wow. Sibylla was right. He was involved in something secret.'

'He certainly was. This highly elite RAF squadron flew modified versions of the Mosquito aircraft, which was why the engine plate wasn't from the usual Tiger Moths at the flying school. Edward was part of a covert mission that involved training for a special sea operation that used a highball or bouncing bomb.'

'No wonder there wasn't any information about what he did during the war.'

Stewart slid the paper that contained a page of printed information over to her. 'Exactly. Not only were the war records top secret, but under the *Official Secrets Act* Edward would have been forbidden to talk about what he did even to family members. Your grandmother wouldn't have really known why he was here.'

'So what happened? His plane must have crashed, even though we can't find any proof?'

'Unfortunately it did, just after take-off. There was a dust storm and poor visibility. The incident was recorded as a general RAAF crash so as to not alert the Japanese via the press that the

618 squadron was in Australia. When I found that record I knew something didn't add up, so I started digging.'

Neve stared unseeingly at the paper in front of her. She could only hope that Tanner had been right and that Netta and Edward had fitted a lifetime's worth of living into their too-short time together.

She focused on the section of information that listed Edward's war record. 'So this isn't all top secret now?'

'No, the veil of secrecy was lifted in 1975. It's incredible how many stories could then be told.'

'I can imagine. Especially Edward's. Thank you. This helps answer so many questions.'

'You're very welcome. I'm glad to have been able to help you find some answers.' Stewart smiled across at Meredith. 'If your offer of a room still stands, I'd like to accept it.' He then nodded towards Tanner. 'I'll have a rest before seeing this fancy horse of yours that's splashed all over your website.'

Stewart's overnight stay turned into three nights. When he left Tanner had already booked a plane ticket from Sydney to Dubbo for his father's next trip. They'd planned to drive out to see the hideaways and also to take a look at the old wartime airfield. Having his relationship with his father restored removed the last of the shadows from Tanner's eyes. The time Stewart spent with Tanner also seemed to have lifted a burden from him. On his final day at Claremont he'd needed no help negotiating the front veranda steps.

Intrigued by the revelations about Edward Jones's secret bouncing-bomb mission, Neve looked further into the 618 squadron that had been given the codename 'Oxtail'. Edward and her grandmother must have met sometime after the squadron arrived in January

1945, the ball was March, which was perhaps when he'd proposed, and then by April they were married. Now all she needed were the more personal details about how they met and why the marriage had been kept hidden.

The answers arrived in a large envelope with United Kingdom postage stamps. As hard as it was Neve waited until the girls had left and Tanner had arrived before opening the letter. They sat on the lounge, in front of the open fire, while she read the contents.

Edward's youngest sister, Alice, had been thrilled to receive Neve's letter. She'd known about her brother's marriage. After the *Official Secrets Act* had been lifted, a 618 squadron member had contacted her to fill her in on what her brother had done during the war. As she was family she was then able to obtain Edward's official military service record from the Ministry of Defence, which she had included.

Before the war Edward had been a fingerprint expert. His sister remembered him as being loyal and compassionate and a real gentleman. He'd written to her that he'd met someone, Netta, while playing tennis at a local hall. In his next letter he'd revealed he'd asked Netta to marry him at a ball and had proposed with a posy of flowers instead of a ring. In a subsequent letter he'd contained photos of the wedding along with a personal note from Netta.

Neve stopped reading to examine the full-length wedding photos Alice had sent copies of. The beautiful black-and-white images further showed how much her grandmother and Edward had loved each other.

Alice then detailed how her family had been notified about Edward's death. Straight away she'd written to Netta and the two had exchanged letters. It was what Alice then revealed about Netta that answered the questions as to why her grandmother's first marriage had been wiped from Neve's family history.

Before the war, Netta's parents had pushed her towards the son of prominent family friends. When war started, faced with uncertainty and pressure from both families as well as the son, Netta had agreed to be engaged. But before they were able to marry, her fiancé was posted overseas.

While he was away, she met and fell in love with Edward. Wanting to do the right thing by both men, she'd written to her fiancé and broken off their engagement. She returned her engagement ring to his family who, along with her parents, refused to speak to her or to acknowledge her marriage to Edward. Neve reached for Tanner's hand when she read that this treatment continued even after Netta had lost Edward.

When her ex-fiancé returned injured from the war, mired in grief and with nowhere to go, Netta again faced pressure from both families to marry the man she'd jilted. They believed it would be the only way to make the scandal disappear. Her ex-fiancé had been prepared to take her back on the condition she never mention the name of her first husband. Alice then wrote that once Netta was remarried her letters stopped. She'd never heard from her again.

Neve re-read the last paragraph. Here was proof that her grandparents hadn't been a love match. It was also clear why her grandfather had never gone to Reedy Creek Hall and why, when her grandmother had gone, she'd appeared almost young and carefree.

As for why her grandfather had been prepared to still marry her grandmother, she could only hazard a guess. Maybe it was because with her red-gold hair and gracefulness, Netta had been considered the beauty of the district. Or maybe it was because as the only surviving child, she'd stood to inherit bluestone Bundara and its productive farm land.

Tanner's arm encircled her and he kissed her temple. 'You okay? This is a lot to take in.'

'It is. I just feel so sad for my grandmother. All those years of silence and secretive visits to Edward's grave. I also feel anger towards my grandfather … but I think in his cold, unemotional way he loved her. My mother said he asked for her before he passed away.'

'I wonder why your grandmother's memento box stayed hidden?'

'I wonder too … she didn't live long after my grandfather died.' Neve leaned forward to place the envelope and its contents on the coffee table. 'The farm was in debt after years of drought and grandfather's mental and physical ill health. My mother always blamed the stress of getting Bundara ready for sale for my grandmother's stroke. Perhaps she simply didn't have a chance to dig the box up again?'

'Your grandmother's love for Edward might have been hidden for decades, but now it's no longer a secret. In a way they're together again and can now rest in peace.'

Neve turned to kiss the man whose integrity, strength and unselfishness had not only enriched her life, but had also brought her so much peace. 'Have I told you today how much I love you, Tanner Callahan?'

# EPILOGUE

Autumn had segued into winter and now bare branches swayed against the backdrop of an airbrushed sunset of apricot orange.

A hint of wood smoke tinged the air as the bonfire Neve had helped Tanner build took its time to burst into life. Around the large pile of wood, checked blankets covered hay bales and lanterns hung on poles to push back the incoming night. Neve counted the marshmallow packet stash she'd hidden in the basket beneath the bread rolls. Tanner had already snuck one packet and Maya and Kait's cheeks resembled those of the wombat she'd discovered on her morning ride.

Tonight was the first celebration of many at the site where their dream home would be built. Thanks to heavy financial losses, Claremont's stockbroker neighbour had abandoned his plans to renovate his small farmhouse. When Tanner had approached him about buying the farm, contracts had been exchanged within a month.

She moved the marshmallows to a new hiding place in another basket and stared out over the picturesque Bell River Valley to the distant hewn ridge. She could understand why Tanner loved this elevated plateau and had wanted to wake up every morning to the breathtaking view.

As well as finalising their house design, Neve had worked with Meredith to plan a water-wise garden. Fliss had already potted up cuttings from the Bundara garden that Neve's grandmother had once planted.

To the left of where the house would sit there would also be enough space for a vegetable garden as well as smaller paddocks. When Dell's foal arrived she would need space away from Bassie and Skittles, who had become partners in pony crime. Add into the mix two big-eyed alpacas and their animal family was growing.

Further down the hill there was room for stables and a round yard, where Arrow and Jazz would have their own larger paddocks nearby. She couldn't wait for when Tanner could teach his own little redheads to ride in the circular yard. The contentment he'd always found whenever he'd worked in a round yard now encompassed the other arenas of his life. He'd hung up his droving hat to focus on his horse training and to start a campdrafting school. Now the only trips he took out on the long paddock were with Neve and were for enjoyment, not escape.

She glanced across to where Tanner laughed with his father as they sat side by side on a hay bale. Stewart flew from Sydney once a month to stay for a week. He'd consented to wearing boots, even if he kept them polished and pristine. It always made Neve's heart light seeing them together and the closeness of their father–son bond. As the relationship with his father had repaired, the final barrier that had stood between Tanner and his Woodlea life had fallen. No longer did Meredith look at him with worry in her eyes, only love.

Neve searched for Cressy, who sat next to Fliss, Drew and Freya on some nearby hay bales. Fliss and Hewitt's wedding plans were underway, but Fliss was being very mysterious about what she was organising. Knowing Fliss, every little detail would be perfect.

Neve's attention centred on Cressy. She was worried about the cowgirl. Cressy was again looking too thin and insisting she was fine, even when her cheeks were as pale as the frosts that blanketed Rosewood's lawns. But this time Neve suspected what was wrong with Cressy had nothing to do with taking risks and everything to do with why Denham hovered and insisted on carrying anything heavy.

Reassured Cressy appeared okay, Neve went to the table to check there would be enough plates. Over on a portable gas barbeque, Hewitt and Denham were cooking up platters of steaks and sausages. Giggling sounded and she glanced over to where Taylor and Ella chatted. As Edna approached, they stopped talking. With Bethany and Mac together, everyone was nervous about whom Edna would now turn her matchmaking focus on.

Meredith caught her eye and smiled. Neve smiled in return. Meredith's kindness and companionship made Neve feel as though she was once again woven into the fabric of a loving family. Her new life had both meaning and purpose. She took the cover off the rice salad she'd made from her mother's much-loved cookbook. She was working her way through the recipes and each one brought back treasured memories of the mother and grandmother she'd cherished.

She stifled a yawn. She was now the proud owner of the disused Woodlea fire station. Between supervising renovations and getting organised to open her new occupational therapy practice, she'd skimped on sleep. Sibylla had been the first specialist to rent out a room. The audiologist had welcomed the opportunity to be part of a collective health service to support local and rural families. Now all they needed were some more health professionals to occupy the spare rooms.

Last night she'd stayed up late to talk to Alice and her daughter in the United Kingdom over the internet. Plans were underway for Alice's daughter to bring her mother to Woodlea in the spring to see her brother's final resting place.

A hand linked with hers before Tanner led her into the shadows and away from the bonfire that now shot sparks high into the darkening sky.

'You look tired,' he said, pulling her close for a tender kiss.

The care and concern he showered on her never failed to make her feel precious and loved. She rested her cheek against the solid warmth of his chest and his arms tightened round her.

Once Woodlea's current wedding fever subsided, there'd be a new wedding for the yarn bombers to prepare for. Except this one would be held in Reedy Creek at the small corrugated-iron hall, a place of community, belonging and new beginnings.

# ACKNOWLEDGEMENTS

It's been so wonderful to again spend time in small-town Woodlea as well as to be able to give Tanner his story.

As always thanks goes to HarperCollins and the incredible and very lovely Harlequin Mira imprint team of Rachael Donovan, Julia Knapman, Alex Nahlous and Sarah Fletcher. Thanks to your expertise, insights and attention to detail the inside of *The Round Yard* shines as bright as its beautiful outside. Thanks so much also to the design team who create stunning cover after stunning cover.

Huge thanks to my special writing buddies who have been such a steady constant in what has been a tough year. Your support and friendship are very much treasured. Thank you to my children, Callum, Bryana, Adeline and Angus, for providing me with countless memories. A part of you is woven into every book. Last but not least, thanks to Luke, my hero, my inspiration and my go-to for farm machinery information. I couldn't do what I do without you.

Finally, thank you to my readers. It's such a privilege to be on your virtual and real-world bookshelves. Your enthusiasm and passion for the books that I love to write keeps the ideas fresh and the words flowing. Until next time, take care and happy reading.

Turn over for another Woodlea story.

# THE
# PURPLE
# HILLS

by

# ALISSA CALLEN

# THE
# PURPLE
# HILLS

ALISSA CALLEN

*For Luke*

Sibylla Elliot could have sworn a miniature pony ambled past the kitchen window.

She collected a teaspoon from the cutlery drawer before scanning the view beyond the oversized glass. Apart from the autumn wind swaying the leaves of the jacaranda tree and a magpie swooping down from the top of the pergola, nothing else moved. She made sure she didn't look at the paved outdoor area that once had been her mother's prized bed of fragrant mauve roses.

She added one spoonful of sugar instead of the usual two to her father's favourite mug. Her stepmother might have erased as much as she could of her gentle mother's presence but Bernice hadn't tackled her father over his sugar consumption. That task had been left to Sibylla.

As she reached for the kettle, the click of small, hard hooves on concrete had her swing around. Abandoning her father's mid-morning coffee, she headed for the next-door sitting room. A breath-misted pane of glass on the French doors failed to obscure the big pony eyes looking in at her. The door rattled when the pony's knee bumped the glass as she pawed the ground.

'Shhh Jelly Bean.' Sibylla turned the glossy brass handle and stepped outside. 'If Bernice sees you, she won't be happy.'

The bay pony, with a white snip on her nose, turned to face her. Sibylla rubbed her warm neck. With her thick winter coat Jelly Bean resembled an adorable fluff ball. 'What's up? Where's Riley?'

She looked left past the open garden gate to the track the pony had taken from the neighbouring farm. Usually her freckle-faced partner in crime wasn't far behind. While some rural kids had puppies, five-year-old Riley had a tiny pony as his shadow. Smaller than a great dane, Sibylla was sure Jelly Bean thought of herself as more of a dog than a horse.

Heavy breaths sounded to her right before the soles of Riley's running boots slapped against the concrete. Even with energetic Riley taking the shortcut, Jelly had worked out where he'd been going and had arrived first.

Sibylla's smile slipped. This was no normal visit. Dried tears streaked Riley's dusty cheeks. She bent to catch him as he threw himself against her. His small, wiry frame was as rigid as a corner fence post, his chest heaving.

Concern caused her arms to tighten around him. Pragmatic and cheerful, she'd never seen Riley upset, even when his eardrum had perforated or when his mother had failed to call last week for his birthday. 'Where's your dad, Riles?'

His words rushed out as a breathless torrent of anguish. 'On the ground. Jelly bit his boot … he won't wake up.'

'Where? Near the house or in the paddock?'

'Near the shed.'

Sibylla had her phone out of her jeans pocket even as she straightened. While she made the emergency call she kept her arm around Riley's narrow shoulders.

'Everything okay?' her father's voice rumbled from behind them.

Sibylla took her time to return her phone to her pocket. She couldn't allow her father to glimpse how worried she was about Hugh. She also had to hide the fear that never left her whenever there was a farm accident. Her father's recent stroke and vulnerability was why she'd temporarily left the coast to return to the family farm. She couldn't remind him of all they'd lost on that long-ago summer day.

'Yes.' She took Riley's hand. 'Hugh's somehow knocked himself out. The ambulance is on its way.'

Her father nodded as he shuffled from the room. The intense expression on his weathered face communicated how hard he was concentrating to move as quickly as he could.

She squeezed Riley's fingers. 'Dad's gone to get the gator key and then we'll check on your dad.'

When her father returned he was only halfway across the living room when he nodded. Sibylla lifted her hand to catch the key he threw across to her to save time. A bittersweet happiness briefly shouldered aside her worry. As strained as their relationship was, in a time of crisis they were still the team they'd been in her childhood.

'Thanks,' she said, voice quiet.

He gave her a barely-there smile before lowering himself into a nearby chair.

With Riley's hand in hers, she headed for the side-by-side gator in the corrugated-iron shed. As fast as her heart beat and thoughts raced, she kept their pace even. Riley would be exhausted and she wanted her composure to reassure him. When she clicked in his seatbelt, he looked over his shoulder, his eyes teary.

She dropped a kiss on his tousled nutmeg-brown head. Even covered in red dirt he smelt like fresh, sun-dried cotton.

'Jelly will be okay, she'll be right behind us.'

When Riley nodded and sought Sibylla's hand, she blinked to keep her own emotions at bay.

It had been only three weeks since she'd stopped at her neighbour's front gate to chat to the boy and his pony who were waiting for the mail contractor. It had only taken three visits for motherless little Riley to sneak into the space she always made sure her small audiologist patients never accessed. Brave, curious and intellectually-gifted Riley was special. She turned on the gator before the thought could follow that his slow-smiling father was too.

As she'd predicted, the bay mini-pony cantered behind them as they made their way through the boundary gate between the two properties. But the closer she drove to Hillside the less she turned to see where Jelly was. Her attention fixed on the shiny roofline of the large shed beyond the green expanse of the back garden. She then focused on where Hugh's white farm Hilux was parked in front of the end bay. As it was the weekend, the local horse chiropractor would have been busy doing farm work with his tan kelpie, Diesel.

Her fingers locked around the steering wheel as she searched the ground. But the only thing out of place was a fallen branch from the old gum that stood between the shed and the stables. There also didn't look to be any ominous patches of blood darkening the dust.

Riley tugged at her arm. 'Dad's gone.'

She turned the gator towards the house. 'He'll be inside.' She failed to keep the relief out of her words. 'Look, there's Diesel by the back door.'

It made no sense that Hugh being conscious should ease the tightness in her chest. As much as Riley had welcomed her into his life, his distant, taciturn father hadn't been as open. She could count on one hand the times he'd said more than two sentences to her. It was only when he was with his son that she glimpsed the warmth and humour beneath his reserve.

Riley had his seatbelt unclipped even before the gator engine noise quietened. She made sure she took his hand before they entered the back door. The kitchen appeared empty. Then, a crash sounded down the hallway.

'Dad.'

Riley ploughed his way through the open door. Sibylla slowed him when she saw Hugh leaning against the wall outside Riley's bedroom. Dirt and grass covered his left side and his usual wide-brimmed hat was missing.

'Ril—'

Sibylla may as well have not spoken. When father and son saw each other, Riley dragged his hand free and Hugh pushed himself away from the wall. It was only Riley's tight arms around his father's waist and Sibylla grabbing Hugh's shoulder to hold him upright that stopped him from slumping forward.

'Let's get your dad into the kitchen,' Sibylla said, working hard to get Hugh's arm around her shoulders.

From her previous stealthy glances she knew he was all bone and work-hardened muscle, but the reality of supporting his large frame rendered her breathless. When they made it to the kitchen and he was finally in the closest chair, she left her hands where they were on his shoulder and chest to drag in a breath.

She caught the scent of cedar and registered the stubble softening the firm line of his jaw. Beneath her palms, the heat from his skin bypassed the cotton of his green work shirt. Beneath her fingertips, corded tendons rippled as he reached for Riley's hand. Never could she have imagined what it would feel like to touch Hugh. Even dazed and unsteady, his vitality and strength flowed into her.

She swallowed. It was too soon to appreciate the irony. All her friends said she was too fussy. But when her parents divorced she'd made a vow to never settle for anyone who didn't tick certain boxes. Finally, here was a man that her head and her hormones approved of. Yet he barely acknowledged that she existed.

She needed to lift her hands and to step away. But it was as though she were anchored to him like metal to a magnet. The steady rise and fall of his broad chest reassured her that he was, for the most part, okay.

Muscles again flexed as he shifted in his seat. Then, his whisky-brown gaze met hers.

Hugh Mason was living his own personal nightmare.

The woman he'd been battling to ignore ever since Riley brought her home to show her the solar system hanging from his bedroom ceiling stood close beside him. Even with a raging headache and blurred vison, the beauty of her ebony hair, pale skin and large grey eyes moved him. Her blue shirt and dark jeans hugged her in all the right places and further reminded his testosterone that he was a man.

The gentle pressure of her hands on his shoulder and chest did nothing to ease the world spinning around him. Knowing she was touching him only heightened the dizziness stealing his stability. Before all he'd smelt was dust and now all he could smell was the fragrance of spring flowers. All he needed was for her to smile and the self-control he prided himself on would snap. She had a soft mouth made for kissing.

But as she carefully lifted her hands and stepped away, her expression remained serious and unsmiling.

'Dad?'

Riley's scared, thin voice brought the world back into focus.

'I'm okay.' He touched Riley's smooth, grubby cheek. He'd give his life for his son. Even now, every day he said a silent thank you that Clarisse hadn't contested his request for sole custody. 'You went next door?'

'Jelly came too.'

Hugh tried a smile but the wave of nausea turned it into a grimace. He risked a glance at Sibylla. 'Thanks for coming over, I'm fine.'

Her only answer was a lift of an eyebrow.

He tried to come to his feet. Suddenly Sibylla was by his side. 'Sit tight. Dr Fliss will soon be here.'

He silenced a groan and settled back into his chair. He couldn't stand even knowing that Fliss was on her way. The local doctor wasn't to be messed with. Her do-what-you-are-told stare had worked on patients who were far less confused than he was. Right now he was trying to remember what Riley's Jelly looked like. He had a feeling she could be a pony.

Sibylla bent towards him and he stiffened thinking she would touch him. But all she did was examine the left side of his head. He didn't have the energy to lift a hand to work out why his temple pounded like it did.

'What happened?' she asked, voice low.

He went to shake his head, then stopped himself. 'I think I was … at the shed.'

Riley nodded. 'A branch fell. Jelly and I heard it.'

'What day is it?' Sibylla asked.

Hugh repressed a sigh. He'd had a concussion at the start of the rugby season and knew low-order questions were important to clarify the extent of any injury plus to keep a patient awake. But he had no idea what day it was. It hurt to think but if Mrs Poole wasn't there looking after Riley, it meant it had to be the weekend. He made a guess. 'Saturday.'

Riley smiled. Sibylla didn't.

'Okay,' she said, her eyes never leaving his. 'What's my name?'

'Sibylla.'

Not even a knock to his head would make him forget who she was and how her quick smile made him feel.

'Can you say these words after me?' Sibylla said. 'Bird, rabbit, cat?'

The crunch of tyres saved him from making more of a fool of himself. Even when not concussed, Sibylla Elliott disturbed his equilibrium. It was bad enough she'd been privy to his physical weakness. She'd now lost him after the word *bird*.

Before she left to walk to the front door, she gave him a last intense look.

Alone with Riley, Hugh relaxed the tense line of his shoulders. He ruffled the top of Riley's hair. 'Remember how last time I had to go to the hospital? I'll have to go there again.'

'Okay.'

Hugh thought hard. It was as though a thick winter fog had engulfed his brain. An elusive thought half-formed and then disintegrated. 'Mrs Poole will look after you until I get back.'

Riley didn't answer, just turned his head towards the sound of footsteps at the kitchen door. Instead of the paramedics, Sibylla and Dr Fliss walked in. Fliss, with her symmetrical features and shiny brunette hair, was a taller image of her cowgirl sister, Cressy. Both lived on historic properties on the other side of small town Woodlea.

Fliss's smile flashed as she greeted Riley. 'How's my favourite little astronomer?'

'Good.'

'And your sore ear?'

'Better.'

'Can I take a look at it after I check over your dad?'

Riley nodded and looked towards Sibylla. When she held out her hand, Riley squeezed his fingers before moving to sit on Sibylla's knee.

Hugh was glad of the sudden quiet. Even normal speaking voices were too loud.

Just like at the rugby ground when he'd taken a hard hit, Fliss asked him questions before she examined him.

When she was done, she considered him with a slight frown. 'I don't need to tell you you're concussed. What I don't know is whether the branch knocked you out or if it was the impact of your head hitting the ground.'

He didn't answer. He had no idea. Another wave of nausea hit him.

'You'll need another CT scan.'

'Okay.'

'This is your second brain injury. No cheating again by going back to work early.' Fliss's voice firmed. 'And absolutely no driving until I give you the all clear.'

This time he didn't reply because he had no intention of sitting around doing nothing. He had a business and a farm to run but most of all Riley to take care of. He'd recovered quickly last concussion. He would do so again.

As the silence stretched, Fliss gave him her take-no-prisoners stare. But between the light being too bright and trying to watch Sibylla and Riley out of the corner of his eye, he missed the full impact.

Another engine sounded. The ambos were here. He went to stand but Fliss's hand was already on his shoulder to keep him in his chair. No wonder her fiancé, pickup rider Hewitt, made sure he didn't injure himself again. Perceptive Fliss was wise to country boys who hated fuss, let alone being out of action.

When she was sure he'd remain seated, she left to update the two paramedics who entered the kitchen.

Riley came to his side. Hugh pulled him close to drop a kiss on his forehead. 'Love you to Neptune and back.'

'Love you to Neptune and back too.'

'Be good for Mrs Poole. I'll be home soon.'

When Sibylla approached he fought through the fog in his head. He couldn't let her, or Riley, know how much she occupied his thoughts. If he remembered what happened he wouldn't be surprised if he'd been thinking about her instead of taking notice of strong wind gusts and falling branches. There was a reason why gum trees were known as widow makers; their branches could just give way.

'Hugh?'

Sibylla's soft voice hit a sweet spot that was a perfect volume level.

'Yeah.'

'It's Saturday, remember.'

He pressed his mouth shut. He didn't.

She spoke again. 'Mrs Poole isn't here. Riley also said she's not coming next week as Mr Poole has been in hospital. You were taking the week off to put up a new fence.'

The half-thought formed into a coherent sentence. Sibylla was right. That's what his subconscious had been trying to remind him.

She placed a hand on Riley's arm. The need to also feel her touch hit him hard. He closed his eyes to blank out the intense longing. He and Riley were fine on their own. They didn't need anyone else, even if the woman before him fired his blood.

'Hugh?' Again her soft voice sounded. 'I'll stay.'

His eyes snapped open and, uncaring of the pain, he shook his head. Finally, he could think clearly. This nightmare was not continuing. He wasn't having her sleeping two doors down from him. He wasn't seeing her every day. He wasn't having her laughter wrap around him, stirring the yearnings he'd long ago discarded.

'Thanks. We'll be fine.'

'No, you won't. You can't drive.' Their gazes locked. 'To be honest, I'd welcome coming to stay. Things have been a little ... tense at home.'

The moment the light in her grey eyes dulled, he knew concussion or no concussion, he'd be making a critical error in judgement. Riley had mentioned something about Sibylla's stepmother not being very nice to her.

He spoke slowly. 'If you're sure, I'd appreciate it.'

She smiled her radiant, sunrise smile. It wasn't his imagination that the world tilted around him.

'I'm sure.'

# CHAPTER

## 2

Beyond the conservatory glass walls of Hugh's farmhouse the early morning sunlight warmed the garden that was draped in the russet hues of autumn. As much as Sibylla enjoyed her sea change, she was glad to be back in the bush. She missed the vibrancy of the colour display when the seasons changed.

Her gaze travelled to the undulating hills that gave way to the distant ridge that marked the edge of the fertile Bell River valley. The view was similar to the one that could be seen from the wide veranda of her family home. She also missed watching the hills she loved being bathed in purple when the sun slowly set.

She answered a work-related text from the audiologist filling in for her before taking a sip of her tea. Riley wasn't yet awake, and in the two days since she'd slept in the spare room, Hugh appeared to be following Fliss's instructions to rest. From the washing up neatly stacked in the drying rack each morning, she guessed he slept through the day so he could be awake in the quieter, darker night. His frequent blinking indicated he was still experiencing light sensitivity.

A kookaburra cackled from deep in the garden. Jelly Bean lifted her head from where she was grazing. Tiny hoof prints criss-crossed the dew-soaked lawn, showing where she'd ambled. The mini-pony had her own small paddock, but she spent most of her time around the house. Her favourite place was standing at the kitchen screen door to watch what was happening inside.

Sibylla again sipped at her tea and, just like the day before, her attention strayed towards the photographs on the table against the back wall. Riley's mother might only barely be in his life, but pictures of them together could be found amongst the family photos. She was yet to see one of Hugh and Clarisse on their wedding day, though. Even before she'd discovered that Clarisse had been blonde, model-slim and stunning, she'd had a sense about what she'd been like. The sleek, minimalistic house renovations didn't match Hugh's home office that was filled with books and decorated with Riley's bright artwork.

Riley's bare feet padded on the floorboards before he climbed into her lap. She snuggled his warm, sleepy body close. The sight of his father out cold continued to worry him. When Hugh was awake, he stayed by his side.

'So what shall we do today? Go to story time at the library and then keep working on our papier-maché planets after lunch?'

'Will Dad come?'

'We can ask, but he might still need to sleep.'

Riley nodded before tugging at his left ear.

Even in the short amount of time she'd known him, he'd already had one ear infection. From what he'd said, he'd had quite a few last winter as well. 'Your other ear sore?'

His forehead scrunched while he thought. 'Not now.'

Which meant it had been. After the number of ear infections he'd had it wouldn't be surprising if his pain threshold were quite high. 'Before we go to town how about we do some of those things we did last week?'

She'd put her audiologist hat on and together they'd blown up balloons to clear his narrow Eustachian tubes. She'd also made sure he knew how to blow his nose properly by focusing on one nostril at a time.

'Okay.' He touched his ear again. 'Dr Fliss said if my eardrum gets a hole again I might have to have comets in my ears.'

Riley and his planet obsession always made her smile. But not this time. She hoped he'd latched onto a similar-sounding space word and not that his multiple ear infections were affecting his auditory processing. 'Dr Fliss was talking about things called grommets. If you keep doing everything I showed you, hopefully you won't need them.'

The creak of water pipes sounded. Hugh must be awake and taking a shower.

Riley scrambled off her lap. 'I'll ask Dad if he wants to come with us.'

Sibylla only nodded. Riley had already sprinted out of the conservatory. She cupped her hands around her mug and finished her tea. It was unlikely Hugh would accompany them but if he did she'd need every drop of caffeine. No one could know how he affected her. Especially Hugh. It was a secret that had to follow her back to her regular life.

When she'd gone home to pack and to tell her father she'd visit each day, she'd made sure her emotions were carefully concealed. Her father had only given her a quick look before Bernice had gushed about how wonderful it was that she was helping out and that she might need to stay longer than a week.

Riley and Hugh's voices brought Sibylla to her feet. She flexed the fingers on her right hand. It ached now that it was away from the warmth of the mug. After her last ride, she'd slipped and hit her hand against the wash bay rails. That would teach her to not watch out for puddles when hosing down Cloud.

She headed for the kitchen. When Hugh was awake, the busier she kept the less she caught herself listening out for him. The husky timbre of his voice resonated with something deep within her. As for his laughter, she wasn't going to think about how good it sounded or how the corners of his smiling eyes crinkled when he tickled Riley.

She was leaving the walk-in pantry with Riley's box of cereal when Hugh and Riley entered. Hugh's dark hair was shower damp and instead of his usual jeans and cotton work shirt he wore a charcoal-grey T-shirt and faded jeans. Like Riley, he didn't seem to feel the chill and his feet were bare.

'Morning.' She kept her voice low in case he was still having trouble with noise.

He gave her a too-brief smile before flicking on the electric kettle. His attempt at appearing normal didn't fool her. The hollows defining his cheekbones and the pallor beneath his tan suggested he should still be in bed. He rested his hip against the kitchen bench and loosely crossed his arms.

Sibylla concentrated on pouring Riley's cereal and not on the muscled strength of Hugh's forearms.

'Dad said he'll come.' Riley stood beside her as he snuck a piece of crunchy cereal.

Sibylla looked across to where Hugh was now making a coffee. His carved profile was unreadable. 'Like another cuppa?' was all he said.

Jelly Bean appeared at the back kitchen door. The screen door rattled as the pony flicked it with her front hoof. Riley stuck his hand in the cereal box before racing outside. The mini-pony would munch on her cereal treats while Riley took off her purple rug.

'Thanks.' Sibylla walked over to where Hugh stood at the bench. 'I would.'

If he was conscious that they were now alone it didn't show in his casual nod.

'Are you sure you want to come with us?' she asked, trying to glimpse the emotions behind his reserve. 'Riley will understand.'

'I'll be fine.' He draped a teabag in her mug. 'I don't want to make this any harder on Riley than it already is. Besides, I keep putting off seeing Taylor ...' He rubbed the back of his hair. 'She might be able to give me a haircut as well as Riley.'

Distracted by the curl of his biceps, Sibylla took a moment to reply. 'If she can't, we can always go in on another day.'

He nodded as he added milk to her mug. She ignored the pang of pleasure that he knew how she liked her tea.

His eyes met hers. 'Thanks again for staying. I haven't recovered as quickly as I'd hoped. I wouldn't even trust myself behind the wheel yet.'

She took hold of the mug handle. It was either that or reach out to smooth the lines of tension that bracketed his mouth.

'Getting over concussion can take time. I know when James knocked himself out it took at least two weeks until he felt normal again. It was strange seeing him without his nose in a book.' As hard as she tried she couldn't strip the pain from her voice. She turned away to hide her expression.

'Sibylla ... I'm sorry about your brother. His birthday's coming up, isn't it?'

She stilled before placing her mug on a round coaster on the kitchen table. 'It is. Has Dad ... talked to you about James?'

Ever since her seventeen-year-old younger brother had been killed in a quad-bike accident, talking about him had become taboo in her family. Perhaps if they had communicated their anguish and kept James's memory alive, then her parents' marriage might have survived.

'He did.'

'That's unusual … but a relief. It's been nearly ten years and every conversation I start gets shut down. Whereas Mum and I can at least reminisce now.'

'We've talked about James a few times. Maybe it's because your brother also liked to stargaze like Riley.'

'That could be it. Thanks … it means a lot to know Dad's talking to someone.'

She thought a muscle worked in Hugh's jaw but as Riley raced across the room to slide into his chair Hugh looked across at his son.

She took her time to pour milk onto Riley's cereal. Hugh's empathy and compassion ticked yet more of her boxes. To think she'd been worried about him discovering how much she was drawn to him. What she should have been fearful of was how perceptive he was about the entire spectrum of her emotions.

She shouldn't have underestimated his steady, all-seeing stare. From here on in, she wouldn't again. Her heart was at stake.

Concussion was not his friend.

Jaw tight, Hugh stared through the dark lenses of his sunglasses at the bitumen road that would lead them to Woodlea. The fog still hadn't lifted in his head, his sea legs continued and he was flat out focusing on anything for longer than a minute. He glanced sideways. Unless that something was Sibylla.

She'd changed out of her jeans and shirt into a white, long-sleeved dress that even with his sensitive eyes he kept wanting to stare at. With its fitted lace top and flowy skirt, it clung to her neat curves. Her long ebony hair fell loose around her shoulders, calling for him to tangle his hands in the silken strands. So strong was the need, he'd had to fold his arms.

As for his emotions, it was as though his feelings were on steroids and his decision-making abilities had gone AWOL. That was the only explanation for the way he'd reacted to the earlier sadness stripping the vibrancy from her voice. The impulse to hold her and comfort her had been insistent and strong. His hands fisted beneath his crossed arms. He hadn't felt this out of control even when around Clarisse.

'How's everyone travelling?' Sibylla asked in a soft, soothing tone.

'Good,' Riley said from the back seat where he was re-reading his library books.

Hugh stifled a sigh. So much for his usually reliable memory. He'd forgotten the book list the Reedy Creek school teacher had given him. As Riley could already read, Freya was helping with suggestions. The friendly redhead would be his teacher when Riley started school next year. Hugh had no doubts his son's needs would be met in the inclusive one-teacher school. Riley wouldn't feel isolated like Hugh had when he'd been academically accelerated as a child.

Realising Sibylla was looking at him he said, 'I'm good too.'

When her pink lips curved, he faked interest in the windmill out the side window to allow his testosterone to settle. A rainbow-coloured woollen scarf decorated the windmill's base. Guerrilla knitters had put small town Woodlea on the tourist map. Thanks to Woodlea also being the town of windmills, there was no shortage of structures to be yarn-bombed.

'That scarf wasn't there the other day,' Sibylla said with another smile that only dragged his attention back to the full sweep of her bottom lip. 'I love seeing what the knitters come up with next. There seems to be either a white winter or a white wedding theme happening in town.'

To his relief, after passing two more woollen-clad windmills, they reached Woodlea. As Sibylla drove along the main street, the sight of a woman dressed in a stylish navy dress and wearing a thick string of pearls had her take the first turn left. Sibylla may have left Woodlea years ago but Edna Galloway, the notorious town gossip and matchmaker, obviously hadn't changed.

Sibylla shot him a telling glance and he nodded. With Riley listening in, they didn't need to discuss the implications of Edna seeing them together. They'd be Woodlea's latest couple before they'd even unclipped their seatbelts.

At the end of their side-street detour, they turned past the double-storey Royal Arms. The white wrought-iron work on the historic verandas caught in the mid-morning light. He stifled a sigh. Apart from no driving Fliss had also said no alcohol. Having a relaxing cold beer anytime soon would have to wait.

Sibylla parked outside the old railway station that now housed the local library. Hugh turned to look at his son. The cream weatherboard building was Riley's favourite place.

Brown eyes bright, Riley stared through the car window at a small boy who stood in a line of people waiting to head inside. All the children wore an orange vest to signify they were from the local early learning centre. 'Steve's here.'

The infectious excitement and energy in Riley's voice pushed back Hugh's fatigue. He smiled. 'I thought he might be.'

It wasn't long before Riley was sitting cross-legged on the floor in front of the story time librarian. Beside him sat Steve and every so often the two boys would turn and smile at each other. As Leanne opened the book to read, Hugh moved away. He wasn't joining the other parents who had made use of the chairs behind the children. As quiet as the library was, his head was already pounding.

He looked for Sibylla and when he saw her near the non-fiction space section, gave her a nod. After she'd smiled in return, he headed outside. From his seat on the shaded bench out the front of the library, he had a clear view of the main street.

He'd spent his childhood further south where the hills stretched into mountain summits, but his home town had possessed a main street similar to this one.

The first thing he'd done when he knew he was going to be a father was ensure that his and Clarisse's child would grow up away from the city. In the beginning Clarisse had shared his dreams. When he mentioned their plans to an old Sydney boarding school friend, the outcome had been the purchase of Hillside. His friend hadn't wanted to carry on his family legacy and was now a London merchant banker.

A horn blasted. Hugh masked a flinch and gave a brief wave as Edna's four-wheel drive sped by on her way out of town. Heels clicked on the path before Sibylla joined him on the bench.

She sat the full bag of library books in the space between them. 'How are you?'

He went to say he was fine but the narrowing of her grey eyes called his bluff. 'I've been better.'

'Would a coffee help?'

'Thanks, probably not.'

Conversation lapsed as they stared at the busy main street. The tree-lined road ran through the heart of the town, past the stone church to the top of the hill where the red-bricked Woodlea hospital stood. After the spring floods it was good to see locals and tourists supporting the town's shops and businesses.

Sibylla lifted her phone to snap a photo of the closest yarn-bombed lamppost. Just like she'd mentioned, the recent yarn bombing was predominantly white. 'I know this sounds silly ... I live on the coast where everyone wants to be ... but I miss this place.'

'It's not silly at all. I wouldn't live anywhere else.' He paused. 'I'm sure, if you wanted to, you could come back.'

'I could in theory, but I have my business as well as other commitments to think of. Plus things would only get worse between Bernice and me. I'm sure she has a calendar marking off the days of my two-month visit.'

Hugh kept his expression from changing. While Sibylla hadn't said she had someone waiting for her, she had mentioned other commitments. A woman like her couldn't possibly be single. 'Have things always been difficult between you and Bernice?'

'They have. When Mum and Dad split I stayed with him because I thought he needed me more. Turns out I was wrong.' Pain edged her tone. 'I came home from boarding school to find he'd filled his life with another woman. Bernice never had children ... I think perhaps she just doesn't like sharing my father.' Sibylla gave him a small smile. 'But things have been better since I've been staying with you.'

It shouldn't make him feel content that she was happy being with Riley and him.

'Families and relationships are complex.' He didn't usually talk about his marriage but having such a conversation with Sibylla felt natural. 'Clarisse and I moved here for a better life but she ended up hating the isolation and slow pace. Primitive and unsophisticated were the words she used. By Riley's first birthday she was gone.'

Compassion softened Sibylla's mouth. 'I'm so sorry.'

'It was tough at the time but looking back it was inevitable that Clarisse and I would have our problems. Riley was a … surprise, quite early on in our relationship.' Sibylla nodded as he continued to speak. 'Riley knows that, in her own way, Clarisse loves him. She's the first to admit she wasn't meant to be a mother. She's remarried, to an older man, and lives in an apartment in Switzerland with a lake view. We've been to visit but to be honest it's a relief for all of us when we leave.'

Chatter sounded as the pre-schoolers exited the library in a long orange line. Story time was over.

When he went to stand, Sibylla put her hand on his arm. 'I can get Riley, if you like. There was a book the librarian was tracking down for me.'

'Okay. Thanks.'

He hoped she put his strained words down to his head injury and not the intense effort it took to appear unaffected by her touch.

When she'd disappeared into the library he released a tense breath. Concussion had a lot to answer for. If he wasn't careful, his heightened emotions and confusion would have him falling for a woman who'd made it clear moving back here wasn't a possibility.

He'd worked hard to create stability for Riley; he wasn't going to now jeopardise his son's happiness. The safest and most logical way to keep Riley's world predictable was by making sure there would only ever be the two of them. He glanced in the direction Sibylla had taken. Even if it meant denying the deep longings that the knock on his head seemed to have unleashed.

# CHAPTER
## 3

Hugh's insomnia was proving contagious. Sibylla smothered a yawn as she packed banana muffins into a picnic basket. She hadn't slept this poorly since her father had had his stroke.

She didn't know if it was because it would soon be James's birthday, or that yesterday Hugh had again kept to himself, or that she couldn't stop thinking about him raising Riley alone, but she'd tossed and turned until the birdsong had welcomed in the dawn light. After what he'd been through, no wonder he could appear guarded and hadn't ever remarried.

She added a container filled with cut fruit to the basket. This morning she was taking Riley into the hills she'd roamed as a child for a picnic by the river. She wasn't spending another day on high alert listening for Hugh or hoping he'd appear for longer than five minutes before he left to feed Banjo and the other stock horses.

'Found it.' Riley raced into the kitchen, a black cap now on his head. On the front was a picture of a planet and stars. After his haircut in town, brown hair no longer peeked from beneath the cap edges.

'Great. We're almost ready to go. How about you blow up another balloon for our papier-mâché?'

'Okay.' Riley sped into the living room. To her relief his sore ear no longer seemed to be troubling him.

Sibylla turned to talk to the pony watching her through the screen door. 'Sorry Jel, it's too far for you to come with us. You'll be fine here. Diesel also needs some company.'

The tan kelpie was keeping watch for Hugh as much as she was.

After she'd written Hugh a note to say where they'd be, she flexed her right hand to ease the stiffness. She didn't know what it was that made her turn, but when she did Hugh was standing at the doorway. His sunglasses made seeing his eyes impossible but he smiled as he walked into the kitchen. 'Morning.'

'Morning.'

She hoped her greeting didn't sound breathless. The fight to remind her hormones that he was off limits had only intensified. Taylor and her scissors had also worked their magic on Hugh. While his hair wasn't as cropped as Riley's, the shorter length showcased his high cheekbones and strong jawline.

'You look like you've been busy?' She eyed his jeans and dusty blue work shirt. When she hadn't seen him for breakfast she'd assumed he'd been asleep.

Hugh opened the container of banana muffins she'd left out on the bench for him. 'As busy as I can be when I forget why I went to the shed in the first place.' He nodded towards the packed basket as he peeled off the muffin paper. 'Where are you headed?'

'To the river for a picnic. Would you like to come?'

'Thanks. Maybe we could take a look at the wheat and go around the cattle on the way?'

'Sure.' She turned away to collect a third water bottle before he could sense her happiness.

Instead of taking the farm Hilux, they piled into Hugh's pewter-blue Land Cruiser. He automatically went to the driver's side and then took hold of the bull bar to steady himself as he walked around to the passenger seat.

As she followed the dirt track through the farm, Hugh and Riley took it in turns to open the gates. Along one fence line ran a knee-high mass of golden tumbleweeds. Hairy panic grass was going to be bad this autumn.

They drove into the cattle paddock. A handful of Black Angus cows stood in a small dam. Thanks to the wet spring, water and feed remained plentiful despite the hot summer.

Once Hugh's breeding herd had been checked, he gave directions over to the green crop on their left. When they arrived, row upon row of tiny winter wheat shoots rippled in the breeze. Sibylla snuck a glance at Hugh's profile. He no longer appeared pale beneath his tan and the grooves beside his mouth weren't as deeply etched.

The flat cropping land soon gave way to the meandering tree line that followed the Bell River. Beyond the trees, the timbered hills rolled in gentle waves. If she looked hard enough she could make out the white glint of the dome that stood on top of a distant hill on her family farm. Hugh followed her gaze and she made sure her expression remained neutral. She didn't know if he knew what the building was or not.

Raucous calls sounded as cockatoos flocked to the tops of the red river gums. The taut line of Hugh's jaw confirmed loud noises still bothered him, but by the time she parked beside the river bend, the cockatoos had quietened.

Hugh helped her carry the basket and picnic rug along the short track that led to the river's edge. Where they'd have their picnic might be sandy and pebbled, but the opposite steep bank towered high above the willows.

When Riley and Hugh went in search of flat stones to skim, Sibylla unpacked the morning tea. The gurgle of running water and the rustle of leaves eased her tiredness. She smiled as a willie wagtail darted nearby looking for insects. Leaving the house hadn't just been good for Hugh, but her too. Out here, surrounded by nature, she could think.

As Riley and Hugh exchanged a hug, she weathered the tug on her heartstrings. She'd spoken the truth about how difficult it would be to return to Woodlea for good. But if she were honest, coming home had been on her mind before she'd made the mad dash to her father's hospital bedside.

As much as he didn't want to admit it, her father was getting older. While he did have a workman, and had contracted out the sowing of this year's wheat crop, there was always work to be done. She and Cloud were needed next week to help muster cattle. What would happen when her father could no longer run the farm was another thing he refused to talk about.

She hadn't realised she'd sighed until Hugh said quietly from behind her, 'Everything okay?'

She nodded as he joined her on the rug. She didn't miss the way he sat on the opposite side of the red tartan. She offered him a muffin before looking over to where Riley was standing beside an impressive pile of skimming stones. 'That's quite a collection.'

'It is. I hope you're in no rush to head back?'

'No. Are you?'

Something indefinable flittered across his face before he spoke. 'Not at all.'

Hoping that her cheeks weren't as flushed as they felt, she again looked at Riley. 'Ready for some morning tea, Riles?'

He sent her a quick grin. 'Nah.'

Hugh chuckled. 'Let's hope we make it home before dark.'

She nodded and reached for the container that held the fruit. She'd had no defences against a reserved and distant Hugh, so stood no chance when he was relaxed and at ease. She went to open the lid but changed hands when her right one twinged.

'What have you done?' he asked, his gold-flecked gaze intent.

'Nothing. I'm just a klutz and hit my hand on a rail when washing Cloud.'

'Can I take a look?'

Her senses said yes and her head said no. She didn't need to be a rocket scientist to know that Hugh touching her was a bad idea. She was supposed to be hiding the way he made her feel. 'It's nothing, really.'

'I know what I'm doing. I promise.' He smiled again. 'I'm not just a horse chiropractor, I'm also a human one.'

She kept her voice light. 'I've no doubt you know what you're doing. Riley showed me all those framed degrees you keep in a box in your office.'

Hugh rubbed at his chin. 'Did he?'

'Yes, he wanted me to frame the sun picture he did for you the same way.'

'Riley might be interested in all things astronomical but for me it's always been bones.'

The unexpected vulnerability furrowing his forehead and deepening his tone had her hold out her hand. 'I'm sure it's only bruised.'

Even knowing that he'd take her hand in his, she wasn't prepared for the jolt when his fingers brushed against hers. His touch was warm and gentle as he took his time to learn the secrets beneath her skin. She forced her breathing to remain regular and prayed the frantic pulse at her wrist didn't betray how fast her heart was racing.

She flinched as he found a tender spot. His eyes briefly met hers before he massaged her palm and made some small manipulations to her fingers.

'How does that feel?' he asked, releasing her hand.

As relieved as she was that he was no longer privy to her every shake and tremor, she missed the comfort of his touch.

She flexed her fingers. The earlier stiffness had eased. 'Thank you.' She smiled. 'It does feel better.'

It was just a micro-expression but she could have sworn need eclipsed the gold in his eyes. Then, as his attention dipped to her mouth, she had no doubt he too felt the pull of attraction. Her stomach swirled and her breaths grew shallow.

But before she could fully gauge his intent, Riley flopped onto the rug beside them. Automatically she reached for the fruit container. In her peripheral vision she saw Hugh inspect the patterns on the rock Riley held out to him. Only the darkness of Hugh's eyes as he flicked her a quick glance proved she hadn't imagined the intensity between them.

The verdict was in. The knock on his head had done more than injure his brain. It had annihilated his self-control. Not only had he been a heartbeat away from kissing Sibylla earlier by the river, he'd have done so in front of Riley.

Hugh's low groan echoed around the silent lounge room, which was lit only by the flames that danced in the fireplace. So much for all those weeks of appearing immune to Sibylla. If she hadn't known he was attracted to her, she did now. He stared at the glow of the fire coals.

The way her lips parted as their gazes held said the chemistry wasn't one-sided. The knowledge only made him curse his weakness more. She already had enough things to deal with. She had her father to worry about, Bernice to contend with and her brother's birthday to get through. If that wasn't enough, she also wasn't looking to stay.

He settled back on the lounge and tried for the third time to get past the opening paragraph of a book that had been on the top of his to-read pile. It had been hours since he'd tucked Riley in and the sliver of light beneath Sibylla's bedroom door had disappeared.

His phone pinged, providing a welcome distraction. He'd been limiting his screen time like Fliss had instructed after his first concussion, but it must be important if someone was contacting him so late. He checked his mobile. The message was from Mac Barton asking if he could see his young chestnut gelding who'd injured his shoulder.

Hugh went to text a reply but when he couldn't think of the right word to type, he hit the call button. He'd leave Mac a voice message.

Instead of the phone going to voicemail, Mac answered. 'I thought I was the only fool awake at this hour.'

From the echo, Mac had to be using his phone via bluetooth in his ute. A man's voice mumbled in the background.

Hugh grinned. Mac's twin brother was with him. Mac must have texted as they'd left the Royal Arms and was now driving Finn home. 'Let me guess. You drew the short straw.'

Mac sighed. 'Tell me about it. Yet again we were the last to leave.'

'Who was Finn trying to impress with those dance moves of his?'

'Whoever it was they were long gone before he did his signature spin, twist and shake.'

'How did it end?'

'Same as last time. He'll need to see you again for that back of his.'

'No worries.' While he was a horse chiropractor these days, he made sure he completed the necessary amount of clinical hours in a Dubbo practice to keep his human registration current. 'I won't be back on deck until next week though.'

Finn's voice again mumbled before Mac chuckled. 'He says not only to hurry up getting back to work but also on the rugby field.'

They were all members of the Woodlea Wallaroos and Finn particularly took his rugby seriously. 'Getting back to work won't be a problem ... but getting clearance from Fliss to play might be.'

'Which is the way it should be,' Mac said, voice sombre. 'I'll never forget Riley's face when he saw you carried off the field.'

'Trust me, I'm done with scaring Riley, let alone with knocking myself out.'

'I would be too. Just the thought of answering to Dr Fliss keeps me in one piece.' The phone line crackled as Mac drove into an area with patchy signal. 'Don't forget to give me a call if you need help with anything. Otherwise I'll see you next week.'

'Will do and Finn ... if you really can't move tomorrow let me know.'

The only reply was Mac's deep sigh. 'He's sleeping like a baby. I'll be the one with a sore back after having to lug his great weight inside.'

Hugh chuckled. He was glad he was on Finn's rugby team and not the opposing side. Finn was nothing but solid muscle. 'Good luck with that.'

When Mac didn't answer, Hugh ended the call. The phone line had dropped out.

Firewood popped in the night-time silence before light footsteps sounded at the doorway. 'Hugh … everything okay?'

He came to his feet, glad he'd pulled on tracksuit pants and a T-shirt. 'Sorry, did I wake you? Everything's fine. That was Mac Barton on the phone.'

Sibylla rubbed at her upper arms as she nodded. Her attention focused on the flickering flames. 'I thought I smelled wood smoke.'

'I figured it was time for the first fire of the season.'

He was standing between her and the fireplace, so he moved away to share the warmth. After only a slight hesitation she went over to the fire and held out her hands. 'The days might feel like summer but you're right, the nights definitely have a winter feel. I hope Riley has enough blankets.'

'He does. I put a second one on earlier.' Even to his own ears his voice came across as husky.

He was having trouble concentrating on anything but the oversized white T-shirt Sibylla was wearing. The too-big neckline had slipped off one shoulder to expose the delicate, pale jut of her collarbones. The hemline hit her mid-thigh. In the room's darkness the firelight played over her smooth, bare legs.

As she turned to look at him, her heavy hair slid over her shoulder and he inhaled the subtle scent of fresh flowers. Her shirt had the words *The BEST Audiologist Ever* sprawled across the front in a pink, swirly font.

'Don't believe everything you read,' she said when she noticed him looking at the caption.

'I've no doubt it's true.' His eyes met hers. 'Appreciative client? Or … other half?'

Her gaze didn't waver. 'Client. There's no other half, despite Bernice making a big deal about me attending a conference with a doctor I work closely with.'

The tension gripping his shoulders eased and he grinned. 'I did hear something along those lines.'

She didn't smile in return. Instead the grey light in her eyes turned serious. He didn't break eye contact as the intensity that had earlier gripped them again took hold.

He might be concussed but he wasn't a coward. They had to talk about the connection between them. He spoke again. 'I'm glad there's no other half. I'm sorry too that I was so standoffish when we first met.' He touched the curve of her fine-boned jaw. She had such beautiful bone structure. 'The truth is I was aware of you every moment you were here ... and also when you weren't. It's just ... Riley has to come first.'

She half smiled. 'Just as well you ignored me, otherwise we'd found ourselves where we are now sooner.' Vulnerability widened her eyes. 'Not that I exactly know what *this* is or where we are exactly.'

'That makes two of us.' His voiced rasped as he framed her face. 'All I know is that if I don't kiss you, thinking straight will never be possible again.'

Her hands lifted and flattened against his chest. He felt their heat right down to his bones.

'We can't have that happening,' she murmured as she closed the distance between them. 'Dr Fliss will never give you the all cl—'

His mouth covered Sibylla's. Somewhere there'd been the thought to make sure that their kiss stayed lighthearted and that they both remained in control. But the instant her lips parted beneath his it was as though he went into a freefall. Rationality, logic, caution all ceased to exist. There was only the woman pressed against him, who bewitched his senses and filled the part of him he'd never acknowledged was empty. He tightened his arms around her and lost himself in her sweetness.

They drew apart to drag in ragged breaths. Her tousled hair fell around her flushed face and her T-shirt had dipped lower off her shoulder. On the skin of his lower back he felt the brand of her hands, which she'd slipped beneath his shirt. She stood so close that every breath they took only made their upper bodies connect further.

He dropped a kiss on her bare shoulder before resting his forehead against hers. His disorientation had nothing to do with his brain injury.

For a long moment they stayed that way before she pulled back to give him her sunrise smile. 'I think we established one thing.'

'What's that?'

'We should be alone more often.'

His laugh was hoarse and low. 'We should and ...' He paused. 'Maybe we could?'

Her hands left his back to slide into the hair at his nape. 'If you're sure?'

'I'm sure. I know you have enough to deal with being home, and I have Riley to think of, but there's still a few weeks until you leave ...' He snuck a kiss before continuing. 'I'm not going to be able to pretend nothing has happened between us.'

She placed her palm against his chest. The unsteadiness of her fingers matched the shaking of his own hands. He couldn't be any more out of his depth than if he'd fallen overboard on a weekend fishing trip.

'Me either. But it's our secret and we keep things ... in perspective so no one gets hurt.'

'Agreed.'

This time he made sure their kiss was both tender and controlled, even if a voice inside his head said he was already well down the road of risking his heart.

# CHAPTER
# 4

Lost in thought, Sibylla dipped her brush into the orange paint. The papier-mâché planet in front of her was already covered in random splashes of yellow and red.

She didn't realise Riley had asked her a question until his own paintbrush lowered as he looked at her.

'Sorry, Riles? Did you say something?'

'Can we make moon sand?'

After breakfast they'd looked on the internet for some more space craft ideas now that their planets were almost finished. 'We sure can. I checked and there's baby oil in the bathroom cupboard plus plenty of flour in the kitchen.'

Riley's smile shone brighter than a shooting star.

They both went back to painting. This time she forced her thoughts to stay in the present. It was only the second morning after her and Hugh's fireside kiss but she needed to get herself under control. She had to stop reliving the moments when he'd pull her into the pantry for a heady kiss or would simply grin at her and wink. If she wasn't careful Riley would sense there was something going on between her and his father.

She again dipped paint on her brush. If she wasn't careful she'd also flag to Hugh that despite her line about needing to keep everything in perspective, she was already fully invested in their connection. She'd only added such a caveat to ease his fears about things becoming too serious. She'd be naive to think that after the failure of his first marriage it was only Riley he was protecting by maintaining his single status.

The mobile beside her rang and her father's name flashed onto the screen.

'Hi Dad.' Worry quickened her words. He rarely called.

'Hi. Sorry I missed you when you all visited yesterday afternoon.'

'That's okay. Bernice said you were resting?'

She didn't add that Bernice had made it obvious she hadn't wanted her father to see anyone by not inviting Hugh or Riley inside. After they'd all left, she'd made sure she texted him to let him know they'd dropped by. Bernice wouldn't have mentioned anything about their visit.

'I was. Is Riley with you?'

'Yes. Why?' She smiled across at the five-year-old whose forehead was furrowed as he concentrated on painting the shape of Australia on his green and blue papier-mâché Earth.

'I was on the Reedy Creek auction website and they have a telescope for sale today.'

'Do they?' She checked the time on the kitchen clock. 'Do the auctions still start at ten?'

'They do. The poultry starts at nine, followed by the livestock and then the general auction. You have about an hour, so plenty of time.'

'True. I'll let Hugh know.'

'No worries … Sibby, when are you coming home?'

She swallowed as her father used her childhood name. Nowadays it was only Riley who called her by the shortened version. 'Maybe tomorrow. Fliss will be here this afternoon to check on Hugh. As soon as he's given the all-clear to drive, I'll be back.'

'Okay.'

'Was there anything else you liked the look of?' The auctions sold everything from can openers to roosters to bales of hay. She and James had loved going to the monthly sales as kids to see all the animals and poultry.

'No … not really. I'll talk to you later.'

'Okay.' But her father had already ended the call.

She stared at her half-finished planet, this time her thoughts not on Hugh. It wasn't just her father calling her Sibby that had been unusual, there'd been a gravity to his tone that she hadn't heard in a long while.

She glanced at the clock and came to her feet. 'Riles … I'm just going to see your dad. We might need to pop out to Reedy Creek.'

He nodded before adding a green dot for Tasmania.

She headed for Hugh's home office. Through the open door she saw him working on his computer. His concentration seemed to have improved along with his light and noise sensitivity. Her pace slowed as loss twisted inside. Even if Fliss did clear him to drive this afternoon, there was no reason why she couldn't still spend time with him and Riley once she returned home.

She hadn't reached the doorway before Hugh turned in his chair. The whisky-brown of his eyes changed to a golden amber. After a quick look past her to confirm she was alone, he snagged her waist and pulled her onto his lap. She looped her arms around his neck and breathed in his fresh cedar scent.

'How's the planet painting going?' he asked, giving her no time to reply before he kissed her.

'We're almost done,' she managed a breathless minute later. 'But Dad called and there's a telescope at the Reedy Creek auctions if you wanted to take a look for Riley.'

'I do.'

When Hugh's gaze dipped to her lips, she grinned and slid off his lap. 'Which means we have to go now.'

The regret in his eyes made her senses sing the whole way to the small village of Reedy Creek. Once they'd passed the community-built corrugated-iron hall with its twin tennis courts, she took the first turn left towards the local showground. There, she joined the dusty cars parked in the shade of the grey box trees.

Hugh left the passenger seat to help a woman load a crate containing three white ducks into the back of her ute. While he went to register so he could bid, Sibylla walked with Riley along the rows of items. The livestock auction was still on and they had a little time to explore. She'd had a quick look at what else was on offer via the website. An idea had formed but she wasn't yet sure if she should go through with it.

The aroma of steak and onion being cooked on a barbecue wafted through the air as they strolled by welders, a claw-foot bath and farm gates. When Riley saw the black telescope on a silver stand he suddenly stopped before breaking into a run.

Hugh grinned as he joined them. 'What do you think?' he asked Riley.

Riley's high-wattage smile said it all. As Riley again inspected the telescope, Hugh turned to Sibylla and spoke softly. 'I was planning to get him one for Christmas but this might be a good first telescope.'

'It's the perfect height.'

She had trouble keeping her voice casual. As she'd spoken two boys had sprinted past and Hugh's hand had settled into the small of her back to make sure she wasn't jostled in the narrow space. His care and consideration made her feel safe and cherished.

The idea she'd had earlier returned with an insistence that couldn't be ignored. 'Hugh … I'll find you and Riley in a little while. I just need … to do something.'

Steps urgent, she went to register and then joined the crowd gathered around the auctioneer as he worked his way to the end of the livestock for sale.

On the auction website there had been two long-haired Jack Russell puppies that reminded her of her childhood dog Spud. It hadn't mattered if his legs had been half the size of the working kelpies, when he wasn't at home with her and James, he was in the ute or truck with her father.

Before common sense could talk her out of what instinct told her to do, she bid on the puppies. There was a brief flurry of bids but she held firm. It didn't seem real that she was the winning bidder until the crowd melted away to move to the next pen that contained a Galloway cow and calf. She stood alone in front of the puppies that rolled on their backs as they wrestled each other.

Riley suddenly appeared at her side and grabbed her hand. 'Sibby, did you buy the puppies?'

'I did. One's for me and one's for my dad. I have a big backyard and have been meaning to get one for a while now. Dad also needs a little doggy friend.'

'Does your father know?' Hugh asked as Riley crouched down to look at the two Jack Russells.

She shook her head. 'Hearing the way he spoke today … I think he's … lonely.'

Riley's laughter sounded as both puppies tried to lick him through the wire. 'Can one stay with us? They could live with Diesel?'

She took a second to answer. In a perfect world it wouldn't just be a puppy staying at Hillside but also her. 'They both can stay for tonight but in the laundry. I'll have to call Ella and see when she can fit them in to have their needles and to be microchipped.'

Hugh put an arm around Riley's small shoulders as he bent to take a closer look at the puppies. As one tiny nose pushed towards him, he smiled and scratched the puppy's white-and-brown head.

Sibylla looked away before the rawness of her emotions made her eyes well. There was a word for the feelings that consumed her whenever she was around the man showing such tenderness towards his son and the two puppies. Love.

She headed towards the tin-roofed building where she'd need to pay. But the admission didn't bring with it any happiness. She'd fallen for a man who didn't appear to want any form of commitment, let alone a future together. The harsh reality could be that their lives were only destined to intersect for a short while.

Her chin angled. She wasn't losing hope that they couldn't somehow find a way to make things work despite the physical distance between them. Just like her faith that there would come a time when her father could talk to her about James, she'd remain optimistic.

She glanced back to where Hugh and Riley still played with the puppies. But if all she could ever have with Hugh were a few special weeks then when she returned to her coastal life she'd at least have a small, warm bundle of cuteness to love.

'Puppies are such great time wasters,' Fliss said with a smile as she gazed out over the back garden of Hillside.

Hugh only nodded. The doctor had caught him staring through the kitchen window when he should have been remembering the three numbers she'd mentioned.

ALISSA CALLEN

He looked away from where Sibylla and Riley sat on the green lawn, with Jelly Bean standing close by, while the two Jack Russell puppies chased each other. Where they got their energy from he had no idea. They'd either wrestled or chewed on anything within reach the whole car trip home.

'The numbers were three, eight, seven,' he said, voice casual.

He hoped the twinkle in Fliss's hazel eyes wasn't because she'd worked out it was Sibylla he'd been focused on.

'They were.'

While Fliss asked him more questions and had him do such physical tasks as balancing on one leg with his eyes closed, he made sure he didn't again look out the window.

When Fliss was done she gave him a smile. 'The good news is you're cleared to drive as well as to return to *light* work duties.'

'Thanks. And the bad news ... no rugby?'

'Absolutely.'

'No worries.' He came to his feet. The lawn beyond the window was now empty.

The clatter of boots sounded as Riley rushed inside. He'd promised to show Fliss his telescope. While Riley took Fliss into the living room, Hugh went to the laundry where Sibylla would be taking the pups to have a rest.

It had been on his mind that once he was given the okay to drive, there would be no more reason for her to stay. As much as he didn't want her to go, he had to push aside his selfishness. The reason why she was back in town was because her father needed her.

'Hey,' he said as she walked out of the laundry door.

'Hey, yourself.' Her serious eyes searched his. 'You're back on the road?'

'I am.'

Her fingers linked with his. 'I thought you'd be.'

His thumb caressed the back of her hand. 'You don't have to …
race home.'

'I know, but I'll go tomorrow. Dad was asking when I'd be back.'

The murmur of Riley and Fliss's voices silenced his reply that
it wouldn't be the same without her there. Instead he lifted their
hands and pressed a kiss to her knuckles before letting her walk
ahead of him along the hallway.

Now that he had the green light to return to work, he spent the
next hour in his office lining up clients for the week. Mac's chestnut
wasn't the only horse that would be in pain or discomfort until he
treated them. He'd make sure he finished his day early to pace himself.
He also checked with Mrs Poole that her husband was recovering
well and that she'd be back to look after Riley on Monday.

Despite his weekly calendar filling up, it soon became obvious that
he could no longer blame his poor concentration and restlessness
on concussion. In between phone calls, he listened for any echo of
Sibylla's voice. In between emails and texts, he kept his head half
turned towards the door for any sound of her footsteps.

After he'd again found himself staring at his calendar, he silenced
his groan and pushed back his chair. From all the laughter coming
from the kitchen, Sibylla and Riley had to be doing something fun.
While Sibylla might physically still be at Hillside, he already missed
her. Tomorrow she'd be gone.

He stopped at the kitchen doorway and looked in at a white
world. Whatever they were making, it was either going very wrong
or it was meant to be messy. Flour dusted the benchtops and floors
and coated the front of their shirts. Even as he watched, Sibylla
touched Riley's nose and left a large white dot. Riley laughed so
much he almost fell off his stool. He reached out and drew a white
moon shape on Sibylla's cheek. This time Sibylla couldn't stop her
laughter as they looked at each other.

Hugh leaned against the doorframe, needing something solid for support. He'd been delusional in thinking that stability was all that Riley required. His son needed more people in his life than his father. The son he loved so much needed the gentleness of a woman's touch and the understanding only a woman could give.

It hadn't been Riley he'd been protecting by believing all they needed was each other ... it had been himself. He hadn't wanted to risk opening up his heart again. He'd shut himself off from ever loving anyone. Except it hadn't worked. Sibylla, with her beauty, compassion and warmth, had dismantled every barrier he'd put in place. It hadn't been concussion making him feel more emotional, or so out of control, just the woman he'd fallen for.

He pushed himself away from the doorframe. He had only a few weeks to see where the connection between them could lead. There had to be a way of keeping her in his and Riley's life. In the meantime he couldn't waste another moment of what time they had left together.

Both Sibylla and Riley turned as he approached.

'We're making moon sand,' Riley said, clapping his hands so that flour floated through the air like dust motes.

'Remind me if I ever go to the moon to wear white.'

Sibylla shot him a sweet smile. 'There's a spare bowl if you want to make some too.'

'Okay, I'm game.'

He hadn't taken more than two steps when Sibylla and Riley exchanged a look. Within seconds their white handprints decorated the front of his blue shirt.

By the time the kitchen was again flour-free, the sun had painted the golden hills in a soft mauve and wood smoke tinged the air. At the first opportunity after Riley went to bed, Hugh planned to talk to Sibylla. He had no idea what he'd say, but he couldn't allow her to leave without letting her know that while they'd agreed to take things slow and to keep things in perspective, what they had was worth fighting for.

But between phone calls from clients who'd heard he was back at work, to two unsettled puppies, it was as though there was a conspiracy to keep him and Sibylla apart. Add into the mix Riley's excitement at being able to use his telescope to stargaze, along with his ability to negotiate a later bedtime, and Hugh knew he was fighting a losing battle.

When quiet finally cloaked the farmhouse, Sibylla came to sit next to him on the lounge. He tucked her beneath his arm and, smothering a yawn, she laid her head on his shoulder. He kissed her silken hair and let the easy silence continue between them.

Her even breathing soon told him she was asleep. His arm firmed around her. He could spend a lifetime having her lie warm and soft against him and it would never be enough. When the flames in the fire dulled to a glow, he carried her into her room before heading to his own bed.

The protracted howl of a puppy woke him. After flipping back the covers, he pulled on tracksuit pants and a T-shirt. Despite the portable heater the puppies could be feeling the pre-dawn cold. When he opened the laundry door, the light from the hallway spilled into the room. Tiny paws scampered on the floorboards as the Jack Russells ran over to him. He scooped up their wriggling bodies and they snuggled into his arms.

He shook his head. If he wasn't careful he'd be seriously considering Riley's request that they get a puppy so Jelly Bean wouldn't be lonely when he started school in the summer.

The door creaked as it opened wider and Sibylla stepped inside. She held a hot water bottle covered in a knitted red cover that Riley had found for her. He'd also donated a soft toy for the puppies to cuddle with. By the looks of the tiger's ear, the Jack Russells had been more intent on playing than sleeping.

Sibylla smiled when she saw where the puppies were. 'I wondered why they were suddenly so quiet. Sorry they woke you. I never realised boiling an electric jug could take so long.'

She moved past him to place the hot water bottle in the blankets of their basket. When he carefully settled the puppies into their bed they cuddled against the new source of warmth. He backed away and followed Sibylla out of the laundry. As the door clicked shut he waited for any puppy noise, but all remained silent.

He turned to find Sibylla watching him. After he'd put her in her bed she must have woken and changed out of her jeans. Just like the other night she wore her *The BEST Audiologist Ever* shirt. And also just like then, the way the oversized neckline left one of her delicate shoulders bare made his testosterone burn.

'Thanks for carrying me to bed,' she said, eyes searching his.

'Anytime.'

'I can't believe this time tomorrow night I'll be home. Where has this week gone?'

'I know.' He gave in to the need to touch her. His fingers lingered as he smoothed her tousled hair from off her cheek. 'I'm going to miss you.'

'Me too.'

She lifted a hand to entwine her fingers with his. 'But ... we still have a few more weeks.' He'd never seen her eyes so large or so dark. 'And tonight.'

He had no idea who moved first. All he knew was that she was in his arms and this time kissing her wasn't going to be enough. When her mouth left his and she grabbed his hand to tug him along the hallway towards his room, he knew that she'd had exactly the same thought.

# CHAPTER

# 5

'It won't be so cold tonight.' Bernice's quiet and well-modulated tone didn't match the sharp look she sent Sibylla behind her father's back. 'The puppies could sleep outside?'

Sibylla counted to ten. She and the two tiny Jack Russells had only been home two days and it already felt like a life sentence. As soon as she'd told her father to close his eyes and she'd put the squirming puppies on his lap, Bernice had been on a mission to evict them.

Her father spoke from where he sat finishing his morning coffee at the kitchen table and reading an article on the tablet she'd given him last Christmas. 'I'll check the weather but they aren't any trouble in the laundry.'

Beside him, against the nearby wall, lay a dog bed in which the white-and-brown puppies were snuggled together and fast asleep. Her father had asked Sibylla to move their bed into the kitchen during the daytime.

Bernice's lips pressed together but she didn't make any further comment as china rattled while she looked for something high in a kitchen cupboard.

Sibylla's heart warmed as her father looked over at the puppies and smiled. Yesterday she'd caught him laughing when one had pounced on a stick and again when they'd tried to chase their tail.

He'd also been outside more in the past few days than he had in the weeks she'd been home. If he wasn't taking the Jack Russells into the garden to ensure there were no puppy puddles inside, he was taking them to play and explore. He'd even come with her to town when the pups had visited Ella, the local vet. His Dubbo physiotherapist would be pleased next visit to hear that he'd been so active.

Sibylla curled her hands round the warmth of her mug. She'd done the right thing for her father and for herself in buying the Jack Russells. The larger puppy had attached himself to her father and so he'd called him Shadow. She was more than happy with the smaller, quieter male that Riley had named Nova. She just didn't want to think ahead to the day when the puppies would be separated.

She took a sip of too-hot tea to hide the flush colouring her cheeks. Not that leaving was on her mind. After the night she and Hugh had shared she wasn't going anywhere in a hurry. She couldn't look at him now without wishing they were again alone. Nothing could have prepared her for the feel of the heat of his skin against hers.

Her hope grew that he too knew how good they were together. While there hadn't been time yet for a serious discussion, his affection and the tender way he held her communicated that they were on the same page.

Realising that her father was staring at her, she took the last gulp of her tea. 'I'd better get Cloud saddled. The cattle in the creek paddock won't muster themselves.'

He nodded before Bernice's voice sounded. 'If you're looking for your boots I put them out the back door. There was dust in the hallway.'

Sibylla again counted to ten. It was just the little things her stepmother had always done to reinforce her unspoken message that Sibylla wasn't welcome.

She didn't bother glancing at her father. She didn't know if he was unaware of Bernice's intent, or whether he didn't know how to intervene and didn't want to appear as though he was picking sides. As physically and mentally strong as he'd always been, when it came to dealing with emotions he simply avoided them.

'No worries,' was all she said, tone composed as she came to her feet.

Irritation flittered across Bernice's face. Apart from not wanting to give Bernice the satisfaction of knowing that anything she said or did had any impact, it wasn't her place to cause trouble. Her father appeared content in his marriage.

He briefly looked at her. 'Once Tony's changed the oil in the ag bike, he'll muster the top paddock with the dogs. Let him know if those steers give you any trouble.'

'Cloud and I'll be fine. We'll just take things slow.'

As she went outside to collect her banished boots, she sent Hugh a text to see how his morning was going. He'd left early to work on some horses over near the rodeo grounds before he'd head to Cressy's. His quick reply of a thumbs-up and a bunch of flowers made her smile.

Cloud nickered in greeting as she opened the gate to the paddock behind the stables. His Appaloosa spots gleamed snow-white against the darkness of his glossy brown coat. Years ago, she'd thought about taking him to the coast but he wouldn't be happy in a small agistment paddock. There also were weeks when she'd get so busy it was a struggle to find time to grocery shop let alone ride.

She scratched his favourite spot on his neck. 'Sorry, your peace and quiet is over for the morning. We've work to do.'

She soon had the gelding saddled and they were making their way to where clusters of black cattle dotted the slopes of the creek paddock. Tony had a steeper and larger area to muster, so it made sense he'd need the dogs more than she would.

Despite the sun warming her shoulders and Cloud's placid, easy stride, she blew out a tense breath and forced her shoulders to relax. It had been over a decade since she'd fallen off her horse while jumping and had lost her nerve, but old fears still haunted her. She smoothed Cloud's warm, velvety neck and drew confidence from his calm.

After leaving the paddock gate open, she headed for the back fence. Curious cattle lifted their heads before moving in the direction she wanted them to go. When the smaller group she'd bunched together joined a bigger mob, a heavy-set steer made a dash to her left. Cloud spun around and they cut off the runaway. When he rejoined the herd, she kept a close eye on the edgy Black Angus. There was always one who had to be different and not follow the crowd.

The open gate was in sight, the cows ambling along the fence line, when the steer again made a run for it. This time he managed to reach the trees at the edge of the gully before lumbering down the dry creek bank and up the other side. Sibylla and Cloud followed. She kept their pace steady to avoid the wombat holes dug into the gully banks, but when the pasture flattened into open space she gave Cloud his head. The gelding's hooves pounded as he closed the distance between them and the steer.

Then, she remembered that somewhere along the gully there'd been an old fence line. Then, she registered it was here that her father had had his stroke while taking down the fence. She pulled on Cloud's reins to slow him. Surely there weren't any posts or fence wire left in the long grass?

The answer came with a stumble and a pitch and then the impact of the hard earth slamming against her side. Winded and with dust tainting her mouth, she lay still. Concern for Cloud had her push herself to her knees. The Appaloosa stood to her left, reins dangling and red dirt coating his shoulder.

She stood and hobbled over to the gelding. With each step her back straightened and her movements steadied. She hadn't done any major damage and could only hope he hadn't either.

She collected the reins and smoothed Cloud's trembling, damp neck. 'Everything's okay. You just tripped.' To their left, tangled in the thick summer grass, lay a twisted line of fence wire. 'Let's get you home where Hugh can take a look at you.'

She slid out her mobile and when she held it to her right she had enough service to make a call. While she waited for Hugh to pick up, she looked around for the Angus steer, who was nowhere to be found. Behind her, cattle bellowed as the once neat mob dispersed. She'd come back with the motorbike and dogs once she got Cloud to the stables.

When Hugh's phone went to voicemail she left a brief message to ask if he could come over to check out Cloud. She then left another message on her home phone to say what had happened and that she would be walking the gelding home. She banished the little voice that said the first rule after any fall was to get back in the saddle. Instead she rationalised her decision not to ride with the concern that Cloud could have sustained an injury that wasn't yet obvious.

They'd just started to walk when her mobile rang. Hugh's number flashed on the screen.

'Sibylla, are you okay?'

The urgency and rawness of his words made her throat ache. There had to be a way to make sure she never stopped hearing his voice. 'I'm fine but Cloud took a fall on his right shoulder. I'm walking him home.'

'I'm on my way. Where are you?'

'Creek paddock, but don't rush. We'll be a while.'

'I'll come and find you. You're a long way out. Cloud might be okay and you can then ride the rest of the way home.'

She didn't realise her hand was shaking until her phone bumped against her cheekbone. 'Thanks but he'll be bruised and sore so the last thing he needs is me on him.'

'I've just left Cressy's front gate. See you soon.'

Sibylla didn't reply as she ended the call. She stopped and bent to rest her head on her knees as nausea hit her. She'd spoken the truth. She was fine … physically. But the shaking and queasiness were old and familiar friends. She'd experienced them every time she'd even thought about getting in the saddle after her teenage fall.

Something wasn't right. Hugh took his time running his hands over Cloud's shoulder, feeling the solid weight of the Appaloosa's bones. But it wasn't his equine patient he was concerned about.

To his right Sibylla sat on a tree stump, her arms wrapped around her knees. They hadn't made it halfway home before he'd found them. Her pale skin was paper-white and she was far too quiet. But it was her eyes that unleashed a feeling of dread that settled low in his gut.

Her grey gaze, which was usually alight with laughter and life, was now as dull as a bleak winter sky. Even though he'd already checked her over and reassured himself that she was fine, the reality was that she wasn't.

He'd thought the brittleness to her words when he suggested that she ride Cloud home had just been the poor phone line. But now he'd witnessed her sheer relief when he'd removed Cloud's saddle to better examine him. The fall had rattled her. Deeply.

He forced himself to focus on Cloud. When he was certain the gelding was unscathed, he led him over to Sibylla.

She slid off the stump. 'He's okay?'

'Yes.'

'Thank goodness.' She stroked the Appaloosa's nose. 'Thanks for coming out so quickly.'

He nodded. The angle to her chin was at odds with the way she wouldn't hold his gaze. As desperate as he was to pull her close, instinct told him she was working hard to keep herself together.

She took hold of the reins. 'There's no point putting Cloud's saddle back on. I'll keep walking him home. It isn't far.'

'Or …' Hugh paused as he turned to scan the track he'd driven along. He'd heard the sound of the gator. 'Let's see who this is.'

'Hugh.' Her hands shook so much the metal on Cloud's bridle jingled. 'If it's Dad, I don't want to worry him … but I … can't ride back.'

He turned towards her to make sure his back hid her from whoever was approaching. He brushed his thumb across her cheek. 'It's okay. I'll make sure you won't have to.'

'Thank you.' When her lips pressed together he thought she wasn't going to say anything more but then she spoke, her voice low and strained. 'I've been here before. I will get back in the saddle. It will just take time.'

Despite the gator sounding almost behind them, he again caressed her cheek. 'I've no doubt you will.'

Dogs barked and he turned to see Gary and his young workman, Tony, arrive.

Gary had always been a well-built and strong man, but as he eased himself out of the gator, Hugh had never seen him look so frail. Even after his stroke he'd retained an air of capability. But now Sibylla's fall had appeared to age him. He shot her a concerned and anxious look but by the time she faced him, his expression had assumed its usual gruff cast.

'I only just got your message,' he said, his words a little rougher than usual. 'Everyone okay?'

Sibylla nodded.

When Sibylla didn't elaborate, Hugh spoke. 'Yes, everyone's fine.'

'Where's the wire?' Gary asked, his attention never leaving his daughter.

Sibylla waved a hand to her right. 'Near the wombat holes.'

Her father grunted. 'I don't know how it was missed, but Tony will get it now.'

The workman whistled to the black-and-tan kelpies sniffing the tyres on Hugh's ute. They jumped onto the back of the gator before Tony drove away.

Sibylla looked over to where a single steer walked along the side of a hill towards the cattle now grazing on the flat. 'I'll come back on my old bike.'

'Okay,' was all Gary said before he turned towards Hugh's ute. 'Sibylla, how about you drive me home. I left the puppies inside.' His faded grey eyes briefly met Hugh's. He read the unspoken question about such a plan being okay. Gary knew full well his daughter's fears about getting back onto a horse had returned.

'Sounds good.' Hugh ran a hand over Cloud's shoulder. 'It'll just be you and me, buddy.'

Except when he reached for the Appaloosa's reins, Sibylla didn't relinquish them. 'Is riding something you should be doing?'

The worry widening her eyes shouldn't have moved him as much as it did. 'Yes, my balance is back to normal.'

Sibylla slowly passed him Cloud's reins. He led the gelding a little distance away before vaulting onto the Appaloosa's bare back and turning him towards home. It wasn't long until Sibylla drove past and gave him a wave. While she was still more white than pale, her accompanying smile was genuine.

But as the red dust behind the ute settled, the knowledge that she was feeling a little more like herself didn't reassure him. He scraped a hand over his face. Now he was alone, his emotions refused to cooperate. They coursed through him with the force of spring floodwater. He forced himself to relax as Cloud's ears flicked back and forth. The Appaloosa would sense his agitation.

It wasn't just the thought of Sibylla being injured that flayed him but also what he'd seen in her eyes. He knew what abject fear looked like. He'd never wanted to see it again.

When he and Clarisse had moved from Sydney he'd explained that western brown snakes were common. He'd also reassured her that if she saw one they'd want to get away from her as much as she would them. The snake she'd seen on the lawn near the clothesline had done exactly that. It had slithered into the garden bed and then away into the paddocks.

But Clarisse's fears hadn't been assuaged. He'd been powerless against their strength and their persistence. Having the snake so close to the house had been the tipping point. Her bags had been packed within a week.

Now seeing the same fear in Sibylla's eyes triggered his own fears. He was reminded of how unpredictable life could be and how it could change in a heartbeat. Despite the warmth of the breeze he felt as cold as he had when he'd woken at dawn and Sibylla wasn't beside him.

All the happiness and contentment of the past days wilted and withered. As much as he loved Sibylla, what had he been thinking letting her into his and Riley's lives? As much as she had been a willing participant, what right did he have to assume being with him was the best thing for her?

His thoughts continued to roil until he and Cloud reached the stables. There was no sign of Sibylla but her father was sitting on a garden bench beneath the jacaranda, the puppies playing around him. Hugh checked Cloud over a final time before letting him loose in his paddock.

Gary came to meet him as he closed the gate. 'Sibby's gone for a shower. Thanks for helping out.'

Hugh only nodded. The older man had something on his mind. Deep furrows creased his forehead and his tone had been more brusque than usual.

'It's my fault the wire got missed.' Gary's shoulders moved in a sigh. 'After my ... turn ... things were a bit of a blur.'

'Which is understandable. Gary, this wasn't anyone's fault. It was an accident.'

The older man didn't reply as he stared past the horse paddock towards the far off ridge. Then he cleared his throat. 'Did Sibylla say anything about not wanting to ride or you work it out?'

'Both.'

'I thought so. She had a bad fall when she was sixteen. She was jumping a log she'd jumped many times before, but this time it went wrong. To this day I don't know how the only thing that was broken was her spirit. She was black and blue for weeks.'

'She's strong. She's got back in the saddle once, she'll do so again.'

'I hope so. But life has knocked her a few times since then. We lost James … and then Carol and I didn't make it.'

When Gary paused and his stare hardened it was obvious the topic of conversation had changed. 'I want your word you won't let her down.'

Hugh didn't try to misunderstand. 'You have it.'

He grunted. 'I know you won't but I needed to hear it. She's all I have left.'

Gary's hoarse, emotional words stayed with Hugh the drive home. He had lunch with Riley and Mrs Poole and when his afternoon client called to say she had sick kids, he went to the woodpile. As he split and chopped wood he attempted to restore order to his emotions. But the more he thought the more he kept coming back to a single truth that he wasn't yet ready to accept let alone follow through on.

He'd texted Sibylla to see how she was going. She'd been about to head out on the bike to bring in the cattle. Since then he'd heard nothing more, but he had left his phone on the kitchen bench. He'd finish this last log then give her a call.

He split the thick piece of wood and when he straightened he caught a flicker of pink. Sibylla and Jelly Bean were walking towards him through the carpet of auburn leaves surrounding the liquid-amber tree.

Relief took the edge off his tension. Colour had returned to Sibylla's cheeks and she moved without any sign of stiffness or pain. 'Hey,' she said, voice bright as she stopped in front of him.

'Hey.' He hoped his reply only sounded husky to his ears. It was so good to see her. He scratched Jelly Bean's forehead before the pony went off to sniff the newly chopped wood.

'You and Riley won't be cold this winter,' Sibylla said with a smile.

'That's the plan.' He added wood to the neat pile that ran alongside the shed wall. It was either keep busy or kiss her. 'How's all the bumps and bruises?'

'Going okay. The cattle are finally in the yards.' She hesitated. 'I also talked to Dad … and told him I won't be riding for a while.'

Hugh folded his arms against the deep need to comfort her. He didn't trust himself. His emotions were too unsteady and he needed to stay in control to be able to think. 'Whatever I can do to help you get back in the saddle, let me know.'

'Thanks. I will.' When her eyes searched his he realised he hadn't been successful at hiding his instability. 'Hugh … is everything okay?'

He unfolded his arms and tried to appear relaxed even though his jaw felt as hard as the wood he'd worked up a sweat splitting. 'Your fall gave me a fright.'

'I'm fine. Really.'

He nodded and took his time to answer. The promise he made to her father replayed in his head. 'The thing is … I'm not.'

She stilled. 'You're not?'

'No. If anything ever happened to you …' Mouth dry, he unfolded his arms and sought her hand. 'I know we were supposed to take things slow and to keep everything in perspective but, for me, that was never going to happen.'

'Me either … but that shouldn't be a problem if we both feel the same way?'

'It shouldn't, but after today, I also feel … fear.'

'I mightn't know much about all the emotions we're feeling but this is one I do know about.' She touched his cheek with gentle fingers. 'The trouble with fear is that it's a control freak … but we can choose whether we fight, freeze or take flight.'

He swallowed. Her perceptiveness and strength humbled him. 'A control freak, huh?'

Her lips tilted in a smile that didn't quite reach her eyes. 'It sure is.' She traced the line of his stubbled jaw. 'It's been a big day ... for both of us. Let's not dissect things too much. Tomorrow's a new day. Anything will be possible.'

He drew her against him before she could read his face. If only he could share her optimism. Tomorrow the world would be the same risky and unpredictable place it was today. He'd also given his word to her father that he wouldn't let her down. The worst possible way he could ever do that was if he didn't put the brakes on what was between them. It was the only way to protect each of them from all hurt.

He tightened his hold and pressed a kiss to the top of her head, deluding himself that this wasn't the last time the woman he loved would fill his arms.

# CHAPTER

# 6

The new day Sibylla had spoken of arrived with the gentle creep of light beneath her bedroom curtain and the cheerful call of a kookaburra. She groaned and pulled the covers over her head. It felt far too early to be the morning.

It hadn't been her aching side that had kept her awake, or worry about how she'd ride Cloud again, but thoughts of Hugh. As upbeat as she'd been when she'd seen him yesterday afternoon, the reality was that, inside, the flicker of her hope had dimmed to a feeble glow. Of all the emotions that could threaten what lay between them, fear would be the most destructive. She knew the power it could wield. She knew the tenacity of its unrelenting grip. But most of all she knew how hard it was to fight against the pull of its undertow.

It hadn't mattered how quickly she'd shut down their conversation, he'd already distanced himself from her. She could feel it in his touch and see it in the bleakness of his eyes. When he'd waved her off, and then remained still while he watched her leave, she couldn't shake the feeling she was driving out of his life for good.

She kicked off the bedcovers and rubbed her gritty eyes. She could only hope that when she saw him today her fears would be put to rest. After a quick shower she entered the kitchen to the fresh aroma of French toast. The breakfast had been one of her childhood favourites.

Her father was sitting at the table, the puppies wrestling beneath his chair as he checked the weather on his electronic tablet. Bernice was nowhere to be seen.

'Something smells good,' she said, as she looked at his empty plate.

'I thought it was a French toast kind of morning.' Her father went to stand. 'How many pieces would you like?'

She waved at him to stay in his seat. 'Not sure, but I can make the—'

She stopped as Bernice entered the kitchen carrying the puppies' bed from the laundry. Without looking at her, Bernice placed it in its usual spot beside the wall near her father's chair.

As her stepmother straightened, she slowly faced Sibylla. 'I owe you an apology.'

From the corner of her eye she saw her father look up from his tablet. His attentive expression indicated that Bernice's words hadn't come as any surprise.

Bernice wiped her hands on her white slacks. 'I want to apologise for not always remembering that this was your home before mine. You see ... it's been very hard to compete with the bond between a parent and a child.'

Sybilla didn't hesitate. It had never been her intention to not accept Bernice or to come between her and her father. 'Apology accepted. Can I make you some French toast?'

Bernice went to shake her head and then gave a small smile. 'Thank you. I'll just have one.'

While Sibylla prepared the French toast a text came through from Hugh. She made sure she read the message over near the bench while Bernice and her father were engrossed in conversation. He said he hoped she was feeling okay and that he'd be around tonight to see her. Even though he'd added his usual flower emojis, she wasn't fooled. Things were serious if he was coming to her. She always went to Hillside.

She forced herself to concentrate so her French toast peace offering to Bernice wouldn't burn. It didn't matter for her own breakfast. She'd lost all appetite. After the puppies were asleep in their bed and Bernice had left after her second piece of French toast, a small figure waved through the window.

Sibylla went to greet Riley at the kitchen door. Her heart ached as he gave her a tight hug. She couldn't lose either him or Hugh. 'No Jelly Bean today?'

'Your dad said to come by myself.'

Sibylla turned to look at her father who'd gone to get a key from off the hook in the wall cupboard.

He nodded. 'There's somewhere I need to take Riley … and you. It's okay with Hugh and Mrs Poole.' He handed Sibylla the key to the dual cab ute. While he could drive the gator, he wasn't yet confident about driving a larger vehicle.

'I'll just get my boots,' she said, glad of the distraction.

At first, as her father directed her through a series of gates, she wasn't sure where they were headed. But when he said to take the road past the river she shot him a look. He didn't meet her gaze. Instead all he said was a gruff, 'I'm sure you know where we're going now.'

She nodded, not trusting herself to speak. The only thing at the end of this road was a single white dome on top of a hill. Her grip tightened on the steering wheel.

As far as she knew her brother's solar-powered observatory hadn't been visited since the day they'd lost him. Filled with precious memories of having sleepovers in their swags and stargazing, it was the one place she hadn't been able to visit. Then, as time passed, she couldn't go back as seeing James's special project neglected and derelict would have only broken her heart even more.

She glanced in the rear-view mirror at Riley's excited face. But with her father being willing to take Riley there perhaps James's legacy could now be treasured. Fingers crossed the dome wasn't beyond repair.

She stopped at the observatory gate and frowned. She didn't know what she was expecting but it wasn't this. The grass in the small yard had been slashed and an unfamiliar tree stood to the left of the dome. Beneath the tree sat a solid wooden garden chair. The tree's breadth and height meant that it would have to have been planted around the time of James's accident.

When Riley raced to open the gate, she turned to her father. 'Dad?'

He didn't look at her. 'I come here.'

She nodded, incapable of words. By the neat look of things he did more than come here. All this time she'd thought he hadn't kept his son's memory alive. She briefly covered his hand with hers before driving through the open gate.

For the next two hours they lost themselves in memories and created new ones. Riley's enthusiasm and constant questions kept them busy with explanations and demonstrations. Riley's awed expression as the dome slid open above them was one she wanted to hold on to forever.

When he sat cross-legged on the floor to read a book on meteors, she went outside to where her father was sitting in the shade of the new tree.

Apart from a quick glance, he didn't appear to register her standing beside him. Then he spoke. 'Sibby, I also owe you an apology. I should have told you I spend time here to feel close to your brother. I should have always made sure that you felt as though Avonlea was your home.'

'You don't need to apologise. We've all been dealing with things in our own way.'

'Yes, I do. This stroke has made me see things … differently.' His eyes met hers. Unfamiliar emotion tensed his weathered features. 'I always felt guilty that you chose to stay because of me. I wanted you to be, I don't know, free to live whatever life you wanted. So I made sure the ties that bound you were as loose as possible.'

'It wouldn't have mattered how loose they were, this is where I belong. I have no regrets about going to university in Sydney and making a life on the coast, but the truth is, and I know we've never talked about it, but I've always been working towards one day coming back.'

When her father offered her his calloused hand she took it. His grip was warm and strong like she remembered from her childhood.

'I'm glad. Whenever that one day will be, this will all be here waiting for you, Sibby.'

'Thank you. I'd like nothing more.'

Her father squeezed her fingers. 'Me too.'

A companionable silence settled between them as they stared over the rolling hills and river flats towards the distant roofline of the farmhouse.

When she returned inside the dome, she found Riley flipping through a book about comets. She took a closer look at the narrow shelves beside him. She'd assumed her father had packed away all their family photos the day they'd disappeared. Instead, here they were.

She picked up a silver-framed picture of her and James. In the photograph they wore their swimmers and had their arms around each other. Covered in mud, they'd been playing in the hollow near the cattle yards that filled with water after a big storm.

Her fingers shook as she returned the photo to the shelf. If she'd learned anything from losing a loved one, it was to hold on to those who remained.

She'd waited so long to find a man like Hugh. She wasn't now relinquishing what they had without a fight. As worried as he'd been about her falling off Cloud, his fear had to stem from already having had his and Riley's hearts broken. Somehow she needed to find a way to prove there was nothing to fear from what lay between them. She wouldn't walk out of their lives like Clarisse had.

Her resolve only strengthened as she drove everyone home. While Riley sat with her father in the kitchen having morning smoko, she went to answer some work-related emails. After the morning's high emotion, she needed some alone time. She wanted to have a clear head so she could have an answer for everything she suspected Hugh would say tonight. But as she finished an email and went to start another, the deep timbre of a new voice in the kitchen made her stomach flip.

Hugh hadn't waited until after work. He'd come to talk to her now.

The sight of his son's animated face and his breathless excitement failed to ease the tension constricting Hugh's chest. Until he spoke to Sibylla and did what he had to do, he'd have no respite from the tension that hammered at his temples.

He hoped his smile didn't appear forced. 'It sounds like you had a great morning.'

Riley nodded before taking a huge bite out of a lamington.

'Coffee or tea?' Gary asked from over at the kitchen bench.

'Nothing, thanks. I'll see Sibylla, then Riley and I'll head home.' He turned as Sibylla entered the kitchen.

Today she wore her usual jeans and cotton shirt but the sight of her still made his world spin. Her ebony hair was pulled back into a ponytail to reveal the smooth pale skin of her nape. He ground his teeth. He'd memorised every delicate contour and satin-soft curve and still he'd never be able to get enough of her.

While her lips tilted in her sunny smile, the solemn intensity of her gaze scored him to his soul. She somehow knew what he'd come to say.

'Have you got a minute to check on Cloud?' she asked, voice casual.

'Sure.'

'No need to rush,' Gary said, without looking at them 'Riley's going to help me look for my missing slipper in the garden that a certain two puppies have taken. That will teach me to leave the veranda door to my bedroom open.'

Hugh followed Sibylla out of the kitchen. She didn't say anything as he fell into step beside her. It was only when they were out of earshot of the house that she glanced at him. 'The stables will be the best place to … talk.'

As if by mutual agreement they didn't again speak until they'd reached the elongated building that featured a wash bay at one end. Sibylla leaned her hip against a wooden post. When she faced him, she lifted her chin and arched her brow.

The gestures reminded him of the reasons why he loved her. Beautiful, resilient and strong, her only response to fear and to being let down would be to fight. The last thing she needed was protecting. Whatever justifications he'd spent the night and day preparing fled. He'd allowed his own fears to control and compromise his thinking. Words wouldn't be enough to convey how foolish and wrong he'd been. He stepped forward, cupped the back of her head and kissed her.

Her response was instant. She fitted herself against him and wound her arms around his neck. Urgent, honest and raw, their kiss banished the last of his doubts. Whatever form their relationship took moving forward, there would be a way to make it work. He wasn't not having her in his and Riley's lives. He'd already wasted the past twenty-four hours giving into his flight response and running. He wouldn't waste another second.

When he lifted his head, the grave intensity of her grey eyes hadn't dimmed. Her hands slid down his back to his waist. Through his shirt he could feel the determination in their clasp.

'Hugh Mason, if you now tell me that you're walking away from what we have then I'm calling Dr Fliss to tell her you're not thinking clearly and must be still concuss—'

He silenced her with another kiss. This time when they broke apart her eyes were filled with laughter and a beautiful softness. 'You know … if this is how you plan to keep on talking, I don't have any complaints.'

He traced her lower lip with his thumb before easing himself away. While they stood so close, talking would be the last thing on either of their minds. She only let him go so far before her expression turned serious and the grip on his back firmed.

'It's okay.' He paused to brush his mouth across hers. 'I'm not going anywhere. But we do need to talk.'

'We do.'

'You were right. Fear is a control freak. It can make you expect the worst and only see things through a certain mindset. To be honest, I didn't come here today to … kiss you.'

'I know and I understand why.' Her earnest, solemn tone matched the tension he could feel vibrating through her. 'But we can work through all the things worrying you.'

'There's nothing we need to work through. There are no more things holding me back. Not now. Not ever. Sibylla … I love you. I need you in my life and in Riley's.'

The joy in her smile warmed him like a physical touch. 'I love you too. You have no idea how much. There's nowhere else I'm ever going to be but with you and Riley.'

Knowing further words would be futile, he kissed her again.

They still had time before she returned to the coast to work out the practicalities of merging their two lives. Whatever the solution, all the fears that had brought him to see her no longer existed. The bleak, dark space they'd occupied was now filled with happiness, peace, and, most of all, love.

# EPILOGUE

'What are the odds?' Humour edged Hugh's words as he took the first turn left to avoid Woodlea's main street.

Sibylla smiled. Just like their last visit to town the first person they saw was Edna Galloway. This time the notorious town gossip stood outside the bakery talking to Mrs Knox. Edna made no attempt to hide her interest in every car that drove by. 'I think we can stay off her radar for a little bit longer.'

The wink Hugh sent her made her senses hum and her heart light. Since their stable talk two days ago they'd been inseparable. Being with Hugh was more than she could have ever imagined. She still couldn't believe that she'd found a man who made her so happy and who she felt so complete with. All her boxes had been well and truly ticked.

She glanced over her shoulder to where Riley sat with a bag of library books on his lap. He gave her a wide grin.

After they'd returned from the stables they had a quiet talk to the five-year-old. His first comment was that he and Jelly Bean already knew they loved each other. His second was that Nova could sleep in his room if he wanted.

Her father too had shown no surprise. Rare emotion had welled in his eyes as he'd hugged her and said that Hugh was a good man. Bernice had given her a perfunctory embrace. Even though things were better between them, they'd never enjoy a close relationship. A call to her own mother had led to a video chat with Hugh over the internet. Plans had already been made for a road trip next month to visit her in Melbourne.

When Hugh turned past the Royal Arms, he nodded at the distinctive blue ute parked outside. 'Tanner's home from droving. He could help you out with Cloud.'

She nodded as she forced her hands to untangle in her lap. The thought of riding again still stole her sleep. Hugh and her father had both made multiple offers to help but she didn't want her stress to transfer to them. While she could lunge Cloud and generally be around him, she was going to need professional help to get back into the saddle. As well as being a drover, Tanner was a horse trainer and both Fliss and Cressy said there was no one better to help restore her confidence. 'When I'm back, I'll give him a call.'

Hugh's smile flashed white.

There was no doubt now how their lives would combine. The audiologist who had been looking after her coastal practice had become invested in the vibrant local community and had offered to buy her out. Sibylla would go home as planned but then her return to Woodlea would be permanent. She'd heard the Dubbo mobile children's ear clinic was looking for an audiologist.

Hugh parked outside the library. When they unclipped their seatbelts, he snuck a last kiss. 'See you at the Windmill Café in half an hour.'

As she crossed the road to enter the main street she waved to Fliss and Cressy as they drove past in Cressy's battered silver ute. Edna had now moved to position herself outside the post office where she was talking to a pretty young woman with red hair. Sibylla made sure she stuck to the other side of the street before crossing over to the pharmacy. She had a list of things her father needed.

The autumn-gilded leaves on the plane tree beside her rustled. She slowed to appreciate the tree's amber beauty. She'd now have a lifetime of watching the seasons change in the bush. White crocheted squares covered the midsection of the tree's smooth trunk. Behind her a lamppost was also decorated in delicate white wool. There definitely was either a white winter or white wedding theme going on.

She stopped to touch the soft yarn bombing wrapped around the plane tree. But she really knew what the white stood for … it was stars. She looked through the golden leaves at the vivid, cloudless sky. Somewhere up there James was looking down and smiling.

COMING SOON

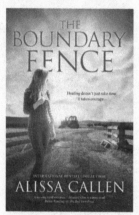

# THE
# BOUNDARY
# FENCE

by

# ALISSA CALLEN

Available February 2020

mira

Other books by

# ALISSA CALLEN

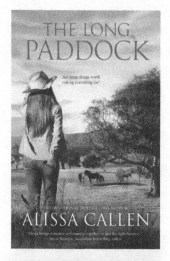

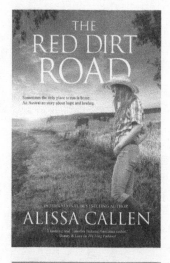